CLOVER

Clover Beckitt is surprised when her mother announces that after fifteen years of widowhood she is about to be married. Clover finds herself with a new 'pop', Jake Tandy, and a stepsister, Ramona. Despite her initial fears, all seems settled in the household and new plans for the family's brewery promise to bring wealth and prosperity. When love blossoms with Tom Doubleday, the photographer Clover met at her mother's wedding, she feels that things have turned out just right. Then Jake's younger brother Elijah joins the business and both Clover and Ramona find their lives changed forever...

CLOVER

CLOVER

by

Michael Taylor

WARWICKSHIRE
COUNTY LIBRARY

CONTROL No.

Magna Large Print Books
Long Preston, North Yorkshire,
BD23 4ND, England.

British Library Cataloguing in Publication Data.

Taylor, Michael
    Clover.

        A catalogue record of this book is
        available from the British Library

        ISBN   0-7505-1904-5

First published in Great Britain in 2001 by Hodder & Stoughton
A division of Hodder Headline

Copyright © 2001 by Michael Taylor

Cover illustration © Stewart Lees by arrangement with
Hodder & Stoughton Ltd.

The right of Michael Taylor to be identified as the author of this work
has been asserted by him in accordance with the Copyright, Designs
and Patents Act, 1988

Published in Large Print 2002 by arrangement with
Hodder & Stoughton Ltd.

All Rights reserved. No part of this publication may be reproduced,
stored in a retrieval system, or transmitted in any form or by any
means, electronic, mechanical, photocopying, recording or otherwise
without the prior permission of the Copyright owner.

Magna Large Print is an imprint of Library Magna Books Ltd.

Printed and bound in Great Britain by
T.J. (International) Ltd., Cornwall, PL28 8RW

All characters in this publication are fictitious and any resemblance to real persons, living or dead is purely coincidental.

To the memory of my mother and father –
Gladys and Eric

Chapter One

What she'd just been told shook Clover Beckitt rigid. How greatly it would change her life she did not know, but change her life it would; irredeemably. Maybe it would change it for the better – there was plenty of room for improvement – but maybe it would not. Time alone would tell. And that time would not be long coming, for the change was to commence one week from tomorrow. Preparation, however, was about to start right now. And with a vengeance.

'Get your hat and coat on, our Clover,' Mary Ann, her dour mother instructed. 'I'm taking you to the dressmaker's. Zillah has promised to look after the taproom till Job comes on.'

'I'd better change into something clean, Mother, and wash my face and hands. I've just got in from work. I'm filthy dirty.'

'Well make sure your underwear's decent and all. I don't want folk talking about me behind me back, saying as how me only daughter's riffy.'

'You'd be riffy as well if you had to work in a foundry making cores,' Clover complained as she headed for the stairs. 'Why can't I have a nice clean job in a nice posh shop?'

'Because the pay's better in a foundry,' Mary Ann called after her. 'As you know well enough.'

In her spartan bedroom, Clover unfastened her

home-made working frock and underslip, took off her headscarf and unpinned her dark hair. She placed a sheet of newspaper over the podged rug at the foot of her brass bed and vigorously brushed her hair over it to dislodge any bits of sand that sometimes penetrated to her scalp. Tiny grains of black sand rippled gently onto the newspaper, which she screwed into a ball to throw away in the miskin outside. She washed her face, her ears and neck, and then her feet in cold water which she poured from her ewer into the bowl that adorned the wash-stand. Dried, and feeling immensely more presentable, she rummaged through her wardrobe for a clean dress, in the drawers of her dressing table for a decent underslip, for clean drawers and clean stockings. She loathed dirt, especially foundry dirt, and it was such luxury to change into clean clothes. When she was finished, wearing dainty shoes and all, she returned to the parlour.

'I'm ready.'

'I'll just tell Zillah we'm off then. Wait outside for me, our Clover.'

Mary Ann, her hair tied back severely with a black ribbon, was wearing the long black coat she'd owned ever since Toby, Clover's father, had died in 1892 – fifteen years ago. It was profoundly unfashionable, but fashion was a luxury they could not afford. The coat, however, was not the only Victorian thing about Mary Ann. The stern, unsmiling, tight-lipped demeanour prevailed, as did the total rejection of anything that was not orthodox or had not been entirely sanctioned by the Good Book. For Mary Ann was also a devout Christian. However, as a licensed victualler, her loyalties were often divided, especially when the intolerant aims and ideals of the Band of Hope were thrust in her equally intolerant face, as they so often were.

Still reeling with consternation from the news her mother had imparted, Clover walked outside into George Street and stood with her back to the Jolly Collier, the public house her mother owned and ran. It was a red-brick affair, dingy on the outside from the smuts of heavy industry and intensive coal mining. The roof was missing one or two slates and the window-frames were shedding their dull green paint in brittle, curling flakes. Inside, the curtains reeked of cigarette smoke and stale ash and even the wallpaper on the upstairs landing was yellowing with nicotine stains from the thick smoke that drifted upstairs from the taproom. The stale smell of beer was pervasive. But it was home.

As Clover turned her face to the slanting sun to consider once again this monumental change that was facing them both, she heard the tap-tap of her mother's footsteps on the quarry-tiled floor of the inside passage. She turned, ready to go. They walked briskly up George Street and turned the corner into Brown Street. Clover had a thousand questions she needed to ask her mother, but there was no time now. They arrived at the door of Bessie Roberts and entered her front parlour that had been converted into a shop-cum-sewing room many years earlier. Inside was a stout woman with grey hair and spectacles.

13

'Mrs Beckitt, how lovely to see you again,' Bessie Roberts greeted obsequiously in her thin voice that was incongruous to her size. 'How long's it been?'

'A year or two, Mrs Roberts, by anybody's reckoning. Our Clover here wants a new frock. Suitable for a wedding.'

Bessie looked Clover up and down with a well-practised look of admiration. 'Oh, a wedding-dress, eh?' She smiled professionally. 'Very nice. Oh, she'll make a lovely bride and no mistake. I reckon I've got the very thing.'

'It's me that's getting married, Mrs Roberts, not our Clover,' Mary Ann pronounced self-righteously. 'And I know what I'm gunna be wearing. Like I said, it's me daughter as wants the frock.'

'Forgive me, forgive me, Mrs Beckitt. I naturally thought... Well, fancy ... that's nice as you'm getting wed again. Let me congratulate you. Shall you be staying on at the Jolly Collier?'

'Oh, yes, we shan't be going nowhere. So what have you got in the way of material, Mrs Roberts? Something blue or green, I fancy.'

'Oh, blue to match your daughter's eyes,' Bessie Roberts affirmed. 'I reckon I've got the very thing.' She hunted beneath her counter and flopped a roll of azure-blue satin material on top. 'This is beautiful stuff, Mrs Beckitt. Just feel... And the colour would contrast beautifully with her lovely dark hair... Don't you think?'

'Have you got e'er a pattern what I can look at? The fashion seems more for fitted bodices and skirts these days from what I can see of it.'

'I've got the very thing, Mrs Beckitt.' She hunted again in a cardboard box. 'When is the happy day, Mrs Beckitt?'

'A week on Saturday.'

'Good Lord! So soon?'

'Yes, we'll all have to get our skates on, I'm a-thinking. I take it as read that you can accommodate we, Mrs Roberts?'

'It'll be a bit of a rush but, yes. Ah... Here we are...'

Mrs Roberts placed the printed sketch of the dress on top of the roll of material.

'I like it,' Clover said, taking the first available opportunity to get a word in. 'I think it's perfect.' She looked at Mary Ann for consent. Mary Ann nodded and, without further ado, the decision was made.

'I'd better take some measurements, young Clover. Would you like to slip into the back room with me and take your dress off? I like to take an accurate measurement.'

The three women trooped into the tiny back room. Clover took off her dress and stood in her clean underwear while Bessie Roberts produced her measuring-tape from her apron pocket.

'Such a lovely figure you've got, Clover,' Bessie commented. 'Doesn't she, Mrs Beckitt? It takes me back to when I was as slender... Just lift your arms a little bit, please... That's it. Now your waist ... I see you don't wear a corset, Clover.'

Clover thought she detected disapproval in Bessie's tone. 'I don't need to, Mrs Roberts.'

'It's one thing we can never agree on, Mrs Roberts,' Mary Ann complained. 'I'm a firm

15

believer that all women should wear a corset.'

Clover smiled secretly as she alone caught the unintended humour in her mother's words.

'Oh, as you say, Mrs Beckitt, but your daughter's very trim.' She gently prodded Clover's belly. 'Just look ... I wish my belly was as flat... Can you hold the end of the tape for me, Clover?... At your waist ... while I get the length?... That's lovely.'

It was half an hour later when they left. Mary Ann had paid a deposit on the dress which would be ready on Good Friday, provided Clover could come for a fitting about the same time next Wednesday.

When they returned to the Jolly Collier Mary Ann placed two plated dinners in the oven to be reheated. The meal had been cooked earlier by Zillah Bache.

'Are you marrying for love, Mother, or convenience?' Clover asked pointedly as she sat down in front of the coal fire. The question had been troubling her.

Mary Ann shut the oven door of the cast-iron grate using a rag and stood upright. 'Do I seem the sentimental sort, our Clover?'

'That'll be the day.' Clover scrutinised her mother's expression looking in her eyes for a clue as to her true feelings. 'I just wondered. It's all so sudden. It's such a shock.'

Mary Ann pulled a chair from under the scrubbed wooden table. She sat down opposite her daughter and sighed. 'Ever since your father passed away fifteen years ago next November I've run this place on me own, pub and brewery. I've

16

tried to bring you up to the best of me ability and all, but it ain't bin easy. I had to take Zillah on to help in the house and look after you. But folk cost money to employ and money's scarce, Clover. It's always bin scarce.'

'Our beer's still as good as ever it was,' Clover encouraged.

'Because I know what I'm a-doing when I brew it and because it has to be, else we'd sell none. By this time last year though, our Clover, I'd had enough. I know I never said nothing to you but I was ready to pack it all in. I'd been working me fingers to the bone eighteen hours a day. And for what? What with a mortgage on this place to pay off, bills for malt and hops, for coal to heat the copper and the mash tun, the excise man to pay, as well as Zillah and Job Smith, that bone-idle cellarman. And God knows who else. It's no wonder I insisted you went out to work. We've needed the money, Clover.'

'And it's not every girl's dream, working in a foundry,' Clover commented as one of the cats, Malcolm, came in and rubbed itself gently against her shins, a sensation she enjoyed.

'Anyway, when I thought about it hard, our Clover, I had to admit to meself that the only way we could live in anything like comfort and peace of mind would be for me to marry, cause there's no sign of you getting wed.'

Clover peered through the window onto the back yard and saw that it was raining. 'Well, that's not my fault. When have I ever been given the chance to do any courting?' she said, throwing right back in her mother's face the prejudice she instinctively held against any of Clover's likely suitors. 'You've never allowed me to go out with lads.'

'It's been for your own good,' Mary Ann said soberly, picking her fingernails. 'I never wanted you getting mixed up with any damned scruff. I always wanted you to wait till the right chap came along.'

Clover shrugged off the subject. Her mother knew well enough her feelings. 'So did you ask Jake Tandy to marry you?'

'Me ask him? As if I would.' A hint of a smile teetered on the brink of Mary Ann's eyes at that. 'I didn't have to, thank the Lord. He asked me. I've got to know him over the six months he's been a regular here. He's had a stall on Dudley Market and he ain't short of a bob or two. He'll have a house to sell as well. He wants to put money into the brewing, to expand that side of the business. He reckons we can sell our beer to free houses and off-licences. Not only that, he reckons them as owns the pits and the ironworks will buy barrels of the stuff off us. As he says, a hammer driver in a forge can sink twenty pints or more on a hot day. For every worker that amounts to a tidy lot of beer, our Clover.'

'So tell me about Jake, Mother. I hardly know him.'

'He's younger than me – by four years...'

'So he's what? Thirty-eight?'

Mary Ann nodded, either ignoring or failing to recognise the trace of disapproval in Clover's voice.

'And he's never been married?'

18

'Oh, he's been married afore, Clover. He's a widower.'

'A widower? Does he have children then? Children who are coming to live here?'

'Just a daughter. Seventeen. Two years younger than you.'

'Mmm...' Clover mused. 'Does she work?'

'She'll work here – serving, helping out in the brewery.'

'While I have to work in a foundry.'

The main room of the Jolly Collier was the taproom, but it also boasted a snug with a fireplace where the women were more likely to congregate on Saturday and Sunday nights. The taproom was devoid of a bar counter; the beer pumps were built into a wooden construction that hugged one wall. So, when you wanted your glass refilled you hailed Mary Ann, or Clover, or Job Smith or whoever was serving, ordered your drink and they would deliver it to your table. A low, cast-iron fireplace framed a hearty coal fire at one end of the room, around which the older men huddled for warmth in winter.

Clover realised that running a busy public house and brewing sometimes in excess of thirty barrels of beer each week had indeed tended to keep Mary Ann at full stretch. But Clover did her bit to help despite her day job. By five each morning she would be up, lighting the fire in the taproom ready to receive the first ironworkers and miners when they called for their threepenny rum and coffee on their way to their morning shift. They would yawn and gossip like old biddies with their colleagues who also called in for a drink when returning home, tired from the night shift.

That evening, Jake Tandy turned up in the taproom with his younger brother, Elijah.

'How am yer, my flower?' he greeted.

Mary Ann smiled with pleasure at seeing him. 'Rushed off me feet, as ever. But all the better for seeing you, Jacob,' she replied. 'Usual?'

Jake nodded. 'And a pint of pale for our Elijah. Here, I've bought our Elijah to meet you, Mary Ann, seeing as how he's gunna be me best man.'

Elijah stood erect and held out his hand formally. 'I've been looking forward to meeting you, Mrs Beckitt. Jake's said some fine things about you.'

'Well, that's just as well in the circumstances,' Mary Ann replied. She turned to Jake. 'And now is as good a time as any for you to meet our Clover properly. She's always gone to bed by the time we've finished serving, so there's never been a chance for her to get to know you.'

So Mary Ann issued them with a pint of beer each and led them into the living quarters, leaving Job Smith, the part-time bartender to serve the customers.

'How do you do, Clover,' Jake said agreeably when he saw her.

Clover smiled back and blushed. 'Nice to see you again, Mr Tandy.'

'Hey, *Mister* Tandy, eh? Now that's summat as'll have to change. It'll be no good calling me Mr Tandy when me and your mother am wed. Why not call me Pop and start right off? Sounds better than *papa,* I always reckon.'

Clover continued to smile politely.

'I bet you'm wondering what sort of a chap I am, eh, Clover?'

'I'm bound to wonder, Mr Tandy. I hope we can all live together contentedly.'

Clover had been aware of Jake Tandy for months, serving him pints of bitter in the tap-room of the Jolly Collier. He had started loitering after closing time, collecting glasses, washing up, sweeping up the old sawdust and putting the spittoons out to wash – generally currying favour, by which time Clover had usually gone to bed ready for her early start next day. It galled her that she had not known he was to be her step-father till today. Even though the banns must have been read, nobody had thought to mention the fact to her. Typical. Still, Clover couldn't help wondering what Jake saw in Mary Ann and her stone-faced demeanour.

'I've got a daughter meself, you know,' he said and took a swig from his glass.

'Mother said.'

'Ramona. You'll like her. There ain't that much difference in your ages.'

'I'm sure it'll be very nice having a stepsister,' Clover said equably. 'Especially if she's of an age.'

'Well, she's a nice lass, though I say so meself... And this is me brother, Elijah...' Jacob turned to him. Clover shook his hand and said hello. She guessed him to be in his early thirties. He was smart, with dark hair and engaging brown eyes and a confident smile. 'He's going to be me best man at the wedding, Clover. I hope you've got a

21

nice new frock to wear for it. Has your mother treated you?'

'We've been today to order it, Mr Tandy. I'm sure it'll be very suitable.'

'It's costing enough,' Mary Ann commented typically. 'But the wench has got nothing else.'

'I bought one for our Ramona,' Jake said. 'Cost me a fortune, it did. But what's money? Why worry about it?'

'It's only them as ain't got money what worry about it,' Mary Ann remarked. 'And you know how we've been fixed, Jacob.'

'And all that's coming to an end, Mary Ann,' Jake declared with a grin. 'All that's coming to an end.'

Good Friday in 1907, as well as being a holiday, was a perfect day for flying. A light south-westerly breeze was panting warmly as it ran up the side of Rough Hill, where Ned Brisco sat apprehensively in a weird contraption he had built, confident it would fly. His older brother, Amos, sat crouched beneath the fragile wings on its port side waiting for Ned's signal.

Ned gazed into the distance. Distance was his challenge. From these heights he overlooked the Clent Hills to the south, lush and green in their spring finery. In the far distance he could discern Worcestershire's Malvern Hills, colourless on the hazy south-western horizon. Towards the north-west, beyond the furnaces of Ironbridge and Coalbrookdale, the Wrekin lay like a stone pushing up through Shropshire's greenery. Ned imagined himself flying effortlessly in his

machine over the vast expanse of gently undulating terrain that lay between himself and
these yet unvisited outposts. Once beautiful
countryside, it was now pockmarked by scores of
pit-heads and slag heaps and quarries, and by
chimney-stacks that spewed endless palls of filthy
smoke into the hazy, white sky that was struggling to turn blue in the spring sunshine. As well
as these effigies to the industry and enterprise of
man, the inevitable stone structures loomed that
were erected to the greater glory of God. The
spire of Top Church in the middle distance to the
north-west pierced the atmosphere like a tintack,
while St John's and its square grey tower occupied a ledge on Kates Hill to the north. Beyond
St John's stood Dudley Castle, hoary, crumbling,
derelict, yet defiantly majestic.

The girl with him looked striking, despite being
plainly dressed in a home-made blouse and skirt.
Her eyes were intelligent, as blue as summer
cornflowers. Her skin was fair yet her lush hair
was as dark and shiny as the coal they mined
thereabouts. When she smiled her face lit up and
you couldn't help but smile with her, for she
seemed then to throw off the shackles of reserve
and shyness that normally confined her. Clover
Beckitt was Ned's soul mate.

As well as Clover and his brother Amos, both of
whom gave Ned much needed encouragement, a
smattering of ragged children had attached
themselves to the band and their cart. They
looked on in incredulous silence and wonder,
hoping they would witness the miracle of man
and machine in flight.

'All right, Amos,' Ned called. 'Let her go.'

Amos quickly pulled a chunk of wood from under one of the thin-spoked bicycle wheels on which the contraption stood. The ensemble began to roll downhill over the stubbly grass that cloaked that side of Rough Hill between two disused quarries, gathering speed quickly. Ned held his breath as his stomach seemed to rise into his mouth.

'Be careful, Ned!' Clover called, hearing the creak of struts and wire and stretched canvas. 'Don't crash into the pepper-box.'

'Let's hope he gets that bloody far,' Amos said dubiously, seeing that the Dudley Tunnel's air shaft of which Clover spoke was directly in Ned's path, but unreachable. 'If he ended up in Warren's Hall pond, even that would be summat to crow about.'

Clover chuckled at the mental image Amos's words conjured, then remained silent for seconds that seemed like ages while they watched Ned's progress. The contraption had reached about thirty miles an hour and was almost at the place where the steep hill was levelling out when Clover whooped with excitement.

'Look, Amos, look! He's flying! He's flying.' She turned round to catch Amos's reaction, a delighted grin on her lovely face. Behind them, the group of ragamuffins cheered boisterously.

'By Christ, he is and all... He's airborne, Clover... Whoops!... Oh, Jesus Christ... Well, he was airborne.'

She saw the contraption stall and hit the ground. At once she hitched up her long cotton

24

skirt and ran for all she was worth down the hill in her buttoned-up boots, her dark hair flowing like a mane behind her.

'Ned!' she called. 'Are you all right? Are you all right?'

As she hurtled towards him, she watched with relief as Ned disentangled himself from the wires, broken laths and strips of sailcloth that had come adrift from the wooden frame. Eventually, breathless, she was within hailing distance. Ned slid down from what remained of the lower starboard wing, onto his feet.

'Ned, are you all right?' she gasped again.

He watched her as she approached, and grinned, his brown eyes alive with exhilaration. 'I did it, Clover – I did it. I flew – I actually flew.'

She ran the last few steps towards him and flung her arms around his neck with pride at his brilliant achievement. 'I know,' she shrieked, as happy as he was. 'I saw you.' Then, self-consciously, she let go of him, for fear he should presume too much. 'Are you hurt?' she earnestly asked.

'No, Clover,' Ned said, pulling his gloves off. 'I'm as good as new. I think I know what went wrong. As soon as the thing started to lift it climbed gently for about thirty or forty yards then came down again nose first. It *stalled*, that's all. I should've fixed in some ballast. Ah well – next time, eh?' Ned stood with his hands on his hips looking thoughtfully at the tangled wreck before him and shook his head.

'How did it feel, Ned, gliding above the ground?'

25

'I – I can't describe it, Clover... Smooth... Incredibly smooth. Like being on a magic carpet, if you can imagine that.'

'You're going to try again, then?'

'Course I am. If Wilbur and Orville Wright can do it, so can I. And now I've got this far...'

Clover looked at him with admiration in her wide eyes. Although he was not her sweetheart he was ... well, he was dear to her. Oh, he wasn't handsome, nor was he particularly elegant. She didn't fancy him in that way, yet in a sisterly sort of way she liked him. He was ordinary with reddish hair and gawky in his tallness, but he was so clever and such a gentle soul. And so determined. Like other lads that had left school at twelve because their parents could not afford to send them to the Dudley Grammar School, Ned Brisco could have developed into one of the finest engineers of his time. Of that, Clover was certain. As a moulder at the Coneygree Foundry where she also worked, he was wasted and frustrated. Exercising his mind with the seemingly insuperable problems of flight was his only outlet.

Clover looked back up the hill towards Amos and waved. He was carefully leading the pony and cart down the steep, grassy hill, followed by the posse of assorted youngsters. Earlier, the cart had hauled the flying machine, still in sections, up Oakham Road and past the hangman's tree to the top of Rough Hill.

'What are you going to do with what's left of your flying machine, Ned?' Clover asked.

Ned inspected it cursorily. 'Oh, there'll be some

bits I can salvage. Perhaps by Whitsun we can try again. I'll have built another machine by then. A better one.'

So, Ned started to disassemble his damaged machine. He had unfastened the rigging that secured both pairs of wings to the flimsy frame that was the fuselage by the time Amos heaved to with the borrowed horse and cart. With Clover's help, Ned stacked the separate assemblies onto the inadequate transport as best he could, considering the wings' deformed leading edges and the nose that prevented it all sitting squarely. When it was all in place and tied securely, Ned invited Clover to sit alongside him on the cart while Amos led the horse.

'We can get onto the New Rowley Road if we follow that path down,' Ned claimed, pointing. 'If we go that way it'll save trying to lug this lot back up Rough Hill.'

Amos waved his acknowledgement and the horse blew his lips as if in thanks.

'It's back to the drawing-board, Clover,' Ned said stoically. He turned and smiled at her, the warm smile of a good friend.

'It's a good job you've got the patience, Ned,' she replied, signalling her approval. 'But what do you hope to do with all this if you're successful?'

'I'd patent my design,' he answered at once. 'I'd start my own factory building flying machines. I reckon there's a big future in flying machines if you can get them to stay up a decent time and make them controllable. Course, I'd need a decent engine and that would cost money. But just think of the possibilities, Clover. Just imagine the possibilities if only I could build flying machines big enough and strong enough to carry freight or passengers.'

'Well don't ask me to fly in one,' Clover said. 'I'd be scared stiff. But at least this is a start. At least you got the thing off the ground, even if you did crash. I'd like to help you, if I could. I'd like to help you build the next one.'

He turned to her again and she saw the admiration he had for her in his eyes. She was certain he wanted to be her sweetheart, but was thankful he'd never asked. He was her pal and they talked like pals. She enjoyed being his pal. If she became his sweetheart it wouldn't be the same. She would have to kiss him and somehow, she just didn't fancy kissing him. Being his friend was one thing, but kissing him was another. Whenever she thought he was about to broach the subject of them courting, she astutely introduced some topic to distract him – like now.

'My mother's getting married again, Ned.'

'Never!' He regarded her again, but disconcertedly. 'Who's she getting wed to?'

'A man called Jake Tandy.'

'What's he like?'

'I hardly know him,' she answered wistfully. 'It's funny, when I was a child, most of the kids in my class at school had a father and I didn't. I always felt a bit jealous, a bit out of it because my father had died when I was so young. I only ever had my mother and Zillah to go back home to and all the time I wondered what it must be like to have a father. My friends at school all used to speak of their fathers with such reverence, yet all I had of mine were a few vague memories. Well, I suppose being faced with the prospect of a new father – one I don't really know – makes me a bit apprehensive. He's a widower, by the way.'

'A widower? Does he have any kids then?'

'Just a daughter, seventeen.'

'What's she like?' Ned asked. 'Is she pretty?'

Clover shrugged. 'How should I know? I've never seen her.'

They were trundling past the Warren's Hall pond that was brimful of frogspawn. To their left sat grim pit banks, the same roan colour as the horse, where any grass feared to prosper. The headgear of pit shafts, some derelict now, stood like gallows in the ravaged landscape, their unturning wheels the halos of their victims.

'She can't be as pretty as you, Clover,' Ned said kindly. 'I bet you any money.'

Clover shrugged again, but smiled at the compliment.

'When are they getting married, Clover?'

She sighed. 'Tomorrow... From tomorrow it'll be a whole different way of life. A new stepfather, a new stepsister...'

'You sound as if you're not relishing the prospect.'

'It's just that ... I don't know what the future holds, Ned.'

Chapter Two

Mary Ann Beckitt, née Scriven, and Jacob Tandy were married at noon on Easter Saturday. The Reverend John Mainwaring, the recently installed and increasingly popular vicar of St John's, Kates Hill, officiated. Outside in the spring sunshine the party posed for photographs with Mary Ann in the centre in her new red velvet dress. Clover looked radiant in her sky-blue satin dress and her blue satin hat with its white lace brim. Jake said he wanted this marriage, unlike his first, to be a proper do and insisted they have a proper record of the event. So he engaged the services of an enterprising local young photographer called Tom Doubleday who had his own studio and darkrooms in Hall Street near the centre of the town. Tom was about twenty-five, or so Clover Beckitt estimated. With increasing interest, she watched him changing plates in the huge wooden camera that looked top-heavy stuck on its wooden tripod. When he'd finished Jake asked Tom if he would like to return with the rest of the party to the Jolly Collier, where they were providing a meal and free beer. Clover was secretly delighted.

In addition to Clover and her mother, there were nine Scrivens in the form of the bride's brothers and an unmarried sister. On Jake's side, there were only four relatives in addition to himself and his daughter Ramona; his elderly mother and father, and younger brother, Elijah with his betrothed, Dorcas Downing, who was the daughter of a wealthy local industrialist. Old Man Tandy hacked in a corner and expectorated the product of his miner's cough into the fireplace where it bubbled and hissed, only to be castigated by Elijah for making Dorcas, who was sensitive to such vulgar mannerisms, feel sick. Old Mrs Tandy unfastened her boots and slipped them off and presented her bunions, which were killing her, to anybody that was interested in inspecting them. Tables had been laid in a line down the middle of the taproom and trestles spanned the lot. When everybody had supped their first glass or two of free beer, this is where they sat. Zillah Bache, who was generally sober but not quite today, unsteadily served up the roast beef, Yorkshire pudding and vegetables. Job Smith, shifty-eyed, served the beer.

Clover sat next to her new stepsister, Ramona. Ramona, to Clover's relief, was neat and tidy. She was also exceptionally pretty with a mop of fair hair that was unruly with self-willed curls, even today, despite the determined attempts she'd obviously made to tame them. Her eyes were big and the colour of the sherry she was drinking. She seemed friendly and made conversation easily. Maybe Ned Brisco would like her. They talked, comparing their lives, comparing their likes and dislikes, interspersing their verbal explorations with comments to Tom Doubleday, the young photographer, who sat opposite. Tom's blue eyes creased into the most pleasing smiles and, as his participation in their conversation increased, Clover was torn between his charm and the certain knowledge that she must get to know and befriend Ramona.

'How long have you been a photographer, Mr Doubleday?' she asked politely, placing her knife and fork together on her plate, for she had just finished her dinner.

'I'm not sure,' he replied, pleased with the interest he was getting from this lovely dark-haired girl with the smiling blue eyes and beautiful nose that looked so appealing in profile. 'It's something I drifted into. Even as a small boy I was interested in photography.'

'Is it fiddly?' Ramona chipped in, not about to be excluded. 'It looks fiddly to me.'

'Yes, it is a bit, Miss Tandy—'

'Oh, please call me Ramona, Mr Doubleday.'

'Yes, er ... Ramona.' He smiled into her alluring brown eyes. 'It's even more fiddly in the dark-room.'

'In the darkroom?' Ramona's voice had an appealing, girlish croakiness about it. 'I don't know if I'd like it in a darkroom. Would I be scared, do you think?'

'Not if you're with somebody else.'

'Would I need to be scared with somebody like you?' Her eyes darted knowingly from Clover to Tom and Clover thought her new stepsister was maybe trying to be just a little provocative.

'Do you have to work in complete darkness?' Clover interjected, seizing the opportunity to get back into the conversation before Ramona completely hijacked it.

'Yes, otherwise you'd fog the latent image on the plate,' Tom explained. 'It's light-sensitive, you see, Miss Tandy.'

'Miss Beckitt, but you can call me Clover,' Clover corrected with a broad smile. 'Ramona and I are stepsisters. That's why we have different surnames.'

'Oh, I beg your pardon. But Clover... Mmm, what a lovely name that is.'

'Well, thank you, Mr Doubleday.'

Tom Doubleday nodded his acknowledgement. 'Well now – with all this informality, I'd be obliged if you'd call me Tom.'

'All right.' Clover smiled delectably. 'So, to get back to my question – Tom – does all this working in darkness mean you have to go through the whole process of developing your plate without even knowing your photo's come out all right?'

'Not just developing, Miss ... er, Clover. To make the image so it's not sensitive to light any more, you have to thoroughly wash off any developer – after a given time – then fix it in another solution we call hypo. But listen, forgive me. The last thing I want to do is bore you.'

'I'd like to see it done,' Ramona said. 'It sounds ever so interesting.'

'Well, it's more frustrating than anything, Ramona,' Tom said pleasantly. 'Especially when you enlarge or make prints. You're never quite sure how long to expose the paper to the negative. You waste a lot getting it right, and it's expensive stuff.'

Zillah Bache served the pudding, hot apple pie and custard, and the girls' conversation with Tom

Doubleday continued. Clover was drawn to him inexorably. He was clean-shaven and his teeth were beautiful and even. As he spoke, she watched his lips and imagined how his kisses might feel. But she would dearly have preferred it if Ramona had not been there. She felt Ramona was a rival when she wanted her as a friend. Trouble was, she did not know the girl well enough to tell her to keep her pretty nose out of it.

Meanwhile, Job Smith tapped a firkin of old ale and presented everybody with a glassful. Elijah Tandy got to his feet and set about doing his duties as best man. He made a clever speech that made everybody laugh and asked them all to drink the health of the bride and groom. Then Jake Tandy thanked them all for their good wishes and said how lucky he was to be wed to somebody like Mary Ann. Mary Ann summoned a rare smile and Clover even thought she detected a blush in her mother.

While the tables were cleared and the trestles taken away, the guests drank more old ale, stretched their legs and stumbled about from one to the other, noisily putting the world to rights. The women complained about their men while the men cag-magged about work, feeling obligated to denigrate their gaffers. Job Smith meanwhile tapped a second firkin of old ale and began doling it out. Ramona Tandy, to Clover's surprise and disappointment, played an old accordion adeptly while many sang along raucously to the tunes.

'They reckon as all the steam engines at the pits

am gunna be replaced by 'lectric motors afore long,' said one of Mary Ann's brothers to another above the hubbub. It was Frederick, a miner, who had just been given a fresh glassful of old ale.

'Like the trams,' remarked the other.

Frederick took a swig from his glass. 'And the sooner the better as far as I'm concerned. Bloody stinking, noisy articles, steam engines. Why, you cort hear yourself think when you'm a-standing by 'em. And somebody's gorra be shovelling coal in night and day.'

It was at this point that Zillah Bache dropped a tray of glasses and the room went eerily quiet.

'Zillah!' Mary Ann shouted in her most intimidating voice.

Zillah froze. She faced Mary Ann and affected a toothless smile that was intended to project innocence.

'Zillah, are you drunk again?' Mary Ann asked admonishingly. 'Have you been a-guzzling me best ale behind me back?'

'I don't know what you mean, Mary Ann,' Zillah responded defiantly. 'It was just an accident. I'm sorry.'

'Right,' said Mary Ann. 'Get your hat and coat on. You'm sacked.'

'Please missus...' Zillah pleaded, suddenly remorseful. 'I said I was sorry. I lost me balance. It wo' happen again. Let me pay for what I'n had.'

'You'll be paying till kingdom come from what I can see of it,' Mary Ann bellucked. 'No. Up the road. Get on with you, you drunken swopson.'

'Mother, will you let me talk to Zillah?' Clover interceded diplomatically. 'I think I can sort this out a different way. You go and look after your guests... Please?'

'All right, but don't be soft with her, our Clover.'

Clover escorted Zillah into the scullery. She thought the world of Zillah. Zillah had been like a mother to her. Zillah had soothed the cut and grazed knees of childhood, mopped her tears and held her in her fat, dimpled arms when Mary Ann was too busy. When Clover had started her monthly bleeding and believed she was terminally ill, Zillah had explained about womanhood, how babies were conceived and brought into the world. She could talk to Zillah. Just because Zillah had helped herself to a glass or two of beer was nothing afresh. It had never bothered Mary Ann before. So Clover felt justified in sparing Zillah the belittling glare of attention from her mother's guests when Mary Ann doubtless felt she should be seen to be doing something about the offence.

'Take your coat off, Zillah,' Clover said kindly. 'You're not going anywhere. Come on, there's work to be done.' Zillah took off her coat biddably and rolled her sleeves up, relieved that she'd been reprieved. 'Now listen, Zillah. Can you understand why my mother is so upset about you?'

'I reckon so.'

'Right. Well, when you come to work in future there'll be no drinking behind her back. We all know you do it. Mr Tandy's here now and he

36

won't stand for it. But if you bring a clean bottle with you every day and give it to whoever's serving, I'll see as they fill it up with free beer for you ready for when you go home. I can't be fairer than that. Agreed?'

'Oh, God bless yer, Clover. God bless yer, my wench. I need the money from this job and I should be in dire straits if I lost it. And I've always loved workin' here, yo' know that. Not another drop'll touch me lips again while I'm at work. May the Lord strike me down if ever it does.'

'Good. I don't want to see you go, Zillah. You've always been like a mother to me. I've always been able to come to you with my troubles. I'll never forget how kind you've been.'

'God bless you, Clover. But what about Mary Ann?'

'Don't worry about my mother, Zillah. She only wanted to put on a bit of a show in front of her guests. She's probably a bit tipsy herself by now. I'll straighten it all out with her and Mr Tandy tomorrow.'

On the morning of Easter Sunday, the day after the wedding, there was a gleam in Jake Tandy's eyes as he sat at the table in the scullery and smiled fondly at Mary Ann. To Clover's amazement, there was a corresponding gleam in Mary Ann's eyes too, as she smiled fondly back. Mary Ann delivered a plate of bacon, eggs, fried bread, fried tomatoes and sausage to her new husband with something approaching a smile.

'There you are, Jacob. Start the day with a good

37

breffus, I always say.'

Jake nodded and smiled back gratefully. 'Thank you, my flower. I could do with it. I'm clammed.'

'Are we going to church this morning, Mother?' Clover enquired, sitting facing Ramona who had arisen that morning as fresh as the dew.

'We're all going to church, our Clover,' Mary Ann replied piously as she placed a full plate in front of Ramona. 'It's Eucharist today. I always go to Eucharist. Have you been confirmed, Ramona?'

'Yes, when I was eleven, Mother,' Ramona replied. She had already been coached by Jake to call Mary Ann 'Mother'. 'Me and Father always went to Top Church.'

Mary Ann placed a plate in front of Clover. 'Our Clover you could've got up yourself for this, save me stretching over the table.'

Clover thought it unfair that she'd not made the same comment to Ramona who was just as awkwardly placed. 'Marmaduke's on my lap. I didn't want to disturb him.'

'Oh, sod the cat, Clover.' Mary Ann frowned and placed her own plate on the table, sitting down opposite Jake, with Clover on her right. 'Well ... now we'm a family we'll have to decide who's doing what in the pub afore we open. What do you say, Jacob?'

'Quite right,' Jake responded, nodding and chewing bacon rind. 'It's good if we all have a routine. Ramona, you can bottle up while Clover sawdusts the floor and polishes the tables. I'll stoop any barrels and mek sure as there's plenty oil in the lamps and coal in the scuttle. What'll

38

yo' be doin', Mary Ann?'

'I reckon I'll have me work cut out cooking we dinners when I get back from church, Jacob. But have no fear, I'll come and serve while it's a-cooking.'

'Well at least Zillah will do the spittoons for me now,' Clover informed them. 'After yesterday she'll be glad to do anything.'

'And serve her right,' Mary Ann remarked. 'Still, I liked the way you handled it, our Clover. Good idea to give her a pint of beer every day. Save her pinching it and more.'

'But I don't think we should put on her, just because of what's happened,' Clover stressed. 'She's been a good friend to us in other ways. You know she has.'

'And in a day or two it'll all be forgotten, I daresay,' Jake said.

Clover turned to Ramona. 'I'll show you all round the house after, Ramona, so you know where everything is. How did you find your bed, by the way?'

'Lumpy, if you want the truth.' She dipped a piece of fried bread into her egg yolk. 'I didn't sleep very well. I'm not used to a lumpy bed.'

Clover watched for her mother's reaction.

'Then we'll go down the town to the Worcestershire Furnishing in Wolverhampton Street in the week and order you a new one,' Mary Ann said with a finality that was unassailable.

Clover could hardly believe her ears. Such sudden and unbounded generosity. 'Can I have a new bed as well?' she asked, not wishing to be outdone.

'What do *you* want a new bed for, our Clover?' Mary Ann asked, evidently irked that her daughter might be trying to take advantage. 'They cost money and the one you've got is best feather and down.'

'But it's all lumpy and hard, Mother. Same as Ramona's is.'

'Try giving it a good shake. How come you've never moaned about it afore?'

''Cause I knew you wouldn't buy me a new one. But if Ramona can have a softer bed, I don't see why I shouldn't.'

Jake stuffed a forkful of best back bacon into his mouth and it amazed Clover how so much food could pass his huge moustache without leaving its mark upon it. 'If the wench wants a new bed she can have one, Mary Ann, as I see it,' Jake adjudicated fairly. He looked at Clover and smiled. 'Nobody wants to kip on a hard bed, do they?'

'Thank you ... Pop.' She was having difficulty getting used to calling him that.

'Huh!' Mary Ann tutted indignantly. ''Tis to be hoped you'm as finicky when you get married, our Clover. Lord help whoever it is as gets you.'

Conversation paused while the family, all self-conscious of each other in their new situation, concentrated on their breakfasts. Despite Clover's concern about just how radically the presence of a new stepfather and stepsister might affect her, it seemed that things might not be so bad after all. Maybe she was going to like her new stepfather. He seemed very fair.

'Are you courting, Clover?' Ramona asked,

tackling her food with determination.

Clover shook her head and smiled self-consciously, glancing at her mother. 'No, no, I'm not courting.'

'Not courting at nineteen?' Jake sounded incredulous. 'Why they must be a-queuing up – a fine-looking madam like thee.'

Clover smiled demurely and continued eating.

'Oh, there's one or two that come in the taproom and ogle at her all soft-like,' Mary Ann admitted. 'But I wouldn't give tuppence for e'er a one.'

'I'm a-courting,' Ramona stated proudly. 'I've been courting more than six months now.'

Jake burst out laughing. 'Courting at seventeen, eh? What d'you think about that, Mary Ann?'

'I think seventeen's a bit young to be a-courting, Jacob,' Mary Ann declared disapprovingly. 'I take it as you ain't serious with this chap, Ramona? Whoever he is.'

'No, I ain't serious, Mother,' Ramona felt inclined to confirm. 'It's just a chap I know.'

'There's no harm in the wench stepping out with a young chap a couple of nights a week if she wants to, Mary Ann,' Jake said. 'As long as she's back home afore ten.'

'What they can do after ten they can do afore it, Jacob,' Mary Ann argued. 'I don't hold with young women being out nights on their own with men, as our Clover knows. Specially at seventeen. But if you'm content, Jacob, then I'll be ruled by thee.'

'She'll come to no harm, Mary Ann.'

Clover smiled to herself. Things were really

looking up, because whatever Ramona could do, she would be able to do also under this new regime.

The terraced buildings that lined both sides of George Street and Brown Street on Kates Hill were made up mostly of dwellings, but were interspersed with little shops. Brown Street, generally the busier of the two, boasted shops that sold lamp-oil and clothes-pegs, sweets, haberdashery, greengrocery, as well as a barber's shop, a fish-and-chip shop, a couple of butchers' shops and several public houses. George Street hosted a newsagent, a pawnbroker, a coal yard, and a grain merchant. A mere three pubs vied for trade in George Street; the California Inn, the Jubilee Inn which was the headquarters of the pigeon club, and the Jolly Collier. But then it was less than a hundred yards from one end to the other.

Clover proudly showed Ramona around Kates Hill that afternoon to help walk down their Sunday dinners. Groups of children tumbled through the narrow streets on their way to Sunday school, and courting couples strolled hand in hand. All were wearing their Sunday best.

'It'll be nice having a sister,' Ramona said chirpily as they ventured up Cromwell Street, and Clover began to feel she was getting close to Ramona already. 'Course, with my mother dying when she had me there was no chance of a brother or a sister after.'

'Oh, I didn't realise your mother had died in childbirth,' Clover said sympathetically. 'So your dad's been on his own all these years.'

'More'n seventeen years now. I worked it out – they had to get married, you know. They'd only been married five months when I was born.'

'But that's tragic,' Clover remarked with the utmost sympathy. 'Your poor father. He's hardly known any married life. And he must have reared you by himself.'

'With a bit of help from my two grandmothers. When I was little, I used to go to one of my gran's when he went to the market.'

'I like your father,' Clover proclaimed. 'He seems very fair.'

'He's all right. Your mother don't smile much, though, does she?'

Clover chuckled good-naturedly. 'She was smiling this morning at your father...'

'I know... What if she gets pregnant, Clover?'

'Pregnant? At her age?'

'Well, I know she's forty-two but women do have babies at that age.'

'No, not my mother, Ramona. Not Mary Ann. She wouldn't. That sort of thing wouldn't interest *her*.'

'It interests every other woman. Why should she be different?... Anyway, Clover, tell me about your father.'

'I can hardly remember him. Just a few vague impressions, that's all. He was called Toby. He and Mother became licensees of the Jolly Collier in 1890 when she was twenty-five and I was just two. He died of pneumonia when I was four.'

They passed the Sailor's Return on their left, which fronted the Diamond Brewery.

43

'So who's this Ned Brisco you mentioned?' Ramona asked.

'Oh, Ned? He's just a friend. But a good friend. I'll show you where he lives in a minute.'

'Isn't he your sweetheart?'

'My sweetheart?' Clover burst out laughing. 'No, I don't fancy him that way.'

Ramona registered surprise. 'Have you ever had a lover? Have you ever done what lovers do?'

Clover shook her head, half resolutely, half apologetically. 'No. I'd wait till I was married before I did anything like that.'

'I have.' Ramona paused for Clover's reaction.

'You mean...?'

Ramona smiled smugly.

'Ramona! You never.'

'It's nothin' to make a fuss about, you know. Plenty of my friends do it.'

They were silent for a few seconds, hearing only the sound of their footsteps on the Ketley blue paving-blocks with the criss-crossed pattern, while Clover mulled over this surprising information.

'Does it hurt? They say it hurts.'

'A bit. The first time. Made me bleed a bit as well, but it didn't stop me liking it. I really liked it, Clover.'

Clover was intrigued. 'So who did you do it with? That boy you're courting?'

'Course. Sammy.'

'How long since the first time?'

'Last Christmas. I *was* seventeen, Clover,' she said reassuringly. 'I mean, it's not as if I was a child.'

'But where did you do it? I mean, if it was Christmas?'

'Me and my father were going to my gran's for our Christmas dinners, but he wanted to go to the Jolly Collier first for a drink. So he left me in our house by myself getting ready, and I was supposed to meet him at my gran's after. Anyway, Sammy called to bring me my Christmas box. I gave him a big kiss for it ... you know ... and one thing led to another ... I locked the door and we ended up on the hearth in the front room, me with me nightdress up round me waist.'

'God... But what if you'd got pregnant, Ramona? Think of all the trouble, the disgrace.'

'Oh, I won't get pregnant. Sammy pulls it out a bit sharp when he's ready to ... you know...'

Clover digested this thought-provoking information for a few seconds while they turned the corner by the Junction Inn. Watson's Street, where Ned lived, stretched narrowly to their right, a steep hill that took you to the top of Cawney Hill and its tiny twisted streets, its back-to-back cottages and its disused quarry. But Clover decided not to point out Ned's home; it would be too distracting and she wanted to explore this fascinating subject more. So they began the climb up Hill Street with its row of terraced houses on the right and its allotments on the left behind a small row of cottages.

'Some of the girls I work with at the foundry do it with their sweethearts,' Clover admitted at last. 'They tell me all about it.'

'And do they like it as well?'

45

'They must do. They're at it every chance they get.'

Ramona chuckled. 'See. It ain't just me then, is it? You'll have to get yourself a chap, Clover.'

'I think I'd be too scared to let him do anything, though. My mother's never allowed me to have a chap. She'd have a fit if I ever got into trouble. Maybe now, now you've come she'll allow it. Especially if your father allows you to see this Sammy.'

'But he don't know we do *that*, Clover. Lord above, he'd kill me if he knew, so keep it under your hat.'

'Oh, don't worry, Ramona.' She smiled reassuringly. 'Anything you tell me is just between the two of us.'

Ramona chuckled. 'It'll be nice sharing secrets, won't it?'

Chapter Three

It had been some weeks since her mother's wedding when Clover walked to the Coneygree Iron Foundry in Tividale early one sunny morning in May. In a week, it would be her twentieth birthday and she wondered what present her mother might afford her. A new summer dress for best would be nice if she were allowed to choose it herself. As she walked on, past St John's church and over Brewery Fields to the Birmingham Road, she pondered how her life had surprisingly changed for the better since Jake and Ramona had become a part of it. Clover had always lived in the shadow of her mother's domineering, had accepted it with resignation, but now she felt a new freedom. Jake was in charge and, if nothing else, he was even-handed where she and Ramona were concerned – so far at least. Mary Ann could no longer impose her restraining and often unfair moral and social code on Clover any more than she could on Ramona. It allowed for a certain latitude she had never enjoyed before. She was even allowed to visit Ned Brisco's workshop nights where she helped him construct his new flying machine. And she did not have to return till ten o'clock.

She clambered over the stile where the stubbly field met the highway. Three young beaux on bicycles wished her flirtatious good mornings before she stepped, smiling in response, onto the cobbles to reach the other side of Birmingham Road. A carter hauling sacks of coal steadied his horse while a tram rattled past and she caught up with it while the conductor alighted to change the points. She walked on, not heeding the passengers who turned their heads to look at her. In the middle distance, the black, foreboding headgear of the vast Coneygree Collieries loomed like the artificial skeletons of huge automatons. As she passed the grim Coneygree Brickworks and its great marl-hole like a giant pockmark on the landscape, she wondered whether working as a brickmaker might be cleaner than coremaking. She dearly wished she could get away from

47

coremaking. She felt she was worthy of work more dignified, cleaner; a job where she did not have to wash her hair every other night because of the filthy atmosphere. Maybe, now Jake was in charge, now they no longer seemed impoverished, she would be allowed to find a job working in a nice shop. Even working in the brewery with all its steam would be better than the foundry.

As she reached the gates of the Coneygree Iron Foundry the familiar, acrid smell of scorched sand and burning metal filled her nostrils. She headed for the time office and had her time-card stamped. In the ablutions block where she donned her headwear and her dusty brown coverall she greeted other girls who worked alongside her with a chummy smile. Conversation was generally robust and Clover indeed learned much more about life in their company than she would if she'd stayed at home helping her mother. Despite the overtly strict moral conventions that were supposed to inhibit sexual activity outside of and before marriage, it never ceased to amaze Clover just how many young women she knew who were manifestly flouting it. Ramona's confessions had only served to confirm the notion. But where did all these girls find out about such things? Who coached them?

'Have you and that Ned Brisco started courting then?' one of her friends, Selina, asked.

Clover was changing her boots, for it would not do to be seen walking in public in unsightly working boots. She smiled reticently and tugged at the laces. 'We're just friends, Selina.'

'You seem to spend enough time with your

48

heads together. I wonder as you ai' wed the chap a'ready.'

'He hasn't asked me. Besides, he's too pre-occupied with his own interests to worry about the likes of me,' Clover answered tactfully.

Selina's expression suggested she did not believe her. 'Would you marry him if he asked you?'

'He's not likely to ask... Hey, come on. Look at the time. Old Ratface Mason will be docking us a quarter-hour if we don't hurry.'

So Clover, Selina and the others trooped across the dusty yard to the core shop. Their machines were already set up to produce the cores that were required later for insertion into moulds that were to fashion gear casings, electric motor housings and the like. The atmosphere was dense and smoky and the constant roar of the blast furnace, that melted the concoction of iron ore, scrap, coke and limestone ready for casting, meant they had to shout to each other to be heard.

Clover pressed a foot pedal and the two halves of the corebox that bore the impression of the core she was making closed together with a sibilant hiss of compressed air.

'Me and Charlie have decided to go to the seaside at Whitsun, Clover,' Selina shouted over the din.

Clover pulled on a lever and black sand, like a sudden fall of soot, was forced into the iron corebox under air pressure, filling the precisely machined space inside it. Black sand these days was a mixture of Bromsgrove red loam sand and fish oil, and smelt none too savoury. It was soft and easy to work and, by the time the cores came to be used, they would be cured hard and dry. In any case, oil sand was eminently preferable to muck sand, a mixture of coal dust and sand, with strands of hemp and horse manure to bind it together. When Clover opened the corebox again, when the sand had taken on the shape of the intricately engineered recess, the result was called a core. Exactly located at a predetermined position in the mould, such as Ned Brisco would make, the molten iron when poured into the mould, would solidify around the core. By the time the iron cooled, the core would have disintegrated leaving its impression; a hole through the casting that its design and purpose ordained.

'Where to?' Clover asked. 'Which seaside town?'

'We thought about New Brighton. There's a train early from Dudley Port.'

Clover carefully eased the fragile core from its mould, inspected it and set it down gently on the table behind her. Then she began the whole process again. In a day, she would produce up to a thousand such cores.

'Let's hope the weather holds, Selina,' she called.

'Why don't you come with us, Clover, you and Ned?'

'I doubt if he'll have time. Besides, I'm supposed to be helping him with some work. I'll ask him though.'

'Yes, ask him. Too much work's no good for

50

nobody. Going to the seaside would be a nice change.'

At half-past twelve they had a half-hour break. Clover spent it with Ned outside in the warm sunshine, eating sandwiches as they sat on a crate of castings that were destined for Indian Railways, Lahore. She asked him if he fancied accompanying her to New Brighton with Selina and Charlie.

'If the weather's fine I'd rather try out the model of my new flying machine,' he replied predictably. 'I've done some wing-load calculations, Clover, and I reckon I need to increase the wingspan a bit.'

Clover took a crunching bite out of a rosy apple.

'I'm making some changes to the tail as well.'

'Oh?'

'I'm incorporating hinged flaps.'

'I see.' She didn't. She never did when he launched into his technicalities.

'I've been going over and over everything I've ever read about flying machines and one thing's struck me, Clover.'

'What's that, Ned?' She bit into her apple again.

'The Wright Brothers have a patent for controlling direction and height by warping the wings in flight. All it does is induce drag – and it's drag that gives you control. After four years of knowing about it, none of the Continental aviators have taken any notice at all and that's why they can only get their machines to hop a few yards at a time. But I reckon I can get the same effect by incorporating flaps in the wings and the tail wings. Something a bloke called Sir George Cayley suggested a hundred years ago.'

'A hundred years ago?' Clover repeated, incredulous.

'Oh, Sir George Cayley dedicated his life to the pursuit of flying. As long ago as 1809 he flew a full-size glider, unmanned at first but later with a young lad on board. Everybody seems to have forgotten the work he did. But I haven't.'

'Does that mean all my good work covering the wings was for nothing if you're increasing the wingspan?' she asked.

'No, not all of it. Just bits. I need to test it all first on my new model, though. I'm certain it'll work. I'm modifying the rudder as well.'

'I hope all this will be worth it in the long run,' Clover said. 'Mind you, I have to admire your patience, Ned. And your determination.'

He smiled warmly. 'It'll be worth it, Clover. I'll be rich one day from making and flying these machines. You'll see. Then I might even ask you to marry me.' He said it as if in jest but Clover knew that this attempt at flippancy was merely a device to disguise how earnestly he meant it.

She laughed dismissively. 'Is there any fear of you achieving it in this century then?'

'Well if I don't, it won't be for want of trying.'

The hooter sounded and Clover picked up her lunchbox and the empty bottle that had contained her tea. 'See you later, Ned. Shall I come and help you tonight?'

'If you want. It'd be nice to see you.'

Clover returned home to the Jolly Collier just after six o'clock that evening. Although she had had a good wash in the ablutions block at the foundry and thoroughly brushed her hair, she felt she did not look her best. So when she popped her head round the door from the passage that led into the taproom and saw Ramona talking to none other than Tom Doubleday, she found herself in a dilemma: whether to stop and say hello and risk Tom's silent disapproval of the way she looked in her working clothes, or allow Ramona, who looked delightful in a clean, pale-blue cotton dress, to have him to herself.

But before she could escape, Tom had already spotted her. He smiled over Ramona's shoulder and hailed her to join them.

'Oh, I daren't. I'm filthy. I must have a decent wash down and change before tea. And my hair...' Clover rolled her eyes.

'It's lovely to see you,' Tom assured her, seeing nothing untoward in her appearance at all. 'Let me buy you a drink.'

'He's brought the pictures of the wedding, Clover,' Ramona chipped in. 'Come and have a gander. They're ever so good.'

Self-consciously, Clover stepped into the tap-room and sat next to Tom. There were possibly a dozen other men in there, smoking, drinking, cursing, some playing crib. At one table a group were playing shove-ha'penny and beneath their table a mangy German shepherd dog lay, keeping a weather eye on the begrimed boot of one of the more animated players whose foot shot out unwittingly from time to time in his excitement.

Tom picked up the album from his lap and handed it to Clover. Smiling with anticipation she opened it and looked at the first photograph.

'God! Look at Mother. She's actually laughing,' she said, delighted. She flipped over to another. 'Oh, 'struth, look at me. I look awful.'

Tom craned his neck to see the offending photograph. 'To tell you the truth, Clover, I thought how nice you looked.'

With a glow of satisfaction, she looked first at Tom then at her stepsister. 'Has he been flannelling *you* like this, Ramona?'

'He says I look like Ellen Terry,' Ramona answered flatly.

'Ellen Terry?' Clover pulled a face of disapproval.

'I said you look more glamorous than Ellen Terry, Ramona.'

'I should hope so,' Ramona said, her voice characteristically croaky. 'She's older than a flippin' conker tree. She's older than Mother.'

'I only meant,' Tom explained, 'that you have similar poise. You must admit that Ellen Terry has poise. She's very elegant.'

Ramona smiled and looked at Tom warmly. 'I believe you. Thousands wouldn't.'

'This is a good one of you, Ramona,' Clover said generously and held a photograph up for her stepsister to see. Ramona agreed that she liked that one.

'Let me buy you a drink, Clover. May I?'

'Thank you, Tom. A glass of lemonade wouldn't come amiss. It's thirsty work I've been doing all day.'

Mary Ann appeared at the door from the passage, in stern mode. 'Clover. Come and help me with the tea now you'm back,' she said curtly.

'Have you seen the photographs, Mother?' Clover waved the thin album at her to buy more time with Tom.

'Yes, I've seen them,' was the terse reply. 'Now I could do with some help in the scullery.'

Clover looked disappointedly at Tom and then at Ramona. 'I'd better go. Shame about the drink.'

'Another time,' Tom suggested, his face manifesting equal disappointment.

'Yes, another time.' She smiled her apology. 'Coming, Mother.'

Tom Doubleday appeared again in the taproom of the Jolly Collier a couple of days later. Clover spotted him as she returned home from work. Self-conscious about her dowdy working clothes, she flitted past the door hoping to be unseen, but Tom caught sight of her and waved. She waved back but scurried out of sight into the security of the scullery. Later, as she was peeling potatoes at the stone sink, she peered through the window and caught sight of Tom Doubleday talking and laughing with Ramona outside. A pang of jealousy seared through her. Never in her life before had she experienced jealousy and it was not a pleasant feeling. Suddenly, her heart was beating fast and she felt hot; she hated Ramona for being in Tom Doubleday's company, for luring him away. Just as suddenly she hated Tom Doubleday for spurning her by being so obviously taken with her stepsister. She'd hankered for Tom Doubleday since the day she met him and Ramona must have known that. Ramona surely didn't want him; she'd got this Sammy she'd talked about. Could the girl really be so thoughtless, so selfish as to take the man *she* wanted?

At tea Clover hardly spoke and didn't even acknowledge Ramona. But nobody seemed to miss her contribution to the conversation that was growing more intense by the minute.

'Six more free houses will take our ale, Mary Ann,' Jake announced. 'And an off-licence in Castle Street. As soon as we can brew the extra beer they'll start selling it. Things am really looking up.'

Mary Ann sighed and swallowed a mouthful of rabbit stew. 'It's all well and good finding places what'll take the stuff, Jacob, but can we brew it fast enough? That lot in the taproom can soak it up as quick as ever I can brew it.'

He picked a small piece of bone from between his teeth and set it on the side of his plate. 'We need a bigger copper boiler. Six hundred and fifty gallon capacity wouldn't be amiss. That's eighteen barrels a brew, Mary Ann. Brewing six days a week, that's one hundred and eight barrels. Course, we'd need half a dozen new fermenting vessels and all. And that grist mill we've got is buggered.'

'And where d'you suppose the money's coming from, Jacob?' Mary Ann asked astutely. ''Cause I don't suppose for a minute as it'll stop at a new boiler and fermenting vessels. I daresay we'll

56

need an extension to the brewery, eh? Then we'm gonna need a new horse and dray *and* somebody to drive it.'

Jake dipped a piece of bread into his stew and popped it, dripping, into his mouth thoughtfully. 'Well, we've made a start,' he said. 'You see, Mary Ann, what you've gorra consider is the potential. In five years, if everything goes according to plan, we could own six or seven licensed premises besides this'n. You only have to see what Hanson's have done to see as there's money to be made.'

Clover displayed little interest in the schemes and aspirations of her new stepfather. Let him get on with it. It was a different world to the one she inhabited. She was more concerned about Tom Doubleday and how he now seemed out of her reach. She excused herself from the table and went to her room sullenly. There, she sat on her new bed and sighed, full of frustration, full of animosity over Ramona. She gazed at the washstand with its ewer and bowl set and saw her face reflected in the mirror at the back of it. She was frowning. Yet she was not given to frowning. She must be in love with Tom Doubleday, else why would she feel like this? Her inborn common sense, however, suggested she had no prior claim over him. Ramona had just as much right to him.

She stood up and rummaged through her wardrobe for a frock that was suitable attire for sewing canvas pieces onto wing sections. A home-made one presented itself and she changed into it. If Tom Doubleday fancied Ramona who was she to complain? She could hardly blame him. After all, Ramona was a fine-looking, vivacious young woman. Doubtless, in no time, they would be doing together eagerly what Ramona had been doing with Sammy. Naturally, the thought did not please her. It did not please her at all. Deftly, she buttoned up the dress, then shook out her long dark hair, brushed it thoroughly and tied it up again. At least Ned would be glad to see her. At least she could rely on Ned.

When she called for Ned at his home in Watson's Street his mother, as usual, made a huge fuss of Clover. No, he'd gone half an hour since to Springfield House. He'd had another idea and couldn't wait to get cracking on it. He said to send her over when she arrived, but would she like a cup of tea first? Clover replied that she'd not long had one and another would ensure she'd be dying to pee in an hour, when there was nowhere for a woman to pee at the stables of Springfield House since they'd demolished the old earth closet. She didn't like to bother Mr Mantle, either, when he was so good anyway about them using the old stables to construct Ned's flying machine.

So Clover bid goodbye to Florrie Brisco and carried on down Watson's Street, turning right at Percy Collins's greengrocery store. When she reached the top of Hill Street where it levelled out, she could see the blue slate roofs of Springfield House in Tansley Hill Road, a narrow, descending lane that was overhung like a grotto with tall trees.

Now that Joseph Mantle had bought a Sunbeam motor car and housed it in a newly constructed garage on the other side of Springfield House the old stables were redundant and the horses and carriage long since gone. The stables comprised one building that used to be sectioned into stalls on one side and was long enough to accommodate a forty-foot wingspan. Ned realised he was lucky to have such a fine facility, and with no outlay. His mother had been instrumental in arranging for him to use the stables through her connection with the Mantles; she had been in service there for years before she married, and was highly thought of. She still called regularly and the Mantles welcomed her like any old friend. Indeed, Joseph Mantle took a keen interest in Ned's project and often put his head round the stable door to check on progress.

Ned smiled when he saw Clover. He had already taken off the sailcloth coverings at the wing-tips, ready for extending the wingspan.

'So what do you want me to do, Ned?'

'I want you to cover in the fuselage behind where I sit,' he told her. 'There's no advantage anyway in leaving it open like a frame. Enclosing it can provide storage space and protect the control wires to the tail and rudder.'

'All right.' She set about measuring up for the first piece.

'Look here's the model. It's nearly finished already. What do you think?'

'It looks a bit different to the first flying machine you made,' she said fingering the tail. 'It's less like a box kite.'

He grinned with satisfaction. 'And it'll perform

better than any box kite design.'

She smiled at him with admiration. He was so engrossed in his machine and how he could make it fly. His determination was formidable. Nothing would deter him from his goal. Oh, he would succeed, of that she was certain. He read every scrap of information there was to read about the progress of other aviators all over the world and utilised their best ideas.

Clover moved to the trestle table and rolled out the expensive canvas sailcloth. She measured it and marked it out with a piece of blue chalk, then began cutting with a huge pair of scissors. Meanwhile Ned sawed and sanded the lath of wood that was to become an extended spar on one of the wings and offered it up to the construction. They worked companionably, speaking little, while Clover's thoughts were about Tom Doubleday and whether he was supposed to be meeting Ramona that evening.

It depressed her to think about it. Ramona and Tom Doubleday... What if she got pregnant and he had to marry her?

If only he had asked her, Clover, to be his, she would be the happiest girl in the world. Oh, she was not without admirers, that much was obvious. Often she caught men looking at her covetously in the Jolly Collier when she was helping to serve. Men looked at her in church on a Sunday, they ogled her at the foundry. When she was walking to work she would attract many a wolf whistle. Yet no other man had really appealed. Nobody had ever made her stomach churn like Tom Doubleday. She'd never looked at a man's lips before and known she wanted, more than anything, to be kissed by them. She'd never looked at a man's hands and wondered what sensations they would elicit if they explored her body. She'd lain in bed at night imagining it and all sorts of other very private things, and could not sleep for ages after because of it.

The nearest thing she'd experienced to romance was Ned Brisco, but that was too one-sided to be any good for him. It was time to be honest with Ned, time to make him realise there could never be anything more than that which already existed between them. Some day, she would meet a man and fall head over heels in love; somebody other than Tom Doubleday who was occupying her thoughts now. Ned had to be prepared for that. It was only fair.

'Why is it that you like me to spend my time here with you, Ned?' she asked, breaking the concentration.

Ned stopped what he was doing and turned round to face her. 'That's a funny question, Clover.'

'But I'd really like to know.'

'Well, because I enjoy your company, I suppose. It's nice being with you. And because you help me a lot.'

'You enjoy my company, you said. But you hardly ever speak while I'm here.'

'I still enjoy your company, Clover. I feel comfortable with you. We don't have to talk all the while.'

'No, I suppose not,' she answered softly.

'What's the matter, Clover? You sound real fed

up.' He sounded uneasy. 'Aren't you interested in the flying machine anymore?'

'Course I am,' she admitted. 'I still want to see you succeed. I want to see the thing fly and know that I had a hand in it. But, as regards anything else ... I mean *us* ... you and me ... we see each other here, yet we don't talk much, you have to admit.'

He sighed with dejection. 'I admit I'm not such a brilliant conversationalist, Clover.'

She smiled affectionately. She couldn't help but like him. 'Well you do seem to be limited to one topic...'

'Yes, I know I'm a bit preoccupied with it. Sorry. It doesn't mean I'm not interested in you, Clover. I think the world–'

'So how would you feel if you saw me with another man?' she asked straightforwardly. 'Because if another man I liked asked me out and I liked him, I'd most likely go. I mean, it's not as if you and me are courting or anything like that.'

'No,' he said and she perceived his dejection. 'I agree, it's not as if we're courting. I had hoped though, when–'

'So it would be a mistake for you to regard me as anything other than a friend – wouldn't it? Even though plenty folk think we're more than just friends.'

He shrugged again disappointedly. 'So have you met somebody you like, Clover? Is that why you mention it?'

'No, no. I haven't met anybody, Ned. But I might. And if I do, I don't want you to think that

I ... I don't want you to think you have any claim on me. On the other hand, I'd hate you to think I don't care anything for our friendship, 'cause I do. 'Cause that's what we are – friends.'

'Yes, we are friends, Clover. I'd like us to be more than that but... Dammit, I might as well say it, since we're talking about it ... I'm in love with you, Clover. Always have been. All right, I know you're not in love with me, so...' He shrugged again and turned back to the wing he was modifying. 'Well, at least we work well together, don't we?'

Clover's twentieth birthday came and went and no great fuss made. She was privately delighted when she received a birthday card from Tom Doubleday which she secreted away in her bedroom away from Ramona's prying eyes. She had a lovely new white two-piece summer dress made at Bessie Roberts's, who already had a note of her measurements. It had a high-necked bodice, pouched in front; she chose the style and paid for it herself. Mary Ann gave her a new prayer book, Jake handed her a sovereign to spend as she wished, and Ramona bought her a new parasol for the summer to go with the new dress.

The new dress re-exposed a recent bone of contention that Clover had hoped was buried for good: to Mary Ann's reaffirmed dismay, Clover still refused to wear a corset to pull in her waist. She insisted that her waist was small enough at twenty-four inches, so she didn't need a corset. 'Brazen faggot,' her mother called her. 'Wait till you've had kids and you'm my age and it all

63

starts to puff out like a bladder full of wind,' she told her. But Clover perceived some humour in her mother's eyes. Perhaps envy, too, that she could not be so brazen as to face the world corsetless, especially as her younger husband was fond of patting her rock-hard backside, when he might well have preferred patting untrussed feminine flesh that yielded more temptingly to the touch. Ramona, too, embraced Clover's attitude to corsets. It made perfect sense not to constrict your movements and make yourself uncomfortable and hot, especially now that summer was coming. In any case, at work she was bending down so much, reaching for bottles on low shelves, stretching up for glasses and spirit bottles. It was bad enough having to wear all the uncomfortable things a woman was expected to wear, let alone corsets. Besides, Ramona's waist measured only twenty-three inches, so she needed a corset even less than Clover, being so petite. So corsets they did not wear and, since corsets were not a fit topic for discussion at the meal table in any case, the subject was finally abandoned.

Whitsun came and went in days of perpetual sunshine and the scaled-down model of Ned's flying machine proved to be a big attraction in Buffery Park on the Sunday, watched by a gathering clutch of highly curious Sunday afternoon walkers. The modifications he deemed necessary he carried out the same evening and put them to the test next day, to the delight of a chattering of children who were astonished, and a cete of grey old men whom nothing would surprise. It only remained to incorporate these changes into the full-scale biplane he had almost finished constructing.

Tom Doubleday, Clover knew, called in at the Jolly Collier two or three times a week nowadays, but since it always coincided with her return from work when she looked her shabbiest she seldom spoke to him. Occasionally, he would spot her drifting through the passage but there was no opportunity for conversation. And besides, she did not want to antagonise Ramona.

Apart from one or two days of squally rain early in June that left the uneven cobbled streets of Kates Hill dotted with inky puddles, the weather became more settled again. Ramona enjoyed her eighteenth birthday and she, too, had a card from Tom Doubleday which she kept in her room away from Clover's prying eyes. Her father bought her a new accordion.

A new copper boiler with a capacity of six hundred and fifty gallons was installed in the brewery along with a larger mash tun. But Jake could make full use of neither yet; three more fermentation vessels were required to give them the capacity they needed. Lack of capital was proving to be the problem and his house remained unsold, making matters worse. Mary Ann seriously distrusted all banks so, out of respect for his new wife's wishes, Jake was reluctant to apply to one for a loan. However, some progress had been made, inasmuch as several outlets had signed up to take deliveries of Beckitt's Beers, as the products were being branded.

It was time for Jake to implement his back-up plan.

On the evening of Wednesday, 5th June, he left the Jolly Collier's customers in the care of Mary Ann, Ramona and Clover while he headed for the Dudley Arms Hotel in the Market Place. The Dudley Arms was where Elijah Tandy lived, enjoying his wealth in lordly fashion, in a fine room that offered him easy access to all the card schools in the town. As a soldier Elijah had served unscathed under Kitchener, first in the Boer War from 1899 to 1902, and in India during 1903 and 1904 and had seen something of life. He returned from India somewhat better off than when he departed, thanks to a skill he acquired during countless off-duty hours playing poker. Nowadays, Jake often referred to him as the Nabob. Since his soldiering, he had done little other than gamble successfully. Jake considered the time had come for Elijah to make himself useful and be a more responsible citizen.

He found him in his room, fastening a collar to his shirt in front of the mirror.

'Off out, our Elijah?'

'A spot of courting.'

'Can you spare me half an hour before you go? I doubt if Dorcas will mind.'

'Why, what's up?'

'The brewery, Elijah. I was counting on having sold the house by now and the money from that subsidising the expansion of the business a bit further. Well, it ain't sold, as you know and we need money for more fermentation squares.

66

Otherwise we can't get no further forward. I wondered if you'd got a few hundred I could borrow meanwhile.'

Elijah struggled with his collar stud but managed to attach the collar at the back. 'This brewing business, Jake... Is it sound? I mean is there money to be made?'

'Sound? I should say it's bloody sound. Already I've got off-licences and free houses clamouring to buy our stuff. You know what Mary Ann's beer's like – beautiful. The blokes love it. Then there's the ironworks we could supply. Have no fear, Elijah, your money would be safe enough.'

Elijah pondered while he tied his necktie. 'I ain't so sure as I want to lend you money, Jake,' he said at last and noted the disappointment that registered on his brother's face. 'But I'll come into the business as a partner, if you'll have me. And I'll put money in.'

Jake's face lit up. 'And you're welcome, our Elijah. Listen, if you come to work in the business it makes sense to come and live at the Jolly Collier. After all, you couldn't live here still when the place belongs to a rival brewery. And there's a spare bedroom. We could soon get it ready for you.'

Elijah studied the proposal for a few seconds while he adjusted his necktie in the mirror. 'All right. There's just one small consideration, Jake...'

'Which is?'

'Dorcas.'

'Oh. Are you getting wed at last then?'

'Me wed? You're kidding, mate. I ain't about to

67

get wed. But I do like to claim me conjugal rights from time to time.'

'Oh, I see...' Jake looked pensive.

'There is one way we could solve it, Jake...'

Jake looked up at him hopefully. 'How?'

'By you allowing me to use your house a couple of nights a week for me courting. They turn a blind eye here when Dorcas comes back to me room at night, but I can't see Mary Ann turning a blind eye at the Jolly Collier, can you?'

Jake shook his head. 'Besides, there's the two girls...'

'As you say, there's the two girls,' Elijah agreed.

'Well, I've got no objection to you using my old bed to get your wicked away a couple of nights a week, our Elijah. Far be it from me to get in the way of that. In fact, I'll call in myself and get it all made up for you.'

Elijah smiled. 'Let's go down to the bar and have a drink on it then, eh?'

'It's all settled then?'

'It's all settled. How much money do you want off me, our Jake?'

'Let's say a thousand for now if you can spare it. We'll have a deed of partnership drawn up, legal like, and agree later the final figure. Wait till I tell Mary Ann. She'll be beside herself.'

'With joy or despair?'

Jake laughed. 'You can never tell just by looking. But she's all right. I wouldn't swap her for crock of gold.'

Chapter Four

On 10th June, a Monday, Clover and Ned walked back to Kates Hill together from the Coneygree. Whichever route they took they had a steep uphill climb at some point. Today, though, they decided to take the Bunns Lane route.

'Did you read about that attempt in France yesterday to fly?' Ned asked as they ambled past the Bunns Lane brick works on their left.

'No, tell me about it.'

'Some chap called Alberto Santos-Dumont. Yesterday, on its first test flight he wrecked some weird concoction of aeroplane and airship he'd put together.'

'That's a shame,' Clover commented. 'Just think of all the work he must've put into it, if what you do is anything to go by.'

'Well I don't feel sorry for him, Clover,' Ned said trenchantly and slung his knapsack onto his other shoulder to underline his point. 'Serves him right for not sticking to one configuration. He tried his luck first with a biplane he'd built in March and that didn't work. So he cobbles together this latest daft combination and that don't work either. Well, I ain't surprised. Now he's said he's going to try and fly with a monoplane arrangement. Why don't he make his mind up?'

'You mean he should try and master one thing

at a time?'

'It's obvious. We know biplanes'll fly 'cause the Wright Brothers have flown 'em. Why didn't he just stick with his biplane and try to master that shape. That's the trouble with the Continentals. They keep hiving off in different directions. I bet any money I'll fly sooner than they do – and further.'

The exertion of brisk uphill walking in the warm muggy evening air made them both hot and they were at the point in Watson's Green Road, by the wooden cowsheds of Roseland Farm that reeked of farm animals, where the climb started to get steep.

'If the weather stays fine this weekend I want to try and fly the *Gull*.' The *Gull* was the name he had given to this, his new biplane. 'It's as good as ready, Clover, and Amos can borrow the horse and cart again so we can transport it.'

'Are you going over Rough Hill again?' she asked.

'It's the best hill facing south-west. And not much in the way of trees if I come down a bit sudden. Shall you come?'

'Course I'll come. You don't think I'm going to miss it after all the hours I've put in, do you?' She laughed and pushed her hair away from her forehead that was bearing a sheen of perspiration.

'I'm ever so confident it'll fly, Clover, I'm thinking of inviting the *Dudley Herald* to send a reporter. I want local factory owners to take an interest. I want the world to know about my efforts.'

'Good idea,' she said enthusiastically. 'You deserve some recognition for all the work you've put in.'

'That's what I thought. Even the French get loads of publicity and they generally fall on their arses. What are you doing tonight, Clover?'

'I'm going to stay in tonight. I've got some ironing to do.'

'I just wondered if you fancied going out with me... If you're going to be busy though, it don't matter.'

They reached the Junction Inn with its rounded façade, said cheerio and parted. Holding her coat by the loop with which she hung it up, she flung it over her shoulder and walked briskly down Cromwell Street. She was hungry and wanted her tea. She hoped it would be ready when she arrived home. As she reached the bottom of Cromwell Street, she could see the rotund figure of Zillah Bache in her long skirt ambling towards her in George Street. She waved and smiled and Clover crossed the road at Brown Street to intercept her.

'I'm just on me way home,' Zillah announced. 'It's warm, int it?'

'It is warm,' Clover agreed. 'Too warm. What's for my tea, Zillah? I'm famished.'

'I'n done yer a nice meat-and-tater pie, my babby.'

'Ooh, lovely.'

'It'll be in the oven at the side of the grate. The others'n had theirs.'

As she made to continue her journey, Clover noticed a solitary bottle of beer frothing in Zillah's basket; her daily reward for not helping herself. 'I'd better go, Zillah. I don't want anybody else pinching my pie. See you tomorrow.'

'I er ... heard your mother and that Jake talkin' today, Clover...'

'Oh?' Clover checked herself.

'He was on about 'em needing more money to finish what they'm a-doing in the brewery.'

'God knows where they'll get it. You know what Mother's like about the banks.'

'Well that Jake was saying as how they've got to the point where they can't turn back. They've got to go forwards, he says. So he's asked his brother Elijah to come in with 'em. He ain't short of a copper or two by all accounts.'

'Well, if that solves the problem, Zillah, all well and good.'

'Yes, but you ain't heard the best of it,' Zillah gloated, bursting with this opportunity to impart even more astounding information. 'He's taking up lodgings with you. He's moving into the spare bedroom. From next Sunday. I gorra spruce it all up and air the bed.'

'You mean he's coming to live at the Jolly Collier?'

'That's about the size of it, Clover, my wench.' She pressed her lips together tightly and nodded once, her expression suitably grave.

'Thanks for letting me know. I don't suppose Mother will tell me till the last minute. She never tells me anything. I sometimes wonder if she knows I exist.'

'Well, she seems a bit took with Jake, your stepfather and no two ways. I 'spect she can't keep

72

her mind on nothing else yet awhile.'

'As long as she's happy ... I'll go, Zillah. See you tomorrow.'

'Yes, see you tomorrow, Clover. Keep out the hoss road.'

Clover carried on, smiling and acknowledging people who were walking in the opposite direction. As she reached the Jolly Collier, Tom Doubleday rushed out and almost knocked her over.

'Oops!... God, I'm so sorry, Clover,' he said full of remorse.

'Oh, hello, Tom. Fancy bumping into you.' Standing on one leg, Clover tried, hidden by the length of her skirt, to secretly rub her shin with the upper of her shoe at the spot where his foot had caught her.

'I hope I haven't hurt you, Clover.' He placed his hand on her arm in a gesture of concern and the sensation of his hand, warm upon her, set her pulse racing. 'I ought to start looking where I'm going before I wreak too much damage. I'm such a clumsy clot.'

'It's all right, Tom, I'm fine,' she assured him.

He took his hand away. 'Did I hurt your leg?'

'Just my shin,' she admitted and raised the hem of her skirt to reveal a well-turned ankle. 'It's nothing. Are you just leaving?'

He smiled with a warmth that churned her insides. 'I've got work to do.'

'Oh... Is Ramona all right?' she asked awkwardly.

He turned his head momentarily as if to check inside the pub. 'Yes, she seems all right. Why? Is something the matter? Are you worried about her?'

'No, no...' She shook her head, tongue-tied, and hoped he would be able to think of some comment to make, for she could think of none.

'How's your friend,' he blurted, almost as dumbstruck as she was. 'Isn't his name Ned? I think that's what Ramona told me.'

'Oh, Ned...' She nodded, flustered. There was no sense in denying Ned if Ramona had made it her business to mention him. 'Ned's all right ... thanks.'

'He's building a flying machine, isn't he?'

'Yes, that's his real passion.' She smiled then looked abashed at her shoes that were poking out daintily under her skirt, silently cursing herself for blushing so vividly. 'I help him. I help him build it. He's going to fly it on Sunday morning over Rough Hill. Tis to be hoped the weather stays fair.' She looked up into the sky as if it would yield some clue.

'Let's hope so.' He found it difficult to avert his eyes from her face. 'Are you helping him tonight?'

'Oh, no, not tonight. I'm having a night in tonight. Ironing.' She uttered a little laugh of embarrassment and rolled her eyes.

He nodded. 'Well, it's nice to see you Clover. I seldom get the chance to talk to you ... which is a shame. Still ... I'll see you again soon, I hope.'

She smiled demurely and nodded again. 'Yes ... I hope so.'

'See you then, Clover. Sorry about your shin.'

74

'It's all right, Tom. I can't feel a thing.'
And she couldn't.

As the week wore on Clover thought more and more about Tom Doubleday. Meeting him so unexpectedly and talking to him had triggered dreamy thoughts again which, because of Ramona, she dared not foster. The week also brought a steady dribble of cardboard boxes and a couple of suitcases; Elijah's belongings that were in the course of being transferred from the Dudley Arms to the Jolly Collier. And still nobody mentioned to Clover that his permanent arrival was imminent.

'Do I take it that somebody is coming to lodge with us, Mother, seeing how somebody's trankel-ments are cluttering up the passage and the stairs?' she asked, pretending she did not know, peeved that nobody other than Zillah had mentioned it.

'Elijah Tandy,' Mary Anne responded eco-nomically. 'Sunday.'

'Why has nobody mentioned it?'

'Oh? I would've thought that Jacob or Ramona might've said.'

'Nobody's said. I would've thought you might have said, Mother. So how come he's moving in here?'

'He's investing some money in the brewing venture and coming to work with us. Jacob said that if he did, he might as well live here.'

'Why doesn't he go and live in Jake's house till it's sold?'

Mary Ann laughed scornfully. 'I imagine he's

afeared that if he does, young Dorcas will take it as a sign to go and live with him. That'll mean him getting wed and he don't want to get wed. You'd think she'd have the gumption to take the hint. He's only been engaged to the wench three years.'

'Will he be paying rent here?'

'Lord, no. He's Jacob's brother, our Clover. Besides, you could hardly ask him to pay rent when he's coughing up a load of money.'

'I suppose not. How did he make his money, Mother?'

'I shouldn't ask.' Mary Ann lowered her voice. 'Gambling, if you want the truth,' she muttered distastefully. 'Cards. Not as I hold with it, as you know. But if it can do Jacob some good...'

Clover finished her ironing by eight o'clock that night and, looking neat and tidy in a white blouse and navy skirt with her hair done up, went into the taproom to help Ramona. The number of young men that were patrons these days suddenly struck her, young men she had not seen before, many more than there ever used to be. They all had eyes for Ramona but, when Clover herself appeared, many of them fastened their eyes onto her too. Ramona spoke familiarly to those who addressed her. She giggled at their flirting and her repartee was equal to the wittiest.

'You seem to have quite a few admirers, Ramona,' Clover commented ungrudgingly.

Ramona grinned. 'Well, they'll all be disappointed when Sammy comes.'

'Sammy?' she queried, thinking of Tom and

76

how it might affect him. 'Is he coming?'

'I ain't seen him for ages. But I had a letter from him yesterday. He says he wants to see me again, so I wrote back and asked him to come tonight.'

Clover was tempted to say well what about Tom Doubleday. She felt inclined to comment that it seemed hardly fair on him, especially if she intended resuming her shenanigans with this Sammy. But she thought better of it. It was none of her business. It was best to keep well out of it.

'When he comes, Clover, would you mind covering for me while I go out with him, seeing as you're down here?'

'I don't mind,' Clover replied. 'Just as long as Pop doesn't mind you going out.'

'Oh, he won't mind.'

'Is Tom coming tonight?'

'He's already been and gone, Clover.'

A group of young men on one table called Ramona's attention. They wanted their glasses replenished. She made a show of provocatively swinging her narrow hips as she approached them and it seemed to Clover that her stepsister was deliberately flaunting herself. She seemed to enjoy it when they gawped at her. She revelled in their looking her up and down wantonly, making lewd signs to each other. She played up to them, laughed at their ribald comments while she collected their glasses ready for refilling.

'You seem to enjoy egging those men on,' Clover remarked with disapproval, helping her fill a couple of the glasses from another beer pump. 'Do you think that's wise?'

'Wise?' Ramona queried, as if such wisdom was irrelevant. 'It's good for business, Clover.'

'You mean...?'

'I mean, I couldn't give a sod for any of them, but as long as they think they've got a chance with me they'll keep coming in here and spending money.'

Clover laughed as the realisation struck her. 'Yes, I suppose...'

'You could help the cause as well, you know, Clover. You can fetch the ducks off the water. I've seen how men look at you.'

'Do you think so?'

'I know so. You're different to me but that don't mean they like you any less. What one bloke likes, another won't. What one bloke don't like, another will. One man's meat, Clover.'

Clover smiled to herself. They *were* different, Ramona and her. Ramona was so much more worldly than her years suggested. But then, she had always had the freedom to do as she pleased. She was canny and uninhibited. Clover was neither. Ramona understood love, life and how to manipulate. Clover did not. Ramona's big brown eyes, her curly, flaxen hair and her dimpled grin she could use to gain ascendancy over anybody she wished and she was not reticent about doing it. A couple of inches taller, with dark hair and blue eyes, and with an innocence Ramona lacked, Clover certainly was different. But she was no less appealing. Each had something the other did not possess.

Clover oozed innocence. Although she was two years older, compared to Ramona she was a

78

novice, never allowed to go out alone at night before Jake and Ramona came along. She had led a sheltered life and she was beginning to realise just how sheltered it had been. Clover had never been loved by a man – not truly loved. How could she be a complete woman when she was lacking such experience? How could she truly know what men appreciated in a woman when she had never been allowed to mix freely with attractive, eligible young men who might teach her? She had obediently succumbed to her mother's will in all things, seldom challenging; not that Mary Ann had been tyrannical – indeed, she had not, but she brooked no opinion contrary to her own. Sometimes Clover wondered whether Mary Ann's decisions were derived for Mary Ann's own benefit and the daughter's considerations were secondary. Well, times were changing. Things were going to be different.

The front door latch clattered and a youth walked in with an expectant look on his fresh face. He was about nineteen, Clover estimated, with short-cropped dark hair and a cheeky grin. He had a pretty face for a boy, features that many a young girl would have been glad of. With an indisputable cockiness he stepped up to Ramona who had her back towards him.

'Ramona?'

At once she turned around, a grin of anticipation on her face. 'Sammy. You came. How are you?'

'All the better for seeing your lovely face, Ramona,' he replied. 'Can I have a pint?'

'Have it on me,' she said and immediately

79

pulled him a pint of mild. 'When you've drunk it we'll go out if you like. Clover here will cover for me, won't you Clover?'

'I said I would. So this is Sammy.' She smiled politely.

'Clover. My new stepsister,' Ramona explained.

Sammy shook her hand and smiled broadly. 'I bet you fetch the ducks off the water,' he commented.

The two girls broke into a fit of giggling.

Dorcas Downing and Elijah Tandy appeared in all their finery at the Jolly Collier on the Saturday night. They drank in the snug with Jacob, Mary Ann and Ramona by turns, when customers in the taproom would allow them a few minutes from serving.

Elijah Tandy was celebrating his thirty-second birthday that very day and bought everybody in the pub a drink. He oozed confidence and had a way with women. He was not excessively handsome, but he was fit and solid and his pleasant and polite manner, his easy way with a compliment, won him the admiration of many a girl.

Dorcas Downing, his woman, was twenty-five, dark and strikingly beautiful with enormous brown eyes. Her father, who owned a hollow-ware factory at Eve Hill in the parish of St James, was also a magistrate and highly respected. His affluence ensured Dorcas could indulge herself in expensive clothes. They lived in a fine house in Ednam Road on the rural north-west side of the town. Whether Mr Downing approved of his prospective son-in-law, nobody knew.

'Can I interest anybody in a cheese sandwich?' Clover was carrying a tray into the snug. She looked a picture of fresh-faced femininity with her dark hair shining, done up in loose curls on top of her head. She wore a crisp white blouse with a high neck and a long black skirt that emphasised the youthfulness of her hips and gave her bottom some attractive contours. 'There's some Spanish onion as well, look, if anybody wants some.'

'Yes please, Clover, my babby,' Elijah said amiably. He put down his pint and took a couple of sandwiches.

'Dorcas?'

Dorcas sighed heavily as if the world and all its problems had suddenly come to roost on her shoulders. 'Well if Elijah's having cheese and onion I suppose I'd better.'

'I should,' Clover urged with a friendly wink.

'You'd better,' Elijah agreed and there was a twinkle in his eye, 'else you won't want to kiss me after.'

'Who would not want to kiss you, Elijah?' Clover said flippantly. 'Onion or no onion.' At once she realised she had been tactless. She was not that familiar with Elijah, yet his easy-going nature had allowed her to believe she could get away with such innocent innuendo.

Elijah chuckled but Dorcas's face was like cold marble. She was evidently not so easy-going. 'Does that mean that when my back's turned others will be trying to usurp me?' she asked Clover, her eyebrows raised in pique.

'Not at all,' Clover apologised earnestly. 'I was

just being frivolous, Dorcas. I didn't mean anything by it. You shouldn't read anything into it.'

'It's all right, Clover,' Elijah said, and others
had cottoned on to the chill atmosphere that was
suddenly pervasive. 'Dorcas can be a bit touchy,
can't you Dorcas? Time of the month, I reckon.'

Dorcas looked at him with scorn. 'Don't be so
coarse, Elijah. But how do you expect me to feel
now you're coming to live in the same house as
two frivolous young fillies who can't keep their
eyes off you?'

'I think that might be a bit of an exaggeration,
Dorcas,' Clover said, and left to fetch another
tray of sandwiches for the taproom.

Ned and Amos had already loaded the flying
machine onto the borrowed cart by the time
Clover arrived at Springfield House. Mr Mantle
appeared in his dressing-gown and night-cap and
wished Ned the very best of luck, to which Ned
replied that he was getting nervous about the
whole thing. But at least the weather remained
warm and sunny.

'I hope there's a bit more wind up on Rough
Hill,' Ned commented apprehensively as they
walked alongside the cart down Tansley Hill
Road. 'I'll need a bit o' wind to keep me aloft.'

'The wind's kept me aloft all sodding night,'
Amos said sombrely and Clover giggled. 'That
Millard's bloody mild up at the Gypsy's Tent
serves me barbarous. And what with having to
run up the yard when I was took short...'

'It's all right for you to mock, Amos,' Ned
complained, 'but what about if I fail today? I've

asked the *Dudley Herald* to come and report on this attempt.'

'Well I don't suppose he'll mind, the Dudley herald, specially if you crash, our Ned. It'll give him summat to shout about... Who is he, anyroad, this Dudley herald?' Amos winked conspiratorially at Clover.

'Who is he!' Ned scoffed. 'The *Dudley Herald* is the newspaper, you fool...' Then it dawned on him that Amos was pulling his leg. He laughed, embarrassed. 'Swine!'

All three laughed and it relieved some of the tension they all felt. This was going to be a day of great significance. If Ned and his machine covered any distance and it responded to his new control mechanisms, he could be on his way to more important things. Powered flight would inevitably be next and the search for a suitable engine. If he failed... No. Failing was not to be contemplated. Even though he had to scrimp and save so he could afford to buy the materials to build his machines, it really was a labour of love.

Folk on their way to church stopped and gawped at the strange contraption that was strapped in sections onto the cart. One or two of the more enlightened men guessed that it might have been a flying machine but, for all some of them knew, it could have been a giant bedstead.

Eventually they trundled past Oakham Farm and, on a lane known as Turner's Hill, they arrived at the broken gate that led into the high field that crowned Rough Hill. To Ned's relief it was blowing significantly harder up here than it had been in Tansley Hill Road that lay in the lee of Cawney Hill. They off-loaded the flying machine and Ned began by bolting the under-carriage, which was a pair of bicycle wheels attached to a wooden frame, to the fuselage. While Clover held the assembly steady, Ned bolted the wings to the fuselage and began the complicated routine of fastening the bracing and the rigging between the top and bottom wings that afforded some stability and tension to the structure. By this time, the reporter from the *Dudley Herald* had shown up and began asking Ned all sorts of questions. Ned answered them patiently while he worked, but he would not stop what he was doing. He fastened the stiff wires that joined the wing flaps to the levers by his seat and within an hour, the *Gull* was ready to fly.

'Steady as you go,' Ned urged as they trundled it ungainly towards the launch point, holding it back so that it shouldn't run on its own down the hill and fly off unmanned; that would be the ultimate embarrassment with a reporter there to witness it. Amos was chocking the wheels with a large piece of wood when they heard a man's voice calling from behind them, its sound almost carried away from them by the stiff breeze.

'Clover! Clover!'

She turned around. Tom Doubleday was rush-ing towards them carrying his camera, a case and a tripod. Her heart leapt into her mouth but she waved at him, blushed and grinned. Guiltily, she looked at Ned.

'Ned, there's a photographer here to take your picture,' she said. 'Don't climb aboard yet.'

Tom was panting when he reached them. 'I'm

glad I caught you... Didn't think I'd get here in time... Which one's Ned, Clover?'

Clover introduced them.

'You're just in time, mate,' Amos informed him. 'Two more minutes and you'd have missed all the fun.'

'Do you mind if I take a photograph of you and your machine, Ned?' Tom asked. 'It's for my own interest really.'

'I've got no objection,' Ned replied.

'Maybe the *Dudley Herald* would like a copy?' Clover suggested to the reporter. 'It could illustrate your article.'

The reporter nodded. 'That'd be perfect. We could make a proper feature of it.'

'What's your name, by the way?' Ned asked.

'Julian Oakley.' Julian smiled. 'At your service.'

'Welcome to this little gathering. Let's hope you get something worth reporting.'

'I have every confidence, Mr Brisco,' Julian replied diplomatically. 'And a picture will certainly help, if it comes out.'

'Great,' Tom said. 'It'll come out all right, have no fear. Now, if you can just bear with me a minute while I set up my camera and put in a plate...' When Tom had found a suitable place to stand that showed the biplane off to best advantage, he adjusted the legs of his tripod to compensate for the uneven ground. 'If you like, I'll take one of you, Ned, standing at the side of the machine, then another with you sitting in it.' He hid his head under the black cloth that enabled him to see an inverted image on the ground glass screen. He focused it, then inserted

85

a photographic plate into the back of the camera and pulled out the dark slide that protected it from unwanted light. He screwed a shutter release bulb into the body of the lens. 'Smile, please.'

'Can I have one with Clover and Amos on?' Ned asked. 'Have you brought enough plates?'

'No trouble, Ned,' Tom said obligingly.

So Amos took his place by Ned and Clover self-consciously shuffled into the frame. Ned suggested she stand between them. Tom took out the exposed plate and inserted a new one.

'Right... Look into the lens and smile, please.'

The shutter clicked, the group dispersed, Ned clambered up onto his machine and posed for another photograph.

'If I can get one of you in flight as well... Give me one minute to swap plates...' Tom rushed to finish his task then thanked Ned for waiting.

'I think we're ready now,' Ned called. 'Amos, shift the chock... Wish me luck, you lot.'

'Good luck,' Clover called, echoed by the rest of them.

Amos removed the chock and the biplane rolled downhill, rapidly picking up speed. Clover saw Ned gently pull the levers that worked the flaps on the trailing edges of the wings and tail and, magically, the glider lifted into the air. She watched, mesmerised, unable to speak as its trajectory levelled out. Momentarily the wings dipped from side to side as Ned played with the controls and Clover was reminded of a heron she'd once seen floating with absolute grace and composure over a field not unlike the one she could see now below her. The biplane seemed to climb a little, but from these heights it was difficult to tell how much. It turned slightly to the right, then to the left and Clover knew that Ned was testing his controls for response. Smiling, her eyes sparkling with tears of admiration at Ned's achievement, she turned briefly to Tom. Her only fear now was that Ned was going to run out of terrain. He was rapidly approaching the New Rowley Road and the Springfield Colliery.

Suddenly, Clover was anxious. 'What's he going to do now, Amos?'

'Practise landing a bit sharp, I wouldn't be surprised,' Amos replied sardonically.

Clover realised that of course, Ned had never been able to practise a landing, for he'd never got that far before. Last time he'd crash-landed.

'Think he can do it, Amos?'

'He's gunna have to try. The ground's a bit rough down there though, all them great tufts of grass and gorse bushes and pit shafts... And that bloody stupid hoss, look...'

Clover held her breath. The next seconds seemed like hours. The aircraft looked small in the distance now but she discerned it descending, lower and lower. From where Clover stood it looked as if the tail end touched down first and she realised his wisdom and foresight in fitting a tail wheel. Then the narrow bicycle wheels made contact with the ground and the whole assembly seemed to shake and flop about as it came to a halt over the rough field.

She breathed a sigh of relief. 'He's done it!' she yelled, ecstatic at Ned's success. She turned to

Tom Doubleday and Julian, jumping up and down with excitement. 'He's done it. Did you see that? He's done it.'

'That was pretty impressive,' Julian declared. 'Wait till our readers hear about this. Ned Brisco will be a hero. He was in the air about fifteen seconds by my reckoning.'

'What d'you reckon that is distancewise?' Tom asked.

'Gettin' on for two hundred yards,' Amos estimated. 'At least. We can easy pace it out. Come on, Clover, we should be getting down there to him. We'll have to congratulate him.'

'Yes, we'd better.' She turned to Tom Doubleday as Amos went back to fetch the horse and cart. 'I'd best get down there,' she said apologetically.

'Do you mind if I come with you?' he suggested. 'Maybe we could walk down together.'

Clover smiled happily. 'All right.' Her elation all at once took on a new perspective. 'Would you like me to carry something for you? Your case, maybe?'

'Thanks.' He handed her the case that contained his plates. 'It's not too heavy is it?'

'Not at all,' she said and they began the steep descent down Rough Hill.

'That was quite a spectacle,' Tom said, 'seeing man and machine fly. Quite a spectacle. Something I'll never forget. Something to tell my grandchildren about.'

'Quite a spectacle,' Clover agreed. 'I'm so pleased he succeeded. He's worked ever so hard for it, you wouldn't believe. He lives and breathes this aviation lark.'

'But you obviously share some of his enthusiasm?'

'Oh, I do. Because he would never allow it to beat him. He's read everything about what the Wright Brothers have done and wanted to prove to himself that he could do it as well. He knew he could. You have to admire such determination, such faith. I suppose his enthusiasm has rubbed off on me a little bit.'

'So how long have you been courting, Clover?'

'Oh, we're not courting, Tom.' She looked at him earnestly and almost tripped over a tuft of grass.

'You're not? But I got the impression from your stepsister that you were.'

Clover shook her head and, with her fingers, brushed aside her hair that was blowing about her face. 'I don't know what Ramona's told you about me and Ned, but we're definitely not courting. We're only friends. Good friends, but only friends.'

She could see Ned scrambling out of his glider that looked like a small toy from here. He walked round to the rear of the craft, fiddled with the tail and checked the tail wheel.

'Well she seems to think you're courting, Clover.'

'No, she doesn't, Tom,' she answered decisively. 'She knows very well that Ned is only a friend. She knows very well we're not courting.'

'So why would she...?'

Clover looked at him and saw a flicker of realisation in his eyes.

He caught her look and smiled dismissively. 'So what's the next step for Ned as regards aviation?'

'For Ned? Oh, powered flight, he reckons. Obviously, he's going to need an engine.'

'Well there are plenty of firms locally who make engines. He could use a motor car engine, I daresay.'

'I don't think they're suitable,' she replied. 'Too heavy and not enough power – so he says. The other problem is that he pays for all this out of his own pocket. The reason he asked the newspaper to come and report it was so that he might get some factory owner interested enough to sponsor him somehow and contribute to the costs.'

'Good idea. I hope he succeeds in that as well. It would be a crying shame if the project had to stop through lack of money.'

'It would,' Clover agreed. 'Ned has a dream. He wants to develop these machines – these aeroplanes – enough to carry freight and even passengers. He wants to start his own factory building them.'

'Well, what a dream, eh, Clover?'

She looked at him and smiled. 'I know. What a dream. You have to admire it. But he sees such potential.'

After a few seconds pause, Tom said, 'Can I ask you something, Clover?'

'Yes,' she said. 'Ask away.'

'I can see you're very attached to Ned but ... well, if you're not courting, may I ask if I could take you out tonight?'

She thought he would hear the sudden pounding of her heart and she was sure she must have coloured crimson, but she smiled delightedly, wide-eyed. 'Oh, I'd love to. But what about Ramona?'

'Ramona?' he queried, a puzzled look clouding his handsome face.

'Yes. She won't be very pleased.'

'I don't understand. What's she got to do with it?'

'Well...' She uttered a little laugh of embarrassment. 'Aren't you and Ramona supposed to be–?'

Tom laughed out loud. 'Me and Ramona? Has she told you that?'

'No, she's said nothing. I just got the impression that... You always seem very close, Tom. Heads together in the taproom ... you know?'

He laughed again. 'Well, it's an illusion, Clover. There's nothing between Ramona and me.'

'I'm sorry, Tom. I really was under the impression.' She smiled, embarrassed but so relieved. She was relieved on two counts; one, that he and Ramona were not courting and two, that he was therefore not being two-timed on account of Sammy.

'Oh, Ramona's always very bright and friendly. I like her. And she's a fine looking girl. I flatter myself to believe that if I asked her out she would accept. But you're the one I've always set my cap at, Clover. Why else d'you think I've been calling so regularly at the Jolly Collier? To see you. Trouble is, you've been so elusive. You kept hiding yourself away.'

She laughed and her eyes lit up like bright blue crystals. 'Only because I didn't want you to see

91

me all scruffy.' Then she was stumped for words again.

'You look good in anything, Clover.' He paused, certain she would savour the compliment. 'So can I call for you at say eight o'clock?'

'Yes, eight o'clock would suit well. What shall we do, though?'

'I don't know yet. Go for a walk maybe? This weather seems very settled. It should be a pleasant enough evening.'

'All right.' She smiled and there was a skip in her step now.

Julian, the *Dudley Herald* reporter, had tagged along with Amos who was leading the horse and cart carefully down the steep slope. They remained a good sixty yards or so behind Clover and Tom and Amos furnished him with a few background details that he would be able to use in his story. Eventually they all reached the grinning Ned who could scarcely contain his joy. He'd inspected the aircraft and declared it free of damage.

'Tonight, you lot, I'm having a celebration and you're all invited.'

Tom's eyes met Clover's and they both smiled with resignation that their planned evening stroll might have been thwarted.

'Where at?' Amos asked.

'At the Jolly Collier. Is it all right, Clover if we all pile into the snug at your place tonight? I want my mother and father to come, and Amos's wife.'

'I expect it will be all right,' she replied, catching Tom's look again. 'Is Tom invited?'

'Yes and you, mate...' He nodded at Julian. 'Bring your wives as well.'

'Thanks,' said Tom. 'Tell you what. I'll develop and print the pictures I've got and bring them with me.'

'That would be lovely,' Clover enthused. She would see Tom after all. 'I want to be first to see them, Tom,' she said with a wink. 'Can you bring them about eight?'

Chapter Five

Tom Doubleday showed up in the taproom wearing a smart grey suit with a subtle stripe. His plain royal blue tie contrasted well with his white cotton shirt and starched round-edged collar, and the silver chain of his pocket watch hung glistening across his waistcoat.

'Well, you look smart tonight, Tom, and no two ways.' Ramona greeted chirpily.

He smiled gratefully at the compliment. 'Thank you, Ramona. That's exactly what I needed to hear.'

'So who's the lucky lady?'

He glanced around to see if anybody was listening, then leaned forward conspiratorially, as if to divulge some deep secret. 'Your stepsister,' he whispered.

'Clover?' Ramona's expression changed and she paused while she took stock of this vital news. 'She never said.'

'Would you do me a favour and let her know I'm here?'

Stunned, Ramona left the taproom. In a few seconds she returned, her demeanour unusually aloof. 'She'll be a minute or two yet. D'you want a drink while you wait?'

'Not for now, thanks, Ramona. Later.' He smiled pleasantly but Ramona did not return it. He turned around while she tended to somebody else's needs and he nodded at those regulars he was already familiar with. 'Lovely evening,' he said to somebody. He scrutinised the ends of his fingers and nervously creased the flap of the brown envelope he was holding that contained the photographs of Ned's triumph. He wondered what Clover would be wearing.

Of course, she wore the new white dress she'd bought herself. Her dark hair she'd piled up in the Pompadour style that emphasised the youthful set of her head and the elegance of her neck.

'You look beautiful.'

She smiled demurely. 'I'm glad you approve. Thank you.'

'I've never seen you looking so lovely.'

'Perhaps you can appreciate why I always hide away from you when I get in from work all grubby in my scruffy clothes. I *can* look decent. I'd much rather you see me looking decent.'

He looked her up and down admiringly. 'I've seen you decent before – at the wedding, if you recall. But decent is a bit of an understatement, Clover. You look delicious enough to eat. Come on, let's go for a walk so the world can witness me at the side of somebody so lovely.'

She smiled again and felt her colour rise at his compliments.

'You don't mind walking out, do you?' he asked and she shook her head. 'There might not be much opportunity to talk later. What time did Ned say he would get here with his family?'

'About nine.'

'That gives us an hour. Shall we head for Buffery Park? It's a lovely evening.'

'If you like. Give me a minute, though, to get my hat on.'

She went out again and returned wearing a beautiful Leghorn hat, trimmed with field flowers. She wore it tilted slightly to one side, in the manner of the fashionable women she'd seen in pictures in newspapers. Tom said how elegantly she wore it as they stepped out of the Jolly Collier into the warm evening sunshine of George Street and she felt like a queen. They talked at first about Ned's achievement that morning and how Amos made her laugh with his irreverence. Before they knew it they were near the hothouses of Buffery Park.

The flowerbeds were ablaze with chrysanthemums and dahlias. Clover said how she wished they could have a garden at the Jolly Collier instead of the dreary brewery that overlooked and overwhelmed the rear of the pub.

'Do you like living in a public house?' Tom asked.

'I don't know any different,' she replied, stepping over a crack in one of the paviours to avoid bringing bad luck. 'But I like all the company we get. I see different people all the time. It's nice getting to know lots of people.'

'Yours is a decent pub, you know, Clover. It has a reputation for being a good house, as well as for the beer.'

'Yes, I know. It's because of my mother, I suppose. The way she's always run it.'

'Do you get on all right with her?'

Clover chuckled. 'Funny woman.'

'Oh? How is she funny?'

'In the sense that she seldom smiles, her attitude to folk. She has some funny ideas, mostly about me it seems. She's not been so bad since she's married again. Jake keeps her in check.'

'What do you think of him?'

'I like him. He's very placid, very down-to-earth. He's certainly good for my mother. Good for me, too. Before he came along I wouldn't have been allowed to walk out with you, without somebody else with us.'

'A chaperone? God, how old-fashioned.'

'Like I say, she's a funny woman – old-fashioned – a dyed-in-the-wool Victorian. But Jake's changing all that. Ramona was always allowed to go out apparently, so now I am as well.' She smiled with the satisfaction of having won some great privilege.

'So you've had no chance to meet sweethearts?'

'I didn't say that,' she answered coyly, half teasing. 'There have been one or two boys I've been sweet on...' She looked away for she found herself blushing again. 'How about you?' she said, diverting him. 'How many sweethearts have you had?'

96

'Oh, hundreds...'

He grinned first and they both burst out laughing.

'Oh, you have to be truthful, Tom,' she said. 'Have you really had lots of sweethearts?'

'About two.'

'You mean two hundred?' she suggested mischievously.

She loved how he laughed at that, how his eyes crinkled at the edges so deliciously.

'Just two,' he answered. 'A girl from Sedgley who was my sweetheart for two years and a girl from Brierley Hill.'

'Oh? What went wrong?'

'Well ... with the girl from Sedgley there were too many instances where we didn't see eye to eye. Too many arguments over nothing, too many unreasonable requests, too many times I was taken for granted when I'd gone out of my way to do things for her and her family. There was too much incompatibility, Clover. We would never have made each other happy. So I ended it.'

'And the girl from Brierley Hill?'

A couple of sparrows descended into one of the flowerbeds they were approaching, twittering angrily at each other as they squabbled over a worm, then just as rapidly took flight again, the one hurtling after the other.

'Maud...' He sighed. 'Maud didn't play quite by the rules. While I was conscientiously trying to nurture our relationship she sought extra attentions in the arms of one of my friends.'

'She was being unfaithful?'

'Yes, she was being unfaithful. Seriously unfaithful as it turned out. Six weeks after we split up she married the bloke, already pregnant. And the child certainly wasn't mine.'

'I imagine you were upset, Tom.'

'I was engaged to be married to her. I was in love with her. Yes, I was upset.'

'And you had no idea what was going on behind your back?'

'Not then. Oh, looking back now I can see there were lots of clues, but I was oblivious to them. I imagined her not wanting me to touch her was a passing phase – something all women go through. I thought the reasons she gave not to see me sometimes on our regular nights were genuine, and I never challenged them. Oh, there were lots of little things – insignificant on their own, but when you view them as a whole, a different picture develops.'

'It's a shame you had to go through all that... Good for me, though, Tom... Otherwise you wouldn't be here now.'

'No, I don't suppose I would.' He smiled cheerfully to indicate he was over the trauma. 'The trouble is, Clover, when something like that happens, you tend to lose confidence in yourself, in women, in human nature. I'd never allow it to happen again. I'd know the symptoms another time and at the first signs I'd ... well, I'd just walk away.'

'Only right, Tom,' she agreed. 'A couple has to be committed to each other if they want their relationship to work.'

They fell silent for a few moments while they

each digested what the other had said. The shadows were lengthening and the low sun, directly in front of them, was promising a rhetorical bedtime for itself.

'How old are you, Tom?'

'Twenty-five. And you?'

'You should never ask a girl how old she is,' she said feigning indignation. 'But I'll tell you anyway. I'm twenty. I was twenty last month.'

He laughed at the way she changed direction so quickly. 'That's a nice age gap between a man and woman, five years. Don't you think?'

'I hadn't thought about it. Ned's two years younger than you.'

'Ah, Ned, eh? Good old Ned ... I must say, he seems a decent sort. The sort who wouldn't hurt a fly.'

'He's too wrapped up in what he's doing to hurt anything,' Clover mused. 'So how did the photographs turn out?'

He waved the envelope that contained them. 'Let's sit on that bench over there and I'll show you.'

'Are they good?'

'They're fine.'

'Do you live with your folks, Tom,' Clover asked, changing tack again.

'Yes, I do. I have a sister, Lily, the same age – no, a year older than you. She's getting married soon, so she'll be leaving home to live with her new husband. I have another sister, called Frances who is already married and pregnant, and a brother called Cedric who is married with children.'

'So where do you live? Nobody's ever mentioned it.'

'Stafford Street, towards the top. By Top Church. That damned great clock of theirs often wakes me up in the middle of the night, striking.'

She laughed, a sympathetic laugh. 'You poor old thing.'

By this time they had reached the bench that looked out onto shrubberies where rhododendrons blossomed in profusion. Clover dusted off the bench with her handkerchief to protect her new white dress, then sat down expectantly, her back gracefully erect, her knees drawn towards Tom. Tom sat down casually and opened the brown envelope. He drew out the pictures and handed them to her.

'Oh, yes, they're really good, Tom... Look at Amos's expression here. He's such a nit.' She laughed at them, at how ordinary they all looked, at their incongruity with what they had achieved together – especially Ned. 'That's a good one of Ned. He looks so serious – he always looks serious... God, don't I look awful?'

'Actually, I think you look beautiful,' Tom answered, his voice low. 'I took the liberty of enlarging that portion of the photo to show just you ... the very bottom one ... I thought I'd keep it for myself, if you have no objection...'

She pulled it out and glanced at it, then hid her face with it giggling girlishly. 'I look so stupid,' she said self-effacingly, and blushing for she felt his eyes hot upon her.

'Why do you have such a low opinion of yourself, Clover?' he asked seriously. 'You're really a *very* beautiful girl.'

'Lord, I'm not,' she countered flatly. 'My nose is too long for a start.'

'You have the most scintillating nose I've ever seen,' he said sincerely. 'It was one of the first things about you that really struck me.'

'About ten minutes before the rest of me came into view, you mean,' she said with humour brimming in her eyes. 'Stop laughing, for God's sake. It's not that funny.'

'Yes it is.' He spread his arms across the backrest of the bench so that one was behind her.

'You wouldn't think it was funny if you were stuck with it.'

He couldn't help but laugh for quite some time. He had never anticipated that Clover Beckitt could be so amusing. 'You're a jewel, Clover.'

'A jewel, eh?'

'Yes, a jewel. Don't denigrate yourself. Few girls are as lovely as you are. And you know what's most appealing about you?'

She rolled her eyes, wondering what gem he would come out with next. 'Don't say my nose.'

'You don't acknowledge your looks. You're not affected by them. You're just natural.'

'You mean that's good?'

'It makes you different, Clover. I get young women all the time in my studio, come to have their photographs taken for their sweethearts or husbands. Most are nowhere near as pretty as you. Yet they have such a bob on themselves, some of them. They really think they're something special when they're not at all. You are the exact opposite. That's refreshing – and appealing.'

Clover tried hard not to blush, but she couldn't help it. 'Anyway, I think Ned will be pleased with these. And that Julian chap, the reporter.'

'Yes,' he said. 'I just hope they do Ned some good. I reckon he deserves recognition for what he's achieved already. It seems there's nobody else in this country seriously attempting flight. I wonder why it should be left to some ordinary bloke with no great education and little money to do all the groundwork for something as important. Such apathy is unforgivable.'

Clover shrugged. 'Makes you wonder, doesn't it?'

'Here we are, the richest country on earth and nobody cares tuppence about aviation, except Ned Brisco.'

'And me.'

He laughed. 'Yes, and you.'

'Are you a wealthy man, Tom?' she asked.

He looked at her curiously. 'God, Clover! Why do you ask? Does it make any difference?'

'No, no difference at all, but you always wear such nice clothes. I mean, look at this suit your wearing...' she fingered the material of his lapels admiringly and he enjoyed the intimacy of it. 'You always look so smart. Even when you came to Rough Hill this morning you looked smart.'

'Well, to answer your question, Clover, I'm not a wealthy man. I wear decent clothes because I come into contact with the public who spend money with me. If I was a scruffy article, people might assume my work would be scruffy. I can't afford for people to think that. But I've worked up a decent little business and I earn enough to buy nice clothes and to put a bit by.'

'My mother always says you have to put a bit by.'

'What happened to your father, Clover? If you don't mind me asking.'

She smiled wistfully as she told him.

'Do you remember him?'

'Not really. I've got a picture of him. I know what he looked like.'

'Will you show me sometime? I'd like to see it.'

'Course... Hey, what time is it?'

He took his pocket watch from the fob in his waistcoat. 'Nearly nine according to this.'

'Maybe we should head back to meet the others.' She smoothed the rear of her skirt with her hands and stood up, ready.

'I suppose you're right, Clover.' He put the photographs back into their envelope and stood up with her. 'Look, I might not get the oppor-tunity later, so do you mind if I ask you something now?'

The sun was going down and the sky was shot with streaks of orange and magenta. Distant clouds that had settled on the horizon were caught in the blaze, daubed with the same vivid colours. Tom and Clover started walking, casting long shadows across the neat lawns of the park.

'What did you want to ask me, Tom?'

'If I can see you again – another evening.'

'Yes, please, I'd like that,' she answered softly, sincerely, looking into his eyes. 'When?'

'Whenever you can. How about Wednesday?'

'All right, Wednesday. Eight o'clock again?'

'Eight o'clock would suit very well...'

He smiled, took her hand and her heart starting beating noticeably faster.

Clover, her bright eyes alive with the exhilaration of one hour alone with Tom Doubleday, walked buoyantly down the passage and through the door of the snug. When he saw her, Ned looked at her in disbelief and unwittingly stood up. He'd never seen her looking like this, like a princess all in white, with her hair done so elegantly beneath the pretty hat that was adorned with flowers. The Brisco family were already supping their first drinks with Julian Oakley and a mousy young woman who was evidently his wife. Ned looked disconcerted standing there, trussed up in a stiff collar and necktie as he supped a pint of mild ale. Florrie Brisco wore a grey dress that she'd evidently bought when she was a stone and a half lighter, and Old Man Brisco wore a striped shirt with a mismatched, crumpled collar beneath his unpressed serge suit.

'Clover!' Ned greeted. 'Where've you been? Your stepsister said you'd gone–'

Then he saw Tom.

He watched Tom follow this princess in. He watched her turn to him and smile enigmatically, as if they shared a thousand secrets. Ned's mouth fell open with disappointment that was rapidly spiralling into an abyss.

'I went for a walk in Buffery Park with Tom,' she said casually, as if it was an everyday occurrence, trying to make his fall gentler. 'He wanted to show me the photographs he took this morning. They're ever so good.'

He nodded unsurely. Maybe he was jumping to conclusions too quickly. 'I'll get you a drink, Clover. And you, Tom,' he added, trying to hide any animosity. 'What would you like?'

'A half of shandy, please,' Clover answered.

'A pint of bitter, Ned, if that's all right,' Tom said.

'Can we see the photos?' Julian asked, lighting a cigarette. Tom handed him the envelope and Julian opened it with a professional keenness. 'Oh, yes... This is exactly what I need to illustrate the report I've written,' he said when he'd looked at them. 'Can I have these, Tom?'

'You'd best let Ned see 'em first. They're for him. I could bring some prints round to your office tomorrow.'

Meanwhile, Amos was keen to introduce Clover to his wife. 'Clover, come here a minute and meet our Ida... This is Clover, our Ida. Dint I tell yer as she was a bit of a bobbydazzler?'

'What a beautiful frock,' Ida commented, scrutinising Clover's lovely outfit. 'You never work in a foundry?'

Clover laughed generously. 'Not in this outfit. But yes, I work at the Coneygree – when I'm not helping Ned build his machine.'

'Dint he do well, eh? Amos is that proud ... I wished as I'd sid it meself.'

'Well, I daresay there'll be other opportunities, Ida,' Clover assured her. 'He's not going to give up now.'

'And him getting his name in nex' wik's paper and all.'

'And his picture,' Clover added.

And so it went on. Amos fetched a round of drinks from the hatch in the passage that opened into the taproom, then Tom paid for a round. The party was beginning to get noisier, the room smokier and soon Elijah joined them. He, too, paid for a round while Jake came in carrying a lighted spill and lit the oil lamps. Mary Ann put in an appearance on her way to the taproom and Ramona joined them later.

'Ramona, you haven't met Ned before, have you?' Clover said.

'No.' She looked around. Tom Doubleday smiled his good wishes but she failed to acknowledge him and her eyes settled on the only man other than Elijah who was not ostensibly with a woman.

Clover introduced them and Ned stood up. He shook Ramona's hand uncertainly and sheepishly avoided eye contact. 'Nice to meet you, Ramona. Clover's told me about you.'

'Nice things, I hope.'

'Nothing bad.' He smiled self-consciously. 'Er – can I buy you a drink? It's my celebration and I think I've bought everybody else one.'

'There's no rush, Ned,' Ramona replied easily. 'I've not long had a drink. Somebody bought me one in the taproom. Tell me about your flying machine first. It sounds really interesting.' She smiled, a warm, open smile.

'What do you want to know?' he asked, at once feeling comfortable with Clover's pretty step-sister.

'Oh, I dunno... How you got started, why you decided to build your own machine. Things like

106

that. I think it's really interesting. I think you've done wonders, Ned, I really do.'

'D'you want to sit down, Ramona?'

'Thank you.' She sat beside him and Ned shuffled along the settle to make more room. 'You're a real gentleman, Ned and no mistake. So what a day you've had. What a triumph. Are you going to let me see the photos Tom Doubleday took?'

Ned retrieved them and opened the envelope. 'Here, look. Here's one of me actually in flight...'

'My God...' She looked up from the photograph and glanced at him, catching the pride in his eyes. 'How did it feel, to be actually flying?'

Ned shook his head. 'I can't describe it, Ramona. I haven't got the words. All I can tell you is the human race should've done it a long time ago.'

She looked at him again, her clear brown eyes meeting his with all the appeal she could summon. He could not maintain the eye contact, however. Her look seemed brim full of veneration, of wonderment. No girl had ever looked at him like that before – with such beautiful eyes. He did not know how to react. He glanced towards Clover; she was intent on something Tom Doubleday was saying.

'So what gave you the inspiration, Ned?'

'Well, when I was about ten years old my father bought me a book called *Progress in Flying Machines*. It was written in 1894 by an American called Octave Chanute. Ever since then–'

'Did they build flying machines that long ago? In 1894?'

'Even before that. Years and years before.'

'Oh?'

'Yes. In 1809 Sir George Cayley, a man dedicated to aeronautics, built and flew a full-size glider...'

While Ned and Ramona became acquainted, Elijah amused Tom and Clover with tales of his experiences in India. Florrie Brisco, perspiring under her several layers of necessarily unfashionable over and undergarments, familiarised Julian and the plain Mrs Oakley with the fine detail of Ned's childhood, his youth and his adulthood. As she eulogised over his dietary peculiarities and on the regularity of his bowel movements Julian yawned. 'I just hope as he axes young Clover to wed him afore it's too late,' Florrie added with a sideways glance at Tom Doubleday.

Julian excused himself and made for the dismal but obnoxiously aromatic urinals at the rear of the pub. A solitary candle standing in an old jam jar afforded meagre light. Julian lit a cigarette off it and unfastened his fly as Tom Doubleday appeared at the door.

'Tom!' Julian greeted, his cigarette hanging from his bottom lip while he looked up at the wall directly in front of him to avoid smoke going up his nose. 'Fancy seeing you here.'

'I know.' Tom stood alongside him, keeping a discreet distance. 'It's funny how you have to keep running off when you drink beer.'

Julian laughed. 'Blessed relief. God, that's better.' He gave himself a brief shake and fastened his buttons. 'It's the volume, Tom. Never could drink much beer. Now whisky – that's a different kettle of fish. Hey, about them photos. How much shall we owe you?'

'How many shall you want?'

'Just two, I reckon. That one of the three of them standing in front of the flying machine, and that one where you've caught it in flight.'

'How much are you prepared to pay?' Tom asked. He turned away from the wall and buttoned his fly. 'After all, it's a bit of a scoop.'

'How about a guinea a picture?'

Tom shook his head. 'Three guineas more like. Surely your newspaper can afford to pay for exclusive photographs?'

They settled on five guineas for the pair and shook hands on it. Tom said he would bring them round tomorrow with his invoice.

When they returned to the snug Ramona was standing near the door strapped to her new accordion. She gave it a squeeze and, with an expectant smile, played a chord to get everybody's attention.

'What yer gunna play then, our Ramona?' Elijah called and swigged his beer.

'I know,' she said, at once decisive, and launched into 'Wait Till the Sun Shines, Nellie', while Tom and Julian resumed their seats.

The sound of the accordion, like an unrefined organ, filled the little room. Then Ramona sang and her singing voice, like her speaking voice, had an appealing catch in it, far removed from the clear warbles of a soprano or contralto. The only other sounds to be heard were the occasional spit and crack of the fire as the coals shifted further into their basket. When she'd finished everybody applauded noisily. 'More! More!' Amos yelled.

'I think Clover ought to sing us one,' Ramona proclaimed, pleased with her success and the attention she was eliciting. She beckoned her stepsister to stand alongside her, knowing her shyness would inhibit her. This was Ramona's golden opportunity to demonstrate to the two men who meant something to Clover, her own pre-eminence in confidence, talent, and her supremacy over Clover's innate reticence.

Clover, predictably, shook her head. But attention was suddenly focused upon her and hoots of encouragement prompted her to bury her face in her hands with embarrassment.

'Come on, Clover,' Ramona persisted. 'We want to hear you sing.'

'I bet you can sing like a lark,' Tom encouraged, at her side.

'I can't,' she insisted.

But her denial seemed to have no clout.

'I bet you can. Go on, let's hear you.'

All at once recognising Ramona's implicit challenge, vividly perceiving again the difference between them and wishing to obliterate it, Clover emptied her glass. She rose from the settle and went to stand by Ramona. She straightened her back and raised her head defiantly.

'All right. What shall we do?' Clover asked.

'Do you know "Waiting at the Church"?'

Clover shook her head. 'I don't know the words. I do know "How'd You Like to Spoon With Me", though.'

'But I can't play that one, Clover,' Ramona reluctantly admitted. 'I could never get the music.'

'Well I'll start it by myself. See if you can get it as we go along.'

Ramona nodded uncertainly, fearing that her ploy was about to backfire. 'All right, I'll try,' she said.

All eyes were on Clover as she began her soft crooning. The light from the lamp spilled on her young head and rimmed her hair with a soft, dancing yellow glow. Her voice was clear and light, almost soprano in pitch. Everybody fell silent and Clover made no attempt to find favour by singing loud. But when she sang the title, 'How'd You Like to Spoon With Me', she made sure the lyric was a personal message to Tom.

Behind her, Ned stood, fingering his necktie, anxious about the woman he adored, anxious about this romance that he could see budding right under his very nose.

When Clover had finished, she paused a moment and coughed, laughing in anticipation. Surprisingly, everybody merely clapped; surprising, since there was no vocal praise. Clover had taken them all too much by surprise for that. Clapping by itself seemed to demonstrate the most profound admiration.

'That was brilliant, Clover,' Elijah said. 'D'you know any more songs like that?'

'Maybe one,' Clover replied, enjoying the limelight for a change. 'It's called "Sweet Adeline". Do you know it, Ramona?' She was conscious that her stepsister was temporarily in the shade,

111

a situation that would never suit the girl and, with typical unselfishness, Clover wished to bring her to the fore again.

Ramona began to play the introduction. It was a party song and more people joined in with the singing. It was the start of a good old sing-song that had everybody singing at the tops of their voices. Some of the men from the taproom even gathered round the door of the snug and lent their voices too.

When the party was over, Ned lingered. He lingered deliberately so that he might impede any progress between Clover and Tom. The thought of them kissing goodnight was abhorrent to him. But Ramona lingered too and was very sweet to Ned, although her charm was largely lost on him. Rather he began to regard her as a likely chum. Anyway, Ned's ploy met with success and satisfied, he watched as Clover merely waved Tom off from the front door after closing time.

Ramona and Clover met on the landing when everybody had gone. Clover was returning from the scullery with a ewer of water in one hand with which to wash herself come the morning, a candle to light her way in the other.

'We had some fun tonight,' Ramona remarked.

'Yes, I enjoyed it,' Clover agreed, resting the heavy jug on the wooden handrail while she secured her grip of it.

'Did you enjoy your walk with Tom Double-day?'

'Yes, I did, thank you.' Clover was uncertain how much she should divulge.

'He's nice, isn't he?'

'I've always thought so.'

'Are you seeing him again?'

'Wednesday. He's taking me out on Wednesday.' She smiled at the prospect.

'Ooh, lucky you, Clover. Is there romance in the air at last?'

Clover shrugged non-committally. 'I can't tell. It depends on him.'

'I think Ned likes me.' Ramona hunched her shoulders and grinned shyly.

'Ned?' Clover queried, somewhat alarmed. 'Oh, keep away from Ned, Ramona. He's no match for you.'

'What do you mean?'

'You've got Sammy after all. Be satisfied and leave Ned be. I can't believe you're really interested in him anyway. Just don't lead him on.'

'Why not let Ned decide, eh, Clover? Seems to me you're in love with Ned after all, for all your denials. Tom Doubleday had better watch out.'

Chapter Six

Tom collected Clover at eight o'clock on the Wednesday evening. The weather had turned and a light drizzle had set in. Beneath his brolly, she warmly linked her arm through his as they walked along Brown Street and on, down steep Caroline Street and Claughton Road towards the Opera House, absorbed in each other.

Outside the theatre in Castle Hill, people

113

arrived in cabs and stepped off trams in swarms. In the foyer, folk were milling about animatedly, looking at photographs and colourful posters, chatting, laughing. 'Tickets here, please,' somebody in uniform was calling. Tom joined the queue and paid for two seats in the stalls near the orchestra at two shillings each. He smiled at Clover as he rejoined her and his heart skipped as the bright flare of the ornate gas lamps, reflected in her eyes, enhanced their sparkle. An attendant with polished brass buttons pushed open the door into the auditorium and two enormous crystal chandeliers that hung majestically from the high ceiling cast a warm glow. Several men in army uniform, tall, straight-backed, with fine moustaches, turned to stare at Clover and nudged each other as Tom allowed her to go before him.

They took their seats ready for the nine o'clock show and Clover smiled admiringly at Tom. As they sat, he looked at her with profound curiosity.

'Why are you looking at me like that?' she asked with a puzzled look.

'Because you never seem to look the same twice,' he said. 'I thought I'd remembered your face from the last time I saw you, yet you look different. Your cheeks seem rounder, your eyes bigger. Your nose... No your nose is the same ... as beautiful as ever.'

'My nose!' she said with exaggerated scorn and laughed. 'You're always going on about my nose.'

'I can't get over your nose.'

'Because it's such a big obstruction?'

He laughed. 'It's not big. Only *you* think it's big... All right, it's a tiny, tiny bit long, but that's what makes it so exquisite. Don't you see?'

'I'm glad you like it. I hate it.'

'Don't hate it. It's an alluring feature.'

'Let's look at the programme,' she said, wishing to turn his attention. He opened it up between them. 'Have you heard of any of these?'

'I've heard of that comedian, Little Tich, and Casey's Court Circus troupe. They're supposed to be very funny. Nobody else, I must admit.'

'Nor me. I've not seen a variety show before. I expect you've seen hundreds.'

'Oh, I've been here a few times – and to the Empire. I always enjoy it. I imagined you would enjoy it as well.'

'Well, it's a change for me.' She looked about her and was surprised to see how already nearly all the seats had been taken. Another couple asked if they could come through their row and Tom and Clover stood up to allow them passage. 'I do like the atmosphere,' she whispered. 'It seems so friendly and warm.'

The lights went down and the little orchestra struck up. An arc light was trained on the stage curtain and a little man wearing navvies' clothes strutted on and told a few ribald jokes then sang a song. He introduced the magician, who had a moustache bigger even than Jake Tandy's.

Clover's attention was divided equally between the show and Tom's being so close to her. Sometimes she would turn to him and smile and he would tilt his head towards her as she whispered some comment or query. Then she in turn would tilt her head as he whispered a reply, and his breathy words in her ear sent shivers up and down her spine.

She glanced about her, at the ornate plasterwork of the Opera House, and the gilt scrolls and the fluted columns that supported the roof and the galleries behind them. She watched the conductor's baton as it waved about like something from a Punch and Judy show above the dark velvet curtain with its bright brass rod that divided the orchestra from the rest of the auditorium. She shuffled her bottom in the velveteen-covered seats that were so plush and comfortable. She loved the acrobats that tumbled all over the stage and somersaulted off each other's shoulders and tiptoed across a wire that was fastened tight between two posts.

The comedian called Little Tich, who wore a dark suit with large yellow buttons and a shiny top hat, had her in stitches with his smutty jokes that would have had her mother turning her nose up in disapproval. When one of his jokes went over her head, she tapped Tom on the arm, shook her head and frowned. He explained it in a whisper and she put her hand to her mouth in shock, then giggled and nodded that yes, she did understand after all.

His attention was focused almost entirely on her. He loved how she chuckled at what she heard, at her facial expressions that registered shock, surprise and apprehension, sometimes all at once. He loved the way she glanced at him to see his reaction to almost everything, how her eyes creased and sparkled with vitality as she

116

laughed. He was excited at having her so close to him, at having her to himself at last, after yearning for her for so long.

Dottie Baxter, a handsome, round-faced girl with a fine figure and wide hat trimmed with lavender, sang ditties with a streak of blue implicit in them. She had the modest air of a young girl at her first dance, and Clover identified with her. During her first performance she pretended to surprise herself with little fantasies that cropped up in the lyrics of her songs. The audience became mouse-quiet, leaning forward lest they missed any of it.

The next turn was spectacular: Monsieur and Madame Salambo, human lightning conductors. A volunteer was needed from the audience and a self-conscious young man was coaxed onto the stage. Madame Salambo asked him to hold one end of a hollow glass tube while she retained the other end. Suddenly, there was a brilliant flash as the glass tube lit up, and everybody laughed at the astonishment on the young man's face. When he was asked to touch Madame and Monsieur he was just as amazed when a series of sparks shot out from them. The tricks went on, amazing everybody and Clover looked on in open-mouthed incredulity.

When the curtain came down for the interval, Clover asked Tom the time and he told her it was just after ten.

'I ought to go,' she said reluctantly. 'Mother will have been expecting me by ten.'

'But we've only seen the first half of the show. Don't you want to see the rest of it?'

117

'Course I do. More than anything.' More than anything she wanted to remain with Tom. 'Oh, to hell with her, Tom. I'm staying. If I'm late, I'm late.'

'Blame me,' Tom said. 'I'm the one keeping you out late. Anyway, what do you have to fear? You're a grown woman and Jake is very fair. You've said so yourself.'

'It's just that I didn't realise we were coming here tonight. If I'd forewarned her...'

'Well the show won't be over till after eleven. You might as well sit it out and enjoy it. You might as well be hanged for a sheep as for a lamb. What time do they shut the Jolly Collier?'

'Oh, they'll be serving till going on for twelve o'clock. Maybe later.'

'Well then. They won't even notice what time you come in. In any case, I'll come in with you and explain. I'll tell your mother it's my fault. Anyway, you should be allowed to stay out late if you want to. It's not as if you're a child.'

Clover smiled up at him, embarrassed that they should both have to contend with her mother's quaint but annoying idiosyncrasies. She made her mind up to do something about it. Indeed, she would have to if she wanted to be courted regularly by Tom.

So, she settled comfortably into the second half of the show. Robert Fordham, a black American singer with a brilliant dance routine got the second half rolling when he performed 'Chocolate Dreams Cakewalk'. Clover liked the brassy sounds the orchestra made accompanying him, the easy, foot-tapping tunes.

The Court Casey Circus was a knockabout troupe that had the place in uproar and their antics brought tears to her eyes. She forgot about Mary Ann's stern glare. Dottie Baxter did a second spot, this time dressed as a policeman. She sang a song about how the policeman lost his love to the Sergeant, which was poignant and funny all at the same time. Little Tich closed the show and he'd certainly been holding his funniest jokes till last. Even when the orchestra had finished playing 'God Save the King', Clover still had tears in her eyes from laughing.

She turned to Tom, coming out of her happy dream. 'I suppose we'd better hurry.'

He nodded and grabbed his umbrella. She held his hand while he thrust his way through the men that were lingering around the aisle stretching their legs and the women smoothing their dresses. Outside the rain was pouring. He opened the umbrella and, beneath it, they crossed the road, heading towards the Station Hotel and Trindle Road. The street lamps beyond the Station Hotel were not so bright, but the paltry light they afforded was increased as it reflected off the glistening cobbles.

'I've really enjoyed tonight, Tom,' she said, looking up at him as they turned into Claughton Road. 'Thank you for taking me.'

'Thank you for coming,' he answered. 'I hope we can have plenty more nights like it.'

'I hope so too. I just hope my mother doesn't spoil it. I expect she'll be all of a franzy.'

'I told you, Clover. Don't worry. I'll handle it.'

It was after half past eleven when they arrived

at the Jolly Collier. Clover looked at Tom apprehensively while he opened the door and allowed her to go in before him as he shook the water off his brolly. The taproom, full of noise and smoke, was still busy and Mary Ann, Ramona and Jake were all working.

'Is it still raining?' Jake asked Clover.

'Pouring,' she said over the hubbub and smiled at him appealingly. 'I bet Tom would like a pint, wouldn't you, Tom?'

He winked at her. 'I'd love one. Bitter, please.'

'We've been to the Opera House,' she explained to Jake. Ramona, by this time, was standing by her. 'Shall we sit down, Tom?'

'Was it a good show?' Jake asked pleasantly. 'One or two have said how good it is.'

'Oh, it was grand, Pop. You ought to take Mother. You'd both love it.'

'Hear that, Mary Ann?' he called. Mary Ann looked up from the washed glasses she was wiping. 'Clover says as how good the show is at the Opera House this week. She reckons I should tek you to see it.'

'Oh yes. And who's going to serve in here while we'm gone?'

'Well I could, Mother,' Clover said. 'And Tom wouldn't mind helping either, would you, Tom?'

'I'd be delighted. It could be my penance for keeping Clover out so late, Mrs Tandy.'

'Is that an apology, since you mention it?' Mary Ann asked, stone-faced.

Tom smiled steadily, not about to be unnerved. 'If you honestly feel one is necessary, Mrs Tandy.'

Perceiving dissension, Jake waved it aside. 'Christ, Mary Ann, anybody'd think the wench was late in,' he retorted placing a pint of bitter in front of Tom. 'I've told you before, she's twenty now. This time next year she'll be of age and able to do as she pleases. She'll even be able to go and get wed without having to ask you. Think about that. You'd best start letting go of her now.' He winked at Tom and poured a glass of cider for Clover. 'Here, have these on me.'

'As long as she can get up in the morning,' Mary Ann responded, conceding defeat.

'Cheers,' Tom said and raised his glass. 'Here's to you, Jake.'

Jake smiled. He'd won another round by reasonableness and good sense.

Tom stayed in the taproom for twenty minutes before deciding it was time to go. Clover went outside with him in the rain to say goodnight and they stood under his umbrella, facing each other, their bodies touching tantalisingly.

'Thanks for a lovely night,' she said again. 'And for squaring it with my mother.'

He put his arm around her waist and gave her a squeeze. 'Jake did that. Not me.'

She smiled into his eyes then looked at his mouth, so inviting. She had not yet kissed him and the urge to, fuelled by the warmth of his companionship, overwhelmed her. Impulsively, she pursed her lips and turned her face up to reach him, then, standing on tiptoe with her hands behind her back, she planted a kiss on his lips as gentle as a butterfly landing on a petal, lingering just a little.

'There. I've done it,' she said, as she experienced the eminently palpable thrill shuddering through her. 'I've kissed you. I bet you think I'm a right hussy.'

He laughed with delight. 'Oh, unquestionably. But I'm pleased you are. When can I see you again?'

'Friday?'

He smiled with happiness. 'Yes, please, Clover. Friday.'

The family took turns to take baths when they could fit it in, often between brews when the huge copper boiler on the first storey of the brewery was free to heat up water for cleaning with enough left over. Normal practice was to put the tin bath in the scullery and fill it with hot water, fetched in buckets from the brewery. One Saturday evening in August Elijah, sweaty and hot from cleaning the mash tun, the coolers and the available fermenting vessels, decided to take a soak himself before getting changed for a night out with Dorcas, which would finish inevitably with some vigorous courting at Jake's old house afterwards.

In the small brewhouse that housed the mangle that Zillah used on washing day, he lifted the galvanised bath off the whitewashed wall and bore it across the yard to the brewery where he set it on the quarry-tiled floor. He drew off the fresh water that was already heating up, by way of a hose arrangement and, while the bath filled, he returned to the brewhouse to cut himself a cake of soap. On the way back, he fetched a towel from the house and whistled tunelessly as he strutted across the sunlit yard. Back in the brewery he put his fingers in the water to check its temperature. It was too hot so he stemmed the flow of hot water and turned on the cold tap, playing another hose into the bath. He undressed himself, had a good scratch round and dipped his toes in the bath. It was still hot, but bearably so. Having got used to the intense heat of India and enjoying it, bathing in hot water always reminded him of his time there; he liked to get a bit of a sweat up.

He immersed himself in the water, lay back and relaxed. His thoughts drifted back to India and, inevitably, to those beautiful Indian women he'd enjoyed so much there. Such sultry pleasure he'd had in India's fierce heat with sensuously perspiring, dusky girls with sleek, jet-black hair, dark eyes and wonderful bodies, many of them younger than his niece Ramona. Recalling those times aroused him enormously.

At about the same time that Elijah was getting all steamed up, the tea was ready. Clover had taken pork chops out of the oven all sizzling and succulent and smelling divine, and put them on warmed plates along with fresh-cooked vegetables and steaming gravy. But nobody was around to serve it to. Where was everybody?

Ramona appeared. 'Do you need any help, Clover?'

'You wouldn't like to round everybody up, would you? Mother and Pop are serving in the taproom. Uncle Elijah will still be in the brewery, I daresay.'

'I'll go and fetch him,' Ramona said, wiping her hands.

As she stepped into the yard the whine and clatter of a lorry's engine trespassed into the late afternoon air as it chugged up George Street, and a neighbour's pig was squealing discontentedly close by. A dog barked in St John's Street and a flock of pigeons flapped in a great whooshing arc overhead. The door to the brewery was already open and Ramona wondered whether Elijah had left it so to keep the place cool, or whether the breeze had done it. She stepped inside. Just as she was about to call his name, she saw him standing in front of a fermenting vessel, his back toward her, as naked as the day he was born, dripping with water. Her heart went to her mouth and she was suddenly stricken with a strange inertia. His lean, supple, military back looked hard, rippling with masculinity as a shaft of slanting sunlight glinted off the droplets of water that clung jealously to him. The cheeks of his backside were small and tight and muscular and she imagined cupping them in her hands, like she did Sammy's, to feel how hard and firm they really were. She was mesmerised. Water lapped against the side of the bath tub as he leaned forward to grab the towel that was hanging over one of the water pipes. She beheld, with a healthy womanly curiosity, his scrotum dangling loose between his legs as he bent over, like two eggs hanging from a nest but still attached to it. Slowly, as she watched, becoming reconciled to this unexpected vision, the ability to move returned. As he began towelling himself dry, she slid silently to one side to conceal herself behind a pile of stacked beer barrels. Through the gap caused by the curvature of the barrels she continued to gawp unbelieving at her Uncle Elijah. He turned around, presenting himself in profile and she gasped when she saw how well-blessed he was – and standing up so hard and so proud, all ready for action.

Maybe, naked in the bath, he'd been thinking of all the things he liked to do with Dorcas when they were alone, she thought. No doubt Dorcas was very accommodating in bed. No doubt he was very active there too.

Ramona watched, transfixed as he took the towel and dried his hard, extended rod with gentle care and attention; understandably, for it was such a handsome piece of equipment. But he must not see her watching him. She waited for him to turn away, hardly able to divert her eyes from his very excellent tackle. Deftly, but with great reluctance, she silently side-stepped back through the open door and back onto the yard.

'God!' she murmured to herself and smiled impishly as a wayward thought flashed through her mind. 'Oh, my God! Uncle Elijah! You're magnificent.'

Back in the scullery the others had all sat down to their meal. Elijah's was placed in the oven to keep warm. They had been eating for five minutes or so when he returned, his hair plastered down where it was still wet, a sheen of perspiration seeping from his forehead.

'Your dinner's in the oven, Elijah,' Clover said, trimming a piece of fat from her meat.

He grabbed a cloth and pulled the plates, one upturned over the other to keep in the moisture, out of the oven and placed them on the table.

'You've been a while,' Mary Ann commented as he put the covering plate into the sink.

'Sorry,' he said. 'I didn't realise I'd been so long.'

'I sent Ramona into the brewery to look for you,' Clover added innocently.

'Oh?' Elijah turned and looked from one to the other, a light of realisation brightening slowly in his eyes at Ramona's refusal to meet his.

Her face was already rubescent. 'But I couldn't find him,' she was quick to blurt out with a brief but guilty glimpse at her uncle.

'Well, you didn't look very bloody hard,' he said, wilfully catching her glance and evidently finding it amusing.

No, but you did, she wanted to say and lowered her eyes as she ate.

Chapter Seven

Next day, Sunday, Tom Doubleday called after dinner for Clover, as he did every Sunday. By this time they had been stepping out together for two months and love was blossoming. Sometimes, they went for a walk around the fields of Oakham, sometimes, a tram ride into Birmingham where they enjoyed window shopping in New Street and Corporation Street. Today, they intended to take a leisurely walk through the Castle Grounds. The weather was settled, although typically humid for August, and they decided they might find some cooling breeze in the shade of the trees that covered the elevated paths to the castle keep. On the way, it was necessary to pass Tom's studio.

'I've got an idea,' Tom said, stopping outside it.

Still holding his hand, Clover turned to him in a swirl of sleeveless summer dress with a scalloped neck. 'What?'

'You look so beautiful – so fresh and breezy ... I feel inspired to take a photograph of you. It's time I did a really nice photograph.'

She smiled at his compliment. 'I don't mind. If you want to take my picture...'

'Well, we've been courting for ages now, Clover, and it's a sin that I haven't got a studio photo of you. And the light is perfect, look. Bright and hazy. No hard shadows.'

'All right,' she agreed easily. 'As long as I can take one of you as well.'

He laughed at that and said she could as he took the key from his pocket and opened the front door. They entered into a small foyer, with examples of his best work hanging in frames from a picture rail, and a small carved counter facing the door where transactions were concluded. Plush velvet curtains hung from a brass rail along the side wall and similar drapes, tied back, adorned the deep window. Tom led her through the door into his studio which was, by now, familiar in any case, since she'd called on him a few times while he was working. Tom had

had the room extended in the fashion of a conservatory to make best use of the soft north light, with a glass roof and vertical windows that stretched to the floor. Roller blinds had been fitted to the roof windows to adjust the intensity of light, and rich floral curtains hung from floor to ceiling. Two of the solid walls of the studio were decorated to look like the drawing-room of some stately home, even with a false, but very ornate door and frame let into one wall. Odd pieces of furniture stood randomly; props that could be included in a photo as required. A mahogany whatnot stood with a shiningly healthy aspidistra sitting on top in a brass pot. There was a screen, several armchairs in various styles, all ornate, a variety of occasional tables that subjects might rest their backsides on for a jaunty pose, a music stool, a *chaise-longue* that looked soft and comfortable, and a soft bearskin rug on the floor.

'How do you want me to pose?'

'Oh, all ways.'

She thought she detected a sparkle of mischief in his eyes. 'No, you must tell me, Tom. I've never had my picture taken in a studio before. You'll have to suggest something.'

He was fiddling with his plate camera. 'Well, we can have one of you reclining, one sitting, one standing, full length, three-quarter or just head and shoulders. Personally, I'd like one full length and a head and shoulders. You choose the pose, Clover. Just be yourself.'

She stood with her hands on the whatnot, partially hidden by the aspidistra.

128

'No, stand to the side of it, my love. The damned plant's hiding you... Yes, that's better.' He bent down to look through the class screen and pulled the dark cloth over his head. 'Thrust your bosom out a bit, Clover... Ooh, lovely.' He focused the image and emerged from under the black cloth. He smiled as he inserted a plate into the rear of the camera. 'That looks good. Now... A nice smile... Smiling is a part of your nature, Clover, so I want to see a smile.'

She smiled.

'Don't forget to thrust your chest out a little... That's good. Hold that.' He pressed the shutter release bulb and Clover stood perfectly still.

The next was a head and shoulders portrait, three-quarter face, which captured her exquisite nose to perfection, although Tom deliberately did not say so for fear of protest.

'I think I'd like one of you reclining like some Greek goddess now,' he suggested. 'Like those girls in paintings by Alma-Tadema in diaphanous dresses, lounging on animal skins draped over marble. Have you seen them?'

She laughed dismissively. 'Not that I can recall.'

'As lifelike as any photograph, except they're in colour.'

'But there's no marble to drape myself over,' Clover replied.

'I know. Pity. We'll have to make do with the *chaise-longue*.'

Clover swirled over to the *chaise-longue* and sat on it, half reclining. She looked up at him with all her love in her eyes and smiled. She was enjoying this experience, this attention. She only ever received loving, caring attention like this from Tom; only ever kindness and consideration. No wonder she loved him so much.

'You don't look comfortable, Clover,' he said and left his camera to walk over to her. He knelt down and adjusted the folds of her dress as it draped over her legs. 'Rest your head on the headrest and raise one arm languidly above your head... No, that doesn't seem right ... I know, pretend you have a new ring on your finger – an engagement ring for instance – and your lover has had to go away. Now you're wistful and pining for him... Oh, yes, that's beautiful. Can you hold that while I–'

'Tom... Can I not do that? Please? I think it would be a bad omen.'

'A bad omen?'

'Yes, you photographing me looking all heart-broken because my sweetheart has gone away.'

'Oh, Clover,' he said, full of tenderness. He leaned forward and took her in his arms. 'Have no fear, I'll never leave *you*. I'm yours for as long as you want me, my sweetheart.'

'Oh, Tom.' She squeezed him and felt his cheek reassuringly against hers. 'I love you so much. I couldn't bear to think of losing you ... even for a short time.'

'You're not going to lose me,' he said. 'Ever.' He turned his face towards her and kissed her full on the lips, a hungry, searching kiss.

She responded as she always responded, with warmth and enthusiasm. She took his head lovingly in her hands and drank his kisses as if they were some potent wine. She closed her eyes and when his tongue passed between her lips she thrilled to the taste of him. After some minutes they broke off and he whispered how much he loved her. They kissed again, long, luxuriously, sensuously. He was still kneeling beside her and she felt his hand on her breast, gently, lovingly kneading. She made no attempt to stall him. His mouth left hers and traced a cool, moist trail down her throat as he kissed her neck. She was tingling in the most surprising places and, as she wriggled with pleasure, she slid herself down on the *chaise-longue*.

'I wish there was room for me on there,' he breathed. 'Why don't we lie on the bearskin?'

'Is the door locked?' she whispered.

He nodded and kissed her again. 'Come on. It'll be more comfortable. I'll get a couple of cushions to put under our heads.'

As he gathered up two cushions from the other side of the studio, it was a delight to see her lying down on the bearskin waiting for him. The fall of her dress outlined her figure tormentingly. Never before had they been in this position and he'd never thought to engineer such an opportunity. But here she was now, lying on his rug of her own volition; this, the most beautiful girl he'd ever had the privilege of meeting, the only woman he'd ever truly, honestly loved with all his heart. And how he wanted her. By God, he wanted her so much. He could have waited but, maybe now it was time.

He lay down alongside her while she turned her head and smiled with her entire fund of affection. He raised himself up on one elbow and leaned

131

over her, whereupon he traced a line lovingly from her hairline, over her nose and lips, to her chin. As her arms went around his neck and their lips met again in another lingering kiss, she realised she was smiling contentedly.

'Do you love me enough, Clover ... and trust me enough ... to let me make love to you all the way?' he whispered.

'Yes,' she breathed, unhesitating.

He sighed profoundly. 'Are you sure you understand what I'm asking?'

'Yes,' she said again. 'Course I do. I love you, Tom. With all my heart. And I know you love me equally.'

He sighed again, uncertain how he should proceed. Perhaps he should solicit her help. 'Do you think we should get undressed? I mean, you don't want to get your dress all creased.'

'Nor you your suit.' She uttered a little laugh, belying her nervousness.

He took off his jacket and unfastened his necktie. The collar of his shirt sprung open like a metal spring bent back and suddenly released, which made her laugh. He slipped his braces from his shoulders and undid the buttons on his trousers.

'Let me help you,' he said, and gently, carefully unfastened the tiny buttons that started between her shoulders and ended past the small of her back. She slipped the straps down her arms and stood up while she passed the dress over her slender hips and off. She placed it with care over a chair and knelt down gracefully. To her surprise, she felt no embarrassment as she took off

132

the rest of her clothes and lay down again. It seemed the most natural thing in the world.

Meanwhile, he took off his shirt and his underpants and looked into her eyes self-consciously. 'Oh, Clover,' he said, sighing inadequately. 'My love.'

She still had her stockings on. With a pounding heart he kneeled before her and gently slid them down her smooth unblemished legs, garters and all. He thought he would burst with desire at the touch of the warm, inviting flesh of her thighs and the sight of her naked body and skin that looked like cream.

He tossed the stockings aside and lay with her. With heart pounding scandalously, she offered her mouth once more and, as he leaned over her, she felt his leg part her own and she trembled with nervousness.

'I want to kiss you all over,' he said.

'Yes, I want you to.' Her throat was dry, her voice barely audible.

She tingled as his lips floated over her breasts, barely touching, but she felt her nipples harden nonetheless. She began to ache in the pit of her stomach, an ache of profound longing for him. His hand glided over the smooth skin of her belly and his fingers drew a line from her navel to her crop of soft, dark hair. There, he lingered at the hidden flesh beneath, silky and soft with its powerful, tormenting wetness that told him she wanted him as much as he wanted her. But he resisted the urge to hurry. These moments were worth savouring. He kissed her on the mouth again while his fingers teased her, eliciting little sighs of pleasure that fired him up the more.

As he eased himself onto her she parted her legs.

'I think you'll have to guide me in,' he whispered, half apologetically.

She reached for him between his legs. As he raised himself slightly she held him and was delighted and surprised at what she felt; so lovely and soft and smooth on the outside yet with an inner firmness that was also reassuring. Gently, she pulled him towards her and, as she felt him penetrate at last there was a sharp, incisive pain. She gasped as he pushed deeper into her and he stopped, concerned. Again she drew him into her, just a little at a time till she felt his groin hard against her. Then she held him tight as the pain diminished and the pleasure increased.

The photographs turned out well. Tom brought them to the Jolly Collier on the Monday evening after work. Clover was not due to see him that evening but, after their first lovemaking the previous afternoon, she was glad to see him, just to be sure the magic that had bloomed between them then was still there. Clover didn't mind him seeing her in her working clothes any more. He'd seen her stark naked so he knew now how God had intended her to look. Whether she wore her shabby working gear or her new best dresses was no longer relevant.

'They're lovely photos,' Clover admitted. 'Thank you. Have you printed some for yourself?'

'One of each for my bedroom, one of each to go

on top of our piano at home, one of each to go in the studio and one of each to go in the foyer. All framed.'

She laughed happily. 'I never got round to taking one of you, Tom.'

'Next time, eh?' He winked saucily.

'Do you want to stay for tea?'

'I'd love to, Clover, but Mother will be expecting me. I'll finish my pint and go. So I'll see you tomorrow night.'

She smiled and nodded. 'Usual time?'

'Usual time... Hey, I nearly forgot. One of the women from Cook's drapery store came in today with her daughter. She reckons they're after an assistant to work in the fabrics department. I said you might be interested.'

'Cook's?' she repeated, her eyes lighting up. 'That'd be a lovely clean job. I wonder what they pay?'

'Probably not as much as you get now, and you'd have to work Saturdays, but it would be cleaner. Why don't you go and find out about it? Ask for a Mr Butters. You never know.'

'I'll mention it to Mother later.'

Zillah Bache had made some liver faggots for tea that evening and they smelt divine. They had them with grey peas and boiled potatoes with hot, thick onion gravy, a doorstep of bread-and-butter and a huge jug of beer between them. Talk was about brewing and the inroads Beckitt's Beers were making into the local hostelries.

'Elijah's got another forge signed up today and the Earl's ironworks have agreed to take a couple

135

of barrels to try, to see if the blokes take to it,' Jake announced proudly as Clover placed dinners in front of them all. 'Everything's on song, Mary Ann. Already we'm selling fifty barrels a week on top of what the Collier takes. Already the money's rolling in.'

'And no good squandering it,' Mary Ann advised seriously. 'But I don't reckon much to that new drayman you've started, Jacob. I wunt trust him as far as I could throw him. And idle? He's too idle to scratch hisself.'

'I know, I've been watching him,' Jake replied defensively. 'I've got somebody else lined up.'

'Mother...' Clover muttered tentatively. 'If the business is doing better now, can I leave the foundry?'

'And work here in the business with us, you mean?'

'Not in the business. You always said you didn't want me working in the licensed trade. Tom says they're after somebody to work in the fabric department at Cook's in High Street in the town. I fancy applying for it. It would be clean work.'

'I see no reason why she shouldn't, Mary Ann,' Jake proclaimed before her mother had chance to swallow her bit of faggot and shape her lips. 'Like I said, we'm on target and making money. What bit Clover's been contributing is chicken feed now. Let the wench find herself a nice clean job. I certainly wunt like to work in e'er a foundry.'

Clover smiled her best smile and thanked Jake for his consideration. 'I know it'll mean working Saturdays but I don't mind that. At least I'll be able to buy material and things cheap for dresses ... for all of us.'

'I should get the job fust, afore you start planning what you'm gunna get cheap, our Clover,' Mary Ann counselled.

'I think I'll call in tomorrow. There's no sense in letting the grass grow under my feet. I'll have the day off.'

It was on the Tuesday that Clover informed Ned Brisco she would not be working at the foundry for much longer. The tramlines of Birmingham Road glinted like polished silver in the low sunshine as they seemed to disappear into the depths of Dudley Castle, which stood sentinel over this thoroughfare into the town. Trams rumbled past with workers packed tight, while others, preferring to take in the summer evening, walked home. Ned climbed over the stile into Brewery Fields before Clover and courteously handed her down when she clambered over it.

'When are you finishing then?'

Clover shook out her long cotton skirt and continued walking. 'Friday. I told old Ratface Mason today.'

'What did he say?'

'What could he say? Oh, he said he didn't want me to go, but he could tell I'd made my mind up.'

'Did he offer you more money?'

'It wouldn't make any difference if he did. I'd be mad not to take this offer of shop work. It's less money, but shop work is what I've always wanted. I hate working in filth.'

'But I shan't see you, Clover,' Ned complained.

'We'll lose touch, specially now you're courting *him.*'

'Don't be daft. You know where I live. You can always come and have a drink. I'll always be glad to see you.'

'If you could find time on the nights you don't see *him* you could still come and help me with the *Gull*, if you wanted.'

Clover disliked the resentment Ned always manifested for Tom in the scornful tone he used when he said *'him'*. It was unjustified, but she let it pass. 'If you still want me to, I will. Tom won't mind, you know. He's not an ogre.'

'Would you tell him?'

'Course I'd tell him. He knows I helped you before. He admires what you're doing. He says he'd like to take some more photographs when you go flying again.'

'I don't want him taking any more photos, Clover. The last ones he took he sold for five guineas. Julian Oakley, the reporter from the *Herald* told me. It's as if he's pinched all my work and he's the only one to get paid for it. If anybody should be making money from photos of me and my *Gull*, it should be me. The money could go towards an engine.'

Clover was taken aback. 'Is that why you resent Tom? Is that why you're always so scornful when you mention him?'

'Partly. I resent him most because he's got you, though. You know how I feel about you – how I've always felt about you... But he suddenly pops up from nowhere and sweeps you off your feet.'

Clover sighed, feelings of guilt over Ned returning. 'I can no more help how I feel than you can, Ned,' she said gently. 'It doesn't mean I don't care about you.'

Further conversation seemed superfluous after that. So they climbed St John's Road in silence, past the vicarage and its vast garden, almost as big as the churchyard. The forge opposite the church was still working and the great thud of forging hammers shook the earth beneath their feet. Workmen with dirty faces and dirtier hands drifted into the Freebodies after their shifts for a drink before they went home, as they would be doing at the Jolly Collier.

'Aren't you going up Price Street?' Clover asked, at last punctuating their wordless silence, for at this point they normally went their separate ways.

'No, not today,' Ned answered defiantly. 'I'll come and have a drink at the Jolly Collier. I can say hello to Ramona.'

Clover cast a concerned glance at him. 'Won't your mother wonder what's happened to you if you're late?'

'I'm not a little boy, Clover.'

She glanced at him. No, he was not a little boy. He was a man, full-grown. Yet he was perilously immature in so many ways. He lacked the experience of requited love, had never known the joy, the pleasure, the richness it could bring ... or the agonising heartache. He had not experienced the intense, uncontrollable emotions that prompted rational people to behave in totally irrational ways. Maybe he had not known desire either; he had never said.

Ned obviously knew jealousy. But jealousy was not the same as being in love; it was an unwelcome bed partner of love. Clover had experienced jealousy over Ramona when she believed she had taken Tom from under her very nose. It was a cruel state of mind, an injured lover's hell. She wanted no more of it, so she sympathised the more with Ned.

But desire...?

Clover at last was beginning to understood how a timely kiss, exquisitely delivered, could stoke up enough desire to allow you to throw caution to the wind. Desire could turn your world upside down, could make you wanton. She desired Tom now. Ever since those delectable moments on Sunday afternoon when she had lain naked with him on his bearskin, she had been unable to concentrate on anything else. Ever since she'd felt that profound tenderness and exhilaration, which had fuelled the need to give herself utterly in the name of love, the reliving of it in her mind had consumed her. Yet it had been over all too soon. She longed for that absolute and total intimacy and gentleness to last and last. Although spiritually, she had been content, physically she was left still tingling, instinctively wanting more, requiring more. There must be more to it than what she had experienced that first time. But what she'd had was enough to whet her appetite for the next time they lay together on his bearskin – and that would have to be tonight. Whether it was his intention or not, it was hers. The thought made her pulse race and the spittle in her mouth thicken.

Chapter Eight

'It's bloody scandalous, the price of an 'undredweight o' coal,' Noah Fairfax complained to the man sitting on the adjacent stool in the taproom of the Jolly Collier, which was buzzing with laughter and a dozen assorted conversations. 'I've just bin to fetch a load in me barrer and I couldn't catch me breath when old Ma Poxon asked me for the money. One and threepence ha'penny her charged me.'

'Blame the miners,' the other man, Urban Tranter, said and noisily slurped the froth from the pint Ramona had just placed on the table before him. 'They'm forever on strike. Swines. Never satisfied, them lot. Coal's bound to be scarce.'

'Scarce?' Noah queried indignantly. 'Rockin' hoss shit's scarce but nobody's asking one and threepence ha'penny a bloody 'undredweight for it.'

'But nobody wants to burn rocking hoss shit, Noah. Trouble is, when coal gets scarce, the price goes sky bloody high.'

'So what they oughta do,' Noah said withdrawing a tin of twist tobacco from his jacket pocket, 'is let them saft Suffragettes go down the mines when the miners am on strike.'

Ramona returned to the table. 'Your change, Mr Tranter.'

'Ta, my lover,' he said and pocketed it. Urban chuckled at Noah and nodded his agreement as he dipped his nose into his pint mug.

'Yo' can loff, Urban, but if them Suffragettes want the vote like a mon, then let 'em get down the pits and dig coal like a mon.' Animatedly, he rubbed a knob of tobacco between the palms of his hand to break it into smokable strands. 'Then they might get a bit o' sympathy from the likes o' you and me. Eh, Urban? Then we might get reasonable price coal and all.'

Elijah Tandy, who was also serving, heard the discussion and laughed. 'Are you going to argue about the Suffragettes now, Noah?' he asked. 'Ramona will argue with you, won't you sweetheart?'

'Me? I never argue with customers, Uncle Elijah,' she replied pleasantly and pulled another pint. She caught his eye and he winked at her, which had an unsteadying affect. She could not hold his look, for fear he could read her mind and see the image of himself therein, standing magnificently naked in the bathtub in the brewery. Her long eyelashes swept the intensifying bloom of her cheek as she turned away.

'You're blushing, Ramona,' he teased provocatively, for he believed he knew why. And it was easy for him to make gain from a situation that would have mortified another man.

'No, I'm not,' she protested and pulled another pint to keep her face hidden. Since she'd secretly watched him towelling himself dry, she'd seen her Uncle Elijah in a dangerously different light; not as an uncle – her father's brother – but as a man. And an attractive man at that, with all man's hard and healthy cravings for love. She'd been excited at what she'd witnessed so secretly. Oh, he was a man all right, fit and full-blooded. And she'd found it impossible to dismiss from her mind the images of him standing in all his full-blooded glory in the oblique rays of the yellowing sun as it streamed through the brewery window onto his muscular body that evening.

When she thought her colour had subsided she looked up and saw with grateful surprise that Ned Brisco was standing beside her, an expectant grin on his face.

'Ned! What brings you here?'

'Hello, Ramona. I just walked back from work with Clover. I thought I'd call in and have a drink before my tea and say hello.'

'Sit you down, eh, and I'll bring you a pint over.'

'I'll stand here by you, if that's all right.'

'All right. Just so long as you don't stand in my way.' She smiled to soften what might sound like disapproval. 'Clover's back now then, is she?'

'Yes. She said she was going to wash and change. I suppose she's going courting tonight.'

'Lucky girl.' She delivered two drinks and returned with the money which she dropped into the till.

'Are you courting now, Ramona?'

It was a leading question. She began pulling another pint. She could so easily say no and wheedle an invitation out of Ned to go out with him. And, if she answered no, she wasn't courting, she would be telling no lie, for Sammy had

143

joined the Staffordshire Fusiliers and had gone away to commence his training. On the other hand, she could so easily say yes to an invitation. Ned was nowhere near as fanciable as Elijah but what the hell. It could be her way of getting back at Clover for luring Tom away when she reckoned he was so close to asking her to be his girl. Clover cared about Ned, for all her denials. She had even warned her off.

'Well?' Ned prompted.

'No I'm not courting any more, Ned...' She looked him in the eye and handed him a pint of bitter beer. 'How's your flying machine coming on?'

He delved into his trouser pocket and handed her sixpence. 'Oh, all right,' he answered brightly, well and truly sidetracked. 'I shall be flying it again in a week or two to try out some modifications I've done. Why don't you come and watch? I daresay Clover will come if she can drag herself away from that Tom Doubleday.' He took an ample quaff from the glass.

Ramona regarded him with pity. 'You ain't still bitter about him, are you, Ned? What you need is a sweetheart of your own to take your mind off things.'

'I know. I wondered if you'd like to come out with me one night, Ramona,' he said, mustering every ounce of his confidence.

'I don't see why not,' she answered in a whisper. 'But let it be our secret, Ned. We won't let Clover know, eh?'

He smiled conspiratorially. 'That's all right by me. When shall I see you?'

'How about tomorrow night?'

After tea, when Clover had washed up and she was getting herself ready to see Tom, Ramona tapped on her bedroom door.

'Can I come in?'

'Yes, course. How does this dress look, Ramona?' She twirled around in it and looked over her shoulder at her stepsister.

'Depends what you're going to do in it?'

'Do in it?' Clover queried guiltily, turning round to face her.

'I mean, it's all right for walking out, but not for sitting in a theatre.'

'I'm not going to a theatre.'

'Then it's fine, Clover. The colour suits you.' Ramona gave a generous smile. 'The style suits you.'

'Thank you.'

'How's Tom? I don't get the chance to talk to him now like I used to when he would come in two or three times a week after work.'

'He's lovely,' she responded simply, predictably, with a broad smile. She thought it best not to crow that he used to come in just on the off-chance of seeing herself. Now they were courting he had no need.

'He *is* nice, Clover. I think you're very lucky.'

'I think so as well... Hey, I bet it was a surprise to see Ned tonight, wasn't it?'

Ramona hesitated to reply. 'That's why I've come to see you before you go out, Clover ... I wanted you to know...' She sounded very concerned.

'Know what?'

'That he asked me to go out with him... But I said, no, Clover. I told him I didn't have time these days.'

'Poor Ned... But thanks for telling me. In any case, you wouldn't find him very entertaining. You'd be bored to tears, I daresay.'

'That's what I thought. You won't mention it, though, will you? I'd hate him to think I'd broken a confidence.'

'I won't mention it.' There was a shout from downstairs. Tom Doubleday had arrived. 'Coming,' Clover called.

'Uncle Elijah's just gone out as well. I don't know what he sees in that flipping Dorcas. I don't like her very much, do you, Clover?'

'Not very much, no.' Clover adjusted her hat in the mirror and followed Ramona down the stairs.

Ramona watched Clover link arms with Tom Doubleday as they left. Pity Tom had got away. She could have been content with Tom. Tom was all man; smart, courteous, confident, handsome. Ramona sighed. She needed a man. She needed a man to allow her vibrant emotions to enjoy some much-needed exercise now that Sammy had gone and left this void. Well, Ned was patently interested in her now. Clover was no longer apparently the centre of his world. The trouble was, Ned would be no challenge. She could never fall in love with Ned.

As the sun went down behind the roof of the Board School, where St John's Street met Owen Street some distance away, the whole sky flared into vivid hues of apricot and orange. A ruck of clouds that had sneaked up were trapped in the blaze and daubed with its wild colours. The heat of the day remained, uncomfortably humid and warm.

'Where are we going?' Clover asked Tom.

'Where would you like to go?'

She hoped he was fishing for her to suggest his studio, but she would not. Oh, she wanted to go there more than anything in the world, but she must not appear so brazen as to suggest it herself. 'Shall we go for a walk in the town?' she suggested instead. If they went for a walk in the town, logically, they were ever likely to pass his studio on the way back.

So they walked up and down High Street from Hall Street to Top Church, peering in shop windows, discussing this piece of furniture, that dress. Outside Cook's, they admired the window display of fine materials and Clover said how much she was looking forward to working there.

'I'm looking forward to it as well,' Tom remarked. 'I might even get to see you dinnertimes.'

'Dinner-times? You'll be fed up of me.'

'Never.'

'Maybe on my way home at night, then.'

They turned and resumed walking.

'Well, seeing me will be a change from walking back with Ned every night.'

'Oh, poor old Ned,' she sighed. 'He asked Ramona to go out with him tonight.'

'I imagine she turned him down?'

'Yes and I'm glad. He's not fit for the likes of

Ramona. She'd have him wrapped round her little finger. She'd make mincemeat out of him.'

'Yes, I suppose she is a bit wily.'

'He's still resentful over you, you know, Tom.'

'I can't say I'm surprised. But he'll get over it.'

'You know what's peeving him? The fact that you had five guineas as payment for photos of him from the *Dudley Herald*. That Julian Oakley told him.'

'Julian Oakley should have more sense than betray a business arrangement. But that's typical of a newspaper reporter.'

'All the same, Ned thought he should be entitled to the money as he and his flying machine were the subject matter. He reckons the money could go towards an engine.'

'Well, he's not entitled to it, Clover,' Tom said evenly. 'The copyright of the photos belongs to me. They're my property to do with as I see fit. Besides, I'm a photographer and I have a living to make, the same as everybody else.'

'Course you do.'

'If, on the other hand, he had commissioned me to take the photos, that would be a different matter. Then the copyright *would* belong to him. But he didn't commission me. And I asked his permission before I set up my camera, if you remember.'

'So you did. I'd forgotten about that.'

'Still, I sympathise with him, trying to build and develop that thing with no financial backing. It's almost an impossibility without money, I would've thought.'

By the time they had walked back to Hall

148

Street, it was dusk. As if by a common consent that was unspoken, they ambled back towards the studio. Outside, by that same unspoken, mutual consent they stopped as they reached it.

'I've got a teapot and a kettle in the studio,' Tom said. 'We could make a brew here if you're thirsty.'

She smiled serenely. 'If you like. I could murder a cup of tea.'

Once inside, Tom locked the door behind him and they entered the studio. The grey half-light of dusk was permeating the room through the huge expanse of windows. Outside, Clover could just make out the high wall around the back yard that was topped with cemented-on broken bottles to deter trespassers. And she could just discern the bearskin rug on the floor.

She turned to Tom and he took her in his arms.

He bent his head and kissed her, long and lingering. He had been longing to kiss her ever since he'd called for her. Almost every time she'd spoken he'd watched her lips moving sensuously. Whenever she'd smiled he'd ached to feel her soft, sweet breath on his face. He'd longed to taste her again. Now, here she was, once more in his arms, once more in his studio where they'd made love for the first time only a couple of days ago. He had not been quite the same since. He had never known contentment like he had found with this girl.

'I want you, Clover.'

In the dimness, he could just discern the glimmer of love in her eyes as she looked up into his. Again they kissed, probing, deep, passionate.

'You make me so happy,' he said when they had broken off. 'If I just knew how to unfasten these buttons of yours my happiness would be complete. They're so tiny.'

She chuckled. 'I'll do it.'

He stripped off, watching her undress as he did so. He could just discern her pale limbs, slender, beautifully formed, ultimately feminine. He grabbed the two cushions which they used as pillows and placed them at one end of the bearskin rug. They lay down together and clasped each other in a passionate embrace that anticipated the pleasure they were about to give each other.

For more than an hour they made love.

After it, Clover smiled to herself.

After it, she felt content, sated. Now she understood what all the fuss was about.

After it, when she tried to stand to put the kettle on for the cup of tea they had made their excuse, she felt weak at the knees.

In September 1907 Norway's eminent composer Grieg died in Bergen at the age of sixty-four. Two days later, *The Lusitania* left Liverpool to embark on her maiden voyage to New York and arrived on the thirteenth after crossing the Atlantic in a record five days and fifty-four minutes. During a visit to Bengal, the Labour MP, Keir Hardie kicked up a rumpus when he accused the British government of running India 'like the Czar runs Russia', which subsequently caused anti-British riots in Calcutta. However, for Ned Brisco, the most significant piece of news that month came from France where Louis Bleriot flew 184 metres in his powered, tandem wing monoplane, *Libellule*, before crash-landing.

Spurred on by Bleriot's success, Ned stepped up his own efforts. He had made some minor modifications to the *Gull* and had been once more to Rough Hill with Amos and Clover one sunny Sunday morning in early September, where he had become airborne again, but had flown no further than the last attempt. Ned was becoming frustrated. Before he could consider installing an engine into the *Gull*, he desperately needed to practise taking off and landing, as well as actually controlling the machine in flight. He needed to master pitch and yaw and roll. But he was getting no practice. Once he had landed at the bottom of Rough Hill it was a two-mile round trip to return to the top to have another go; and even then, the *Gull* would have to be dismantled and reassembled. What he needed was a good stretch of open, level ground and some device that would tow him into the air – and tow him back again from wherever he landed. Ned was airing his ideas to Joseph Mantle, whose stables he utilised at Springfield House.

'I can see your problem, Ned,' Joseph said sympathetically and rubbed his chin.

'Oh, Mr Mantle, if you could come up with something, I wouldn't half appreciate it,' Ned replied.

'It's just possible I might know somebody who could help you out. No promises at this stage, Ned lad.'

'Can't you tell me more?'

'Patience, Ned, patience. Listen, you've built this wonderful little biplane. Do you think you could build a trailer of some sort to transport it on?'

'I reckon so, Mr Mantle. I could get hold of some wood and a couple of wheels. That wouldn't be a problem.'

'Good lad. You'll need to do that anyway, whatever happens. By the way, Ned – any luck with sponsorship? Has anybody offered to help you out with the cost of an engine?'

Ned shook his head. 'Nobody, Mr Mantle.'

'Nobody? I'm amazed. I'm amazed that nobody can see the potential in what you're doing. After that lovely write-up you had in the *Herald* as well. And the photos.'

Ned shrugged resignedly. 'It's the way of the world, Mr Mantle. If I was a somebody, it'd be a different tale, I daresay.'

'And have you got your eye on an engine, Ned?'

'There's a French engineer called Levavasseur. He builds engines for aeroplanes. He's developed a sixteen-cylinder one called the *Antoinette*. A fifty-horsepower job. God knows how much it would cost, though. A fortune, I imagine.'

'Well, I imagine somebody will come up with the money, Ned, to help you out. But I'd have thought some firm around here building motor car engines would be able to adapt one for you quite cheap.'

Ned shrugged. 'Maybe I'll end up building my own. I could do it, I reckon. Anyway, there's no rush as I see it, Mr Mantle. Nobody yet has designed a decent airscrew. The ones they use

152

now ain't very efficient. I reckon that's where I should be concentrating me efforts now – designing a decent airscrew.'

Chapter Nine

On 21st September, a Saturday, Clover arrived from work looking delightfully spruce. It was such a change to go to work dressed well and to return from it all clean and tidy. She had been working at Cook's for about three months and she loved it. She liked the people she worked with and always had a smile for the folk she served. On her way home from work she would invariably call into Tom's studio and, usually, his kettle was bubbling away on the portable gas ring that adorned his tiny scullery and he would brew her some tea. Sometimes, they would forego the tea and make love, especially if they were not due to meet that night, or if they had been invited somewhere that would leave no time later for such tenderness and intimacy. This particular evening was one such.

When Clover reached home, she appeared in the taproom where Ramona and her father were busy. Jake smiled and asked if she wanted a drink.

'I'd love a glass of lemonade.'

'Help yourself, Clover, my wench.'

'Is it still warm out?' Ramona asked, sidling up while Clover poured herself a drink.

153

'Not really. There's a bit of a nip in the air now.'

'I wouldn't have credited it, looking at you, Clover. You look all flushed.'

'Do I?' Clover knew it was not just the exertion of walking. Making love with Tom at the studio on her way home, with ever-increasing finesse, expertise and zest, had something to do with it.

'Now you're blushing,' Ramona proclaimed, her voice a hoarse whisper. 'I can tell a blush from a flush.' She chuckled. 'What've you been up to?'

Clover smiled coyly and sipped the lemonade, unable to look Ramona in the eye.

'Come on, tell me,' the younger girl persisted, her voice still low.

Clover shook her head, still wearing her abashed smile.

Ramona measured out a half gill of whisky for somebody and poured it into a glass. 'I bet you've just seen Tom...'

Clover's eyes met her stepsister's and the expression in them gave it all away. She nodded and sipped her drink again self-consciously.

'You dark horse! You mean you–?'

'I'm saying nothing, Ramona...' Her smile this time turned into a little chuckle.

'You don't have to. It's written all over your face. So, he's made a woman of you after all...'

Clover nodded again and bit her bottom lip as she smiled reticently.

'Tell me about it then.'

'You don't expect me to give a blow-by-blow account do you? All right, Tom and I have passed the kissing stage. It's enough that you know that.

You're not really entitled to know that much, but you wheedled it out of me.'

They ceased talking while Jake was within earshot at the beer pumps.

'Do you like it?' Ramona persisted when Jake had moved away.

'Oh, Ramona...'

'Well?'

'Can a duck swim?'

Ramona chuckled. 'Well, well. I take it you haven't been doing it in the churchyard across the graves. Knowing you, Clover, you wouldn't want the dirty granite stones next to you or the grit scratching your bare bum. So where've you been doing it?'

'Where d'you think?'

'His house?'

'With his family there?'

'Where then?'

'God! You don't give up, do you?' she replied with faked exasperation. 'At his studio, if you must know.'

Ramona gave a slow nod of realisation. 'Blimey, I was a bit stupid not working that one out. So when was the first time?'

'Oh, Ramona, you want to know the top and bottom of Meg's backside. Let me have some secrets.'

'Has he got a bed there?'

'No, course not.'

'What then?'

'Never mind.'

'Oh, Clover. You have to tell me. I'll tell you all my secrets.'

'I don't think I want to know them.'

'I promise I'll tell you all my secrets, Clover...'

Clover rolled her eyes in mock despair. Ramona was just too persistent to be shaken off. 'If you must know, he has a lovely bearskin rug.'

The two girls giggled at that.

'Haven't you got some boy lined up now, Ramona? It's time you had. Sammy's been gone a while now.'

'There's one or two... As a matter of fact there's a chap who comes in here some nights. I'm seeing him later. He says he's going to take me out.'

Mary Ann thrust her solemn face round the hatch from the passage. 'Oh, you'm back, our Clover. The tea will be ready in five minutes and, as usual, there's no bugger about. Will you go and call Elijah for me?' She closed the hatch and was gone back to the scullery.

Ramona's heart suddenly lurched. Uncle Elijah would be in the brewery. He was bound to be taking a bath in there. She'd tried to catch a glimpse of him a few times over the last few weeks but had been foiled by interceding events and people. Right now, though, she had the strangest feeling she might be lucky.

'Shall I go?' she suggested casually to Clover. 'You stay here and finish your drink. I could do with a breath of fresh air after all the smoke in here. And Job Smith should be here to serve in a minute or two.' She wiped her hands on her apron and hurried out.

From the passage she stepped onto the pavement outside and turned right up the side of the

156

Jolly Collier, into the yard, passing the scullery window where Mary Ann was preparing their meal. Once on the yard she tiptoed towards the brewery. The light of that September evening was quickly fading. The sky above was a rich, royal blue fused with red and orange in the west and the first of the brightest stars were moving up the eastern sky. The door to the brewery was closed. Gently, Ramona depressed the thumb plate on the latch and opened it soundlessly, a move she had already practised several times in readiness for such a moment as this.

Elijah was there. She heard him splashing about in the bathtub. No light was streaming in like the first time she had caught him like this, just the greyness of dusk, but sufficient to see his fit body glistening with soapy water. Like the first time, she hid herself behind the stack of barrels to her right and peered between them. Her heart pounded hard against her ribcage as she stood stock still, desperate to remain unseen and unheard, like all good little girls. For this was so wrong. If Mary Ann knew what she was doing there would be hell to pay. There would be hell to pay if her father knew. And to hell with revealing this secret to Clover; Clover would scorn her for ever after if she knew about this.

But what perversity had drawn her here again to watch her own uncle bathing and towelling himself dry, merely to risk censure if discovered? The fact that he was her uncle had nothing to do with it, however. The fact that he was a man, was everything. He was only thirty-two, at the height of his masculinity and virility. That was what drew her. His body was worth looking at. Every bit of him was worth admiring, uncle or no. He was desirable and it irked her that Dorcas was the undeserving woman who was reaping the full benefit.

He stood up and the warm water streamed off him, rippling back into the tub. With his back toward her he reached out for the towel and covered his head. As he rubbed his hair, she watched mesmerised as his private parts, in perfect profile, bobbed about in rhythm with his arm movements. So drawn was she to this breathtaking scene, that she did not see the little furry creature that had entered the brewery under the door, nibbling conscientiously on a sparse trail of malted barley grains.

Elijah turned his attentions to his chest, then his arms. He flung the towel across his back, stretched it taut and, as he sawed his straight back dry, Ramona was fascinated again by the erotic joggling of his unfettered manhood. She felt a stirring deep inside her, an ache in the pit of her stomach which, she now freely admitted to herself, was her longing for him. It would have been so easy to strip off her own clothes and run to him, to take him in her arms and drag him to the hard wooden floor in a frenzy of wordless desire. But she remained silent, unmoving, in awe, trying to control her breathing that she realised was coming in gasps, trying to regulate the thumping of her heart.

Then she felt a tiny sensation, like an itch, on the top of her foot by the leather strap of her shoe. She ignored it. Uncle Elijah was towelling

158

his groin, facing her full on and it was a magnificent sight. She felt something again, something else, like little claws digging into her stocking at her ankle ... climbing up her leg... She screamed.

'What the bloody–' Elijah was still standing in the bathtub. He jumped out and, wrapping the towel around him, rushed towards the door from whence the terrified scream had come. He heard the scream again – and again. 'I'm coming, I'm coming.'

By the door, behind the barrels he saw Ramona transfixed, pale, a look of absolute terror on her face. Her skirt was pulled up above her knees and a mouse was vigorously trying to detach itself from the tiny mesh of her stocking. 'Get him off!' she screeched. 'Get him off! Get him off me!'

'Just hold still and keep calm,' Elijah said gently, securing the towel by tucking the end in. 'The little mite's as frit as you are. He won't hurt you.' He slid his right hand into the top of her stocking to ease it away from the warm flesh of her thigh, until it was underneath the mouse. 'This might leave a hole or two in your stocking,' he informed her. Then he gently lifted the mouse away till its tiny claws pulled free. 'There. That's got him.' He held the creature up to inspect it. 'He won't hurt you look, Ramona. He's just a little mouse.'

'God! Take it away,' she shrilled.

Elijah held the mouse firmly in his hand and stroked it. 'I told you, he won't hurt you. Look at him, the poor little thing, he's frit to death.' He opened the door and put it outside. 'There. He's just scurried off. I daresay one of the cats'll get him.'

'I've never been so terrified in my life,' Ramona admitted, the colour returning to her cheeks. 'Thanks for rescuing me.'

'What were you doing here?'

'I came to call you for your tea,' she answered unconvincingly.

'Oh? Did you call? I didn't hear you.'

She adjusted the fall of her skirt and looked at her shoes. Embarrassed, she shook her head.

'Have you been peeping at me?' There was sham admonishment in his voice, mirth in his eyes that belied any real concern or judgement. 'Have you been getting an eyeful?'

'I came to call you, Uncle Elijah, like I said.' She endeavoured to sound indignant. 'With that horrible little mouse running up my leg I didn't get the chance.'

'You've watched me before having a bath, haven't you?' His eyes crinkled with amusement now, at the realisation of what it meant. 'Go on. Admit it. I don't mind. As a matter of fact, I'm flattered.'

She looked away, her face crimson in the fading light. 'So what if I have?'

'Like I said, I don't mind. As long as you enjoyed it...'

'I suppose I'm no different to anybody else,' she said, trying to justify her actions now she'd been discovered. 'It's natural to look if somebody's got no clothes on.'

'Course it is. I'd look at you if you'd got no

160

clothes on and was having a bath. I'd get a real eyeful.'

'Promise you won't tell anybody, Uncle Elijah... Not about the mouse... Nothing.'

He laughed. 'Let it be our secret.'

She did not reply.

'Did you like what you saw? You can tell me, you know.'

'I'm ashamed of myself, if you want to know the truth. You're my uncle.'

His timing was perfect. He reached out and drew her to him so that her head was resting on his bare chest. He smelt all fresh and clean and she was moved to put her arms around his waist, to feel him in her arms as familiar as a lover.

'Don't be ashamed,' he whispered. 'It's nothing to be ashamed of. Very often, I look at you and think, Jesus Christ, I don't half fancy our Ramona. She's me brother's daughter, but I fancy her all the same, she's so bloody beautiful. It's the most natural thing in the world to fancy somebody of the opposite sex, you know. Cousins, uncles, nieces. It makes no odds.'

'I fancied you from the moment I saw you in the bath the first time,' she breathed, reluctant to let go of him. 'You were all hard and sticking up...' She uttered a little giggle of embarrassment. 'I thought, God, that Dorcas has that all to herself.'

'Well, there's no reason why she should,' he answered provocatively and she thought she sensed his breathing speed up. 'You've been with a man before then, our Ramona? You've been with Sammy?'

She nodded against his chest. 'Plenty of times.'

'I thought as much. I sensed it.' His voice was still low, intimate. 'How old are you now?'

'Eighteen.'

'Old enough. I've had girls younger than you.'

'Honestly?'

'Honestly.' He pulled her head up gently and planted a kiss fairly and squarely on her lips. 'Go on. You'd better go, else sourpuss Mary Ann will be out here after you, wondering what's become of you. We'd hate her to see us like this, wouldn't we?'

She nodded, squeezed his hand and left, more breathless than when she entered.

Ramona was preoccupied that teatime. She barely spoke and dared not look up at her Uncle Elijah lest anybody guess her guilty secret. Elijah, by contrast, led every conversation; he was sparkling with laughter and little quips that made everybody laugh. But Ramona was glad when the meal was finished and Elijah went to his room to put on his best suit to go a-courting Dorcas, for she was never sure that he would not relate the story about the mouse climbing her stocking.

As they washed up the dirty crockery together, Ramona asked Clover where she was going that evening with Tom.

'We're going to the Empire to see a variety show.'

'Well that's across the road from his studio,' Ramona said in a low voice.

'I know but it'll be late... What time are you

going out?'

Ramona looked at the scullery clock. 'In about three-quarters of an hour.'

'Then you'd better get ready. Go on, I can finish these things.'

So Ramona changed into a warm woollen dress and went out for the first time with a lad of twenty-one called Harry Heppenstall, whose name everybody pronounced, in true Black Country fashion, by not sounding the aitches. Harry mooned over her like a lovesick buck but Ramona's heart was not with him. He was good-looking and pleasant company. At any other time she would have been responsive to him, but she was too preoccupied with thoughts of Uncle Elijah. Nonetheless, they walked the town together and stopped in Lester's, a 'board' pub without a name, known only by the name of the family that owned it. She told Harry she had to be back by eleven. So, by eleven he had dutifully walked her back to the Jolly Collier and went to have a last drink with his pals who were said to be in the Loving Lamb.

Ramona lit a candle and went directly to bed. However, she could not sleep. She heard Clover tiptoe across the landing and go into her room. An hour or so later she heard Mary Ann and her father speaking quietly before they clicked their bedroom door shut. She got out of bed, opened her window and looked out. In the sky the slither of a waning moon hung withered and dry. A dog was barking in Earl Street or thereabouts and another answered it, more distant, somewhere near St John's church. She got back into bed and snuggled down in its warmth, thinking only of Uncle Elijah. Uncle Elijah... Oh, Uncle Elijah... What was he doing right this minute? No doubt doing something totally unsavoury with Dorcas... Lucky Dorcas. Images of him towelling himself dry sprang to mind and she gulped at the enormity of what had occurred earlier that evening. Now he knew. Now he knew exactly the effect he'd had on her. But was it really all right to lust for her uncle, as he'd said it was?

She tossed and turned. She relived the critical seconds when Elijah thrust his hand inside the top of her stocking and for the first time realised the eroticism of that moment. Did he feel pleasure in touching the warm smooth skin of her thigh with his clean, manly hands? Only now was she recalling the way he gently squeezed her thigh then; the horror of the vile little mouse was fading and no longer clouding the sensuality of his action. Sammy entered her thoughts and their youthful fumblings that had gone on in the same house that Elijah was sleeping in, this very night. They had learned their pleasures together, Sammy and her, querying whether she liked it when he did this, or whether he liked it when she did that. It was useful experience and pleasurable. It had come in handy since. It would stand her in good stead with Uncle Elijah.

Ramona realised she was different from the rest. While many girls behaved in the way that was hoped and expected of them where men were concerned, Ramona did not. In the absence of a mother and a mother's influence, her father had allowed her the freedom always to meet boys

164

at night if she wanted to, never questioning her virtue, never advising, never condemning. Many girls were not allowed such freedom; Clover had not been allowed it till Jake's influence had been established. Convention dictated that a girl did not sleep with her man until they were married and, even then, you did what was expected of you dutifully and Lord help you if you displayed any enthusiasm. Well, bugger that. Convention was all cock-eyed. The old women had got it all wrong. Intimacy with a man was the nicest, most exhilarating, most satisfying thing on earth. It made your toes curl, your lips tingle, your breathing come hot and fast. And that pulsing itch in the pit of your stomach that you wanted to last all night, that made you squeal with ecstasy... Oh, there was nothing like it. No wonder girls got into trouble. No wonder they could never say no again once they had tasted it. Why should they want to when it was so natural and felt so agonisingly beautiful?

She thought about Tom Doubleday; handsome, well-dressed Tom. She smiled to herself at Clover's admitting at last that she and Tom ... that she was no longer a virgin. She tried to imagine them together ... on the bearskin rug Clover had mentioned. She tried to visualise herself on the bearskin rug – with Tom... If ever she had to go to Tom's studio she would smile if ever she saw that bearskin rug... Poor old Harry Heppenstall. Maybe some other time she would give him more encouragement; he was worthy of it.

Slowly she drifted off into a fitful sleep. She

dreamed about huge mice with huge phalluses taking baths in soapy water and drying themselves on bearskin rugs. She dreamed about being shut in Lester's pub with a regiment of naked soldiers led by Uncle Elijah, a bathtub in the middle of the saloon and she in it, but nobody looking at her. She dreamed she was in bed with Elijah, but Dorcas was on his other side and he was taking more notice of her... Little nibbling mice scratched about all over her and she woke up in a cold sweat.

What time was it? She yawned and stretched. Elijah had not gone away. He was still there entrenched in her thoughts, him and his spellbinding virility. Softly, silently, she got out of bed, her bare feet padding on the cold linoleum. She peeped through the curtains. The moon and the stars had moved, turning, turning on their eternal carousel. Oh, Uncle Elijah... Damn you for becoming an obsession. Images of him in his bare, masculine magnificence were plaguing her mercilessly. She was a woman and she craved the taste of him – yearned to take him inside her. The spittle in her throat thickened and the blood was coursing through her veins like some hot river in full spate. Oh, Uncle Elijah... She felt that ache deep in her stomach again and knew there was only one way to ease it. There could be only one way.

She opened the curtains and by the dim light that the night afforded, she dressed herself. Blindly, she ran a brush through her hair for a few strokes and dabbed a little scent behind her ears. She picked up her shoes and tiptoed downstairs, as quietly as the mouse that had been the instrument of her confession to him. Downstairs, she lit a taper from the embers of the fire and looked at the clock. Nearly half past five. She picked up her coat that was hanging at the back of the pantry door, collected her key to their old house that had been hanging on a nail in there and went out. As she shut the door as quietly as she could, the pub's two cats, Malcolm and Marmaduke, scurried inside unheard, escaping the chill of the early morning darkness.

The streets of Kates Hill were still and silent. The air was cold with a dampness that prompted her to pull up her collar. She looked up at the stars; coruscations of tiny lights in a jet-black sky. As she walked down Cross Guns Street, she saw a skein of mist that lay motionless below the level of the foliage on Dixon's Green's trees. She wafted through it in her grey coat, like the ghost of some unfulfilled virgin, to get to Bean Road with only the stars to light her way. At the bottom of Bean Road she turned right into Blackacre Road which, in turn, became Constitution Hill with its rows of terraced houses and the gasworks that reeked of rotten eggs in the valley before her. Light from the gasworks spilled onto the steep hill. She stepped into the road where she could see the potholes and bumps better in its rough surface. Where the street began to rise again she passed the Blue Gates where her father used to drink sometimes before he discovered the Jolly Collier. Constitution Hill became Church Street with its grubby little factories, silent now, the underpaid men and girls who worked there asleep in bed at this time. At Vicar Street, she turned into Brooke Street.

Almost there.

A wave of doubt washed over her. What if Dorcas was there? What if everything Uncle Elijah had intimated was just a bluff? What if he politely turned her around and sent her back home with sage advice not to be such a silly girl? What if he thought...? But such thoughts were not enough to daunt her. If Dorcas was there she'd know straight away and make a discreet exit. Besides, she'd had either the courage or the foolishness to have come this far. Why turn back now? So she walked on in the twilight, unafraid of it, her breath coming in steam in the cold night air. She had not seen another soul the entire fifteen minutes she'd been walking.

And then, she found herself outside the house; the house that used to be home. It was a terraced house, but not some two-up-two-down rented house. Her father had earned well as a market trader. No, this was a fine house, bought and paid for – a three-storey family house with a bay window and a tiny walled foregarden.

She took the key from her pocket and inserted it in the front door lock, turned it. It clicked as the tumblers inside fell. She turned the handle, opened the door quietly, closed it behind her. Inside, she took off her coat and, out of habit that was not yet forgotten, hung it over the newel post in the hallway. Silently, she kicked off her shoes and, her breathing rapid, her heart thumping, she slowly, stealthily, apprehensively climbed the stairs.

The door to the room he used was open. She could hear him breathing, slight snores as he lay sleeping, unaware of the intruder. Her eyes were accustomed to the dark and she could see he slept alone. Thank God for that.

For a moment she stopped, reticent again, but forced herself to go on and take the ultimate test.

Nerve.

She had come this far. There was no turning back. She was alone with him in this house. In a minute or two she would be in his bed. He would be nobody's uncle then, nobody's brother, nobody's fiancé.

She shed her clothes and they slipped soundlessly to the floor. For a moment or two longer she stood in her pale nakedness as alert as a tigress stalking her prey, shivering, watching him sleep, listening to his irregular breathing. She took a deep breath and was surprised at her calmness at that moment, despite all; a calmness she'd not felt for ages. She lifted the sheets and slid into bed beside him, grateful for the warmth from his body, resisting the temptation to snuggle up to him to borrow some more, lest she wake him too rudely. So she lay a few moments, unmoving, and the depravity of what she had done and was intending to do with her own uncle struck her, but failed to move her.

She was alone with him, in his bed now. Her yearning heart could soon be at peace. For the next hour or two nobody would disturb them. Nobody would know. He would open his eyes and smile at nobody but her.

His arm came across her, his hand lingered

consciously over the cool smooth skin of her belly.

He snuffled, disoriented.

'Dorcas?'

'No ... Ramona.'

'Oh, Ramona.' He said it as if it were the most natural thing in the world for her to be there. 'Christ, you're cold. Come here, let me warm you up a bit.' His strong arms drew her to him by the small of her back and she yielded to his warmth, to his welcome. His big, warm hand ran up and down her back, over her small bottom, down her thighs as he explored her. 'By Christ you've got lovely smooth skin, our Ramona. But fancy you coming here in the middle of the night.'

'I couldn't help it, Uncle Elijah,' she whispered. 'I couldn't help it. Ever since ... you know ... I've wanted you more than anything else in the world. It's been driving me mad. You're not going to send me away, are you?'

'As if I would. Come here.'

He hugged her and his free hand went between her legs. She was ready for him, even so soon, but he teased her the more with skilful fingering before moving to ease himself onto her.

'In a minute, Uncle Elijah...' She leaned over on top of him and put her face close to his throat and pursed her lips. But she did not kiss him. Instead, she blew gently on an even course from his Adam's apple to the trough of his belly button, her breasts skimming him tormentingly as she moved downwards over his stomach so taut. The promise in her cool blowing stirred the

170

tight, curly hairs between his legs. She rubbed her cheek against them and softly ran her opened lips along the firm length of his erection, gratified that she was having the same wonderful, stimulating effect on him as he had on her. Lovingly, she fondled his sack that was loose and soft and slightly moist with sweat. This prize bundle of gristle, blue veins and fleshy spheroids that felt like shelled, boiled eggs, was responsible for enticing her so recklessly from her own warm bed. She had to caress this bundle to make certain it was real and not just some wild figment of her lively imagination.

Elijah took her bushy hair in his hands and lifted her face towards him. She smiled with anticipation in the darkness as her body, warm now, snaked up over his and found his mouth searching hungrily for hers. He cupped the cheeks of her backside and thrust himself upward and inward and punctured her wetness with one expert lunge. She caught her breath. As she slid onto him, deliciously slowly, it seemed she fitted him like a glove and she groaned with the extreme pleasure of it.

'There's a turn-up for the books, you coming here to me in the middle of the night,' he said as he rested afterwards, his arm around her as she snuggled up to his warm naked body. 'Just make certain nobody ever finds out, our Ramona. There'd be hell to pay.'

They were contentedly watching the first light of day pervade that bedroom.

She raised her head and kissed him on the

171

cheek. 'Don't worry. I shan't tell a soul. It's our secret – remember?'

He chuckled at that and patted her firm backside. 'You'd best be off afore Mary Ann spots that you're missing.'

So she forced herself out of bed and dressed self-consciously while he watched her. Then, when she'd tucked her mass of yellow hair under her hat she kissed him again and was gone downstairs.

'I'll see you later – at the dinner table,' he called, and she detected the same satirical edge in his voice that she'd heard when he realised she'd been peeping on him.

Sammy had never made love to her like Elijah. Nobody had. It was amazing the difference age and experience made. As she walked home, weak from a surfeit of unbelievable pleasure, she pondered these things. Her raging hunger for Elijah was gratified – for now at any rate. He had satisfied her utterly. She was pleased she had got it out of her system. Now she merely had a raging hunger for breakfast. She was not so stupid or so immature as to expect him to give up Dorcas just because of this one encounter. That was it. It was over now, something she'd had to do, something she'd had to get out of her system. She had enjoyed her Uncle Elijah and he had enjoyed her. It might never happen again.

Ramona was astonished at how easy it was to have her way with him. She merely presented herself to him, in his bed, and there was no resistance. None whatever. Oh, she let him know first that she fancied him, flattered him a bit, let him believe he was the only man in the world she was interested in and he fell for it good and proper, especially since he fancied her in the first place. Well, she was finding out about men. And, it seemed, she could have any man she wanted. All it took was a little nerve, a little courage.

Now she needed to get back home and into bed before Mary Ann or her father arose this Sunday morning. Otherwise, she would have to make up some plausible excuse as to where she had been. The trouble was, what could be plausible about returning home at nearly eight o'clock in a morning? As she walked towards the Jolly Collier in George Street she saw the answer. A man was emerging from the paper shop. Of course, she must buy a newspaper. She'd got up to buy a newspaper, if anybody asked. Else how would they explain the cats being inside?

Chapter Ten

By the time Clover emerged in her hat and coat from the Jolly Collier later that morning the temperature had risen appreciably. The beautiful September day was mild with a light breeze and hazy sunshine. She had heard the pulsing of the engine outside and had gone out excitedly, ready to be whisked along in this, her first outing in a motor car. But it was a strange sight she beheld. The motor car, a Sunbeam 16/20, was towing a long trailer made of wood and covered in the

173

same canvas she herself had used to cover wings for Ned Brisco. She knew, of course, that it contained the *Gull*.

'Hop on board then, Miss,' Joseph Mantle instructed matily over the clatter of the idling engine.

'Morning, Mr Mantle.' She smiled and rushed round the car to where Ned Brisco was standing with the rear door open.

'Morning, Ned,'

'Morning, Clover.'

When she was sitting and had pulled a car rug over her legs the car pulled away. The wind, cool around her neck, prompted her to pull up her collar and settle her hat more firmly on her head.

'How far is it?'

'About fourteen miles, Clover, according to Mr Mantle.'

'Will it take us long to get there?'

'About half an hour,' Joseph replied over his shoulder.

Joseph and Ned talked mostly about motors, using words Clover did not understand. They were discussing the internal combustion engine and how nobody in the area was producing one that was suitable for use in an aeroplane.

'Not surprising really,' Ned commented. 'Since there's hardly anybody building aeroplanes.'

'There's several firms constructing motor cars, Ned,' Joseph said. 'Notably Sunbeam – who built this one – and the Star Motor Company. Both in Wolverhampton as you know. But it's my belief that only Star are producing their own engines.'

'I know, Mr Mantle. I already checked.'

174

'You could always import an engine, Ned. Didn't you tell me there's a French one?'

'The *Antoinette*. But I couldn't afford one of them. I bet they cost getting on for eight or nine hundred pounds.'

'For an engine?' Clover queried, looking from one to the other.

'For a specialist aeroplane engine, Clover,' Ned said, turning round in the front seat to see her. 'They only build them in ones and twos. Even the Wright Brothers had to build their own engine. It's a pity a car engine couldn't be modified. I daresay I could pick one up for about twenty quid.'

'It's just a shame that nobody's took interest yet in what you're doing, Ned,' Joseph went on and crashed the gears as he tried to change down to negotiate the corner at King Street. 'Still, there's no reason why you couldn't approach one of the firms yourself. Even one of the motorcycle makers.'

Ned shook his head. 'No, a motorcycle engine would be no good. Not enough power. I like the idea of an air-cooled engine, though. Save on weight. I'd want somebody who could test airscrew design as well. It needs a firm with the right facilities.'

'And the resources,' Joseph suggested astutely.

'Not to mention the will, Mr Mantle... Actually, there's an *Antoinette* engine already in the country. They're using it to propel that dirigible, the *Nulli Secundus*.'

'Couldn't you borrow it?' Joseph suggested seriously.

Ned laughed. 'They ain't gonna lend it me, Mr Mantle. I found out there's a bloke called Cody, an American, waiting to borrow it for trials on a military aircraft he's built for the army – at somewhere called Farnborough. If he can't get his hands on it, I'm damned sure I can't.'

Clover listened, so sorry that she could be of no help in Ned's quest. She knew precious little about powered flight and nothing at all about the technicalities. As they spoke she enjoyed the exhilaration of riding by motorcar, however, the wind in her face, the envious, admiring looks from passers-by, the reassuring, rhythmic thrash of pistons and tappets. Before long they had passed the splendid Georgian buildings of Wolverhampton Street that housed the professional offices of solicitors and banks. Beyond the poorer houses and back yards of Eve Hill she had sight of the countryside. But they would not reach it until they had travelled the rough and undulating road flanked by pit banks and brickyards that led to Himley. After three or four miles, a fine Palladian mansion became visible through a slatted wooden fence, serene in its ochre livery on their right – Himley Hall, residence of the Earl of Dudley. In its magnificent park, laid out by Capability Brown, the sun glinted off the lake between ornamental trees and Clover decided she had never seen any place quite so beautiful.

But even here in this tranquil rurality, the tentacles of industry had spread inexorably. Railway tracks that served the brickyards and the collieries they had already passed scarred the landscape, connecting like an iron web, inter-lacing over and under bridges. Further on in Wall Heath, wheat and barley was being cut and harvested and placed in stooks. In another field a steam-driven threshing machine pulsed and flailed and hissed asthmatically, while a pack of ragged children watched in awe. Joseph slowed the car down as they negotiated lanes that were little more than dirt tracks and little hump-backed bridges built of brick that spanned locks and canals. At one such place, called Ashwood, bargees, the lock-keeper and farmhands alike enjoyed a drink together in the sunshine outside a public house called the Navigation, but all turned to watch the Sunbeam go by with its long, mysterious trailer. The further they travelled the fewer people they saw. Eventually, they reached a village called Bobbington and shortly after came upon a farmhouse with its ancient brick-built barns.

'Here we are,' Joseph announced and drew the motorcar to a halt in the yard.

A man in moleskin trousers and waistcoat and a woman wearing a flowery apron left the house and approached them, smiling. When Joseph and Ned had alighted from the motor car and shaken their hands, they turned to Clover and asked if she would like a cup of tea. Joseph then intro-duced Clover to his cousin, Fred Woodall, and his wife, Amy. When the ritual of tea and lively conversation was through they all trooped out into the yard again and Fred climbed into the motor car alongside Joseph. Ned and Clover sat in the rear. Fred directed them along the lane to a gate and they turned in. The field they beheld was flat and wide and only in the far distance could Clover see a hedge surrounding it. Near the gate stood a barn.

'You can keep your flying machine in there,' Fred announced.

Ned smiled. 'Is it dry?'

'Dry as a lime-burner's clog. And it'll be safe enough. We never see anybody down here.'

Ned stepped down from the motor car and began unpacking and assembling the *Gull*. Meanwhile, Joseph and Fred discussed the towing of the glider. Because the field was flat and fallow, Joseph decided that he would use his car to tow rather than Fred's van, since it was nicely warmed up and they could easily enough attach the rope that Ned had brought to the rear. Clover helped Ned as best she could and soon the *Gull* was ready. He went to talk to the two men.

'I'm not really sure how fast we need to go, but I reckon we'll need to be going more than thirty miles an hour before I get airborne,' he said to Joseph. 'So once you've reached about thirty, check to see.'

So they attached the rope in a coil to the car, and the other end to the tow hook Ned had devised that was situated beneath the aeroplane. By knocking up a lever, the hook would tilt downwards and allow the rope to fall back to the ground once he was airborne. Ned clambered up into his creation and gave the signal to go. Joseph eased the motorcar forward until the rope was taut then, gently, Ned felt the *Gull* move.

His pulse started racing. Never before had he

attempted getting airborne this way. As the speed increased the ride became progressively bumpier over the uneven grass. The *Gull* shook and creaked and rattled until suddenly, as if by magic, it all went smooth and quiet as the nose of his precious craft tilted upwards. A grin spread over his face. He looked around him. The ground was getting further away. The lane that ran along the side of the field seemed to be getting narrower, its hedge thinner. The tension on the rope was beginning to tug at the aircraft so he tilted the lever as planned and peered over the side again to see the rope drifting downwards.

He was flying, he was flying. How high he was, he did not know. He experimented by gently pushing and pulling the lever that controlled the flaps on one side and noticed the difference it made to his trajectory. He played with the rudder and felt the *Gull* begin to yaw. At once he corrected it.

Roll.

Of course, if you wanted to turn you had to roll. Control in roll. He knew that. He'd read about it often enough. But he'd never had chance to experience it before.

All around him the land was flat. He seemed to have miles in which to play, in which to fly. He could fly just as long as he could keep airborne but, without an engine, how long might that be? His speed decreased as the nose went up, as if to stall, so he quickly adjusted the elevators and sent the aeroplane on a slight downward path to pick up speed. Try a roll. Try a turn. He applied the lever that controlled the rudder, and the one that lifted the elevators on the left hand side. The *Gull* keeled over to the right and turned quite sharply. He laughed aloud as he levelled out again. What a sensation! It worked. By God, it worked. He'd never been absolutely certain before that it would – for him. It worked for the Wright brothers, but they used a different method, twisting the wings by warping to achieve the same result. But now he knew this method worked as well...

He was descending and didn't have enough height to repeat the manoeuvre. He must be only twenty or thirty feet above the ground now. Best land. Best land and get Joseph to tow him up for another flight. So he gently allowed the *Gull* to sail downwards until he felt again the bumpiness of the field and heard again the subsequent creaking and groaning of the construction. At least this landing business was easy.

He came to a halt and looked around for the motor car. Joseph and Fred and Clover were all grinning with admiration as the Sunbeam approached across the field.

'Did you see me turn?' Ned yelled over the sound of the motor car's engine as it pulled up alongside.

'Exquisite,' Joseph Mantle called. 'Do you want another tow?'

'Please, Mr Mantle.'

'I'll attach the rope,' Clover said and enthusiastically jumped down from the car.

Joseph Mantle drove the vehicle in front of the *Gull* and Clover grabbed the end of the rope.

'Thanks, Clover,' Ned called. 'Just loop it over

180

the hook. You know, this is going to be so much better than trying to fly off the top of Rough Hill.'

'Yes, but please be careful, Ned.'

Dorcas had been invited to tea for the first time since Mary Ann's marriage to Jake. She arrived wearing an expensive-looking walking costume with three-quarter length jacket that had a fur collar and matching muff. She sat at table next to Elijah, her beautiful brown eyes taking in every detail of the Tandy household. Elijah she loved, Elijah she worshipped; it was such a pity that his family were not as genteel as her own though. The way Mary Ann hummed hymn tunes while she was delivering cakes to the table would not be allowed of a servant in her own home, and Jake wandering about in a collarless shirt and braces was plebeian to say the least. Still, when she was married to Elijah she would be able to ease him away from these people – these vulgar publicans, these licensed victuallers.

She had overcome her initial fear that the two pretty girls of the house might be a diversion for Elijah. Clover, she knew, was courting and evidently preoccupied with Tom Doubleday, whom she'd met, and it was Clover she had seen as her biggest threat since she was not actually related to Elijah. It was naturally unthinkable to even consider there being any liaison with Ramona; she was his niece after all and strictly out of bounds. So, while Dorcas tended to look down her nose at Mary Ann and Jake, she was inclined to regard Clover and Ramona with a little more

181

tolerance. Having shown herself up as a jealous woman once and, fearful she might have lost their respect, she was even attempting to be pleasant lately.

Ramona was loath to speak to her across the table, however. When Dorcas addressed her, Ramona avoided her eyes lest the girl could see through them and read the scandalous secret that must surely be etched onto her brain and clearly visible. Not that she regretted what she'd done; she did not. But if Dorcas had any inkling at all...

'Elijah tells me you've been out with that lad today who's built that flying machine thing, Clover,' Dorcas said, having taken a small bite out of a slice of Madeira cake that Zillah Bache had baked that morning.

'Yes, we went to Bobbington so he could practise flying and controlling the craft.'

Elijah was about to ask about Ned's progress but Dorcas talked over him with a question that was of infinitely more interest to her.

'Does Tom mind you fraternising with this Ned?'

Clover smiled and glanced at her mother. 'Not a bit. Why should he? I was friends with Ned long before I knew Tom. And Tom knows I've always helped him – almost from the start.'

Dorcas delicately rubbed her beautifully manicured fingers together over her plate to remove the tiny crumbs. 'I would have thought he might have objected if he knew.'

Clover lifted her cup and sipped tea. 'Oh, he always knows, Dorcas. I always tell him when I'm helping Ned.' She replaced her cup in her saucer with a chink. 'He doesn't object. In fact, Tom admires what Ned's doing. There's no opposition from Tom. If anything, it's Ned who seems to resent Tom.'

'You mean Ned's jealous of Tom?'

'He was when I first started seeing Tom. Not so much now. I think he quite fancies Ramona now...' Clover flashed Ramona a generous smile, expecting her to confirm the notion. But she guiltily avoided eye contact, instead glancing warily at Elijah.

'Oh, I didn't know you'd been out with Ned, our Ramona,' Elijah remarked mischievously, his mouth full of cake.

'I haven't been out with Ned,' she answered defensively and looked down, trying to hide her rising colour behind her mop of fair hair.

'He asked you though,' Clover prompted.

'So what? Lots of chaps ask me out. It doesn't mean I have to go out with them all. I hardly go out with any at all.'

'Good job an' all,' Mary Ann declared sharply. 'You'd get yourself a right reputation.'

'You went out last night,' Clover proclaimed innocently, and witnessed Ramona's blushes.

'What d'you mean?' Ramona's inherent guilt over Elijah at once put her on the defensive, believing that Clover must know about her nocturnal visit. She looked with alarm, first at Clover, then at Elijah, then at Dorcas.

'With Harry Heppenstall,' Clover prompted.

'Oh, *him*... He took me to Lester's. It was nothing special.'

'You went out with Harry Heppenstall last

183

night?' Elijah queried.

Ramona could not be certain whether he was mocking or jealous.

'To Lester's?' There was a gleam in his eye.

He *was* mocking. Early this morning when the rest of the world was soundly asleep he was making love to her heart and soul. Now he had the nerve to tease her about her going out innocently with a lad, as if what had happened between them meant nothing to him. That did it – Ramona got up from the table leaving an unfinished jam sandwich and scurried out of the room. Nobody saw the tears that were stinging her eyes.

'What's the matter with her?' Dorcas asked.

Tom Doubleday arrived at eight that evening and found Clover at work alone in the taproom. It was too early yet for it to be busy but several folk had already appeared having been to church or chapel.

'Do you mind if we stay here tonight, Tom?' she said apologetically. 'Ramona's not well and Job Smith isn't working tonight. They need me to help out.'

'That's all right, sweetheart,' he replied. 'I can sit and sup with the regulars. Unless you want me to work as well.'

'Oh, we don't expect you to have to work,' she said with a smile, pleased that he'd offered. 'But if we get very busy later you could always wash a few glasses.'

'Course. I don't mind.'

Clover picked up a glass from a shelf underneath the beer pulls. 'Have a pint now?'

'Please,' Tom nodded. 'So how did it go this morning?'

'With Ned? He did well.' She pulled him a pint of bitter and refused to take the money when he tendered it. Instead, she started to relate in enthusiastic detail the events of the morning and her ride out into the country.

'So you liked riding in a motor car?'

'Oh, it was grand, Tom. There are some lovely places to see – and so close as well. We were in the middle of nowhere within half an hour. Away from all the grime and the factories. It must be lovely to own a motor car.'

'I'm sure it must be,' he replied thoughtfully. 'What make does this Joseph Mantle have?'

'I think he said it was a Sunbeam. Leastwise, it was made in Wolverhampton.'

'A Sunbeam, eh?... So tell me, Clover, was Ned pleased with what he achieved today?'

'He was thrilled...' Two more customers entered; Noah Fairfax and Urban Tranter in their Sunday best suits and caps. Urban jangled the loose change in his pocket and sat down at a vacant table. Noah sat opposite him. 'Yes, gentlemen. What can I get you?'

'Two pints of mild please, Clover my wench,' Urban said.

'And can we have the cribbage board an' all, an' a pack of cards?' Noah added.

Tom located them and passed them to the two men while Clover drew their beers.

'D'you want to play crib wi' we?' Noah asked Tom.

'I don't know how to,' Tom answered honestly. 'But thanks for the offer. In any case, I've got a sneaking suspicion I'll be serving beer and washing up before long.' He turned to Clover who was topping up one of the glasses. 'Go on, you were telling me about Ned and how thrilled he was about his morning's work.'

'Yes, Mr Mantle towed him up four times. He practised all his manoeuvres. It was a pleasure to watch, like a big graceful bird sailing across the sky.'

Tom smiled. 'So how long was his longest flight?'

'I counted about thirty-five seconds.' She passed the drinks to Noah and Urban.

'And in that time he actually flew the thing?'

'Oh yes. Turned left and right, got it to climb a short way, then did a roll to turn back downwards to gather speed again. It was really quite a sight. Mr Mantle was amazed.'

'He really needs to get cracking with an engine,' Tom said. 'I read the other day there's a lot of activity going on in France now as regards flying. Everybody's joining the race.'

'This country too,' Clover advised. 'The Army are starting trials according to Ned. Mind you, they haven't got an engine either, he reckons.'

Tom quaffed his beer and said, ''Struth. If the Army have got no engine, what chance has Ned got?'

'I think he's decided to approach one of the local firms. It'll cost him money, of course – money he doesn't have. Money he's got no way of getting either, except what he saves out of his wages.'

186

'You know, Clover,' Tom said, 'it's damned scandalous the way no firm has taken him up on this sponsorship thing he was after. Surely if the Army can see potential–'

'Am you on about that lad what builds them flying machines?' Noah butted in.

'Yes, Noah,' Tom replied. 'Clover went with him this morning, watching him fly it. She was just telling me what a spectacle it was – how well he's doing.'

'I don't know what to mek of this flying machine malarkey,' Urban declared. 'If God had wanted we to fly he'd have gi'd we wings. It don't seem natural to me.'

'What yer talking about, natural?' Noah responded. 'It's no less natural than sailors sailing the seven seas in ships.'

Urban considered this point a moment. 'But with ships they got the wind to blow 'em forward and the wairter to keep 'em afloat. What's gunna keep a flying machine afloat like, if the wind blows it about too much? It'll crash to the ground.'

'That's a good point, Urban,' Noah conceded. 'I hadn't thought about that.'

'But it's the challenge,' Tom suggested. 'Man has conquered the sea. Now we have to conquer the air.'

'You'll never conquer the sea,' Urban said with an authoritative shake of his head. 'The sea's too powerful.' He lifted his pint to take a swig.

'Well, I'm inclined to disagree, Urban,' Tom answered. 'Now that sailors don't have to rely on the winds any longer, I think it's safe to say we've conquered the sea. All right, ships can still sink, but mariners have got some control now.'

'He's got a point, Urban,' Noah said, looking from one to the other.

'And flight in heavier than air machines is a similar challenge,' Tom went on. 'Once these flying machines can be fitted with reliable engines, just think of the uses they could be put to. There could be a whole new world of possibilities opening up if only we had the foresight to see it. Trouble is, suitable engines are rare and expensive.'

'Yes,' Clover chimed in. 'A proper one can cost eight or nine hundred pounds.'

'Eight or nine hundred?' Noah queried incredulously. 'Bugger me, you could buy a row of houses for that. All with their own privies and pig sties.'

'And see some bloody change,' Urban agreed.

'I could retire,' Noah said and emptied his glass.

'I heard Clover mention summat about the Army wanting to try their luck with flying machines,' Urban said. 'Is that right, Clover, my wench?'

'According to Ned Brisco.'

'What the hell does the army want flying machines for?' Urban asked. 'I mean, if they want to fly messages to one another they can use carrier pigeons.'

'It's obvious what they want flying machines for,' Noah responded, as if he were a great tactician. 'So's they can drop bags o' shit on the enemy. Just think – if you was being bombarded

188

with bags of shit you'd soon surrender, Urban. But why limit it to the army?' he went on. 'If I'd got one of them flying machines, I'd drop a great big bag of shit on Mrs bloody Pankhurst and all her Suffragettes.'

'Thanks for helping out tonight, Tom,' Clover breathed as they stood together in the shadows at the side of the Jolly Collier, arms around each other. 'I know Mother and Jake will have appreciated it.'

'Anytime. I don't mind. So long as you're there with me.'

She hugged him. 'Give me a kiss. I haven't had a kiss all night.'

Gladly, he obliged her, savouring her lips and her undoubted love for him. There was a swell of tenderness within him, a growing awareness of just how right she was for him. He'd never doubted it, but the better he knew her the more resolutely it was confirmed. From the outset, from the first time he'd ever seen her at the wedding of Mary Ann and Jake, he had known he was in love with her. He had perceived the honesty in her clear blue eyes, the gentleness in her demeanour. Time had proved his instincts valid. Here she was now, devoted in his arms; she was his, heart and soul; totally committed. She was not yet promised. Her promise, however, was implicit in her unspoken but eminently observable commitment. He could not imagine life without her now. He would find it impossible to exist without her warmth, her tenderness, her love. He wanted to ask her to marry him. He

189

wanted her to be his wife. He had no doubt what her answer would be. And because he knew she would say yes, he declined from asking her yet. In any case, it was too soon.

But he would.

Before long. Before long he would make his intentions clear.

'Goodnight, my love,' he whispered.

'Goodnight, Tom. Sleep tight. See you tomorrow after work.'

He gave her a squeeze and a last peck on the lips before he went from her. When he reached the street he turned and waved. She waved back happily and hitched up her skirt to save her hem dragging in the dirt, and went back inside.

Inside, Ramona had come down from her room. She stood at the sink in the taproom drying glasses alongside her father.

'Oh, Ramona. Are you feeling better now?'

'Yes thanks, Clover. I've been asleep, to tell you the truth. I feel much better for it.'

'Then you must have been really tired. Maybe that's all it was – tiredness. But you were awake early this morning, you said.'

Ramona nodded and began stacking dried glasses on one of the shelves. 'Have you seen Tom?'

'Yes, he's just gone. He helped out tonight.'

'Good job he did,' Jake commented. 'We was ever so busy.'

'Has Uncle Elijah got back yet?' Ramona glanced at the clock as she asked.

'Not yet. But I don't suppose he'll be long.'

'Tis to be hoped not,' Jake said. 'I want to lock up in a minute.'

'There's a new barrel of bitter wanted, Pop,' Clover said. 'It ran out just as we closed, remember.'

'Oh, Christ. I'd forgot. Good job you reminded me. Ramona, come and give me a hand in the cellar, will you? Best do it tonight ready for the morning.'

'All right,' she answered reluctantly.

Clover began mopping the tables when Ramona and her father went down the cellar. The front door opened and closed, then the door to the taproom opened. Elijah presented himself.

'Brrr! It's gone chilly, Clover. It's cold enough for a walking-stick.'

Clover chuckled. 'Well, you haven't got a coat on. It is September – nearly October.'

He walked over to the fire, drew out a chair and sat in front of it. He grabbed the poker and gave the coals a stir and a flurry of sparks shot up the chimney like shooting stars.

'That reminds me,' Clover said, wiping the last table, 'it's washing day tomorrow and I'll have to be up early to light the fire in the brewhouse ready for Zillah. I hate that job.'

'Why d'you hate it?' Elijah asked. 'When I was a kid I used to love lighting fires.'

'I reckon all boys like lighting fires. But I can't stand getting all dirty with the coal. I had enough getting dirty working at the foundry.'

'Pour me a pint, Clover and I'll help you when I've warmed up a bit.'

191

Clover smiled. 'All right. But it'll have to be mild. Jake and Ramona are in the cellar putting a new barrel of bitter on. He'll need to draw some off before it's ready.'

'Is there any old ale?' Elijah warmed his hands in front of the fire.

'Yes.' Clover poured a glass of old ale and took it to him.

'Thanks, flower.' He quaffed it avidly. 'I hate the cold, Clover. Got used to the heat in India, you know. And Africa. I love the heat.'

'I imagine you're not looking forward to the winter then?'

'Never bloody do. I ought to go and live somewhere hot... Someday, maybe.'

'What about Dorcas? Would she like living somewhere hot?'

'I don't suppose she'd mind too much. America would be nice. Somewhere like Georgia for instance.'

'Not India then?'

'No, not India. India has its charms, but I wouldn't like to live there. Nor Africa, come to that... Aren't you having a drink, Clover?'

'I had a port and brandy not too long ago. I ought to sleep like a top. I'd better go and lay the fire in the boiler.'

Elijah emptied his glass. 'Right. I'll come and help you.'

As they were leaving the taproom, Mary Ann was coming in to check the night's takings. Clover explained where they were going.

'I shall go straight to bed when I've done that, Mother. So I'll see you in the morning.'

'Me as well,' Elijah said.

Mary Ann bid them both goodnight.

Clover picked up an oil lamp from the scullery and met Elijah outside. He shovelled a bucket of coal from the coal house and lugged it into the brewhouse while Clover made firelighters by rolling sheets of newspaper and curling the rolls into coils. Then she laid sheets of crumpled newspaper in the fire hole and lay the coils on top of that. On to that she laid sticks of dried wood and then Elijah did the really dirty job of laying the coals.

'There, that dint take long, did it?' he said and washed his hands clean under the cold tap.

'Thanks, Elijah,' Clover said. 'I really appreciate it. I suppose I've got a bit of a thing about coal dust and black sand.'

'Like you say, Clover, it must come from working in the foundry.' Elijah dried his hands on a piece of rag that was hanging from the mangle. 'Come on then. No point in shivering out here in the bloody cold any longer than we need.'

Clover picked up the oil lamp again and they walked back towards the house across the yard. Then Clover tripped over the uneven cobbles and stumbled. At once Elijah turned to catch her as she lurched and, frightened she was going to fall and hurt herself, she held on to Elijah.

It was unfortunate that at that very moment, Ramona had ventured outside in the hope of encountering Elijah. When she witnessed Clover in his arms her heart lurched. She was horrified, desperately hurt and suddenly angry. But they must not see her. They must not know she'd seen them together. So she quickly turned round and, as quietly as she could, ran back into the house and up to her bedroom with tears in her eyes again.

Chapter Eleven

The brewhouse was not to be confused with the brewery, which was a bigger building altogether, four storeys in height and full of tanks and vessels and pipes and sacks of malt and hops. The brewhouse was the small outhouse that housed the mangle, the sink, the maiding tub and the big tin bath as well, and which enjoyed the inglorious privilege of facing the gentlemen's urinal across the yard and fronting the earth privy. The morning after Ned's astounding demonstration of aeronautics over Mr Woodall's flat, fallow field at Bobbington, Clover got up to light the fire under the copper boiler in the brewhouse at her usual five o'clock. It was raining heavily, typical washday weather. Even though she did not have to commence work so early of a morning these days, getting up at five every Monday morning had become a habit and, as far as she was concerned, it was not a habit she disliked.

As well as normal domestic laundry, the public house created plenty as well in the form of towels by the dozen, drip mats, dusters, aprons and all manner of incidental articles. Mary Ann would naturally put in an appearance during the main

194

weekly event and even wring a few token towels through the mangle, as she did this very morning while Zillah was red-faced and perspiring under the heat and steam.

'Have you put e'er a blue bag in, Zillah?' Mary Ann asked coolly. 'I've sid me sheets whiter than this.'

'Blue bag, yes, and plenty soap flakes and all, Missus,' Zillah replied, trying to hide her resentment of Mary Ann's insinuations. 'When they'n dried they'll look as white as the driven snow. Like they always do.'

''Tis to be hoped, Zillah, else they'll all have to be done again. I don't want nobody on Kates Hill saying behind me back as how me washing's riffy. Mind how you put me new grey frock through the mangle, and all. Them buttons was dear. I don't want 'em bosted to smithereens.'

'Don't thee fret, Mary Ann. I'll mind as I don't bost 'em.' She dried her hands on her apron. 'I'll just go an put me line up.'

So Zillah waddled outside in her clogs with the washing line in a coil over her meaty shoulder. With an eye cocked mistrustfully at the dark clouds above, she strung it across the yard between the rear of the house and the brewery, then back again. She bid good day to Elijah in his shirt sleeves who was rushing into the brewery. As she stretched up on tiptoe to loop the line onto an old iron hook, she was gratified to hear the scuff-scuff of Mary Ann's slippers on the cobbles that were still wet and knew she was returning to her licensed victualling.

Back in the brewhouse rinsing towels in the

195

stone sink, Zillah saw Jake cross the yard to the brewery wearing his long canvas apron and dusty bowler hat. It was the same every Monday morning. Even though the brewery was busier nowadays with the coming of Jake and Elijah, it had always been a hub of activity. A horse and cart trundled into the yard, hooves and iron-rimmed wheels clattering over the cobblestones. Zillah fetched a line prop that was tucked behind a rusty drainpipe and raised the washing line so the cart could pass through unhindered. Before she could hang any washing out she had to wait while Elijah and the carter off-loaded sacks of malt, delivered from the malthouse in Dixon's Green. Using a block and tackle suspended from an overhanging arm, they sent them soaring up the outside of the building, while Jake unloaded them at the open door on the top floor.

Zillah at this point was rinsing underwear and wringing it through the mangle. As she worked she sang a song called 'The Only Bit of English That We've Got' that she'd picked up from the Four Ways Inn in Brown Street where she supped in the snug of an evening.

Ramona appeared, looking preoccupied. 'Hello, Zillah,' she said unenthusiastically. 'Shall I peg some washing out for you?'

'If you've a mind,' Zillah answered, and pointed a dripping finger at the back of the mangle. 'You can start with them towels in the washing basket there.'

Ramona forced a smile. 'And then I'll bring you a cup of tea, eh?'

'God bless yer. That'd be grand.'

'Is my Uncle Elijah in the brewery, Zillah?'

'Yes. And your father. They've just unloaded some malt.'

'I'd best bring them one as well, then. I'll do that first, before I help you peg out.'

Zillah turned the big wheel of the mangle with her strong arms. She heaped the sheets in a laundry basket waiting for Ramona to return. After about ten minutes, Ramona came back carrying four mugs on a wooden tray.

'Here you are, Zillah. I've already sugared it for you.'

'God bless yer, my babby.' She took her mug from the tray and sipped it. 'I think I'll have me five minutes now.'

'Can you take mine as well, Zillah. I'll have it in a minute. I'll take these to my father and Uncle Elijah first.'

As she reached the door of the brewery she met Jake on his way out.

'I was just bringing you a cup of tea.'

'Oh, ta, our Ramona. I'll tek it with me back to the taproom. Does it matter which one I have?'

'They're both the same.'

He took a mug from the tray. 'I'm supposed to be at Noah Hingley's forge in half an hour. I'd better get me skates on.'

'Are they going to buy our beer?'

'They'm interested, if the price and the taste suits 'em.'

'Best of luck then, Dad. I'll take this mug of tea to Uncle Elijah.'

'He's right at the top, stacking the bags of malt. See you later.'

So Ramona went inside the brewery and climbed the wooden stairs to the top floor. Her heart was pounding already at the prospect of being alone with Elijah again. But she was not certain what she would say to him after the astonishment and hurt of discovering last night that she had competition from Clover for his affections. It highlighted how fickle Clover could be. All that show of affection for Tom Doubleday was just a front. Well, she would just as soon tell Tom what she thought about her. She would certainly tell Elijah. She had to tread carefully though; she did not know the strength of this unanticipated liaison with Clover.

She reached the top. Elijah was emptying a sack into the grist mill that crushed the malt into a coarse flour to remove the husk ready for mashing. It was always so dusty up here.

'Ramona!' he called over the rumble of the mill. 'Brought me a cup of tea, have you, my flower? God bless you.'

'Here... And I hope it chokes you.' She narrowed her eyes to let him see her pique.

'Christ! What have I done?' He stopped his grist mill and took the mug from the tray.

'You know very well.'

'Do I?' he responded, obviously puzzled. 'As a matter of fact, our Ramona, I ain't got a clue.' He sat down on a sack that was part of a group. 'You'd better tell me.'

She hesitated, poised at the top of the stairs her back towards him, her hand on the shiny unpainted hand rail. She turned to look at him again with as scornful an expression as she could

198

muster. 'Clover ... I never would have dreamed that you and Clover...'

He let out a laugh, induced by the absurdity of Ramona's allegation. 'Clover? What about me and Clover?'

She shrugged. 'Do I need to spell it out?'

'I think you do. This is all news to me.'

'Last night...' She hesitated, having perceived from his genuine surprise that maybe she had got this all wrong.

'Go on...'

'Last night, I saw the two of you in the yard, your arms about each other. I only saw you for a split second and I rushed off. But you were both laughing and there was no mistaking what was going on.'

He sipped his tea. 'Well you are mistaken, Ramona,' he said, his voice low. 'There was nothing going on.'

'Mary Ann told me you'd gone to the brewhouse with her.'

'To help her lay the fire under the boiler for the washing today. Clover didn't want to get dirty and I don't blame her. What's wrong with that?'

'Clover didn't want to get dirty!' she scoffed. 'Who does she think she is? Miss Prim and Proper... Well, I saw you with your arms about each other...'

Elijah laughed when he realised what it was she'd seen. 'Bloody hell, Ramona...' He held his hand out towards her.

'I don't think it's funny after what we did the morning before. I thought that meant something to you.'

Elijah shook his head, still amused by her wrong interpretation of the scene. 'Come here and sit on me lap and I'll tell you what really happened.' Ramona wanted to comply, but wanted also to make a stand on this thing that was a matter of vital importance when she felt so slighted. Elijah still held his hand out invitingly. 'Come on, I won't bite. Sit on me lap and I'll tell you what really happened.' Acquiescently, she walked over to him and sat on his lap. He put his arm around her waist and gave her a reassuring squeeze. 'What you must've seen happened just as Clover stumbled over a cobble while we was walking back across the yard. I caught her and I suppose, because she felt she was about to fall, she clung on to me. Simple as that.'

Ramona made no response. It sounded very plausible. But she must not give in too quickly.

'Listen, Ramona, I don't have to explain to you what I do, but there's nothing going on between me and Clover. Clover ain't interested in *me*. She's got Tom Doubleday to keep her happy.'

She shook her curls, requiring more convincing, needing to be fussed. 'I don't know whether to believe you or not,' she pouted.

'Well, that's up to you, my wench. Ask Clover. See what she says.'

'I might,' Ramona said and got up from his lap. But she didn't move away. She had no wish to alienate him over this thing that seemed so trivial the way he explained it. So she stood there, one leg still lightly touching his knee, waiting to be enticed back.

'You'd look a right fool if you did ask her

though,' he remarked as an afterthought. 'And it could give the game away between us two.'

She sighed heavily and dropped onto his lap again with resignation. She put her arm around his neck and looked longingly into his eyes. 'I can't stop thinking about you,' she whispered earnestly. 'I can't stop thinking about yesterday morning, how we ... I nearly came to your room last night... And I can't stand the sight of that snotty cow Dorcas... Oh, kiss me, Uncle Elijah...'

He kissed her and they both knew at once where they were headed. He ran his hand up her skirt and felt the smooth warm flesh of her thighs above her stockings.

'You must never come to my room at night, Ramona,' he whispered. 'It's too dangerous. We can meet here in the brewery...'

This new, more definite arrangement was just what she wanted to hear. Her response was to kiss him with more passion, so he shifted her off his knee and rolled her onto the pile of sacks that were stacked like a bed. She uttered a soft vocal sound to register her feigned surprise but allowed him to take a handful of hem and lift her skirt above her waist.

'You've got a fine pair of legs, our Ramona,' he said, running his fingers over the exposed parts of her creamy textured thighs. 'I'd love to see you in the buff again. You look a picture.' Deftly, he removed her drawers, feasted his eyes on her, then kissed her belly while his fingers probed skilfully between her legs. When he had lowered his trousers below his knees, he rolled on top of her and pushed into her without further ceremony, and their bodies began rocking in a mutual frenzy of desire.

In the brewhouse, Zillah drained her mug and, with stays creaking, stood up again achingly to continue with her washday exertions. She glanced across to the brewery. A pair of pigeons, that had been assiduously watching the world go by from the beam that jutted out above the loading door on the top floor, suddenly flapped and flew away as if startled. Zillah eyed up the untouched mug of tea that Ramona had intended to drink. 'What's keeping her up there?' she muttered to herself. 'That tea'll be cold if her don't hurry up.'

But it was another fifteen minutes before Ramona emerged onto the yard again, looking flushed. She would have forgotten her mug of tea had Zillah not called her.

'You ain't drunk your tea, Ramona.'

Ramona changed direction and headed for the brewhouse, a smile on her face. 'Blimey, Zillah, I forgot all about it. I was talking to me Uncle Elijah.'

Zillah noticed she was looking far happier than before. 'Where was you talking to him then? You've got all dust and husk stuck to the back of your ganzy. Come here, let me dust you off. You'm covered in it.' She glanced up suspiciously at the loading door on the top floor.

'Oh, God,' Ramona exclaimed and blushed vividly. 'I was sitting leaning against the sacks.'

'Well you can't go back in the taproom looking like this. Mary Ann'll swear you've been sleeping somewhere when you'm supposed to be working.'

When Ned Brisco answered a knock at his back door that evening he was surprised to find himself greeting the reporter from the *Dudley Herald,* whom he had met before.

'Hello, Mr Oakley,' Ned said, his astonishment evident. 'What brings you here?'

Julian smiled chummily. 'How do you do, Mr Brisco?' They shook hands. 'I'm here on an errand actually. I need to talk to you in private. Can I come in?'

'Course you can.' He stood aside and allowed Julian to enter. 'I bet Mother will make us a cup of tea if you fancy one.'

Julian took off his cap. 'Oh, I'll not trouble your mother if it's all the same to you, Mr Brisco. I'm on an errand, as I say, and I'm anxious to get home.'

'Come through to the front room then... Excuse us, Mother, Father...'

Ned signalled for Julian to sit down, so accordingly, he occupied one of the bulky mock-leather armchairs that was becoming unstitched at the piping on one of the arms.

'I hear you had a successful morning yesterday with your flying machine, Mr Brisco.'

'I did. But who told you?'

Julian tapped the side of his nose and winked. 'It's my job to get to know things. It's what they pay me for at the *Herald.*'

Ned sat down opposite him. 'So what's this errand?'

Julian felt in the inside pocket of his jacket and withdrew a fat envelope, which he waved in front of Ned. 'I am the bearer of spondulicks to the value of two hundred pounds in five-pound bank notes, and I am requested to pass them on to you.'

Ned was inclined to grab the money at once, but hesitated. There had to be a catch somewhere. He regarded Julian suspiciously. 'What's it for? Who's it from?'

Julian grinned. 'I can answer your first question but not your second, Mr Brisco. The money is a loan. To be handed over to you only on the strict understanding that you use it to finance an engine for your flying machine.'

''Struth!' Ned exclaimed and his eyes lit up.

'It's to be used for no other purpose, Mr Brisco, and you are to sign this document...' he withdrew a piece of paper from another pocket, 'to that effect, which is legally binding on you. The loan is interest-free and for an indefinite period but, obviously, it must be paid back as early as you are able to pay it back. It's not a gift, you understand.'

''Struth!' Ned remarked again. 'And who's lent me all this money. I mean – it's a tidy sum.'

'It *is* a tidy sum, I agree, but I'm not at liberty to tell you who the benefactor is.'

'Somebody who can evidently afford it,' Ned said. 'Somebody who evidently believes in what I'm doing... Somebody who evidently wishes me well.'

'Evidently.'

'I can probably guess who...' Ned smiled

knowingly. 'Joseph Mantle, I bet. He was asking me only yesterday about engines.'

Julian grinned and took out his cigarette packet. 'I'm sworn to secrecy, Mr Brisco. I daren't confirm it one way or the other... Smoke?'

'Nah. Never bothered, thanks.'

'If you decide to accept the loan, you must sign the document...' Julian lit his cigarette.

'Oh, I accept it all right. I'll get a pen and ink.' Ned got up and went into the scullery. He returned with an old wooden pen and a bottle of ink. 'Where do I sign?'

'Just here...'

Ned placed the document on the table and signed.

'And I witness it just here...' Julian stood up and appended his own signature. 'Now, you're sure you understand the terms, Ned?'

'Yes. It's to be used strictly for an engine for my *Gull* and I pay it back when I can afford to. Without interest.'

Julian handed over the envelope. 'I suggest you count it...'

Ned duly counted it. Forty white, five-pound notes.

'I wish somebody would lend me that much money on the same terms, Mr Brisco.'

Ned grinned, unable to comprehend his good fortune. 'So when I *do* pay it back, presumably I have to pay it back to you, and you'll hand it over to Mr Mantle or whoever it was.'

'That's the arrangement, Mr Brisco.' Julian drew on his cigarette then exhaled the smoke in a blue cloud that drifted hazily round his head. 'Look, I'd better go. Before I can go home I have to deliver this document you've signed.'

'Won't it do in the morning?'

'Fraid not. Well, the best of luck, Mr Brisco. I hope you achieve what you've set out to do.'

'Thanks Mr Oakley,' Ned replied. 'So do I.'

'Keep me informed. We can run another piece on you in the *Herald*.'

Ned lay in bed that night unable to sleep, unable to believe his good fortune. Two hundred pounds. Jesus! Of course he would use it on an engine, as stipulated. And pay back the loan just as soon as he could. But what engine could he get? It was a handsome amount of money, but two hundred pounds wouldn't buy him an *Antoinette,* even if there was one available. Of course, he could always build his own; one of the pattern-makers at the foundry would make a set of patterns, once he had designed the thing; then he could cast his own engine block and cylinder head and get them machined in the pattern shop. Pistons, piston rings, bearings, connecting rods and crankshaft he could acquire from an existing engine and design his block and cylinder head around them. It was a daunting task but he could do it. It would take time, but it would be time well spent. At least he had a knowledge of the power output that was needed, of the extra weight the craft could tolerate. All this could be designed in from the outset.

And he could afford it now.

But then there was the question of an efficient

airscrew... He would have to design and build his own airscrew... That was a daunting task.

The problems never stopped mounting up.

Next day, Tuesday, the weather was unsettled. It had rained again during the night and when the sun broke through the silver-topped clouds it all looked rather false and watery. As Ned walked briskly along Cromwell Street in his best Sunday suit and overcoat, the sun glistened off the wet cobbles and the blue clay paving stones.

Deliberately, he took the route down George Street past the Jolly Collier, in half a mind to call for Clover. He knew she left at about this time to walk to her new job in High Street in the town. They could keep each other company this morning; he had so much to tell her. The Jolly Collier was already open for business and Ned couldn't resist the temptation to poke his head round the door; he might see Ramona as well. Mary Ann was wiping shelves.

'Morning Mrs Tandy ... I just wondered whether Clover had left for work yet.'

No greeting. Mary Ann stuck her head through the hatch and called her daughter. It took a minute for Clover to present herself while Ned, in his smart suit and overcoat, nodded self-consciously to those men in soiled working attire who were already supping.

'Ned!' Clover greeted with a smile. 'What brings you here – and looking so smart in your collar and tie?'

'I'm off to Wolverhampton. I thought I'd walk with you to the town.'

'All right. I won't be a minute...'

Soon, they were out in the uncertain weather.

'I never expected to see you this morning,' Clover commented as they crossed over St John's Street. 'It's like old times walking to work with you, Ned.'

'Something's happened, Clover. Something good. And I'm not going to let the grass grow under my feet.'

She looked at him with eager anticipation. 'What? Tell me.'

'Somebody has loaned me two hundred pounds to get an engine sorted out. So I decided not to go to work today. I'm going to the Star Motor Company in Wolverhampton instead to see if they can help.'

'Two hundred pounds? Who the devil coughed up two hundred pounds?'

'I don't know. Julian Oakley brought it round last night. He's the go-between. He said he couldn't tell me who lent it. He said he was sworn to secrecy. But I got a feeling it might be Joseph Mantle.'

The rain started again and Clover hoisted her umbrella. Ned held the brolly and felt like a king when, as they walked beneath it, Clover familiarly took his arm.

'I'm so pleased for you Ned. I hope this firm in Wolverhampton will be able to help.'

'I hope so as well. I'll know soon enough.'

'What if they don't?'

'Then I'll build my own engine... Like the Wright Brothers had to. If they can do it, I know I can.'

'So how soon do you have to pay back this loan?'

'When it suits. There's no time limit. No interest to pay, either. Whoever lent it, they obviously believe in what I'm doing.'

'Yes...' said Clover enthusiastically. 'I always knew somebody would.'

Chapter Twelve

Wolverhampton was the home of the Star Engineering Company that designed and produced motor cars. The concern was started around 1869 when Edward Lisle began building velocipedes. Foreseeing a decline in the cycle trade and a rosy future in horseless carriages, Mr Lisle decided to manufacture them and, in 1898, acquired a Benz Velo to see how it was done. He improved upon the design and ran around for months in the motor car he subsequently built. In 1899, the first commercially produced Star motor car was offered for sale at £198.

Ned Brisco asked the conductor to put him off on Dudley Road at the nearest stop to Pountney Street. As he stepped down from the tram he pulled up his collar, tugged his cap on his head a little harder and frowned at the rain. He looked about him. The whole area was a hotchpotch of factories and workshops. After the whining of the electric tram as it pulled away, the first sounds he heard were the thuds of stamping presses forcing form into sheets of metal, the shriek of lathes turning brass and steel. Tall chimneys pumped dense grey smoke into the greyer sky while horse-drawn carts carried new consignments of goods both inward and outward. About to cross the road at Bell Place, he looked left and waited while a steam lorry chugged past, loaded with bundles of steel tube. That part of Villiers Street he could see in the distance was lined with fine houses, incongruous with the unkempt clutter of industry adjacent to it.

From where he stood he could already see the Star Engineering Company. He quickened his pace and entered the premises through a wide entry, which opened up onto an open yard. He hesitated to go further when the thrash of a motor car's engine boomed off the red-brick walls and the rafted ceiling. Ned watched the vehicle pull up alongside him. A middle-aged man, wearing waterproofs from head to toe, looked him up and down then hailed him over the rattle of the engine.

'I don't know you, do I?' he asked, lifting his goggles and giving them a shake to dislodge the water.

'No, sir,' Ned yelled back. 'I came to see whoever's in charge – the gaffer.'

'Are you expected?'

'No, sir.'

'So what's your name?'

'Ned Brisco. I want to see about an engine for an aeroplane.'

'A what? Did you say aeroplane?'

He nodded, uncertain of himself. The man

would very likely think he was a lunatic and eject him forthwith. But he drove forward and beckoned Ned to follow. Ned watched nervously as he parked his motor car against the facing wall, jumped out and took off his gauntlets, still unsmiling.

'Edward Lisle... How can I be of help?'

Ned felt he should shake the man's hand but, since no gesture was forthcoming from this Mr Lisle, he considered it might be inappropriate. 'I want to buy an engine for an aeroplane.' Ned smiled, telegraphing to the other man that he realised such a request might sound outlandish.

'Yes, I thought that's what you said. You're not from the Army are you?'

'No, sir, I'm asking on my own behalf. I've built a biplane and it glides beautiful. Now I need an engine to power it. To be honest, coming here is a bit of a wild shot 'cause I didn't really expect you to have such an engine. Engines for aeroplanes need to be light and more powerful than the engines of motor cars.'

For the first time, Edward Lisle smiled. 'You've built a biplane, did you say? And it actually flies?'

'Yes, sir.' Ned felt in his pocket and retrieved the three-months-old cutting from the *Dudley Herald*. He opened it up and handed it to Mr Lisle.

Mr Lisle browsed it with interest. 'That's damned impressive. How come this was never reported in the *Express and Star?*' He looked up at Ned, who perceived friendliness in his eyes now. 'Would you like to come up to my office, Mr ... I'm sorry. What did you say your name was?'

211

'Ned Brisco, sir.'

Mr Lisle led the way, up a narrow wooden staircase to an office with a wooden bay window that overlooked Pountney Street. The room reminded Ned of a verandah. It was a working office and not a showpiece. Blueprints covered every available flat surface and some not so flat. Shiny, precision turned parts acted as paperweights and a wheel and tyre assembly that was caked in dried mud stood against one wall. Mr Lisle sat down in a leather and wood chair behind a desk and invited Ned to sit opposite.

'Tell me about this biplane, Mr Brisco – this *Gull*. Tell me how you became interested in building an aeroplane.'

'I learnt a bit about aviation when I was a lad, Mr Lisle – I read all sorts of things and made models. Then, when I heard of the Wright Brothers' success, I reckoned I could do just as well. And I have, as far as I've got.'

'So who funds all this activity?'

'I do. I'm a moulder at the Coneygree Foundry in Tipton. But somebody's lent me two hundred pounds to get an engine. It crossed my mind that for all I know, you might be developing one that could be modified.'

'I'd like to think we could develop one, Mr Brisco. Tell me – is there a chance that I could have a look at this aeroplane of yours?'

'Yes, if you think you can help. I see no harm in that. When do you want to see it?'

'Would it be convenient right now?'

'Right now? It would mean a trip out into the country, to Bobbington, Mr Lisle. But I couldn't

212

promise to show you the *Gull* in flight today. Not with the weather the way it is. In any case, Mr Woodall might not be about to give me a tow.'

'No matter. The thing flies, evidently, if this photograph is to be believed. I'd like to take a look, though.'

So Edward Lisle drove Ned out to Bobbington and to the farm of Fred Woodall. On the way, Ned spoke enthusiastically about aviation and propounded at length on why the French had not been as successful as the Americans. Edward Lisle was becoming more impressed with this knowledgeable young man with every minute of the journey.

The rain had eased off by the time they reached Bobbington and the farm. Fred Woodall was surprised to see Ned but gave permission for them to visit the barn that housed the *Gull* and even accompanied them.

'I'm impressed, young man,' Mr Lisle said, running his fingers along the trailing edge of the top wing. 'And you say you've seen young Ned perform in it, Mr Woodall?'

'Flies like a bird,' Fred confirmed. 'Never seen nothing like it. Nor never will again maybe.'

'All right, Mr Brisco, I'm convinced. So, let's get back to my office and discuss this a little more.'

They dropped Fred Woodall back at the farmhouse and made their way back to Wolverhampton with the sun piercing the clouds, casting beams of slanting sunlight that made the wet roads glare so fiercely that you couldn't look at them. Ned told Mr Lisle about the *Antoinette* engine, as much as he knew, and Mr Lisle listened intently. Twenty-five minutes later, they were back in his office in Pountney Street.

'Now, Ned – may I call you Ned?... I have two things to say. One is a proposition I'd like you to consider, the other is a confession. First, the confession. For a while now, it has been my intention to investigate this business of constructing aeroplanes and start some trials. I agree with you that the French have made an utter hash of their attempts so far but, at least, they are having a go. I'd like to think we British could do better if we applied ourselves to the problems with our usual tenacity of purpose. Certainly, if we don't do something very soon we're going to be left sadly behind. Which is a pity, because I believe there is a big future in aeroplanes and I'd like to get in on the ground floor, as I believe I have with motor cars. I think, Ned, that you could assist in this. So, to the proposition. How would you like to come and work for the Star Engineering Company, Ned, developing aircraft? I'm sure we could come to a suitable arrangement that would be to our mutual benefit.'

Ned looked uncertain. 'I don't know, Mr Lisle, sir. It's a very tempting thought but ... but what about my *Gull?* There's hundreds of hours of work gone into her. And I mean to get an engine for her. She's a real labour of love. I didn't come here after a job. I only came here to see if you had an engine I could modify. I could build one myself – from scratch. There's folk who will help me with the engineering. I have all this money...'

'A daunting task, Ned. Look, if you want to

develop an engine independently of Star that's up to you. But why put yourself to all that trouble when we can do it together at Star's expense? What I want, is for you to develop with my company some aeroplanes – aeroplanes that can carry freight long distances, aeroplanes that could fly passengers. It's my guess that the Post Office would relish the opportunity to employ aeroplanes that could deliver mail over great distances quickly. Don't you think so?'

'Oh, certainly, Mr Lisle. And I know the Army is already looking at aeroplanes as a means of reconnaissance. Better than those static balloons and kites they've been working on.'

'All potential customers, you see, Ned. All willing to spend money on the right equipment. They could be using equipment you've developed. We could put Britain in the forefront of aeronautical engineering. How proud would that make you, eh?'

Ned smiled and nodded. 'Very proud, Mr Lisle, sir.'

'Then there's another market that could be tapped. Those better-off people who would like to suddenly appear at a friend's country house in a small aircraft. Social flyers, I'd call them. Showing off. There's a whole world of possibilities, Ned.'

'I suppose there is,' Ned agreed.

'So what do you say?'

Ned twisted his cap in his hands as he pondered what to do for the best. It had been his dream to do exactly this, but with his own firm. Now this Mr Lisle wanted to steal his thunder.

215

But Mr Lisle had the means...

'I have to be straight with you, Mr Lisle, sir. My main interest is in the *Gull*. One way or the other I'll get an engine for her. If you help me develop an engine that will power her, you'll end up with a design that can be sold to other firms that might start building aeroplanes...'

'That's so. Any engine you design and develop in our employment would be our property. Any patents arising from it would be ours.'

'But there's also the question of an airscrew, Mr Lisle. That's going to need as much attention. If you've got the facilities and the contacts to design and make an airscrew as well, then I'll come and work for you. Once those two problems are sorted out, building a craft that will fly is the easy bit.'

'Join us and we'll develop an engine and an airscrew together for your *Gull*, first and foremost. As long as we both understand that we shall be able to sell them commercially. That way we can justify funding development.'

Ned smiled. It all seemed very satisfactory. 'Thank you, Mr Lisle.'

Mr Lisle arose from his seat. He walked towards Ned and offered his hand. 'So we have an understanding, Ned. Let's shake on it... We can discuss terms later. First, let me introduce you to my sons.'

'So what should I do about the two hundred pounds I've got?' Ned asked.

'Well, that's entirely up to you, lad. But I suspect you should give it back.'

The third Saturday in October was fine but cold. However cold it was though, it would never stop people going to town on a Saturday. As usual, Dudley was heaving with folk. Market traders hailed at the tops of their voices the virtues and the unbeatable value of their particular wares. Old women, watched by nobody, haggled for a better price and young women, watched by young men with covetous eyes, dodged the trams and the carts as they flitted from shop window to shop window to admire this dress, that hat.

The imminent birthday of Emily Doubleday, Tom's mother, was the reason he'd arranged to meet Clover that dinnertime, to choose Emily a suitable present. So, making use of her mid-day break, Clover met Tom by the fountain in the Market Place. They greeted each other with a brief kiss.

'I've been so busy this morning,' she complained. 'I didn't think I was going to get out on time. Have you been waiting long?'

'Only a minute or two. Have you eaten?'

'Nothing yet. I'll try and sneak my sandwiches when I get back. Have you decided what you're going to buy for your mother, Tom?'

'I'm not at all sure,' he said as they stood facing each other, being jostled by the hoards of shoppers.

'Why not give her a brooch?'

'Hey, a brooch is a good idea. I knew you'd think of something.'

She smiled up into his blue eyes and took his arm. 'Let's see what they've got in Henn's. I'd like to look for some shoes after, if we have time.'

Progress was slow because of the number of people milling about who always seemed to stop to talk in front of them. A drunk lolled from side to side as he stumbled from the Railway Vaults all the way to the Seven Stars, bumping into indignant shoppers. Then it was Clover's turn to stop and pass the time of day with a woman she knew from Cross Guns Street. Eventually, they made it to Henn's in Castle Street and peered into the window for an idea of what was available.

Tom's eyes were drawn to the gold words engraved into the windowsill that said in large letters **'NOTED WEDDING RING SHOP'**. He felt for Clover's hand and she looked up at him with her clear blue eyes.

'Can you see anything that takes your fancy?' she asked.

'I can see a nice wedding ring I'd like to see on your finger,' he said in a low voice.

'Oh, Tom,' she answered dismissively, but felt her pulse quicken as she squeezed his hand.

'No, seriously.' Maybe this was as good a time as any to convey the thoughts he'd been cherishing. 'I'd like to think we'll be married at some time, Clover... It's a bit soon yet, I know, but ... but someday...'

'Oh, Tom,' she cooed. 'I didn't know you were thinking of us marrying yet.'

'Well not just yet...' He smiled adoringly at her. 'But not too far distant...'

'Well...' she said hesitantly. 'You've really taken me by surprise.'

He looked at her, suddenly disconcerted at her

apparent reticence. 'I imagined you'd feel the same. Tell me I'm not wrong.'

She felt herself trembling. This was totally unexpected, yet so very welcome. Of course she'd entertained similar thoughts, similar hopes, but his mentioning it had come as a complete shock. 'Course you're not wrong.' She was whispering, for folk were milling around them and another couple were also trying to look at rings. 'Course I feel the same.'

He smiled proudly, a measure of relief too in his expression. 'You had me worried then. I thought you were going to tell me not to be so daft.'

'Oh, Tom. Course not. I'm flattered... It makes me happy that you feel that way.'

'I've felt that way since the moment I first set eyes on you, Clover.'

'I've harboured the same dreams as you, by the sound of it.'

They moved out of the way to lend the other couple more browsing space, to give themselves more space to say what was suddenly in their hearts.

He looked into her eyes earnestly. 'Then maybe we should make some sort of plan. Maybe we should give ourselves some sort of time-scale.'

'Yes... Tell me what you think...'

He shrugged. 'All things being equal, how about us using your twenty-first birthday next May to announce our engagement, and plan to be wed on your twenty-second. Nobody could say we'd rushed into it, yet it's only eighteen months away.'

'What if I get pregnant in the meantime?' she whispered.

'Don't tempt me, Clover. Then we'll be married all the sooner.'

The other couple moved away. As they turned to enter the shop the girl smiled knowingly at Clover.

'You don't need to marry me, you know, Tom,' she said, feeling an urge to test his devotion. 'You're already getting what you want.'

'Oh, Clover, credit me with some honour. What I want is to be your husband. What I want is for you to be my wife.'

'Do you want us to have babies?'

He laughed. 'Yes, course I want us to have babies. Lots of little girls that all look like you.'

She sighed happily. 'You'd make a good father. I can just see you with our daughter, bouncing her on your knee, throwing her into the air and catching her while she whoops with glee.'

'Let's go inside then and you can try on some engagement rings. That way I'll know your size and the sort of style you'd like, ready for when I buy it.'

She smiled at him, love brimming in her eyes. 'All right. But let's get your mother's birthday present first.'

It was as romantic a marriage proposal as she'd ever envisaged. A complete and utter surprise. All that afternoon she relived the few minutes they'd spent standing in front of Henn's shop window, going over and over in her mind their words to each other. Inside the shop she had tried on engagement rings and held her hand out in front of her, gazing at each one and then seeking approval of it from Tom's expression. But she could not make up her own mind. The amount of choice only served to confuse her. Each successive ring was as beautiful as the one she'd tried on before it; and the more expensive rings did not necessarily mean they were more appealing in design. But there was plenty of time in which to choose a ring. They were not to be officially engaged till next May.

Clover left Cook's store after work and made her way through the town as happy as she'd ever felt in her life. She had a man who loved her, who intended marrying her; and she was head over heels in love with him too. She couldn't wait to get to his studio, to be alone with him again, to wallow in the pleasure of his unbounded affection. But she had one little query and, not knowing the answer was beginning to niggle her.

Tom seemed as happy as she was. He welcomed her with a kiss, locked his front door and turned the sign round to show that he was closed for business. He sat beside her on the *chaise-longue* and they kissed.

'So you'll marry me?' he said when they broke off.

'I will,' she responded, as solemnly as any bride. 'But should we tell anybody yet that we're going to get engaged in May?'

'I don't see the point,' he said. 'Let's keep it to ourselves and then surprise everybody on the day.'

'All right. I can keep a secret.' She chuckled

and kissed him again. Now for the serious bit that was bothering her. 'Where do you suppose we'll live, Tom?'

'It's over eighteen months away, sweetheart. Any number of houses might come up by then. I can't say where we'll live.'

'But not with your folks?'

'God, no.' It seemed that the notion appalled him. 'On our own. In our own little love-nest.'

She smiled contentedly. It was as she had hoped. 'That's all I wanted to know...'

'Well you're easily pleased.'

She smiled at him impishly. 'I'd be even more pleased if you made me a cup of tea.'

'Course I'll make you a cup of tea, my love.'

Chapter Thirteen

That same October Ned Brisco noted with disappointment that Henri Farman, the English-born but not English speaking son of an English journalist, and domiciled in France, flew 771 metres in 52 seconds. If only he could hurry things up with his own new engine he was certain he could beat the French once and for all, rather than lagging behind them all the time. But developing an engine of the calibre required to power an aeroplane was going to take time, even when the professionals were involved. For a start, there were too many other things going on at Star. One minute all attention was on his project but then, either a panic elsewhere would divert everybody, or Mr Joe Lisle, another son, would require attention to his racer. And technical problems were legion. The walls of the new engine block were as thin as they dared make them and yet the weight, Ned calculated, would be still too great when water was added to the cooling system. Pity there was no lightweight substitute available to replace water, some suitable chemical, for instance. Aluminium might be a suitable material in which to cast the engine block and cylinder head but, as Edward Lisle said, although it was significantly lighter, commercial production had been only recently developed. It was therefore expensive, scarce and an unknown entity as regards behaviour and wear in an internal combustion engine. No doubt time would prove it suitable in many an aero-nautical application, but time they did not have.

For Ramona, life moved on, but not suitably. Her ardent encounters with Elijah were less frequent than she had hoped. The top storey of the brewery was not entirely safe, he told her. They could too easily be compromised by her father or by Mary Ann or by Bobby Cross, the drayman; his bedroom also remained taboo. And the more he had to put her off the more she was determined to have him. Her preoccupation was blinding her to the foolishness of the liaison. Had she stopped to think, she would have asked her-self where this incestuous affair could possibly lead to; and marriage was not one of the options. But she did not stop to think. She merely invented schemes, most of which were impracticable, that might enable her to spend an exhilarating hour on her back with Elijah once in a while. Elijah did, however, agree to meet her a couple of times in October at her father's old house and this served to satisfy her and keep her moderately sweet when a pattern of such visits began to evolve through the winter. Other men vied for her attention and, at those times when she felt spurned by Elijah, she sought comfort in them, regarding these diversions as a means of spiting him; but of course they could only spite him if he knew about them; and he did not know. Dorcas, meanwhile, remained obstinately on the scene and seemed no less content with her lot than at any other time before, which suggested to Ramona that she was having little impact on that relationship. The realisation riled her even more.

November passed in a miasma of putrid fogs. Having got lost in a particularly dense one crossing the English Channel in his royal yacht, Germany's Kaiser, the most powerful military monarch on earth, eventually found Portsmouth, paid a state visit to London and made much of his blood relationship with King Edward VII. A French inventor called Paul Cornu introduced a new type of aircraft that managed to lift him one and a half metres vertically off the ground, by means of two rotors situated above his head. Ned Brisco was unimpressed.

Christmas came and went and, in January 1908, the redoubtable Henri Farman flew a circular course for nearly one and a half minutes, covering more than a kilometre and won a prize of £5000 in the process that was much coveted by aviators. Ned's engine showed little hope of being ready before March. In America, the state of Georgia introduced a law prohibiting alcohol which, when he heard of it, induced Jake Tandy to remark, 'Silly buggers!' Jake was further incensed when the Licensing Bill was introduced in February, aimed at cutting the number of drinking licences by a third. Malcolm, the cat, had kittens which everybody regarded as a miracle, and Clover found homes for them before Mary Ann could drown them. In the meantime, Mrs Emmeline Pankhurst languished in Holloway jail after refusing to find sureties for her good behaviour.

Come March and Tom Doubleday was interested to learn that in Paris a process for producing colour photographs had been introduced at the *Academie des Sciences* by a Gabriel Lippmann. The same city offended Ned Brisco further when it was announced that Henri Farman had made the first aeroplane flight with a passenger, whereas his own twelve-cylinder engine failed to perform, but was still too heavy anyway. Rivalry between the navies of Britain and Germany were boosted when Germany launched its own version of the Royal Navy's *Dreadnought* battleship; the balance of power at sea, however, remained with Britain for the foreseeable future.

In April there was cause for some local celebration when Wolverhampton Wanderers beat Newcastle United 3–1 in the F.A. Cup final at Crystal Palace. This made work bearable at Star for Ned, but only until the euphoria had worn off. He began to appreciate the complexities of

225

designing and developing a high precision, high output, multi-cylinder internal combustion engine of light weight. A radical rethink of his own was called for.

Ned's mind was diverted from the problems of his aeroplane engine one day in May when Edward Lisle offered to sell him one of their Stuart twin-cylinder, three-speed motor cars at a knock-down price, due to the model being discontinued. Ned was used to driving motor cars by this time, having spent some time driving those belonging to the Messrs Lisle. He was sorely tempted. The only way he could afford it, however, was to dip into the money he had been loaned anonymously, which he had been loath to repay yet, not knowing if he would need it for further private funding. But all costs were being met by the Star Engineering Company and it looked less and less likely that he would need it. Since there was no time limit set on when it had to be repaid, he felt justified in using it to finance this lovely new Star Stuart. He would of course pay it back in due course. It would mean saving up but he could do that now since the *Gull* was no longer a drain on his resources. Besides, how many other young men in his position were running around in a motor car? Clover would be impressed; Ramona would be impressed.

It was on Tuesday 19th May, Clover's twenty first birthday, that he took delivery of it.

Tom met Clover from Cook's that day to accompany her back home for the party that had been arranged for her birthday. The weather was fine and warm with just a light breeze that kept the air clear of smuts.

'I take it you haven't changed your mind overnight about being engaged to me,' he said as they milled through High Street's crowds, all hurriedly wending their way home.

'Did you think I would?' she asked with a typically sunny smile.

'No, sweetheart. But I'll be more content when the ring is on your finger.'

The fact that she was due to become engaged to be married meant more to Clover this day than reaching her twenty-first birthday. Being promised to Tom was infinitely more important than merely attaining the freedom to marry him, without having to resort to permission from her mother or from Jake. It was a circumstance she had been looking forward to for months; another step closer to the day this time next year when she would walk down the aisle of St John's church in her white bridal gown with Tom waiting for her in the front pew. She had tried, over the months, to visualise it; a bright, sunny day, the church full of fresh spring flowers, her family and his all wearing fine new clothes, their heads turning to watch her glide regally up the aisle on Jake Tandy's arm, for it must be Jake who would give her away. She tried to picture the house they would occupy, their home. Of course, it was impossible, but she harboured some hopes and impressions of what it might be like. She daydreamed about their going to bed at night, their getting up in a morning, her getting Tom's breakfast, cooking his meal in the evening when he'd come in from work. She imagined romantic evenings together in front of a cosy fire. Perhaps later on there would be a baby in a crib.

As they walked, arms linked, towards Kates Hill, they spoke about who would be attending the party later, who might drop by unexpected, what folk would be wearing, and speculated on what gifts she might receive. They spoke about his family, who were also expected, and hers. The subject of Ramona cropped up.

'Is she courting now?' Tom asked. 'I haven't been aware of anybody while I've been there.'

'I'm not aware there's anybody special,' Clover replied. 'I've noticed a change in her, though. Sometimes she seems offish – with me at any rate. I don't know if I've done anything to offend her. Other times she seems distant. You know? You speak to her and it's as if she hasn't heard you – as if she's not been paying attention.'

'I don't know, Clover. She always seems very attentive–'

'Very attentive to you,' Clover interrupted with a sideways glance at him. 'I've noticed that.'

'Sometimes, I grant you. Not only to me, though. She's always responsive to her father ... and to her Uncle Elijah for that matter. Strange that. Those nearest and dearest are often the most likely to be ignored.'

'Familiarity breeding contempt, you mean?'

'Perhaps. But any new male face in the taproom will always elicit a flicker of interest from her. So don't write her off yet.'

'Tom, I wouldn't dream. She's a bit of a conundrum, is Ramona.'

'An enigma. She's not only cool to you, Clover. I've noticed she's sometimes very cool towards Dorcas.'

'Well, she doesn't like Dorcas. Neither do I for that matter. Condescending bitch!'

Tom laughed aloud. 'That's unlike you. You're normally so tolerant.'

'Oh, I'm tolerant of her. For Elijah's sake. I like Elijah. I like him a lot. I don't have to like Dorcas though. He could do much better for himself.'

'Maybe he feels he's done as well as he's ever likely to do.'

'Has he said as much?'

'He doesn't have to say anything, Clover. See it from his point of view. She's a lovely-looking girl who obviously thinks the world of him, brought up to be a lady. Her father's filthy rich and a pillar of society to boot, and she's likely to inherit everything he owns. If he marries the girl all that will become his. What more does he want? All right, I think she is a bit condescending when she's with the Tandys, but she's all right with me.'

A dog ran barking into the road near them and a horse that was in harness shied as it approached. The carter, nodding off as he leaned against his load, took exception to being disturbed and jumped off the cart to take an indignant kick at the mongrel. Clover and Tom watched the incident with detached amusement for a second or two before continuing their walk up the road known as Waddam's Pool. On their left stood The Firs, a large house in its own elevated grounds, on the opposite side stood Hill House, vying for grandeur.

'So just because her father's made a pot of money she thinks she can look down on everybody else,' Clover remarked acidly as they continued their journey. 'If my father had lived maybe he'd have grown wealthy from his brewing. But I'd never have considered myself above everybody else...'

He'd never heard her talk like this before and he wondered why she felt it so strongly.

'...And just think, Tom, what a catch I would have been for you... As it is, I know I'm not much of a catch.'

He stopped abruptly, turned to face her and looked intently into her blue eyes that already had a defensive look about them, expecting a scolding. Well, she deserved one for that. 'Clover, I don't ever want to hear you say anything like that again. I want to marry you because I love you, because you're you. I want to marry you for yourself. I'm not interested in whether or not your family has any money. It's of no consequence. Surely you realise that by now. So don't put yourself down.'

She looked down at the ground. 'Oh, I'm sorry Tom. I just want to be perfect for you.'

'You are perfect for me. If you were not, I wouldn't be intending to marry you.'

The party, naturally, was to take place in the taproom of the Jolly Collier and began as soon as Clover had changed and freshened up. A selection of Mary Ann's relatives had turned up – the Scrivens – made up of two brothers accompanied by their wives and grown-up children and an unmarried sister, Hannah. Old Man and Old Lady Tandy loomed as large as life, as near to the fireplace as they could get, and Elijah finished work in the brewery early so as to fetch Dorcas. The Doubledays of course had been invited and they were due to arrive later. Some of Clover's old school friends appeared as did girls she worked with at Cook's. She'd posted an invitation to Selina, her fellow coremaker from the foundry and her beau, Charlie, and received an acceptance next day. Zillah Bache and Job Smith had been drafted in to serve free beer and cold food.

Since the Jolly Collier was obliged to be open for business, casual patrons and regulars also found it impossible not to be part of the celebration and indeed were encouraged to join in. Among them sat Noah Fairfax and Urban Tranter. Awash with free beer, they had exhausted the topic of Asquith's taking over the post of Prime Minister from Henry Campbell-Bannerman and were by this time well and truly involved in arguing the pros and cons of the government's intention to introduce an old-age pension of five shillings a week.

'Just think,' Urban said, 'me and my ode dutch'll be better off than we am now.'

'You'd be better off six foot under,' Noah remarked nonchalantly and supped his pint as he waited for the inevitable question.

'How d'yer wairk that out?'

''Cause them as have never worked will never get a penny. Nor paupers, nor prisoners.'

'So how does that affect me?' Urban queried,

with a frown.

'Oh, I forgot. Nor the insane, neither.'

The assembled regulars who were on the fringe of this discussion all laughed while Urban assumed a disgruntled look.

'Yo'm the one who's insane, Noah,' he scoffed.

Noah shook his head. 'Not me, me ode tater. If you think as Lloyd George is gunna cough up five bob a wik apiece for yo' and that missus o' yowern you must want yer yed lookin'. Yo' must be insane.'

'That's what they'n said. Five bob a wik to everybody over seventy. Mind you, I've got a year or two yet.'

'For married couples it'll on'y be seven an' a tanner, Urban.'

Urban sucked on his pipe thoughtfully then hawked into the nearest spittoon. 'Seven an' a bloody tanner? Why should we get half a crown less than a widder and her lodger what am sleepin' together under the same roof? Like that Sarah Mildew an' Georgie Pitchford. Where's the fairness in that?'

'That's gunna be the rule, Urban. Like it or not.'

'I've a good mind I'd write to Hooper,' Urban protested vehemently.

'Arthur Hooper? The MP?'

'Yes. Him.'

Noah scoffed. 'Yo've gorra bloody nerve...'

Urban looked suitably offended. 'What d'yer mean, I've gorra nerve?'

'Since when have yo' ever voted Liberal? That's what I mean. Yo'know very well yo' voted for the

Tory at the last election.'

'What's that got to do with it?'

Suddenly, Tom Doubleday called everybody to attention and, eventually, the room became quiet, save for the occasional chink of glass. He called Clover to his side and took her hand. 'Friends, families... We all know why we're here tonight...' There was a hum of affirmation from everybody. 'We're here to celebrate Clover Beckitt's coming of age.' A cheer went up and Tom raised his hand again in a plea to be heard. 'Now I know for a fact that she's had some lovely gifts from you all, some very touching birthday messages and I know that a lot of you already have given her your best wishes in person here this evening. But there's one gift still to come and I want to present it to her now...

'I've been aware for more than a year now of how special Clover is. It's been less than a year since we started courting but in that short time I realised one thing ... that I set my heart on marrying her...' A roar went up that turned into a hum of animated comment between one person and another. Tom once again raised his hand. 'So... So I asked her to marry me...' Another cheer. Another raised hand. 'And, glory be, she said "yes"!' This time, the taproom erupted with cries of 'well done', 'congratulations' and some slightly bawdy comments that did not amuse Mary Ann. Tom felt in his jacket pocket. 'So, I want to give you this special little gift, Clover,' he said, looking into her eyes with a wealth of affection. 'Give me your hand...' He slipped a ring onto her third finger.

She looked at it and gasped, for she had not seen it before, and smiled happily. 'Thank you, Tom.' She stood on tiptoe and kissed him on the lips. When she looked into his eyes again, he saw a tear trembling on her eyelashes and he was moved to hug her.

'Clover, I love you,' he said simply.

'And me you,' she replied.

Already the room was in uproar and somebody started singing 'For He's a Jolly Good Fellow'.

Elijah then stood up and clapped his hands to attract everybody's attention. 'Now I've got something to say...' The place went quiet again. 'For this very special celebration,' he went on, 'I've brewed a very special beer – and I've called it "Clover's Special". I've tried it meself o' course and though I say it meself, it's a drop o' good – like our Clover, here. So I want you all to enjoy it and drink her health and future happiness.'

At first, nobody noticed the familiar figure standing at the door in unfamiliar leather waterproofs. Ned Brisco removed his goggles, nodded to one or two of the more familiar patrons and smiled self-consciously while he removed his leather gauntlets. Then everybody seemed to see him and the room went uncannily silent.

Noah Fairfax picked up a handful of dominoes to resume the game that had been adjourned during their debate and Tom Doubleday's announcement. He scrutinised them before replacing them face down on the table at which he and Urban sat. He caught Ned's eye, nodded to him and tapped Urban on the shin with his foot. 'Bloody'ell, it's that Ned Brisco. Florrie's son.'

'Evening, Mr Fairfax,' Ned greeted pleasantly, stepping forward with hesitation.

Noah duly responded but remained straight-faced. 'That's him what flies,' he explained to Urban. 'Yo' remember.'

Urban gave a look of recognition. 'Christ, yo'd think he was the archangel Gabriel the way everybody's gone quiet. Looks like he's fled here anyroad, struttin' in here like a leather turkey cock.'

Ned pushed forward through the crowd of people, towards Clover who was laughing now with Selina and Charlie and her old schoolfriend, Ivy Turner. Selina, who knew Ned, looked him up and down.

'What the devil yer got on?' she asked irreverently. 'You look like our old coal bucket. That's leather an' all.'

Ned looked deflated and gave an embarrassed smile.

'Is it raining, Ned?' Clover asked.

'No, it's a grand evening, Clover. Happy Birthday ... I see you and him got engaged then. Here ... I've bought you a little present. I couldn't think what to get you so I brought you this. It's a fountain pen. I hope you like it.'

'Thanks, Ned. I haven't got a decent pen. I'll open it later, shall I? What do you want to drink? It's all free.'

'I'll have a pint of bitter.'

Clover herself poured him a pint and Ramona joined the group. She was wearing a new low-cut

235

dress, revealing a tantalising amount of cleavage, predominantly for Elijah's benefit although she cast an eye at anybody to check that they were looking.

'Congratulations, Clover,' she said, smiling generously. 'Tom fair surprised us all with that announcement. Let's see your new ring... Oh, it's beautiful. You must be thrilled. Did you know anything about it?'

'Oh, yes, Ramona,' she said. 'But it's been the hardest thing in the world to keep it a secret. I wanted to shout it from the rooftops as soon as I knew.'

'And who can blame you?' Selina commented.

'You nearly missed Tom's announcement,' Ramona remarked to Ned. 'You're late. But what's all this leather for?'

'I've bought a motor,' Ned announced. 'They let me have it cheap at Star. You need leathers like this when you'm driving a motor.'

'You've bought a motor car?' Clover queried. 'Where is it?'

'Outside. D'you want to see it?'

'Course we do. Don't we, Ramona?... Don't we, Selina... Ivy?'

So Ned obliged and led the way outside, followed by four eager girls. In the cool evening air of May they gathered round the open car giggling and Selina, without being invited, sat in the front passenger seat. With a gesture of self-mockery, she assumed but exaggerated the air of a lady. This prompted the other girls to laugh and occupy the other seats, such was the novelty of the situation. Some of the other folk streamed out of the taproom into the street and stood around, gawping at the car, amused at the girls who were bubbling and noisy from the effects of a drink or two.

'Take us a ride, Ned,' Selina called over the hubbub. 'I've never been a ride in a hossless cart.'

Ramona was perched in the driver's seat. 'Well, Ned,' she drooled. 'You can take me out in this any time you like.'

'I'll give you all a ride,' he said, enjoying this new-found attention and respect. 'But since it's Clover's twenty-first, I think she ought to go first. If you don't mind, that is...'

There was a murmur of approval from those watching, except from Ramona, and so the girls complied, each in turn alighting from the vehicle. Clover moved to the front passenger seat and braced herself, rubbing her arms in anticipation of the breeze that would soon chill her, for she wore no coat. Ned cranked the engine, clambered aboard and they began to move off to applause from everybody. Tom Doubleday emerged from the taproom just in time to see his sweetheart being driven off in a strange vehicle.

'They've only gone a ride,' Selina informed him. 'They'll only be five minutes. He's coming back to give us all a ride. He's done well for himself since he left the Coneygree to build aeroplanes. Them motors don't come cheap, I bet. I doubt if we'll ever be able to afford one, eh, Charlie?'

Tom's disapproval must have shown in his face; for Tom knew about the loan Ned had accepted and had a very shrewd idea where the money had come from to pay for this unexpected extravagance. Ramona stepped up to him, typically misreading his expression.

'Don't look so worried, Tom. He's taking us all a ride, as Selina says. Clover will be back in a minute.'

Tom forced a smile for her. 'Oh, I'm not bothered about Clover, Ramona,' he replied.

It was not a statement that he would have considered ambiguous to anybody who had just heard his announcement. But Ramona was of different stuff, suffering her own trials and tribulations over Elijah. Suddenly she saw Tom as a kindred spirit, likewise tortured, likewise spurned and desired in turn, till she did not know whether she was coming or going. In her twisted perspective, Tom's apparent anguish made sense. In her distorted view of things, it all started falling into place. She seized on Tom.

'It doesn't surprise me her going off with Ned two minutes after you announced you wanted to marry her,' she said, turning away from the others. 'Amazing how fickle a motor car can make a girl.'

'Doesn't it make you wonder where the money came from, Ramona?' he remarked sourly. 'Six months ago he hadn't got two halfpennies to rub together.'

'But they've always been close,' Ramona said, persisting with her theme, ignoring his. 'I reckon if you hadn't come along she would have married Ned. Specially now.'

Tom looked at Ramona quizzically. 'You think so? Somehow I doubt it.'

Unwittingly they started walking, up the side of the Jolly Collier into the yard between the pub and the brewery, away from the rest.

Ramona shrugged. 'God knows what they used to get up to in that stable up at Springfield House when they were supposed to be building that aeroplane. I suppose you never can tell. Not long ago I saw her in Elijah's arms in the yard. He swore it was innocent enough ... but you never can tell.'

They stopped walking and Tom looked at her sceptically. 'Clover and Elijah? Are you sure?'

She noticed with gratification how his eyes were drawn to the soft curve of her smooth young breasts above her bodice. 'P'raps you shouldn't read anything into it, Tom. After all, Elijah swore... Mind you, when you think he's brewed a beer specially for her birthday – gone to all that trouble – then called *her* special in front of Dorcas – it adds grist to the mill, don't you think?'

'Well I'm certain nothing's ever gone on between Clover and Ned. You're imagining that, Ramona. And if you've imagined the one, you could have imagined the other.'

'Have you ever had a look round the brewery?'

'No.'

'Why don't you let me show you? I can show you how beer is brewed. All the changes we've made.'

He smiled at how nimbly she jumped from one subject to another. 'Some other time maybe, Ramona. It'd be interesting to see this brewery but I know how beer is brewed.'

'Fair enough,' she said resignedly. 'They'd been

to the brewhouse together to lay the fire, you know. It must have been a Sunday night.'

'Who?'

'Clover and Elijah. They was ages. I'd just come outside – I forget what for now – and then I saw them, arms all around each other and laughing, as if they'd been lovers for ages.'

Tom sighed, a troubled sigh. His trust in Clover had been complete. He knew her to be totally trustworthy. And yet he could not be with her twenty-four hours a day. What of the time when they were apart? Could it be as Ramona suggested? After all, there was ample opportunity... No. It could not be. Clover was totally, utterly committed; it was plain enough for all to see. Besides, she was not that kind of girl...

'And just look how she despises Dorcas. Jealousy, that's all it is.'

'What about yourself, Ramona?' he asked, dismissing her fanciful notions. 'Are you courting yourself these days? I never seem to see you with anybody.'

'Me? No, I ain't courting nobody, Tom. I'm saving meself for the right man. He'll find me worth having as well, when he comes along...'

'I'm sure. You're an attractive young woman.'

'Thank you, Tom,' she responded, smiling coyly and he watched her bosom rise appealingly as she sighed at his compliment. 'But that's not what I mean. I know what a man enjoys most and I can make sure he gets it...'

The sound of a motor car boomed off the walls of the yard, suggesting Ned had returned Clover. They looked at each other, turned round and

240

went to meet them.

'You'll want a coat on,' Clover said to Selina and Ivy who were next to be driven. 'You'll be frozen.'

'Oh, we'll be all right,' Selina said and jumped into the car. 'See you later.'

'Wait for me, Ned,' Ramona called. 'I'm coming as well.'

Clover smiled at Tom and shivered. He looked into her eyes trying to read thoughts and intentions, guilty secrets that were not there.

'Let's go inside for a warm,' she said. 'God, I'm frozen. If ever you buy a motor car, Tom, get one with a cover... What's wrong?' she asked, suddenly conscious of his troubled expression. 'You look as if you've lost a sovereign and found sixpence.'

'I hope I haven't,' he replied ambiguously, allowing her through the door to the taproom first.

Dorcas and Elijah were just on their way outside. 'We're just going to see this contraption Ned's bought,' he said.

'Brrr! I've just been out in it. I'm frozen solid.'

'Yes, you need to wrap up,' Dorcas agreed. 'Especially in this weather. May can be very deceiving.'

'Oh, Elijah,' Clover said, and put her hand on his arm familiarly. 'Thanks for that special celebration brew. It was a lovely surprise. I'm not sure how to thank you...' She beamed at him, stood on tiptoe and planted a kiss firmly on his lips.

Tom watched and wondered...

Chapter Fourteen

Tom Doubleday arrived home with his mother and father at about half past one in the morning. On the way they discussed the Tandys at some length and in particular Mary Ann. Mr Doubleday Senior insisted she had a face longer than a hop-picking train and his wife said it was hardly surprising, what with all the work she had to do and a grown-up family to look after. Tom hardly contributed to the discussion, save for a couple of words when his opinion was requested. He was deep in thought, and those thoughts were being muddled by the interference of too much alcohol. He didn't normally over-indulge but, since it had been Clover's birthday and the evening of their engagement, he deemed it reasonable to partake of a drink or two extra. So, when they entered the house in Stafford Street, Tom went straight out the back, sought the privy and then retired to bed.

The alcohol ensured that he fell asleep quickly, as he hoped it would. But he awoke about five, much earlier than usual, and had to get up and visit the privy again. Outside the birds were twittering their anthems that celebrated the first light of day. His mind was instantly alert, active, rational and preoccupied with what Ramona had told him. When he returned to his bed, he continued to lie, gazing at a crack in the ceiling, his hands behind his head, mulling over last night.

He did not know how much credibility he should afford Ramona's words about Clover and Elijah. Ramona, he suspected, possessed a vivid imagination and was possibly being no more than a little mischievous. Her telling him in the beginning that Clover and Ned Brisco were courting had inhibited him from pursuing Clover. It had been untrue. Maybe not a deliberate lie, but an unwitting fiction, told out of ignorance and all the more forgivable because, by telling it, she fancied she might secure him for herself. It was a flattering gesture, especially since it was from a girl as desirable as Ramona.

But Clover had been his goal and Clover he'd eventually won. She was a prize worth having, too; or so he'd always believed. From the outset he'd been drawn to her most exquisite looks; that nose that was ever so slightly long and all the more delicious for it, those clear blue eyes that exuded openness and honesty, those soft, succulent lips that he never tired of kissing and which, when he was not kissing them, curved into the most adorable smiles. She possessed a warmth he'd never perceived in any other woman, an easy-going, seemingly dependable nature that made him entirely comfortable with her. She had given herself to him in the first place out of love, out of trust, knowing she would be vilified by every gossip of Kates Hill if she ever became pregnant as a result.

But what if he'd been wrong all along? What if she had given herself too readily? Wouldn't that

243

say something about her virtue – or lack of it? If she had given herself easily with one man she could do so with another. Some women were like that. He'd been caught out with Maud, the first girl he was engaged to. He'd sworn to himself he would never allow himself to be put in that position again. Other women were easy but they had the knack of making you first believe you'd seduced them, that you were the only man in the world for them. Clover's warmth in any case was evidently not reserved just for him; he had witnessed it being bestowed on Elijah; the touching, the feeling. Wouldn't it be just true to form if something was going on behind his back? What a bitter irony if the very day he became engaged to Clover he'd discovered she really was having a fling with Elijah Tandy. Everything he did, with the best possible intentions, seemed to backfire on him.

So ... was there something too familiar in the way Clover kissed Elijah Tandy last night, the way she put her hand on his, touching, feeling with that innate warmth of hers? By doing so, had she inadvertently let slip some evidence of intimacy they'd secretly shared and enjoyed sometime? The unwitting give-away? Look how she had stood on tiptoe and kissed him full on the lips, brazenly, as if she'd done it a thousand times before. Only an hour or two before she had behaved identically with him, Tom. No, Clover evidently did not reserve such shows of affection solely for himself.

Dorcas's presence could even have lent credence to their complicity. Normally, people

244

would try to hide any signs of a closet liaison. Being openly affectionate belied any guilt. So they could afford to show their natural affection with no fear of anybody thinking the worst. Just a show of innocent familiarity as far as anybody else was concerned. There had always been a rapport between them, an informality that allowed them to flirt openly, unashamedly. Maybe Elijah had taken it as a sign of her interest and pursued it. Fancy him, too, going to all the trouble of brewing a special beer to mark her birthday.

Tom wondered if Dorcas was suffering any doubts. Tom did not dislike Dorcas as Clover did. He found her reserved, not snobbish, and he put it down to shyness. Was Clover's dislike fuelled by jealousy? Was that jealousy simply another pointer? Maybe. Tom realised he could not be with Clover twenty-four hours a day. He could not watch her all the time, to study her behaviour like a fly on a wall. God alone knew what little familiarities she practised with Elijah when they *were* alone – when nobody was looking.

Maybe he should ask her point-blank. He had been cheated by Maud and his best friend ... there was no reason why he should stand to be cheated by Clover and Elijah as well.

What an idiotic state to be in. If Ramona had not alerted him he would have gone on blindly trusting Clover. Ramona was evidently more of a friend than he realised. Now he had to rethink his position, he had to be alert to these other probabilities. It was difficult to take in. Maybe he was not so special after all in Clover's eyes. The biggest problem was, it hurt beyond belief to acknowledge the possibility.

Tom kicked the sheets off and sat on the edge of his bed in his nightshirt for a few seconds. He reached up, drew back the curtains and looked out onto the world wistfully. He opened his sash an inch or two further and the familiar smell of Millard's brewery at the Gypsies' Tent permeated his room the more. The realities of life lay in what you could smell like that beer brewing, what you could see, what you could hear, what you could touch. He donned his long-johns and his trousers and went downstairs to wash and shave in the whitewashed scullery. He would have it out with Clover, make her see he was not the soft touch she thought he was. He would tell her exactly what he thought of such liberal behaviour and let fate take its course.

Wort is the name given to the liquor produced by mashing crushed malt, known as grist, with hot water and allowing the starch therein to be converted by enzymes into sugars. That same afternoon, wort in the new mash tun was ready to be drawn off into a vessel called the underback. Jake Tandy was working in the brewery, passing on to Ramona knowledge he had picked up from Mary Ann.

Jake turned the valve that allowed the hot wort to drain through the perforated base plate of the mash tun and it gurgled and sucked.

'Right, now you can sparge the mash, Ramona,' he called out.

Ramona, who was wearing a light cotton frock that kept her relatively cool in the humid heat of this the liquor room, duly picked up the hose from the floor and sprayed more hot water over the mash of grains to remove any remaining sugar and flush it into the underback. 'Is that all right, Father?' she enquired, diligently spraying every square foot.

'Just the ticket, princess.' He chuckled with admiration of her obvious enthusiasm. 'I can see we'll mek a brewer of you yet. I've picked up a lot from Mary Ann. And by God, she knows what she's a-doing when it comes to brewing beer.'

'Well, she's been at it a long time.' She changed the hosepipe to her left hand. 'Tell me when it's enough, Father. This hosepipe's getting too hot to hold.'

'That should be enough now, I reckon. We'll let it drain through and then I'll dig out the spent mash. See that barrow, Ramona?... Shove it over here, will you?'

'What happens to the spent mash?' she asked, turning off the hose.

'When we've collected enough we bag it and it goes for cattle feed, my flower. Him down at Watson's Green Farm generally teks a few bags a wik.' He looked up and smiled at his daughter, pleased with her interest. 'Nothing gets wasted.'

She pushed the cart he'd called a barrow towards him. 'So d'you reckon we've got everything we need in the brewery now?'

'Not by a long chalk. We need a new bottling plant and a new store. But now we've got a buyer for the house, maybe we can set about getting it.'

He looked at her, proud that he could announce this news at last.

'You've sold the house?' she said, trying to hide her concern. 'Why didn't you tell me before?'

'It ain't actually sold yet, Ramona. Not till I've had the money. But I've agreed a sale. You have to admit, the money'll come in useful.'

Alarm bells were already ringing in Ramona's head. 'How soon?' Her trysts with Elijah would come to an end and they would be left with nowhere to lie and make love.

'It'll be a wik or two afore the deeds am handed over, I daresay,' Jake answered gently. 'Now...' He clambered into the mash tun with a shovel. 'While I shovel this lot out and clean the mash tun, go down to the boiler room and see if your Uncle Elijah's ready to fill the copper from the underback. He can show you what has to be done there.'

Partly out of duty, but partly out of an urgent desire to inform Elijah that they were soon to be deprived of their love-nest, she skipped down the wooden stairs. Elijah was shovelling coal under the copper to stoke up the fire.

'Have you come to watch or to help?' he asked matily.

'To help,' she replied. 'I'm supposed to be learning how to brew.'

It was hot there, too. The wort was flowing from the underback to the copper and she could feel its heat and that of the fire that roared under it. She was glad she wore only a light dress.

Elijah called up to Jake that the wort was safely in the copper and he could close off the underback so that he could proceed with cleaning the mash tun ready for the next wort. Then he turned to Ramona. 'Help me with that pocket, eh?'

Together they went to where huge bales of hops, called pockets, were stored and, between them, manoeuvred one towards the copper. When Elijah opened it they lifted it and poured a measure of dry, compressed hops into the steaming wort. The aroma from it all was heady.

'Did you know that father's sold the house?' she asked him as they allowed more hops to fall.

'Yes, I know.'

'So when shall we be able to meet?' she asked in an urgent whisper. 'More to the point, *where* shall we be able to meet?'

They allowed the pocket containing the remaining hops to fall back to the floor.

'We'll work something out,' Elijah said reassuringly and, with a warm smile, pulled her towards him so she was in his arms. His hands roamed over her buttocks, firm flesh under the flimsy, loose dress she was wearing. 'By Christ, you've got a lovely arse, our Ramona. I swear if your father wasn't upstairs I'd have you on this floor right now.'

'He won't be down for ages yet...' She looked at him hungrily. 'And we don't have to get on the floor. We could stand.'

'Either way we could get caught.'

'We wouldn't. Not if we do it standing up over there behind the hopback where he can't see us. We'd hear him coming down the stairs. We wouldn't get caught.'

'I worry about you, Ramona. You're too impulsive – like a pig at a tater. Just bide your time till we know we can be safe... He'll be going back into the pub soon. Anyway, shall you be all right for Saturday?'

She knew what he meant; her monthly bleeding. 'I think so.'

'Good. I'll meet you at the house Saturday morning. I suppose you'll be going shopping to the town?'

She nodded and smiled, happy that he'd suggested it.

'I shall go to the barber's Saturday morning and get me hair cut,' he told her. 'I'll meet you at the house after.'

'I could meet you somewhere else before then,' she suggested hopefully. 'What if we went to the fields over Oakham one afternoon while the weather's fine? It'd be a change. We could go later in the week.'

'I doubt if there'll be time.'

'We'll have to wait till me father's out of the way then. Like we did before.'

It was another hour before Jake finished. After cleaning the mash tun, he immediately began another wort with grist and hot liquor. While it worked he returned to the pub for a cup of tea and a sandwich of chawl. Elijah looked lustfully at Ramona and he signalled with his eyes that they should go upstairs, to the top floor.

They lay on the sacks of malt as they had before Elijah became nervous about being compromised there. At this moment, his thoughts were no higher than Ramona's navel and their being compromised was not uppermost in his mind. But right now it would be safe enough. They kissed ardently while his hands roamed over her lissom body, then up her skirt to savour the smooth, soft skin of her inner thighs that were moist with perspiration. He lifted her skirt above her waist and she raised her bottom while he eased down her drawers, which he allowed to fall to the floor. She unfastened the buttons of his fly, thrust her hands inside and felt his hot, insistent hardness.

'I want to see you naked,' he whispered urgently. 'Get your clothes off and let me see you.'

'Afterwards,' she whispered.

'What good's afterwards? I want to look at your backside and your titties. They hang beautiful when you'm standing up.'

'Why d'you want to look at them when you've already felt them? Besides, what if somebody comes up?'

'That sounds rich coming from you. We'll hear anybody well before they reach us.'

She let go of him, sat up on the malt sacks and pulled her dress over her head. Beneath that she wore a thin chemise and she doffed that as well. She was wearing no stockings today and was as naked as the day she was born.

'Move over there where I can see you...'

She slid off the sacks and moved away, her bare feet padding on the warm wooden floor. She stood with her back towards him and wiggled her backside then looked coquettishly over her

251

shoulder to witness his reaction. His lustful stare pleased her and excited her.

'You've got a fine arse, Ramona,' he said, his words thick in his throat with desire. 'Turn round to face me now ... I love the way your belly curves below your belly button to that patch of hair between your legs. Go over there so's I can see you walk... Now back...' He ogled her for a few seconds more. 'Ooh! Come here you little minx...'

As she rushed to him he caught hold of her and thrust her onto the malt sacks. With a groan he flung his full weight on top of her, burying his face in her breasts, kissing her hard and biting her remorselessly. He pushed himself urgently into her wet softness and, as she felt him fill her up, she gave a whimper of pleasure and they writhed together like wild, frenzied otters. Greedily, Ramona arched her back, pushing against the firmness of the malt sacks and rubbing herself against him till she uttered a profound sigh of relief. The deep ache of longing was sated once more. While her eyes were closed and a satisfied smile played on her face, he withdrew and she felt his hot, sticky seed drizzle reassuringly over the curve of her belly that he admired so much.

They lay for five minutes before Ramona thought she heard him snore. She moved, deliberately disturbing him.

'You can't fall asleep here,' she said in a hoarse whisper, for once wise.

She slid from him and collected her drawers from the floor, giving them a shake to dislodge

252

the dust and the bits of husk they had inevitably collected. She thrust her legs into the openings and pulled them up, then grabbed her chemise. When she had her dress back on she shook her hair out and sat beside him again on the malt sacks and ran her fingers through his hair. Beads of sweat lingered on his forehead. Today, he'd desired her greatly. Today she'd paraded naked for him. Seeing her naked body excited him more than she had realised. At last she knew what lit his candles.

'Tell me, Uncle Elijah,' she said kittenishly, 'who do you enjoy making love to most – me or Dorcas?'

'Why d'you want to know that?' he answered drowsily.

'Because I do. Tell me.'

'It makes no odds to you.'

'How do you know what makes odds to me?'

'Because I don't see as it matters. I like doing it with you. But I like doing it with Dorcas as well.'

'Do you love Dorcas?'

'Course I love Dorcas.' He sat up, put his feet to the floor and tucked in his shirt and hitched up his trousers.

She remained sitting on the sacks, her knees drawn up. She began rocking to and fro like a schoolgirl, her arms around her knees.

'How can you love her if you're not faithful to her?'

'Easy. Like I said, I enjoy doing it with you.'

'Do you love me then?'

'Not in the way you mean.' He dusted off his trousers with the flats of his hands.

'Do you love me at all?' She sounded slighted now.

Her persistent questions irritated him; they were so puerile, so immature. Why could she not just accept that what they did was for pleasure? For them to become emotionally entangled was taboo. 'I'm your uncle, Ramona. You're my flesh and blood. I love you like an uncle. I happen to like you as well, but don't get any daft ideas that I'm in love with you.'

'Well, I don't think it's such a daft idea. How d'you know I'm not in love with you?'

'I hope to Christ you're not, Ramona. You'd better get any such stupid notions out of your head.'

'Why? Just because I'm your niece?'

'Yes – because you're my niece.'

'What if I wasn't your niece? What then?'

'But you are, so what's the point in saying "if"?'

'Clover isn't your niece,' she remarked huffily. 'Do you love her?'

'What's Clover got to do with anything? Come on, back to work now. You're getting on my nerves with your barmy questions – and insinuations.'

'Funny how you always turn funny when I mention Clover,' she pouted, sliding off the bags and following him to the top of the stairs. 'Do you like doing it with Clover as well?' she goaded, persisting with the fixation that still tainted her reasoning.

His back was towards her as he approached the stairs and he rolled his eyes in annoyance. Ramona he genuinely liked but her immaturity was leading him to wonder whether his involvement was worth all the hassle. She could be trouble – big trouble. Sometimes she seemed as unstable as nitroglycerine and liable to explode at any moment. The consequences could be disastrous. Trouble was, he was in it up to his neck. One word from her to Jake that he had made advances towards her, that he had taken her against her will... Maybe it was time to make a tactical withdrawal. Get out while the going was good. So far, they had both come through it unscathed. Better not push their luck any further.

Besides, there was Dorcas to consider...

Clover called in at Tom's studio on her way home from work that evening. He'd been working in his darkroom and when she arrived he was hanging some prints up to dry on a line that was strung up between two walls. He was in shirt sleeves, his collar detached at the front and he looked preoccupied.

'Hello,' he said coolly.

'Oh, Tom, everybody loves my engagement ring,' she trilled and held it out in front of her admiringly for the umpteenth time that day. 'Lucy's really envious. She says she keeps dropping hints to her Harold, but to no avail. Not yet at any rate.'

'Mmm,' he muttered and craned his neck to scrutinise a portrait he'd taken earlier that day.

'Oh, and Sarah Mansell reckons she's getting engaged on August Bank Holiday Monday. I think it's catching all of a sudden, this getting engaged... And one of the girls in Bedding says she's getting married at Christmas ... I can see you're busy, Tom. Shall I make a cup of tea?'

He shrugged indifferently. 'If you like.'

'You don't seem very bothered.'

'I said, if you like,' he answered brusquely. 'If you want one, make one. You know where the kettle and the teapot are.'

'Blimey, who's pee'd in your hypo?' Her mood instantly changed to match his. 'No, I don't think I'll bother if you're in a mood.'

He shrugged again and pegged up another print, avoiding her eyes.

'If you're too busy to talk to me I'll go...' She hesitated, puzzled, awaiting his response.

None came.

'Do you want me to go?' Her feelings were unquestionably hurt. She headed for the door, opened it, hesitated and turned to look at him, disconcertedly. 'Shall I see you later, Tom?... Tom?'

'I'm not sure...'

A cold shudder of foreboding ran down her spine. After all the happiness of yesterday, suddenly something was wrong. Something had happened. Last night when he left her she'd dismissed his detachment as the result of too much drink, but maybe it had not been the alcohol. Somehow she must have upset him. But how? She was not aware of anything she'd done that might make him displeased. With her hand resting on the handle she remained by the door, looking anxiously at him, trying to work out why he was so unexpectedly cold towards her.

'Why are you not sure?' she asked, her voice

256

even. 'What's wrong, Tom? What is it? What's happened?'

He hung up the final print, picked up a piece of rag and dried his hands. 'Spare me the pretence that you don't know, Clover.' He was trying to maintain an outward calm but his voice was thick with emotion and resentment.

'Know what?' she said. 'What is it I'm supposed to know? What's happened, Tom? Why are you so offish with me? What have I done?' Her heart was beating fast, her mind was awhirl with events last night, trying to recall some incident, any incident that might have triggered such coldness. But all she could recall were feelings of joy and contentment, geniality and everybody's kindness and good wishes.

'Clover, I've always tried to be fair with you. I've always tried to be considerate and caring.'

'Always you have been, Tom, yes–'

'Well, maybe you've mistaken that for soft-ness... Maybe I am a soft touch, Clover, but don't ever fall into the trap of thinking I'm stupid.'

She opened her mouth to speak but no words came. What was he driving at? What point was he trying to make? 'I don't know what you're talking about, Tom,' she uttered eventually. 'If I've done something to offend you, I apologise. But you'd best tell me what it is, because I can't imagine what. I can't stand you looking at me with such scorn when I'm not aware I've done anything wrong.'

His chest heaved with a great shuddering sigh and she discerned his anguish.

A marmalade cat stalked cautiously along the

top of the high wall outside, picking its way between the treacherous shards of cemented-on glass that were intended to deter trespassers and thieves.

'What about Elijah?' he said contemptuously.

'What about Elijah?' she replied with a puzzled frown.

'Oh, don't look so damned innocent. I know there's something going on between you two.' There. It was out. 'God, I'm only glad I saw it when I did – before it was too late.'

She uttered a gasp of disbelief then looked at him, her incredulity manifest in her eyes. 'You think–' Her legs were weak all of a sudden, drained by the shock and disappointment of his monstrous accusation. She moved over to the *chaise-longue* and sat down. How should she phrase her next words for maximum impact? Whatever she might say could affect their whole future relationship, however she said it. But in her unforeseen and absolute distress no words would come to protect her, to make her future safe. She just looked at him in horror, her eyes wide, her mouth open in disbelief that he did not trust her, that for some reason known only to him he could not trust her. How could he possibly consider her incapable of fidelity and virtue when all she ever wanted was to spend the rest of her life only with him and bear his children? Hot tears welled up in her eyes and trembled for a second on her eyelashes before trickling down the gentle curves of her cheeks.

'You think that of *me?*' she said, her face an icon of anguish. 'After all we've done together, after

258

all we've said to each other – after all the promises we've made?'

'Actions speak louder than words, Clover. I've seen how you look at him, how you touch him ... how you kiss him. Well, I don't intend to compete. Have him and I wish you the best of luck.' There was acid in his tone, scorn ... and grief.

Clover perceived the grief first and it gave her hope. She looked into his eyes, got to her feet and walked towards him. 'I don't know what demons have got into you, Tom, but how can you possibly think that of me?' Tears continued to run down her face, yet although she made no effort to stem them, neither did she make a great show of sobbing. 'Ever since we met I've entertained thoughts of no other man but you. When I sleep at night I dream of you. In the daytime you're always with me – when I eat, when I drink, when I work. You are on my mind constantly – never out of my thoughts. My only ambition is to be your wife, to look after you, to have your children. I live for you, Tom ... I would die for you ... How can you think otherwise after all we have been to each other?'

The peaceful tick of the real marble clock on the sham, theatrical mantelpiece of the studio falsified the strong undercurrent of emotion that was swirling between them.

'Clover, I know what I see.' He did not look at her.

'God alone knows what you see, Tom,' she said, her voice soft, steady now. 'But whatever you see, you're getting a horrible, distorted view.'

'I see what I see. It hurts like hell, but I know what I see.'

She stood close and took his hand, filled with sympathy for him, bitterly sorry that he was plaguing himself with such arrant nonsense. When he did not flinch away from the contact she felt encouraged, but she shook her head, hardly able to conceive that this was happening to them.

'What can I say to reassure you?' she entreated. 'There is nothing between Elijah Tandy and me. Hell, he has Dorcas. What man would want more? But I like Elijah...'

'Huh!' he sneered.

'Tom, I'm not ashamed to say I like him because it's the truth. But he's not for me, and that's the truth as well.'

'I only wish I could believe that...'

'He's a ladies' man. I'm in love with you, Tom. Not Elijah. Never Elijah. Oh, you might have seen me flirt with him, fuss him up a bit, but that's bravado. It means nothing. Of course I don't love him...You *know* I don't love him. I love *you.*'

He gave a great shuddering sigh.

'How long have you harboured this stupid perception, Tom? How long?'

'Not long.'

'*How* long?'

He shrugged. 'It was especially noticeable last night.'

'Last night? All this has come on since last night? God! The happiest moment of my life was last night!'

'Not just since last night,' he felt he had to say; he did not want to give the impression it had been triggered by something Ramona had said. 'But last night you went off with Ned Brisco in that damn motor car he's got... Then you were touching Elijah and you kissed him in exactly the way you kiss me sometimes. It spoke volumes, Clover.'

She let go his hand, self-righteous anger welling up inside her now. She was utterly innocent of everything he alleged. He was being stupid. It vexed her that he could see something that patently did not exist.

'I feel insulted,' she said softly, trying to disguise her pique. 'I feel insulted that you should think so low of me.' She took a deep breath and wrestled, not only with the engagement ring on her finger, but with her anger also that was mounting inexorably. Now there was only one way to make him see. 'Here... Have your ring back. I don't want it unless you can come to your senses.'

She placed the ring on the table in front of him and turned the other way. Without looking back, she picked up her basket, opened the door and left.

Outside, she walked twenty yards. She felt hot and queasy. She was breathing hard from the shock of it all. She stopped and sat on the front doorstep of a house to garner her thoughts. She was in half a mind to return to Tom's studio to try and reason with him further, to try and make him see how ridiculous his notion was. But her inborn common sense told her it would do no good. In his present state of mind he was beyond reasoning. Never before had she known him so blinkered and so irrational. Normally, he was the absolute soul of logic and moderation – and tenderness as well. But this change in him made her so angry. His accusations were just too pathetic. Hard though it might be, the only way forward was to leave him be and allow him time to come round to seeing sense. It was up to him. She could do no more ... except perhaps pray to God that He might exert some pressure on him – and soon.

Chapter Fifteen

Clover served in the taproom that evening alongside Jake. Naturally, she was preoccupied. The strife that had so unexpectedly flared between herself and Tom had astonished her. Consequently, she avoided conversation and only smiled politely at those patrons who pleasantly passed a few kind comments to her, as some were wont to do. Ramona seemed to keep her distance too, as if she knew instinctively of her pre-occupation. Nearly everybody congratulated her on her engagement and nobody seemed to notice that she wasn't wearing her engagement ring. Leastwise, nobody mentioned it. Most probably they imagined she'd taken it off to save it getting tarnished while she worked.

262

Tom, she hoped, would come to his senses and call for her later, full of apologies, and the sooner the better. He would need to apologise too; such an accusation as he'd made was ludicrous and hurtful. So each time the door from the passage opened she would look up eagerly to see whether it was him arriving. She had never felt so miserable. May it endure only a short time. Let him come and say he was sorry so they could resume their lives and restore their accord to the sublimity they enjoyed before his unfounded suspicions marred everything. Naturally, she would forgive him.

Where had he picked up this stupid notion about her and Elijah? Never before had he shown any tendency towards jealousy, for he knew he had no reason to be jealous. If he had been that way inclined, then surely any jealousy would have been directed at Ned Brisco – and long before now. And yet... And yet he had been displeased that she'd gone for a ride with him in his new motor car... Or, maybe, he was envious that Ned had got a motor car. But this ridiculous idea about her and Elijah... But of course, Tom had been let down before. That girl called Maud, from Brierley Hill... He was bound to be wary of it happening again and who could blame him? But she was not like Maud. She would rather die than make a cuckold of Tom.

The door opened again but Sol Bennett entered, a miner who lived in Cromwell Street. She sighed, a disappointed sigh, but waltzed over to where he sat and took his order. Again the door opened and Harry Heppenstall, one of

Ramona's admirers, stalked in. He would be disappointed tonight; Ramona had gone out again, meeting some other chap, presumably. Pity. They seemed well enough suited, she and Harry Heppenstall. Still, there was time yet... She was free...

The taproom was noisy with raucous laughter, the chink of glasses and a dozen conversations. If only some of it would rub off on her. Smoke wafted about in a pungent, blue mist and Jake opened the sash of the front window to let in some fresh air. The door opened again ... Ben Jenkins and Obadiah Brookes, pigeon fanciers. Normally they drank over the road in the California. Maybe the beer there was off.

Why did Tom not come?

Somebody tapped the hatch and Clover answered it. A small boy handed her two empty whisky bottles and asked for them to be filled with bitter. She'd seen him before but did not know who he was.

'For your dad?'

'No, me granddad – and me mom. I ai' got e'er a dad.'

She summoned a sympathetic smile and took the bottles from him. When she'd placed a funnel into the neck of the first she thrust it under the beer tap and pulled twice on the pump. Each pull drew a half pint. She gave an extra short pull for good measure, refitted the cork and stuck the mandatory neck label over it, then repeated the procedure with the other bottle. The boy handed her a shilling and she gave him his change.

Oh, where was Tom?

Sam Jeavons scuffled in, his face hanging dolefully beneath his greasy cap, with his walking-stick and smelly dog. As he sat down he poked the dog into lying under the settle at the side of the fire grate with his stick and ordered a pint of mild. Noah Fairfax and Urban Tranter appeared, quarrelling as usual, followed immediately by Teddy Guest, the local bobby who was off-duty tonight. The Jolly Collier was getting busy, but where, where was Tom?

The hands of the huge railway clock on the opposite wall to the beer pumps registered half past ten. Tom would not come now. But still she looked up expectantly whenever the door opened. Eleven o'clock ... half past ... midnight. Most of the customers had drifted away, including Harry Heppenstall.

'I'm going to bed now, Pop, if that's all right. Do you mind?'

'Carry on, flower,' Jake said. 'There's just a few glasses to wash and dry. I can manage the rest.

Clover took an oil lamp from the scullery and went upstairs to bed, bitterly disappointed that Tom had not shown. With anger and sadness dwelling symbiotically inside her she undressed herself, realising this problem was more serious than she had at first thought. She was certain he would come to his senses and seek her out; but she'd hoped it would be tonight. She did not believe he would allow things to fester for more than a day, for he would be suffering the same pangs as she. So there was always tomorrow. When he'd slept on it he would realise how ridiculous a notion it was he was harbouring. If

265

he was so serious about it he must have been tormenting himself. Why did he have to put himself through it so unnecessarily? Why did he have to put them both through so much emotional strife over nothing? Damn Maud and her infidelity that was clouding his judgement, making him believe she was capable of the same.

By Saturday Tom Doubleday had still not come to make his apologies. Clover passed his studio every day going to and from work but she was not feeling inclined yet to make any move towards reconciliation. He had created the problem, let him be first to make an approach. That Saturday morning it broke her heart to walk past his studio and she wondered whether he was watching her, hiding behind the velvet curtain of his lobby. She did not dare look. If he was watching, she wanted to appear as nonchalant, as unfazed as possible. Why should she allow him the satisfaction of believing she was grieving mightily, even though it was true? Fortunately, it was not possible to see that her heart was beating faster, that she was aching for him to appear. It was not possible to see by her outward demeanour how much she needed him to fold her in his arms and beg her forgiveness for being so mindlessly stupid.

Maybe today he would come and seek her while she was working. He seldom worked on a Saturday after one o'clock, unless he had to take photos at a wedding. Dinner-time was most likely. If he arrived, her expression must not betray her joy and relief. As the time approached she cast her eyes frequently towards the main entrance of the store. Lucy noticed and asked if she was expecting Tom, but she smiled wistfully and said, 'I wish.'

The clock on the sales floor showed one o'clock and Clover went into the staff room and put on her hat and coat. She picked up her basket and went outside. She waited, scanning heads for sight of Tom, among the hundreds of folk who were walking High Street. For five minutes she waited. There was no sign. She was fooling herself if she thought he was about to appear today when he'd had nearly all week. Besides, she felt conspicuous in front of all her workmates who would be able to see her. So she set off to walk the town, hoping she might meet him accidentally. She crossed to the other side of the street, for that was the side he generally used. A flotilla of trams moving in both directions clanked their bells and cleaved their way through the hoards of shoppers that crowded the town's streets every Saturday. If Clover did happen to catch sight of Tom it would be a miracle with all those folk about.

She had not walked more than twenty yards when she felt a tap on her shoulder and her heart leapt.

'Clover. Fancy seeing you.'

'Elijah!' She tried not to show her disappointment that it was not Tom, so forced a bright smile. 'What brings you up here?'

'I've just been to get me hair cut.' He stroked the top of his head to confirm the fact and her eyes were naturally drawn to his hair that was shiny with fresh brilliantine. 'I was just on me way to the Little Barrel for a drink afore I go to meet Dorcas. Care to join me?'

She looked around just to make sure Tom had not shown up after all. 'If you like. I was just idling my time, window shopping.'

She turned around and shuffled alongside him on the crowded pavement. The Little Barrel stood directly opposite Cook's and in no time they were walking across the threshold where the buzz of conversation, the customary smell of stale beer and cigarette smoke greeted them. The Little Barrel was a busy town pub, noisy, small and cosy, with the barrels of beer lined up on a stillage behind the bar.

'Do you often use this pub?' she queried.

'I know the landlord. He keeps a decent pint. I generally come in here of a Saturday. Sometimes with Dorcas of a night. Shall we go in the smoke room? We shan't get a seat in the bar.'

'Lead the way,' she said.

The smoke room was less crowded with seats available. There were women in there too, so Clover didn't feel quite so conspicuous.

'What d'you fancy to drink, Clover?'

'Oh, just a half of shandy, please, Elijah.'

'Not a pint?' he said with a gleam in his eye.

'You wouldn't care if I was all bloated and running off to the privy all afternoon, would you?' she said, laughing.

While she sat down at a small cast-iron table with a wooden top he stood at the bar and appropriated their drinks. He returned, put hers on the table and sat facing her.

'Thanks,' she said and sipped it.

'Cheers!' He took a goodly slurp from his pint glass and smacked his lips. 'I like this India pale ale, you know, Clover. By God, we used to shift some of this stuff when we was over there. Course, it was that hot we used to sweat it all out right away. Never got drunk, you know.'

'Never?' she asked knowingly.

He grinned and looked into her eyes. 'Well, sometimes... Not on this stuff, though, generally on gin mixed with Indian tonic. I got quite a taste for that when I was in India.'

'What sort of food do they eat in India, Elijah? I understand it's very spicy.'

'It's bloody hot. Hot and spicy. To mask the off-flavours of the meat, some say. It's hard to keep meat fresh for long out there, it's so hot, you see.'

'Ugh!'

'No... Don't knock it, Clover. I tell you, I got quite addicted to curries when I was in India. Pity we can't get your mother to cook us some. I bet you could get most of the spices to do it.'

Clover laughed. 'Can you imagine my mother? She'd be pulling her jib all ways if she'd got to cook something like that. Why don't you get Dorcas to cook them for you?'

'I intend to. When we'm married...'

'Oh? Is there likely to be a wedding soon then?' She picked up her glass and took another drink.

'Well, it's time I made an honest woman of her, Clover. We've been engaged now since Adam was a lad and she reckons it's high time. She's getting a bit broody. Wants to start a family.'

'So, how soon is this going to take place? I'll

269

need a new outfit.'

'Next month.'

'Next month?' she repeated incredulously. 'Nobody's mentioned it.'

'Nobody knows, Clover. You're the first I've told.'

'How come?'

'I've only just decided. In the last week. I want it done quick now I've made me mind up. So I've been this morning to see about a licence – before I got me hair cut.'

Clover smiled with pleasure for him. 'Can I be the first to congratulate you? I'm sure you'll be very happy. I think Dorcas is a very lucky lady...'

'Thank you.' He slurped his beer and lit a cigarette.

'So where are you going to live?'

'Oh, it's all fixed. I'm buying Jake's old house.'

'Oh, it's you, is it? And Dorcas doesn't mind?'

'Dorcas loves the place. She spends enough time there already.' He gave her a wink and Clover knew exactly what he meant. 'Oh, there's things she wants done, but any woman would be the same, I reckon. Women like to put their own stamp on a place, don't they?'

She nodded. 'It's only natural. So when are you going to announce it?'

'I'm biding my time, Clover. I want to spring it on'em at the right moment. So can you keep it to yourself for a bit?'

She laughed. 'Course I can, but it's a tall order. You'll have to let me know what you'd like as a wedding present.'

'Nothing expensive. You save your money for

your own wedding. So what about you and Tom, eh? When are you getting spliced?'

She shrugged and a sad look clouded her eyes. 'It was to have been next May – a year from now... Now I don't know... Maybe never, the way things are going...'

'You and Tom?' he scoffed. 'Pull the other one. I've never seen a couple more suited than you pair. And you tell me maybe never? Pah!'

She sighed profoundly and he knew by the look in her eyes that it was no exaggeration. 'It's true, Elijah. Since we got engaged I've seen him once. And that was to have a row...'

'Row over what, for God's sake?'

She shrugged. 'A misunderstanding.'

'His or yours?'

'Oh, his.' Tears began to flood her eyes and she tried to shove them back. 'I have my own standpoint. I just wish he could see it.'

Elijah puffed on his cigarette and wafted the smoke away with his hand. 'Well, if it's a misunderstanding I'm sure you'll soon get it all back on track. Why don't you make the first move?'

'But it's not up to me to make the first move, Elijah. If you knew what he'd accused me of, you'd know it was all up to him.'

'So what's he accused you of? Infidelity, I suppose.'

She nodded. 'Can you believe it? Me?'

'And who's he accused you of being unfaithful with?'

She was twisting her glass round and round, her eyes transfixed to the amber liquid within.

'I'd rather not say.'

Elijah moved his stool closer to Clover and leaned towards her. 'If he can't see that you'm the girl least likely to go off with anybody, of all the women he knows, then he must have shit in his eyes,' he said, his voice low. 'And, to be honest, if he thinks no more of you than that, then he don't deserve you. Think on that, Clover.'

She sighed. 'Thanks. But it doesn't help much right now. I'm in love with him and I suppose I always shall be. I just wish he'd come to his senses.' Her voice was ragged with hurt feelings and a tear rolled down her cheek. She pulled a handkerchief from inside her sleeve and wiped it away.

'He was engaged before, you know. A girl called Maud. She was having it off with his best friend unbeknowns and got pregnant...'

'I understand him, Clover. Once bitten, twice shy.'

'But I'm not like that. Surely he can see that?'

'Do you want me to have a word with him?' he asked softly, kindly.

'God, no,' she replied with alarm, dabbing her eyes. 'I reckon that would make matters worse – anybody seen as interfering...'

He nodded. 'It was just a thought. If I can help you I will. You know that.' He reached out and put his hand briefly on hers in a gesture of sympathy. 'I don't like to see anybody put in the wrong, specially when I'm fond of that person myself. If there's anything I can do to help, just be sure to let me know ... I mean it, you know.'

She forced a smile. 'Thanks, Elijah.' She tucked her handkerchief back up her sleeve. 'I appreciate your offer, but we have to sort this out ourselves, Tom and me.'

He flicked his cigarette ash into the ashtray on the table. 'I thought I hadn't seen Tom about for a few days. Dorcas was talking about having him to take some wedding pictures for us. I expect you'll be back together by then...'

'I hope and pray...' She nodded and smiled into his eyes, revealing the dejection that was brimming in her own.

'Well, if not, he wants his bloody head looking.'

Tom Doubleday had agonised as much as Clover over his accusations. Since Tuesday he had thought of little else. Ramona's insinuations had plagued him and continued to plague him. But over this last four days or so he'd had the opportunity, alone at night, to ponder on Clover's positive attributes. There is an old saying that first impressions are always right and Tom recalled his first impressions of Clover. Those attributes that were immediately evident induced him to fall head over heels in love with her before they'd even exchanged a word. Gentleness, honesty, candour, forthrightness, were all qualities that applied to her. The question now was, which view of her was correct? She could not be honest and candid if she were enjoying a secret affair with Elijah Tandy; she could hardly be considered forthright if she had lied. He had to rely on his own judgement. In her favour, she always appeared guileless and truthful. But his judgement was known to be impaired. Maud too had seemed guileless and truthful – and look at the heartache she wrought.

Tom knew of course the times when Clover was due to pass his studio on her way to and from work. Every time he watched out for her, concealed behind the thick velvet curtain that adorned the window of his lobby. Every time he saw her, and this Saturday morning had been no exception. She had walked past on the other side of Hall Street and had not even deigned to look in his direction. Perhaps she was untouched by it all, indifferent, which was understandable if there was a liaison with Elijah.

Tom missed Clover. He missed her warmth, her pleasantness, her love. It was possible that he was entirely wrong about this, that Ramona too was mistaken. What a fool he would be if he tossed aside the chance to have this girl, whom his first impressions told him was his ideal, on the mistaken word of somebody else.

He had to see Clover again.

He had to talk to her. He could not settle till he had settled it. So, when he got rid of his last customer at ten minutes to two he locked up and strode towards Cook's, which was only four or five minutes walk away. Her dinner breaks were never constant, he knew that; they depended on how involved she was with serving a customer, who else was taking a break, how busy they were. But he might be lucky. He might just catch her coming out of Cook's. On the other hand, he could just as easily go inside to see her and ask her to meet him later. One way or the other he would get it straightened out today.

High Street was heaving with folk and, as he turned into it, he found himself at once caught in the bustle, constantly side-stepping to avoid brushing and knocking people. He crossed the road to Cook's, dodging a pony and trap, and looked around him before entering the store.

He caught sight of Clover leaving the Little Barrel opposite – but with Elijah. His heart went in his mouth. So there was truth in Ramona's words and his own subsequent perceptions after all. An eternal amount of truth. Actions, as he had said, speak louder than words. As he tried to meld back into the crowd unseen he witnessed how she stood on tiptoe to plant a farewell kiss on his lips, and he knew. He knew finally that she was beyond his reach.

He walked on, devastated, to Stafford Street, and home.

Their meetings at the house in Brooke Street had evolved into a sort of game where, if Ramona arrived first, she would go straight to bed and wait for her Uncle Elijah. He would then arrive like a furtive lover and sneak into the house and into the bed to end up beside her. It was a game they both enjoyed even when their roles were reversed.

Not so today. Ramona remained alone in that old bed, in that big house, for too long. Elijah had realised the folly of his ways. It was time to fight shy of that little liaison and concentrate his time and effort on Dorcas, who was a more worthy cause. The only difficulty he foresaw was explain-

275

ing to Ramona that it was all over between them without inducing her to do or say something stupid that would incriminate them both. That, however, was a minefield he would negotiate when he had to.

So, at the same time that Tom Doubleday was turning his back on Clover and Elijah – about two o'clock – Ramona Tandy gave up hope of enjoying her promised hour or two of horizontal pleasure and pushed back the bedclothes disconsolately. She threw on her clothes, pulled on her boots, donned her hat and made her way home, prodigiously irked that she should be so scorned.

With every step she grew more disgruntled. Never had she known anybody blow hot and cold like Elijah did. It was so confusing. Their last sexual encounter, on Wednesday, had been full of promise for the future. He couldn't keep his hands off her then and she had naturally assumed it would be like that from then on. She had nurtured hopes of ousting Dorcas to become his only true love. Now, just a few days later, he couldn't even be bothered to show up. Well, she would show him who was the more pleasurable in bed. She knew now what lit his wick. She knew it better than ever.

A means of stimulating his interest yet again began to take shape in her mind... A little more titillation was required, and she thought she saw a way of providing it.

Chapter Sixteen

On the Monday afternoon, Ramona made her excuses and left the Jolly Collier with the express intention of calling upon Tom Doubleday at his studio. Having been told so much about it by Clover, and having seen photos that were taken there in what looked like a stately home, she was intrigued to see it. It must be really something.

The weather remained sunny but some ominous clouds loomed and, typical for late May, the winds were getting up strong. The May blossom, blown from the trees that flanked Dixon's Green, eddied like confetti at the junction with Cross Guns Street at the Fountain Inn. There had been no opportunity to speak with Elijah, to ascertain why he had not shown up at the house on Saturday, when he knew as well as she did that their trysts there were due to be curtailed. She had tried to get close and say something on the Saturday evening just after tea, but he'd whispered, 'Not now, Ramona,' out of the side of his mouth and offered no word since. Well, he would be quick enough to talk to her soon.

She entered the anteroom of Tom's studio, knocked on the counter and waited for him to appear. Some beautiful photographs were on display and she pored over them. A couple were of children, several of self-conscious young women posing with wide eyes and coy smiles, including one of Clover. Men, too, had their pictures taken if this gallery was anything to go by and Ramona inspected them closely to ascertain whether she fancied any of them.

Presently, the door to the studio opened and Tom led out a very pretty girl and another woman, evidently her mother. 'Ramona. Fancy seeing you,' he greeted. Then he turned to the women who were just leaving. 'Thank you Mrs Foley, Miss Foley. I'll have the photos ready to collect by Friday. Thank you very much indeed.' He turned back to Ramona. 'Well, Ramona. How's this? Come inside, into the studio.'

She followed him in and looked about her, surprised at how very light it was in there; far lighter than she'd imagined. The whole wall to the outside was glazed, as was part of the roof above it, yet it was not overlooked from outside. She recognised the stately home section that provided the background in Clover's photos and was disappointed to see it was merely painted onto the back wall. She saw the various tables and whatnots and the *chaise-longue* and smiled to herself when she spotted the bearskin rug that Clover claimed they lay on when they made love... Well... If only it could talk...

'Would you like a cup of tea, Ramona?'

'Oh, no, Tom, thank you.' She smiled pertly. 'I don't want to put you to any trouble.'

'It's no trouble. If you're not in a rush, I'm certainly not. I've nobody coming now till after four.'

'Coffee then please... If you've got some.'

'I've got a bottle of Camp. I'll only be a minute.

278

Make yourself comfortable.'

She sat on the *chaise-longue* while he went out into his room at the back where she heard him fiddling about. When he re-emerged she said, 'I haven't see you lately, Tom. And I venture to say that as far as I can make out, I don't think Clover's seen you either, has she?'

He smiled wistfully and collected together some photographic plates that were cluttering a work table. 'You're right, Ramona. I think ours must be the shortest engagement on record.'

'I'm ever so sorry, Tom.'

'No, no...' He waved away her apology. 'I have you to thank, Ramona. If it hadn't been for your warnings I... Well, it's a good job you had the courage to tell me what was going on. It must have taken some courage. It's been hard to swallow but I'm in no doubt as to the truth of it. Especially after Saturday.'

'Oh? So what happened Saturday?'

'I saw them together. Clover and Elijah.' He shrugged, revealing his despondency. 'They'd just left the Little Barrel in High Street. About two o'clock I suppose it was. He must have arranged to meet her for a drink in her dinner break.'

'Fancy,' Ramona replied. The catch in her voice could have given away her resentment but Tom didn't hear it. She concealed well her annoyance that whilst she was languishing in bed, waiting for Elijah, Clover had already commandeered his attention in the Little Barrel. The realisation did not sit well with her. It made her even more determined to win him.

Tom tilted his head towards the door of his darkroom. 'I can hear the kettle boiling... How much sugar?'

'One teaspoon, please.'

He disappeared into the darkroom with his photographic plates and she looked about her once more. His business must be lucrative if he had paid for all this. Photographic equipment was expensive and not limited to just a camera, even she understood that. There were enlargers, chemicals, plates and special papers to pay for, and God knows what else. And Tom always dressed well – he *always* looked so...

He reappeared carrying two steaming mugs of coffee.

'Here we are then...' He handed her a mug and she took it. 'So...' He sipped his own then looked at her with his professional smile. 'To what do I owe the pleasure of a visit from the lovely Ramona?'

'I'd like you to take some photos of me, Tom.'

'Well, that's easy, and it'll be a pleasure. Did you have anything special in mind?'

She sipped her coffee and as she tilted her head forward, the brim of her hat shielded her face from his eyes. 'I'd like some nude photos done, Tom, to tell you the truth,' she said and looked up into his eyes directly, challengingly.

He nearly dropped his mug. 'Nude?'

'Yes. Does that... Does it trouble you?'

'God, no.' He slurped his coffee and put down the mug. 'It's just that... Well, to be frank, I don't get many requests for nude photographs. Not bona fide ones at any rate. And you're the last person… Are you certain?'

She nodded, smiling at his incredulity and his innate reserve.

'So when do you want it done?'

'Well, you said there's nobody else coming till four. There's no time like the present. And the light seems good.'

He coughed and looked at the uncertain sky through the roof lights. 'The light, yes. The light's fine…'

He was suddenly more nervous than she was. It had taken some neck for her to come here and request this but, now she'd got this far, typically forcing herself to be bold, the worst was over. And it was just a customer-client relationship after all… Still, it would be interesting to see his reaction when she stripped off.

'Maybe I should lock the door from the lobby,' he suggested.

'Yes, maybe that would be a good idea.' She took a drink from her mug while he did it. When he sat down again they talked more, about nothing in particular. Eventually, he asked her why she wanted some nude photos taken.

'It's a birthday present to myself,' she said convincingly. 'I'll be nineteen on Thursday–'

'Damn, I'd forgotten it was your birthday, Ramona.'

She smiled warmly. 'I want to satisfy my own curiosity as to how I really look as well,' she continued to explain, to justify her unusual request. She finished her coffee, put down her mug and got up from the *chaise-longue*. 'Where should I undress?'

'Oh... The screen. Here...' There was a screen at one end of the room. He went to it and opened it up. 'Please... Behind here.'

She smiled coyly at him as she disappeared.

He watched her hat appear on top of the screen as he fiddled with his plate camera, setting it up; then her coat, her skirt, her blouse, her underwear, her stockings... A minute or two later she emerged at the side of the screen looking surprisingly unabashed.

'I'm ready.'

He looked up. Oh, God! Oh, *God!* He gulped and attempted a friendly smile to put her at her ease, but realised he was the more nervous of the two and needed putting at ease more than she did. He tried not to allow his eyes to linger on her but it was impossible.

'Shall we try the *chaise-longue?*' he asked awkwardly. Realising it sounded rather suggestive, he tried to disguise his question and uttered: 'Or ... or would you prefer some pictures standing first?'

'Standing, if you like,' she answered easily. 'Where do you want me?'

God! Now *she* was at it. 'Oh, over here... Let's try this whatnot as a foil, shall we?'

'How should I stand?'

He shrugged. 'How do you want to look? Bashful? Brazen?'

She laughed. 'I suppose I'll end up looking bashful, trying to be brazen. I think you'd better come and show me what to do with my arms. How best to pose.'

He approached her, his heart thumping like a drum. She had the most exquisite figure, petite but in perfect proportion. He had never realised. Her breasts perked up deliciously and her skin looked as smooth as cream. Her legs were slender and unblemished with delightful feminine curves and the gentle arc of her narrow hips drew his eye inwards, inevitably, to the pretty tuft of curly hair that flourished below the flat of her stomach. He gulped.

'Try putting your weight on your left leg to thrust your right hip out...' His throat was as dry as hell, his tongue furry. 'That's good. Now lean slightly back and raise your arm above your head... Yes, that looks very attractive, Ramona. Hold that and I'll focus you.'

She held the pose like a professional artiste. He focused, inserted a plate and squeezed the shutter release.

'That should be good.'

'I'll turn around for the next one. You can photograph my bum.' She chuckled at that as she turned around.

He laughed with her. 'Why not?... If you don't mind me saying so, you have a very pretty bum, Ramona.'

'Thank you.' She smiled to herself. *He* always said that, Elijah. Maybe there was some truth in it.

He changed the plate and clicked the shutter. 'I'd like to get in a bit closer, Ramona. There are marks in your thighs where your garters have been, and I can crop them out of the frame,' he explained. 'There are marks around your waist as well where your underwear's been clipping you. We could wait till they disappear but it could take

283

an hour or more. By which time...'

'Oh.' She sounded disappointed. 'I never thought.'

'It doesn't matter. We can hide them with something – an ostrich feather, for instance...' Several stood in an urn on the floor and he reached over, picked one out and handed it to her.

She took it and positioned it in front of her provocatively, but it worked and hid the garment impressions in her skin. 'There. How's that?' she asked, posing in profile now.

'Have you done this before?' he commented. 'You're very good.'

'Never for photographs,' she said with a suggestive gleam in her eye.

He clicked the shutter for another photo as casually as he knew how and laughed as if he were a man of the world and unshockable. 'How many pictures do you want? That's three.'

'Another couple?' she said. 'I'd like one of me lying on the *chaise-longue.*'

'Fine by me. I'll need to move the camera.'

Gracefully, she glided over to the *chaise-longue* and sat on it, reclining. 'Will this end panel go down, Tom?'

''Fraid not. But that's fine. You look very relaxed ... and very sensual, if you don't mind me saying so.'

It was exactly what she wanted to hear. She smiled to herself and said, 'I'll take that as a compliment. Shall I hold the pose?'

He nodded and felt himself getting hotter with the exertion of working with this naked young woman with as fine a figure as he'd ever imagined – who was not in the least bashful in his presence. He hid his head under the black cloth and focused the camera, then inserted a new plate. 'Right. Hold that, Ramona.' He pressed the shutter release.

'Can I have one taken on the bearskin rug now, d'you think? A last one. That should be enough then.'

'As you wish, Ramona...'

She got up from the *chaise-longue* and crept over to the bearskin rug like a lithe young cat. She lay on it, on her side, facing him, her arm propping up her head.

'How does this look?' she asked, deliberately fishing for another compliment.

'No, not on your side, Ramona. That doesn't show you at your best.' He went over to her and stooped down beside her. 'On your back... Right, now raise the top half of your body... Prop yourself up by your arms... That's it, elbows on the rug, but behind you. Now arch your back and throw your head back... Oh, that's classical, Ramona!' Her long fair hair cascaded down behind her appealingly. 'You look gorgeous. You should see how that emphasises the line of your neck relative to your breasts and...' He knew he was breathing harder but tried hard to keep it under control. This young woman was, after all, a client. 'Just raise your leg a little, the one furthest from me... Yes ... toes pointing downwards ... that's fine. Can you hold that?'

He returned to his camera, hotter than ever. It would have been so easy to touch her, to feel her smooth skin. But he could never allow himself to. She was his client... He could have made it appear accidental, a professional tweaking of her pose, but what if she'd been suspicious of his motive? Besides, he could never take advantage of a girl in this position without a chaperone. That would be too unprofessional, too un-gentlemanly. He checked his focus again in the ground glass screen at the back of his camera and savoured secretly the sight of her naked body and the thought of running his hands over her. Did she realise how desirable she really was, the effect she was having on him? He popped in a new plate. 'Ready now, Ramona.' He squeezed the shutter release.

'There. That's it.' He removed the plate and placed it with the rest.

She got up and headed for the screen. 'Thank you, Tom. I'll get dressed now...' She disappeared behind the screen and he saw her clothes being removed from it, in reverse order to how they arrived there. 'How soon can you let me have the prints?' she called, her arms momentarily visible over the top of the screen as she put on her blouse.

'Oh, I can get them done in a couple of days. End of the week at the latest. Would you like me to bring them to the pub for you? Discreetly, of course.'

'If you like. I'll pay you for them then, Tom. Don't forget to bring your bill.'

On the Thursday, Ned Brisco, together with Bill Harris, a colleague, drove a lorry to Fred Woodall's farm in Bobbington. The load it carried was a prototype twelve-cylinder, water-cooled engine, fuel tank, fuel and a carved wooden airscrew, together with some steel bracing for mounting the ensemble into the nose of the *Gull*, plus a block and tackle to help them lift it. Ned was excited and apprehensive by turn. His apprehension was caused by the gut feeling he had that this engine was still too heavy and too slow to provide the power needed to get air-borne. His excitement, however, stemmed more from the hope that he was wrong, as well he might be.

Ned's employment with Star Engineering had not been as satisfying as he'd at first envisaged. It never occurred to Ned that the main differences between his own outlook and that of his em-ployer would be a barrier to their mutual success. Ned was an enthusiast, his enthusiasm driven by an absolute passion for aviation; his employer was a businessman, driven by a different passion – the need to innovate and, by innovation, show a healthy profit. Thus Ned was frequently drawn away from his passion to help achieve the other's. In consequence, he was not, he felt, able to afford sufficient time and attention to the challenge which had drawn him there in the first place.

Ned was not a qualified engineer. His pre-mature departure from organised learning had ensured that. However, he had a gift for engineering and was fascinated by it; a gift no less valid than such as is endowed upon a great artist or poet. He knew without doubt that he could sort out any engineering problem with logic and suitable tools, given the time to do it. If only they would let him get on with it the way he wanted to. Every week, he had to submit a report to Mr Lisle outlining his progress over the preceding week. That in itself consumed precious time, time he could utilise more gainfully.

Bill Harris, who accompanied Ned today, was an engine designer. They worked together some of the time on this project, or were supposed to. The problem was that Bill had only ever considered that his engines would power automobiles, never aeroplanes. They were thus comparatively rudimentary. The entirely different problems posed by powered flight were alien to him and he found them difficult to comprehend; it was even more difficult to understand why such engines had to be so much more refined and sophisticated. 'What problems are we likely to meet in designing a radial engine?' Ned had asked him once, for he'd read about radial engines and they seemed an ideal configuration for an aeroplane. 'What's a radial engine?' came the frustrating reply. So Ned endeavoured to educate Bill Harris on the peculiarities and demands of aeroplane engines, as he understood it. It was all very disheartening.

They arrived at the farm and eventually located Fred Woodall, to let him know they were working on his property. He said he would call into the barn later and bring some liquid refreshment. Ned reversed the lorry into the barn and they set about hanging the block and tackle from one of the great beams that straddled it. Much of the preparatory work on the *Gull* he had already done; sturdy mountings fitted to accommodate and secure the engine and the fuel tank. After much struggling and deft manoeuvring of the lorry, they managed to lift the engine in place and Ned located it precisely on the mountings he had fitted. After a couple of hours it was installed, everything was connected up, including the fuel lines, and they poured petroleum spirit into the fuel tank.

'Let's crank her up,' Ned said, wiping his oily hands on a piece of rag.

'You get up and prime her then,' Bill said. 'I'll give the propeller a swing.'

After a further delay of a couple of minutes, Ned shouted the order to fire the engine. Bill smartly yanked down the blade of the airscrew and stood back at once. But nothing happened. The engine did not fire.

Again. To no effect.

Several times they tried. Of course, the engine had been bench-tested and it seemed to perform satisfactorily then. Bill clambered up onto the *Gull* and checked all the leads. He disconnected the fuel feed and was satisfied petrol was getting into the carburettor. He checked the distributor and each spark plug. Half an hour later they were ready to try again.

This time, the great engine fired up with a deafening roar. A jet of smoke seared through the broad exhaust, filling the barn with acrid fumes, but there was a smile on Ned Brisco's face. He signalled to Bill to open the great doors and, when he had done so, Ned carefully approached the opening, gently increasing the revolutions.

He felt the thrust pull him forward and outside into the field. He could hardly wait to see just how much power there was at his disposal.

He opened the throttle and the engine roared into life. He felt the *Gull* being pulled forward, his speed across the field gradually increasing. He tried to apply more power but the tone of the engine did not seem to change, neither did the force of wind the propeller was generating into his face. The whole contraption was shaking and trembling with the bumpiness of the field as he traversed it and the throb and vibration of the engine. But he could not go faster. Why? He needed more speed. He needed to be doing more than thirty miles an hour to achieve lift. He felt he was not doing thirty miles an hour yet and, even if he was, the extra weight of the engine evidently demanded even greater velocity. He kept going. Maybe a decent gust of wind under the wings would help, would reduce the drag of the wheels over the long grass. Then he saw that he was running out of field. He decreased the power, slowed down and turned around.

Attempt flight in the opposite direction. Increase power. The aircraft gained speed... But not enough, dammit. Hope, pray for that gust of wind that might make all the difference... Keep going... The barn loomed nearer and nearer. He could see Bill waiting expectantly. Ease off the throttle. Slow down... Come to a halt. Switch off.

Damn!

'The engine seems to be working well,' Bill called up to Ned.

'Is that what you think, Bill? Well, I can tell you

it's bloody useless. I wasn't practising taxing. I was trying to take off. There just wasn't enough power – like I feared.'

'Strange that.' Bill scratched his head. 'But we should be able to tease some more power out of her.'

'Yes, but I don't just want torque, Bill. I need extra revolutions. We've got to speed up the airscrew – get it whirling round faster. As it is, it won't pull the skin off a rice pudding.' Ned stepped down from the *Gull,* a dejected expression on his face. 'Here, give us a shove to get the *Gull* back into the barn.'

'So, it's back to the drawing-board, eh, Ned?'

They set about uninstalling the engine and packing it back onto the lorry for more work back at the factory.

Later the same day, Clover was about to walk past Tom's studio just as he emerged from the front door of his lobby. Her heart went into her mouth, for she had not expected it, even though, in her heartache, she had wished for it. Despite the conversations she'd imagined in the event of it happening, she was unaccountably, but typically, lost for words. It was Tom who ineloquently opened the proceedings.

'Clover!'

She blushed vivid red and was flustered. She passed her basket from one arm to the other nervously, looked down at the ground and then at him. 'Tom! How are you?'

'I'm – I'm all right, thank you. And yourself?'

She detected some resentment still, some icy

291

reserve and her heart sank. She knew him well enough to see that, by virtue of his stand-offishness, he still blamed her for their split.

She shrugged. 'If I said I was all right I'd be lying,' she answered, looking into his eyes to better read his thoughts.

'Are you ill?'

'No, I'm not ill.'

'What then?'

'Can't you guess?'

It was his turn to shrug. He looked away, exaggerating a hurt expression, unsure how to proceed next, uncertain quite what she meant.

'I miss you, Tom,' she blurted out. 'Is that so hard to understand?'

'Huh! I can imagine.'

'Tom, I don't tell lies. You know me well enough to realise that. Of course I miss you. You've been a part of my life for nearly a year...'

'But I'm not the only one, am I?'

'Oh, Tom...' She sighed mournfully, frus-tratedly. 'Of course you're the only one. Give me credit for some virtue.'

'I wish I could, Clover. But I know what I know.'

'Tom, you know nothing... Look, can we go inside? I feel conspicuous standing here on your front step, especially if we're about to have an argument.' At least they were speaking. Better to take full advantage of the moment and use it to see if they could heal their rift.

He fished in his pocket for his keys, withdrew them and opened up the premises again. 'After you...'

Inside, she stood by the counter of his lobby, waiting for him to extend his invitation to enter the studio. He cursorily tilted his head in the direction of the door and she took it as a good sign. In the studio she looked around to see if there had been any changes. The photos he'd had of her on the wall were gone. That told her the depth of his conviction in his reasons for their split. She turned to face him, to explain once and for all that there was nothing untoward between herself and Elijah.

'Tom, I know what you think about me and Elijah. God knows I've thought of little else this week and more. But you have to know there's nothing between us. How could there be? I can't imagine where you got such a ludicrous idea. I've only ever wanted you...' She felt her eyes tingling with tears when the Lord above knew how many tears she'd shed already. But she held his disbelieving gaze and hoped the truth was evident in her face. 'I swear, Tom...' She broke down crying, raised her hands over her face, her shoulders shaking.

Suddenly, his arms were around her and she sobbed the more.

'There, there...' He hugged her. He was so sorely tempted to welcome her back into his life, end this misery that had befallen them. But he had seen what he had seen. He had personally witnessed them exit the Little Barrel together, seen their closeness. It had been nothing short of a dinner-time assignation. He was not wrong... He could not be wrong about such a thing. But her insistence now, her demeanour, all told him

293

he had to be wrong.

'You swear?' he said, his voice low.

'Of course I swear,' she blubbered. 'Ask Elijah yourself.'

'I don't think I'd better.'

'No, because you'd know how wrong you've been. Believe me, you'd look such a fool.'

He remained silent for a few seconds, trying to pluck up the courage to risk again his heart and his deepest emotions. At last he spoke and she raised her head from his shoulder to look into his eyes. 'All right. I'll give you the benefit of the doubt... Let's try again. But if ever–' She squeezed him tight, almost squeezing the breath out of his body.

'Oh, Tom, I'll make you so happy.' She laughed through her tears now and he smiled with her, the dark shadow of their mutual heartbreak lifting already. 'I just want to stay with you here for ever, never moving, just holding you like this.'

'I know the feeling,' he whispered. 'Believe me, I do.'

'Let me stay a while, just holding you like this...'

Chapter Seventeen

'You look very nice tonight, Clover,' Ramona remarked as they passed each other on the stairs. 'Quite perky, I'd say.'

Clover stopped and smiled brightly. 'I'm seeing

294

Tom,' she said and there was no concealing her elation.

'Oh! You two back together then?' Ramona tried to hide her displeasure.

Clover nodded. 'Yes, thank God. I've missed him, Ramona. God knows how I've missed him.'

'I take it you're not going to stay here for my birthday then?'

'Do you mind?' Clover looked at her appealingly, seeking her understanding and condonation. 'Save me a piece of cake, eh? I have to see him, Ramona. I just have to.'

'No, course I don't mind, Clover. I daresay you'll have a lot more fun than me. But this time hang onto him. Men like Tom Doubleday don't come along every day.'

'I know. Don't worry, I shan't let go of him quite so quick next time. Are you coming back down to the taproom?'

'I've just come up to change my apron. I've spilled port all down it, look ... I won't be a minute.'

Clover went into the taproom to serve, as she did most evenings, whether or not she was going out. Archie Lloyd, ageing, cranky, one of the regulars, held his glass up cantankerously and she went over with a smile and took it from him to replenish it. As she pulled steadily on the beer pump she wondered whether Tom would give her back her ring later. She'd hardly worn it, but strangely she missed it, as if it had always been on her finger, as if it belonged there. It just felt wrong without it.

Ramona returned wearing a clean apron and

set about wiping the tables. It was early and the taproom was not yet over-busy. Clover began to busy herself putting glasses away that had been washed and dried when Tom came in. He smiled at her at once and she could see he was holding a stiffened brown envelope behind his back, the likes of which he normally used to protect prints. It seemed he was trying to keep it hidden from her. Of course, she must be mistaken; she knew him better than that. But then she thought she saw him look straight at Ramona. Certainly, his eyes dwelt for a second on hers, as if flashing some covert message, a raising of the eyebrows that was almost imperceptible. It must have conveyed some meaning to Ramona, for she at once stopped what she was doing and brushed past him to leave the taproom by the front door. When Clover looked again, Tom was no longer carrying the envelope. She could not be sure exactly what she had seen. Maybe it was just her imagination playing tricks at a time when she was particularly sensitive. So she smiled at him, trying to shove the disturbing impression to the back of her mind.

'Do you fancy a drink, Tom?'

'Just a half, please.'

She poured his drink, still uncertain what had gone on, peeved at what looked like conniving. Clover had hoped and believed she was on course for a happy and lasting reconciliation with Tom but now she was disappointed that perhaps he was sharing some sort of secret with Ramona. Oh, perhaps she was wrong. She hoped to God that she was. It was easy enough to get the wrong impression. Look how Tom had somehow gleaned the wrong impression over her and Elijah. Because of it, she must give him the benefit of the doubt.

She handed him his glass of beer.

'Thanks, sweetheart.' He took a long draught. 'How long before we can go?'

'As soon as somebody comes to relieve me. Maybe Ramona will be back in a minute or two. She seemed to disappear fairly smartish, didn't she?'

Tom made no comment. He merely turned the conversation, mentioning how fine the weather was.

It was ten minutes before Jake came in ready for work and Clover asked if it was all right to go. Of course, he gave her his blessing.

'Where are we going?' she asked as they stepped outside into the warm evening air.

'Do you fancy going to our house? The folks have gone to my brother's for the evening. They won't be back till late.'

'Yes, all right.'

As they walked, conversation was tentative at first, somewhat forced. They fenced with words, trying to draw each other out, trying to get to know each other all over again after their rift, as if each was trying to determine whether the other had changed noticeably. Raw and barbarous wounds, as yet unhealed, afflicted them both and they were anxious not to open them up again. Damn Ramona and Tom for their secret understanding to which she was not privy. It had put her on edge, irked her, provided one more

297

incident that called trust into question and set back the healing process.

Tonight, however, would afford them the opportunity to do some serious making up and she was determined to put any doubts behind her. She had to. For their reconciliation to work they not only had to trust each other, but also respect each other's trust. There was no other way it could work.

When they arrived at Tom's home the house was indeed empty. She fell into his arms as easily as a child and he held her tight, kissing her ardently, which fuelled her desire for him. It seemed so long since the last time they made love and she was hungry for the tenderness love-making always brought, hungry for the reassurance of his renewed commitment.

'You've never seen my bedroom, have you?' he whispered.

'No,' she said with a coy smile, 'but I've got the strangest feeling I'm about to.'

He grinned. 'This way...' He opened the stairs door at the side of the fire-grate and she followed him up the dim stairwell, her heart beating faster.

On the mantel-shelf in his bedroom stood some photographs of her. She felt a warm glow of satisfaction that he still treasured them. It was an indication of his love. She turned to him and held him, her arms going inside his jacket. She snuggled to him affectionately.

'Tom...'

'Yes, sweetheart?'

'I love you... Only you... Only *ever* you. Don't ever forget it.'

He was unbuttoning her dress. 'I know. And I love you. And I want you...'

'Let me...' She took off her dress and everything else she wore, while he undressed himself. 'Damn these light nights,' she said and laughed. 'I always think it's more romantic when it's dark.'

'I don't mind either way,' he replied. 'You're beautiful, you know, Clover...' He ran his hands over the smooth skin of her breasts. 'I've missed you. God, how I've missed you.'

She gave him a hug, turned from him and pulled back the bedclothes. Then, she got in his bed.

Making love in a soft featherbed was a luxurious change. The bearskin rug was all well and good but, underneath it, lay the hard, unyielding floor. This was so much more comfortable, so much more satisfying. When they were married they would have a lovely soft featherbed, just like this. Lovemaking would always be this comfortable.

The anger and the sadness she'd experienced over the past week and more began to fade as she felt the familiar, yet ever-new sensuality warming her again. The doubts over the eye signals between Tom and Ramona evaporated in inverse proportion to the increasing tenderness she now felt. Tom seemed to be loving her hard with a bitterness and sadness all his own that could only be purged by this passion that was endorsing his devotion, and she welcomed it. Finally, both were spent and they relaxed in an opulence of perspiration and fatigue – and mutual contentment.

They were together again. Nothing was going to part them.

Tom delivered her home at about half past ten. Not particularly late, but she always rose early in a morning. Tom also; he was to travel to Birmingham to look at some new photographic equipment and needed to catch an early train. So Clover looked forward to an early night when she could drift into pleasant dreams, where she could recall the mesmeric experiences she'd stored up from this evening. Tom did not even want to come in for a drink before he set off back home, which was unusual but understandable, in view of his trip tomorrow.

Clover put her head round the taproom door and caught her mother's eye to let her know she was back. Jake and Ramona were working at full crack. In the scullery, Clover lit the oil lamp she generally used to light her way to bed and climbed the stairs. As she passed Ramona's room the bedroom door was open. The glow of the oil lamp's steady yellow flame fell on a stiffened brown envelope that lay on top of the tallboy; the very envelope she thought she'd seen make a magical disappearance earlier.

So she had been right. She had not imagined the envelope.

Clover was tempted to sneak a look but her sense of respect for Ramona's privacy forbade her. After all, she would not like somebody sniffing round uninvited through her things. She went to her own room and unpinned her dark hair, letting it fall about her shoulders. But the surreptitious way the envelope passed earlier from Tom to Ramona plagued her and a cold shudder ran down her spine. There had to be something dark, something nefarious in that envelope that Ramona wanted nobody else to see, else why the secrecy? Tom certainly had no intention of showing her. Tom evidently had no intention of ever mentioning it.

Maybe she would take a peek, quickly. Just to satisfy her burning curiosity that there was nothing untoward in there after all.

She took off her shoes and opened her door. By the light of the oil lamp she peered left and right along the landing. All she could hear was the familiar noise of raucous laughter and animated conversation from the taproom below. She crept along the landing to Ramona's room and closed the door. When she had put the oil lamp on the tallboy she picked up the envelope. Its seal was already broken and she could see it contained photographs – of course. And a birthday greeting-card. She drew them all out.

She gasped with incredulity as she thumbed through them and her stomach twisted into a thousand painful knots. She put them down at once and took several deep breaths. She felt an urge to vomit. Ramona in all her brazen glory, baring all, showing everything she'd got. Clover picked them up again, studied each one. That one posing semi-reclined on the bearskin rug ... Ramona knew the significance of the bearskin rug, damn her. How could she do this? No wonder she wanted nobody else to see these pictures. And Tom had taken them. Tom!... God!

It was a certainty that since it was such a secret between them, nobody else *could* have been present. Ramona and Tom – together – just the two of them – and she without a stitch on ... Clover's mind was working overtime. Anything could have gone on. Knowing Ramona, it probably did. Most *probably* it did.

She opened the card and read it:

With love and very best wishes, Tom.

As quickly as she had taken the things from the envelope she put them back and, in a turmoil, left Ramona's bedroom with her oil lamp.

What now? After the delights of making up tonight, after the extreme joy she felt having made up with Tom, she was back in the shadowy lands of limbo. Now she was condemned to lie awake all night, pondering this awful new doubt. Doubt – not knowing – was hell's way of tormenting the virtuous. Anger was overwhelming her. Who did they think they were if they for a moment thought they could fool her? She could just imagine them, their cosy chat: 'Don't tell Clover.' 'Oh, don't worry, she'll never find out.' 'Yes, it'll be our secret.' Well, she had found out and it was no longer their secret.

She put her shoes back on, raced downstairs, grabbed her coat and ran out into the night. If she hurried she would catch up with Tom, have it out with him. She could not go on not knowing, especially after what he'd accused her of. But which way would he go for the quickest? Try the route they walked tonight.

As she turned into King Street, dark, dismal with its ramshackle red-brick buildings and

302

workshops almost black with grime, she thought she saw him in the shadows and quickened her pace. She passed the bottom of the Green Man Entry and two unsavoury men, the worse for drink, called obscenities after her.

'Tom!' she yelled, half scared, half to attract his attention.

He was about a hundred yards in front of her now and he heard her call. He stopped and turned around, waited for her to catch up with him.

'Clover! What is it? You're all out of breath. What's up?'

She could hardly wait to get her breath back before she began her tirade. 'After all the stupid fuss you've kicked up about Elijah Tandy and me ... after all the heartbreak you've caused us both...' There was no doubting the venom in her tone. 'Well, what have you got to say about Ramona and you, eh?'

'What about Ramona and me?' he asked, reeling from the surprise of seeing her so unexpectedly and the acid sting of her unexpected chastisement.

'Well, seeing the photos you took of her is enough... You and her together in that studio of yours. Did you undress as well, Tom, to make her feel at ease? God! And I let you make love to *me* tonight. I believed you when you told me you loved me – because I wanted to believe you ... I was a fool. But no longer. Now I don't believe you ... I can't believe you. Neither can I trust you, knowing you and she have been alone together like that... Intimate... How could you,

Tom? How *could* you?'

'It was innocent enough, Clover.'

'Innocent? How can it have been *innocent?*'

'It was... You have to believe me. I swear...' He saw tears glistening in her eyes by the weak light of the gas lamps. He had never seen her eyes so wild, never witnessed her so distraught.

'You can swear till you're blue in the face, Tom Doubleday. You can swear till your tongue's ragged and frayed. But you're as guilty as sin. Even if nothing happened you're guilty. Just for allowing yourself to be there while she was naked, flaunting herself, makes you guilty.'

'I had to be there to take the photos, Clover, to fulfil the order.'

Before he could protest more she turned away from him.

'Oh, and I saw the birthday card as well. Well, you can keep your damned ring!' she yelled as she wrenched it off her finger. 'I don't *want it.* Give it to *her!*'

She ran back to the Jolly Collier, oblivious to what was going on around her. She did not notice the passers-by watching her in alarm as she ran past them in a frenzy of agitation, hair flowing behind her like the mane of a wild young mare. Her eyes were blinded by the haze of tears, her mind numbed, seized and clutched by desolation. She had no wish to see Tom again. Not after this. If he could be involved with Ramona doing what they were doing she wanted no further part of him. If it had been innocent, as he'd feebly claimed, why hadn't he told her of it in the first place? Why couldn't he have men-

304

tioned, before ever she found out, that he'd taken some nude photographs of her stepsister? He was guilty of lying simply by not telling her. Did he think she would not understand? Did he think that if he confessed an indiscretion she could not forgive him? Well, better that way than this. Now she could never forgive him. She could never forgive him because it was never his intention to tell her.

But why had Ramona done it? To what purpose? Had she gone there and proposed such photos with the intention of seducing Tom? Or had Tom suggested it with the intention of seducing Ramona? There's a thought! Ramona, she knew, was capable of anything where men were concerned, but she'd given her credit for respecting her sacrosanct, profound relationship with Tom. You don't tempt or seduce your stepsister's man just because you can. It was a basic human ethic. Some relationships had to be strictly out of bounds.

She reached home, though she did not recall one step of the journey. The Jolly Collier was still open. Ramona, with her despicable secret, was still serving, still flaunting herself like the lascivious vamp she was in front of the impressionable younger men whose callow eyes followed her everywhere. Harry Heppenstall was there and Ramona seemed to be specially playing up to him. No doubt she would see him later and get her upright pleasure pressed against the wall of somebody's dark entry. Well, now she could see her for what she really was. Ramona, she understood at last, had no scruples. Clover entered, tears still in her eyes, grabbed her oil lamp and went upstairs. This time she did not turn to look into Ramona's room, but went straight to her own. She slumped onto her bed, heaved a great sigh of despondency and took off her shoes again.

How could she continue to live in the same house as Ramona? She never wanted to see her again, certainly she desired never to speak to her again. Yet continue to live there she must, as would Ramona. It was going to be awkward. Her silence would be noticed, her disdain would be discerned. There would be an icy atmosphere; a cold, stony silence between them.

But it was not her fault.

It was Ramona's fault.

Clover hardly slept that night. When she did drift off she woke herself up with images of Ramona, walking about the house with no clothes on, taunting her, of Tom calling and escorting a naked Ramona to the theatre where all men's eyes feasted upon her and her neat body, and the women were embarrassed that she could be so shameless.

Maybe she would sleep better tomorrow night. And, if not then, perhaps the night after.

It was on the Friday morning that Ramona tapped on the door to Elijah's room. She got no reply and, when she opened it quietly to ascertain whether or not he was there, she was surprised to see his bed had not been slept in. Clover had left the house by this time, sullen and unspeaking as she had been for the past day or two, and

306

Ramona breakfasted with her father before commencing the long hard day that the Jolly Collier and brewing promised.

'Where's Uncle Elijah?' she asked, feigning innocence. 'I haven't seen him this morning.'

'He slept at Brooke Street,' Jake replied, spreading a knob of butter over a piece of toast. 'He'll be there most of the morning, I reckon. He's supposed to be meeting a bloke there about half past nine.'

'Oh? What for?'

'Business.' Jake filled his mouth with buttered toast.

'What time's he due back here then?'

'About midday, I reckon. Did you want him for something?'

'Oh, no.' Ramona lifted the caddy off the teapot and poured herself another cup of tea. 'Just curious. But I want to go to the town to get some new shoes this morning. I've seen some I fancy in Freeman, Hardy and Willis. Is it all right if I go?'

Jake smiled benignly. 'I reckon so. Shoes this time, is it? As long as you'm paying for 'em out of your own money.'

'Course I am.'

'Well, be back as soon as you can, else Mary Ann will have something to say.'

They finished their breakfasts in silence, Ramona pondering the best time to catch her uncle so as to avoid seeing anybody else at the house in Brooke Street. Actually catching him there was the only way she would get to see him privately. He didn't seem to want to make any arrangements to meet her there, for some reason

307

that was not clear to her, and Ramona did not take kindly to being thus scorned.

So she left the Jolly Collier at ten, arriving at nearly quarter past. She did not let herself in this time, but tapped tentatively on the front door. It opened and Elijah presented himself in his shirtsleeves.

'Ramona!' He opened the door wide and stood aside to let her through, aware of what she had come for but surprised to see her all the same. 'What brings you here?'

'My dad said I'd catch you here.'

'Oh, he did, did he?'

She walked along the hall to the scullery. Through the window she could see a man measuring up outside between the back door and the brewhouse.

'You can put the kettle on if you want to make yourself useful,' Elijah said, 'while I just see to Enoch outside.'

She did as she was bid and watched the two men in conversation. Elijah nodded at him and they shook hands and the man disappeared through the side gate and she heard his footfalls through the long entry.

'Who was that?'

He laughed and shook his head. 'You want to know the top and bottom of Meg's arse.'

It was obvious he wasn't about to divulge anything.

'I've brought you a present,' Ramona said after a pause.

'A present? It ain't me birthday yet.'

She shrugged sheepishly. 'Well, I get the impression you don't want me anymore ... so I thought I'd bring you a present to get you interested again.' She reached for her basket and withdrew the stiffened envelope which she handed to him.

Tentatively, he took it and opened it up. He pulled out the five photographs, turned them the right way up and studied them one by one while she tried to read both his expression and his thoughts.

'Mmm,' he murmured approvingly. 'Very nice, our Ramona. I always said you'd got a nice arse. That ain't all, neither. Look at you here... That a bearskin rug? Who got you to pose like that?'

'Nobody. I did it myself. I was thinking of you.'

'And who took them? Tom Doubleday?'

She nodded, embarrassed lest he think the worst. 'He's the only one who knows about them.'

'Then let's hope he keeps his mouth shut. It's a fair bet as he will. He wouldn't want Clover knowing he'd done these, would he?'

She shrugged again and smiled. 'Do you like them?'

'Yes, I like 'em well enough.' He scrutinised them again.

'Do you intend to thank me?...'

'Yes, come here, you little minx...' He thrust her against the scullery wall and pressed himself against her. Ardently he kissed her, lifted her skirt and ran his hand up her leg.

'Take me to bed,' she urged and took his hand.

'Yes, and bring the photos.'

As they climbed the stairs she was already

309

divesting herself of her clothes. In the bedroom she kicked off her shoes and shed everything hurriedly, then slid down her stockings.

'Pose for me like you did for Tom Doubleday, while I get undressed,' he said.

She stole across the bed and, lying supine, raised her torso by putting her arms behind her. She threw her head back, arched her back kittenishly and raised one knee.

'You're a bloody temptress, you are, Ramona. Christ! You get what you deserve...'

They made love lustfully, vigorously, satisfyingly. For some minutes afterwards they lay still. He twitched as he fell asleep and, as she eased his exhausted body off her, his limp phallus flopped out of her, awaking him. She smiled as she felt the sheet beneath her drenched with their seeping wetness.

'I love you, Uncle Elijah,' she whispered tenderly. 'I know you don't want me to, but I do and I can't help it.'

'Well don't,' he said sternly. 'Look, Ramona, this has to be the last time...'

She looked at him aghast and sat bolt upright. 'Why should it be? We enjoy our times like this, don't we?'

'Whether or no, it has to stop.' He lay back, his hands under his head, staring at the ceiling, waiting for her next question.

'So explain to me then ... why does it have to stop?'

'Because Dorcas and me are getting married.'

She was silent for a few seconds, alarmed by this wholly unwelcome news. Eventually, she said, 'Even if you're daft enough to get married, we can still meet ... here, in this bed ... like we did before.'

He shook his head. 'No, Ramona. We can't meet anywhere. And this is the last bloody place. I'm buying this house off your father. Dorcas and me are going to live here when we'm wed.'

'Live here?' she asked stupidly. 'So when are you getting married?'

'A fortnight tomorrow.'

'But that's ... that's just two weeks. And you've told nobody... Is she pregnant as you're in such a rush?'

He did not answer, continuing to stare at the ceiling.

She sighed, a great shuddering sigh. 'So what if I happen to be pregnant? What then?'

'If you're pregnant that's sod all to do with me, Ramona. If you're pregnant, look to the other blokes you've been having it away with.'

'What other blokes?' she queried, disconcerted and angry.

'Tom Doubleday, for a start. It's obvious you and him have been very intimate. He took those photos, didn't he?'

'So what?'

'So bloody what? Are you trying to tell me you and him never coupled when you was in his studio with nobody else about and you as naked as the day you was born? Pull the other one, Ramona. I might look like a cabbage, but I ain't that bloody green.'

Chapter Eighteen

Miss Dorcas Downing became Mrs Elijah Tandy in a ceremony at St James's Church, Eve Hill, on the west side of Dudley on 20th June 1908, a Saturday. It had been a hurriedly prepared event but done in some style nonetheless, befitting the only daughter of the wealthy local industrialist and magistrate, George Downing. The service was conducted by the Reverend James Wescot and a lavish reception was held at the Dudley Arms Hotel in the centre of the town.

Ramona had contrived not to be there. She preferred to remain on duty at the Jolly Collier on this day that graphically symbolised the end of her affair with her Uncle Elijah. Clover, keeping a low profile at home and avoiding Ramona as if she had some rabidly contagious disease, had not been allowed the time off work at Cook's. However, she did not regret the decision; Elijah told her that Dorcas had engaged the services of Tom Doubleday as wedding photographer. And Clover certainly had no wish to see Tom Doubleday.

So Elijah moved all his belongings out of the Jolly Collier and into the large terraced house in Brooke Street. As a partner in Beckitt's Brewery he continued to work there every day, returning home to his wife for his meals. Marriage seemed to suit Elijah and he wondered why he had never seriously considered it before.

The disappearance from the Jolly Collier of Elijah's company at mealtimes and leisure times had a lowering effect on the household. However, it soon became evident to Mary Ann and to Jake that there was another reason for the lack of jollity; their respective offspring were not communicating cordially. Indeed, they were not communicating at all. A rift had developed somehow, rendering the atmosphere distinctly icy. Ramona and Clover made sure that they never sat at the table together. They had seldom breakfasted together anyway because of the different times they arose from their beds, but at teatime, Ramona made sure that she ate before Clover returned from Cook's.

Mary Ann tackled Clover about the situation the day after the wedding as they swept the yard together, prior to Mary Ann's attendance at Matins at St John's.

'What's up twixt thee and young Ramona, our Clover?'

'Nothing that I want to talk about, Mother.' Clover replied curtly and continued sweeping.

'There is summat up, I can tell. Your stepfather can see as there's summat up an' all. He's werriting about it and he's asked me to have a word with you. Whatever it is, he wants you to make it up with her.'

Clover stopped her sweeping and looked at Mary Ann. 'I appreciate Jake's concern, Mother. But there's nothing he can do and I'd appreciate neither of you interfering.' She spoke quietly so as not to be overheard.

The early morning sun was already snooping between the brick buildings of George Street. The weather promised to behave for yet another day.

'I reckon it's to do with that Tom Doubleday...'

Clover shrugged. 'How do you work that out?'

'Well, it's only happened since he stopped coming here a-courting you.'

'Mother, Tom Doubleday and me stopped seeing each other nearly three weeks ago. As far as I'm concerned he hasn't started calling on Ramona, if that's what you're implying. The two things are unconnected. Anyway, if she wants him she's welcome to him.'

Mary Ann looked at her daughter knowingly. 'Huh! And if I believe that I'll believe anything. I've seen you moping about over him like a fairy with the ballyache. Well, I hope he's worth it, that's all.'

Clover sighed. 'I don't know if he's worth it or not, Mother. It's irrelevant. He and I have had our differences and they won't change... And that's an end to it.'

Mary Ann leaned on her brush. She felt like saying she wasn't surprised, that he wasn't good enough for her anyway, but held her tongue. Her daughter would disagree.

'All it means, Mother, is that you're stuck with me for a bit longer ... till I can find somebody else who'll marry me. But it's nothing to do with Ramona. So tell Jake not to worry. I daresay we'll get over it... How was the wedding yesterday?'

'Well, there's no flies on the Downings and no two ways. You should have seen Dorcas's mother.

314

Phew! Done up like a shilling dinner, she was. Her father seems a nice person, though.'

'Did Dorcas look nice?'

'Oh, she looked nice enough, as you'd expect. But she was a bit peaky, if you ask me. That, and the rush to get wed... If she ain't pregnant, our Clover, I'll chew coal.'

When Florrie Brisco called at Rudd's in Brown Street for a gallon of lamp oil she heard the news that Clover Beckitt and Tom Doubleday had fallen out and couldn't wait to pass it on to Ned when he returned from work. So Ned made it his business to call at the Jolly Collier that same evening. Through the scullery window that looked out onto the side of the building she saw him approaching, dried her hands and went outside.

'Ned!' she greeted affably. 'How's this?'

'I called to see how you are, Clover. I heard as you've fell out with that Tom Doubleday.'

She wiped the last smears of soapy water from the backs of her hands on her apron. 'Yes, we've parted. It's nice of you to call.'

'I would have called sooner if I'd known, Clover.'

She smiled appreciatively. 'So how's the job going? Oh, and how's the motor car?'

'The job's getting me down, Clover, to tell you the truth. I wouldn't mind if I was getting more money than I was at the Coneygree, but I'm not. But the motor's fine. How do you fancy a ride out into the country? It's a lovely evening and we could talk. We've always been able to talk, Clover.'

Well, she was not averse to that idea. 'All right. Give me ten minutes to get ready. Why don't you go in the taproom and have a drink while you wait?'

'Is Ramona in there?'

She shrugged. 'I imagine so. Go and have a chat to her. I'll call you when I'm ready.'

Remembering her last cold outing in Ned's motor car on the fateful day of her engagement, Clover put on a coat, despite the warm evening sun that was painting everything yellow.

As he drove the vehicle, Ned explained in detail how he was frustrated in his new career. Oh, they had made some progress but everybody thought in terms of motor car engines and clung to the idea that those principles would suffice when applied to aeroplanes.

'Do you wish you'd stayed at the Coneygree?' Clover asked.

'Who knows, I might end up back there.'

'But that would be a real step backwards, Ned. You shouldn't think of such things. Have you forgotten? You were frustrated working there, as well.'

'No more than I am now. At least I could get on with my *Gull* in my spare time in the way I thought fit.'

'You still can, can't you?'

'Not when it's at Woodall's farm in Bob-bington. Nor where the engine's concerned. I'm dependent on Star.'

'But you had that anonymous loan. You could use that. Or did you pay it back?'

He hesitated to answer while he slowly

negotiated a stretch of rough road. 'No, I didn't pay it back, Clover,' he admitted at last. 'I haven't got the money now either. I used most of it to buy this...' He tapped the steering-wheel.

'So how *are* you going to pay it back? You'll have to pay it back some time.'

'I know.' He shrugged and tugged his cap harder on his head to save the breeze lifting it. 'I'll have to save up the money.'

'But that could take ages, Ned.'

'You're telling me...' He sighed. 'Years... It was a lot of money.'

'Don't you think you've been a bit too hasty, using it to pay for this motor car, nice as it is?'

He nodded. 'Perhaps.'

'It's something you could have done without.'

They fell silent for a while and Clover looked out across a landscape utterly ravaged by the hand of man. They were traversing a horse road that straddled Wrens Nest Hill on their right and Dibdale Bank on their left. On both sides the land fell away, dipping into valleys, each with its own characteristics. The valley on the east side, to the right, was pock-marked with slag heaps, lime works and quarries. On the west side, green and yellow fields began to emerge like a half-finished quilt between the tall, red-brick chimney stacks, the furnaces and iron mines.

'Where are we going?'

'Baggeridge Wood.' He turned his head to look at her. 'Ever been?'

'No. I've heard of it, though. Is it pretty?'

'One of the loveliest places I know. I took a girl there a few times. It's high and it overlooks Penn

317

Common. We'll be able to watch the sun go down over Shropshire.'

'A girl, eh?' she queried. 'Who, might I ask?'

'Oh … er … just a … a girl from work, Clover,' he stumbled. 'I thought I might as well, seeing as how you was courting that Tom Doubleday.'

She thought she saw his colour heighten and she smiled. 'Was she nice?'

'She was all right,' he answered sheepishly. 'She gave me up, though.'

'That's a shame. Were you upset?'

He shrugged. 'A bit. Not much.'

Baggeridge Wood was all he said it was. At a place called Gospel End that hosted a smattering of cottages and, appropriately, a church, they turned off the lane that ran from Sedgley to Wombourne village and travelled through an arcade of trees along a narrow track. They might have been a million miles from civilisation. Ned stopped the engine and the silence struck them, a profound, country silence, punctuated only by the singing of birds. Sunlight the colour of saffron streamed in at the edge of the wood, creating long shadows over the soft leaf mould that lay thick on the ground. Through the coppice of straight, dark tree trunks ahead you could see the hills falling away, gathering fields and hedges as they rolled towards the distant border with Shropshire. The smell here was different, too; nutty, woody, earthy, fresh; as far removed from the smell of stale beer and cigarette smoke as it was possible to be, miles distant from the smutty, sulphurous stinks that spewed out from the myriad chimney stacks.

318

Clover climbed down from the vehicle and thrilled to the feel of soft earth under her feet, softer than the softest carpet.

'Let's walk to the edge of the wood. It's not far, look.'

He got down and walked with her.

'Tell me what happened between you and Tom.'

Clover sighed. 'It doesn't matter what happened, Ned, I still love him. I'll always love him.'

Occasionally a dry stick cracked underfoot as they ambled along.

'So tell me what happened.'

She told him. Everything. From the first time they met, even how they made love regularly. She finished by relating his accusations concerning Elijah and the subsequent incident of Ramona's photos.

'Ramona posed with no clothes on?' he queried.

'Can you believe it?'

'When did this happen?'

Clover thought she detected a flicker of interest in his eyes. 'Why? Are you concerned?'

'Me? No, course not.'

'Well, it was over three weeks ago. She's a slut, that Ramona. I could tell you stories about her that would make your hair curl.'

'Tell me then.'

'No. I don't think I could bring myself to.'

'Well Tom must be as bad, Clover. It beats me how you can still be in love with a man who treated you like that.' He ran his hand over the trunk of a tree, feeling the rough texture of the bark. 'It's obvious something must have gone on

319

with Ramona. Especially if she's like you say she is.'

She shrugged and pulled up the collar of her coat. 'Oh, he never treated me badly, Ned. You must never think that. Just the opposite, in fact. He was always so kind and so considerate. I just don't know what got into him at the last. Something to do with a girl called Maud, I think, who he was engaged to before – she ran off with his best friend. I can see how something as horrible as that happening might warp your mind and make you see it elsewhere, like a spectre, even where it doesn't actually exist.'

He thrust his hands in his pockets, hunched his shoulders and looked out over the valley below them, the low sun directly in his eyes. 'You're still defending him, Clover. You're still very loyal.'

She stood beside him, also peering into the sun. He turned to look at her. It hurt him to see that her beautiful blue eyes were welling with tears.

'No, don't get upset, please, Clover...'

'But I love him, Ned...' He offered his arms and she fell into them, thankful for his chest that she could rest her head against while she wept, thankful for somebody's consoling arms around her. It was what she needed. She'd been starved of love and care and sympathy for too long already, starved of somebody to talk to, somebody she could bare her soul to, to help get Tom Doubleday out of her system. 'I'll always love him, Ned. I can't help it. He was everything to me...'

He hugged her with his great reserve of affection, pleased to feel her in his arms. 'I know,

320

Clover,' he breathed. 'I know. And he's the biggest fool that ever wore a pair of trousers for letting you go. I never would. I would never treat you like that, Clover. I'd cherish you for ever.'

On the last Thursday in June, a batch of wort, unfermented beer, had been drained and allowed to cool. George Doughty, the thin excise man, tapped on the door of the brewery and stepped inside. Ramona greeted him with little enthusiasm, for she thought he always took advantage of his position to barge in.

'Is it your day to come already?' She found it hard to hide her resentment.

'Morning, Miss Tandy,' he replied affably. 'So how are you today.'

'I've been better, thanks.'

'Off the hooks, are you?'

'A bit.'

'Not been sleeping?'

'Oh, I'm sleeping all right, Mr Doughty. I had some herrings for me supper last night and they must have been a bit off. I felt rotten this morning.'

'Stomach upset?'

'I expect so.'

'Try some liver salts. That'll sort you out.'

She forced a smile. 'I suppose you want to check the wort, Mr Doughty. There's a batch ready in one of the fermenters, waiting to be pitched with yeast.'

'I timed it right then today, eh?' They walked over to the row of fermenting vessels. Five of them were bubbling away nicely, with a cover of yeast on each that was growing like rampant fungus. The remaining vessel contained the fresh wort. 'Is Elijah about?'

'He's upstairs, I imagine, Mr Doughty. He's due to put hops in the copper.'

George Doughty's job was to check the specific gravity of the wort so that he could calculate the duty to be paid. He could not check every batch but he applied the reading taken today to the week's production and so arrive at a total amount of duty due for the week.

He produced his hydrometer, took his reading and made a note of it. 'I'll go and see your father now,' he said. 'He loves me coming to take money off him.'

'Like he loves pain.'

George laughed. 'See you next week, Miss Tandy. Don't forget... Liver salts.'

Ramona bid him cheerio and reached for the thermometer hanging on the wall nearby. She dipped the thermometer into the cooled wort, allowed a few seconds for it to stabilise and read it off. It was cool enough.

Elijah appeared from the floor above. 'Has he buggered off?'

'He's gone to see me father to work out the excise duty.'

'Can't stand that bloke. Supercilious bastard. Are you ready to pitch the yeast in?'

'I'm just about to do it.'

'Check the temperature then,' he said.

'I already did, *Uncle* Elijah,' she replied, her tone tinged with sarcasm, underlining their new unimpeachable relationship. 'And it's all right.'

Ramona's contacts with Elijah remained cool after his wedding. Even on those days when they worked together in the brewery, when opportunities to sneak away and make love presented themselves, no signal was given any more, no suggestion made.

She felt like an old shoe, discarded when she was of no further use. Trouble was, she could not complain too much. She knew from the outset of their affair that he was already engaged to be married to Dorcas, had been for ages. He'd been engaged to her for so long, with no outward sign of marriage, that nobody believed he seriously intended it. Consequently, Ramona had earnestly believed she could usurp Dorcas. She was confident that Elijah, once he had tasted her younger, sweeter flesh, would become addicted. How wrong she was. Rather, the reverse had happened. His indifference at times had been hard for her to understand, but that same indifference, his ability to turn away, had intrigued her all the more and become the hook that ensured her addiction. And that addiction was increased when he did pay her attention, when he was aroused, for he made love to her with a practised expertise that made her feel like the desirable woman she aspired to be. He did it so much better than anybody else.

However, rigid social conventions, let alone her father, would never countenance an uncle-niece love affair, never mind marriage. Ramona though, had never seriously considered that. She believed Uncle Elijah's ardent wish that the affair be kept secret was so that Dorcas should not get to hear of it and be upset. Well, she could upset Dorcas good and proper now if she chose to. She only had to reveal what had gone on. But what was to be gained apart from the sadistic satisfaction of telling her? Nothing at all. Besides, revelation would upset too many people and particularly hurt her father, when he did not deserve such pain. No, there were plenty more men about, willing and able to divert her, as she knew well enough, even though they might not make her toes curl with ecstasy nor make her whimper with pleasure like Elijah.

It was time to find a new love, time for another romantic adventure with somebody different. Without doubt, the best therapy for overcoming the disappointments of one affair was to commence another. Gaining the attentions of another man was sure to take her mind off Elijah Tandy.

And she thought she knew a likely candidate who might also be glad of a bit of the same therapy. So, when her morning stint in the brewery was over and the dinner-time trade in the Jolly Collier had finished and all was quiet, Ramona asked her father if she could take an hour or so off work. Good-naturedly, he agreed, so Ramona went to her room and prepared herself for the encounter she had in mind.

Tom Doubleday, that afternoon, decided to update the gallery of photographs in his lobby. Some of those on display were a couple of years old and it was time for some fresh faces to be put on display. Likely photographs he kept in a special box and today was as good a day as any to do the work, since he had no further appointments. So, he took the framed pictures off his walls and inspected them all one by one, prepared to remove the photographs within them and replace them with others. One of his favourites, that in a recent fit of pique he'd relegated to the box, was a photo of Clover. He studied it for longer than he intended and, as he looked at those open and honest eyes smiling her love at him he felt an intense sadness that he imagined was never going to leave him. She was beautiful. And not only in looks, with that delightful, exquisite nose that she thought was so awful. Now that it was too late, he realised just how honest and forthright she really was. She was also warm, gentle, invariably pleasant. He would never find anybody who would match up to her.

Now he had lost her. He had lost her and he was not going to win her back easily. He had lost her because of his own spurious suspicions and his failure to confess that session of photography with Ramona. But how could he have confessed? Just by being with Ramona without a chaperone while she was naked was tantamount to outrageous infidelity. Nobody on earth would perceive it any differently. And just because Clover believed he'd seduced her while she was evidently so vulnerable, he might as well have done exactly that. He might as well have played the part she cast him in; he might as well have been hanged for a sheep as for a lamb. Well, it was done now and, though regrettable that he'd been found out, he could not alter what had already come to pass.

He put the photo down. It could go back on the wall. Let it be a reminder of how fortunate he almost was, how he very nearly attained perfect happiness. Let it be a reminder that it always paid to be open and honest in affairs of the heart. If only he'd been open and honest with Clover, even asked her blessing before he'd agreed to do Ramona's photos, she might have understood. Indeed, she could have chaperoned Ramona. If only... They might still be together now.

There were other photos he wanted to replace. He thumbed through his box looking for suitable newer ones; a beautiful portrait of a child, a young woman with her hair elegantly piled up in curls, a handsome young man in his early twenties with a watch-chain looping across his waistcoat. Yes, it was time these other photos were given an airing. There was a recent photo of the Vicar of Dudley in all his regalia, one of the Town Clerk in his grey wig – good to have some notables in the collection to enhance your standing with the rest of your customers...

A picture of Ramona ... and another. He knew copies were in there. He scrutinised them each in turn... Lovely skin... A nice-looking girl. It was a toss-up who was the better-looking, her or Clover... Their natures were so different, as different as developer and hypo. Clover was a lady, demure, relatively conventional but warm, affectionate and immensely enjoyable in bed. Exactly his type. Ramona on the other hand was extreme, impish, flighty and blasé. Funny how two girls so radically different could both be totally desirable. His eyes lingered a second or two longer on the controversial photos of Ramona before he slid them to the bottom of the pile; he could hardly display those, unless he wanted to be invaded by all the guardians of public decency the town harboured.

He had not stashed them away more than half a minute when the front door opened.

'Ramona! I was just thinking about you.'

'Oh, that's nice, Tom. I er ... I came to pay you for my pictures.'

'I hope you weren't disappointed with them.'

'Disappointed? Lord, no. I think they're good. I shall treasure them, even if I have to keep them under lock and key forever.'

He smiled, masking the pity he felt that she hadn't kept them under lock and key from the moment he gave them to her.

'How much do I owe you, Tom?' She took out her purse.

'Does five bob sound fair?'

'Oh, it sounds very fair to me. Hang on, I think I've got a crown...' She searched her purse. 'Here you are...'

'Thanks. Come through into the studio. Have you got time for a cup of tea?'

'That'd be nice, Tom. Thank you.' She followed him through.

Tom went into his darkroom and put the kettle on to boil.

When he came out, Ramona said, 'I take it you and Clover have finished altogether now, since I haven't seen you.'

'Yes.' He attempted not to show any emotion. 'I

think it's fair to say it's all over between us.'

'Pity you'd got as far as getting engaged, eh? But they say as nothing lasts forever. Matter of fact, she was out with Ned Brisco last night. He called for her in that motor car of his. They didn't get back till late.'

'Oh?' He felt a bitter pang of hurt and resentment. 'Did she say where they'd been?'

Ramona shook her head. 'No, not Clover. I don't know what I've done to upset her, Tom, but she don't speak to me now. I must have upset her somehow but, honest to God, I don't know how.'

'Some imagined grievance?' Tom suggested sardonically. 'I'll go and put some tea in the pot.'

He was gone a few minutes, silent, venturing no conversation while Ramona sat on the *chaise-longue*, consumed with her own thoughts. Eventually, he returned carrying two mugs of tea which he set down on his work table.

'I'd like you to take some more photos of me, Tom.'

'Really?' he said, incredulous. 'Some more?'

'Yes ... I liked those others so much... Is there any chance you could do it now? I'm all ready.'

'All ready?' he queried.

'Remember last time?' She lowered her eyes feigning coyness. 'You said it's better not to wear underwear and tight things before you have such photos done. Then you don't get marks in your skin...'

'That's right.'

'Well, look...' She lifted the hem of her skirt.

'You're not wearing stockings. That's good. No garter marks...'

328

Then she raised her skirt higher to reveal her thigh, then her naked hip.

'I've got no drawers on either, look.' She grinned saucily then teasingly, let the hem of her skirt fall back to cover her ankles. 'Only this loose-fitting dress. That's all I'm wearing.' She giggled girlishly. 'If my father knew he'd go mad.'

Tom was dumbfounded. In the ordinary way of things, to get a peep at an ankle was a thrill.

'Do you want to lock the door, Tom?'

Do you want to lock the door, Tom? The way she said it! Suddenly, he felt all hot.

'I think it would be best...' As he reeled to the front door he was not sure what to make of this situation, but his heart was thumping profoundly. He had never expected a repeat performance and right up to this moment he wasn't really sure he wanted one ... but... Perhaps Ramona had called today with something else on her mind. She was not backward in coming forward. This time she seemed even less inhibited; brazen even, provocatively giving him a peep-show of her bare legs, her thighs.

'You've got a fine pair of legs, Ramona,' he commented empirically, hoping it might prompt her to show them again. 'Altogether a lovely figure.'

'Do you really think so?' She smiled with pleasure at his compliment.

'I suspect that few people know it as well as I do...'

She smiled again, but coyly, looking at him from under veiled eyelids. 'Just one other man...'

'Oh?'

'Sammy... Do you remember Sammy?'

'I remember you mentioning him. Isn't he the one that became a professional soldier?'

She nodded, avoiding his eyes now, looking into her lap demurely. 'Yes, months ago... You know, Tom, it's hard for a girl to confess such a thing to another man but... But we used to ... you know...' Her eyes met his calculatingly now. 'Well, we loved each other, Tom. I see nothing wrong in going all the way. Especially if you love each other. Do you?'

'Oh, I'm all for it. And to hell with the gossips.'

'Like minds, you and me, ain't we, Tom? I think I could tell you anythink. I've always felt I could be close to you.'

'I'm flattered.'

'Some men are right hypocrites, you know. They want to have all the women they can and still marry virgins. Well, they'll be disappointed in me, I can tell you. I never intended staying a virgin long and I ain't ashamed to say it.'

'Good for you, Ramona, if that's what you want.'

'I knew you'd understand, Tom. I knew you wouldn't be such a prude. Shall I get undressed behind the screen again?'

'Oh... Yes. I'll open it up for you.'

She stood up. 'But why bother? Who needs a screen? You've already seen me in the altogether.' She laughed aloud at the absurdity of what she perceived. 'What's the point in hiding behind a screen when you already know what I've got?'

There was a logic in her remark that he could not gainsay. He smiled foolishly that he had not considered it himself and watched while she took off her clothes. Her skin was creamy-white and unblemished.

Naked again, she twirled around shamelessly. 'Look, Tom. There's no marks from a liberty bodice, no shift, no garters...' She inspected her breasts. 'Oh, is this one, here?' She pointed to a mark on her left breast that was from a crease. 'What do you think?'

'I don't know ... it must be caused—'

'Feel it... Go on, I don't mind you feeling me there...' She looked challengingly into his eyes, almost as if she would be hurt if he refused.

He must not refuse. He put his hand on her breast.

Ramona gently placed her hand over his. 'Oh, Tom, you've got a lovely gently touch,' she breathed. 'No, don't stop...'

He felt a potent stirring within him, and gulped. 'You have such lovely skin.'

'Thank you.' She moved in closer to him, her naked body touching the coarse cloth of his trousers. 'See if you think my skin's as smooth everywhere.' She put her hands to his waist and looked into his eyes with an expression of such appealing helplessness that he found it impossible to resist.

He knew from that moment he was lost. He knew then that he did not have the will, or indeed the reason any more, to fight such temptation. Nothing could stop them from travelling down this road. His hands went to her waist and to the small of her naked back. He drew her to him. He looked into her eyes and she looked up at him expectantly, her mouth open, waiting to receive his kisses. As their lips met, he allowed his hands to wander over her small bottom and she pressed herself against him, leaving him in no doubt where this was leading. No word of his could prevent this happening. Her next words confirmed it.

'I want you, Tom.'

'Oh, God! I want you, Ramona.'

'Shall we lie on the bearskin rug?'

'Yes,' he said, half choking with astonishment, the speed with which this was happening, and his urgent desire for her.

She took his hand and led him to the other side of the studio, to the bearskin rug. He grabbed two cushions to use as pillows and placed one under her head. Looking into his eyes so appealingly, she lay down and he lay beside her.

'Don't you want to take your clothes off?' she cooed. 'It'd be nice to feel your skin next to me, not your scratchy clothes.'

'Sorry.'

He stood up again and undressed himself, hardly able to believe that all this was really happening. It must be a dream... Well, enjoy it ... before you wake up. Within a few seconds he lay beside her again, as naked as she, and held her tight. The warmth from her body, the softness of her skin lit him up like a gas mantle.

'I've always fancied you, Tom,' she whispered. 'Ever since the first day we met at me dad's wedding. Do you remember?'

'Yes.' He swallowed hard and ran his hand down her inner thigh, relishing the feel of her

332

warm, enticing flesh.

'I knew if I waited long enough... Ooh, God! That's nice, Tom... Ooh, kiss me again...'

They kissed. Long and lingering. Hot and passionate. They were writhing and wriggling, sighing and moaning at these sensations that, with somebody new, seemed so different. Neither wanted to defer the golden moment any longer than they needed, so at last he eased himself onto her. And she let out a long sigh of pleasure and perversity; perversity at feeling the man whom Clover still loved dearly, sliding delectably inside her.

They both enjoyed this lovemaking. Both were practised in the finer points and they brought each other some welcome relief from their recent anxieties. This new intimacy was an emollient to their love-tortured souls and seemed to enhance their rapport. Surely, it was worth nurturing.

They lay for nearly an hour on his bearskin, talking desultorily, laughing, strangely happy at experiencing each other in this surprising new role, in this new-found familiarity. Eventually, reluctantly, they both got dressed and Ramona was ready to go home.

'I have to work most nights, Tom,' she said apologetically, her hand on his arm proprietorily as she stood with him at his counter in the lobby.

'I know and I don't particularly want to bump into Clover at the Jolly Collier. I think it's best if we meet here for the time being. At least we'd have the place to ourselves.'

'I can come tomorrow, if you like.'

'I'd like that.'

'In the afternoon again?'

'That'd be best.'

'What's the best time?'

'Oh, just after four. My last customer will be gone by then.'

She smiled. 'Perfect.'

Chapter Nineteen

On the evening of the third Sunday in July, Tom Doubleday took Ramona to the Empire Theatre to see a variety show. It was after eleven when the show finished and, in pouring rain, he walked her home to the Jolly Collier. The weather had been unseasonably poor for July. Not only was it wet, but it was cold and, as the couple turned the corner into Cross Guns Street, the gust of wind that met them turned Ramona's brolly inside out.

'Me gamp!' she exclaimed. 'It'll be good for nothing.'

Tom took it off her impatiently. 'You're supposed to hold it into the wind, not let the wind get under it,' he chided while Ramona held on to her hat. 'Give's it here, for God's sake.' He thrust it into the wind, pulled on one of the spars and it flipped back into place with a dull thwack, dowsing his face with an extra shower of water.

Ramona laughed. 'Serves you right,' she said. She took his arm again and huddled to him beneath the umbrella as they walked on. 'Anyway, why *are* you in such a mood?'

'I'm not in a mood.'

'Yes you are. You've been like it more than a week now. What am I supposed to think?'

'Think what you like.'

'Are you fed up of me already?'

'Have I given you cause to think that?'

'Could be ... I reckon you're pining for Clover Beckitt.'

'Course I'm not pining for Clover Beckitt,' he protested.

Ramona thought he was unconvincing but let it go. She was aware, despite her best efforts to allure and his best efforts to bluff, that Tom was still not over her stepsister.

'I know what you need,' she said saucily and gave him a nudge.

'Do you now?' His demeanour softened and he looked at her with a smile, noting how the street lamps made tiny catchlights in her wide eyes.

Ramona's sexual favours continued to be the hook that ensured he remained caught. Clover was lost to him, gone forever, but she was always in his thoughts. Ramona could never replace her, pretty as she was. He was not at peace with Ramona. The very thing he believed Clover had been guilty of – infidelity – Ramona could descend into on a whim. He knew that. He was under no illusions. But, while there was nobody else, and while she continued to allow regular and easy access to her more arcane charms, he was prepared to go along with it; because he was flattered and because it suited him. He was not in love with Ramona. She was not somebody he would consider marrying. She was a salve, somebody who was there right now and, by being there, helped soothe his heartache. Nor did he really believe she was in love with him, though she seemed to be trying hard to make him fall for her.

He had not seen Clover since that night when she came screaming after him accusing him of infidelity with Ramona. He guessed, rightly, that she was taking a different route to work nowadays to avoid him. Several people had told him she was seeing more and more of Ned Brisco. He couldn't really believe she had finally fallen in love with that damned fool. He tried to convince himself that she was meeting him for companionship and nothing else, but anything could happen when you were on the rebound from a love affair. Maybe she even saw him for no other reason than he had his own motor car, paid for out of the money loaned him, for all he knew.

Cross Guns Street split into two at the Cross Guns Inn, forming a triangle, of which part of St John's Street constituted the third side. Here, they took the right-hand fork, Ramona picking her way carefully to avoid stepping into the black puddles that lay like pools of ink on the cobbled surface.

'What if we run into Clover?' Ramona ventured.

'If we do, we do,' he said resignedly. 'I think maybe you should confess to her that we've been seeing each other, you and me. Bring it out into the open. I used to enjoy having a pint in the Jolly Collier. Now I daren't even show my face for fear

I see her.'

'Or her mother.'

'Yes, or her mother.'

'I can't tell Clover, Tom. I haven't got the nerve.'

'She's probably already put two and two together. She's not stupid.'

Cross Guns Street was narrow but widened out where it met George Street. They crossed St John's Street and darted up the passage at the side of the Jolly Collier before any customers who might be leaving spotted them.

'Let's go into the brewhouse,' Ramona whispered. 'I haven't had so much as a kiss off you all night.'

When they reached the back yard, Tom held her back. 'Somebody's just come out of the urinal. Hang on...'

The two shire horses that hauled the dray, locked in the stable for the night, clomped about on their straw fretfully and blew their lips at the sound of footsteps. When all was clear Tom and Ramona tiptoed across the yard to the brewhouse. Tom closed the umbrella quickly before they went in and shut the door. Ramona leaned against the mangle and drew Tom to her. She offered him her mouth. He put his hands to her waist and her arms slid compliantly round his neck. His firm body felt pleasant and warm when he opened up her coat and pressed himself against her.

Within the darkness of her closed eyelids she felt his lips brush her neck with soft, gentle touches. As his hands explored her, she enjoyed

337

the shivers that ran up and down her spine.

'I haven't got any drawers on, Tom,' she breathed into his ear and giggled.

'Why?'

'Why d'you think?'

He snorted with laughter. 'God, you're incorrigible, Ramona. You mean you've been sitting in that theatre with me all that time with no drawers on?' The thought excited him. 'If I'd known...' One thing about Ramona, she did beguile him with her unpredictability and her sexual liberality. Lesser men would become obsessed with her, would be loath to let her out of their sight because of it. He took a handful of skirt and lifted it, then slid both hands under it, relishing the warm, alluring flesh of her bare backside as he drew her to him once more.

She closed her eyes and existed in the darkness, where only the tactile senses seemed to matter. Her lips eagerly found his again while she fumbled with the buttons of his fly. She undid them and felt inside and savoured the welcoming warmth of the inside of his trousers on this cold, wet night. He was hard, ready for her. Gently, she withdrew him and guided him towards her with heady anticipation.

The door latch rattled and they froze.

The door opened and the glow of an oil lamp filled the brewhouse, illuminating the carrier's face.

It was Clover. She let out a shriek of astonishment.

Instantly Tom turned away to hide his rudely gaping fly, and the hem of Ramona's skirt fell about her.

'I'm sorry,' Clover exclaimed, her heart suddenly pounding. 'I ... I ... only came to lay the fire for Zillah tomorrow ... I'm so sorry.'

She fled.

Tom discerned Ramona's anxious expression in the dimness.

'I'd better go in,' she said. 'I'd better go and see her. Suddenly, I seem to have found the courage...'

'No, let me, Ramona. I feel I should.'

'Over my dead body, Tom. You'll only make matters worse.'

Ramona put her head round the door of the tap-room. There was no sign of Clover. She skipped through the passage, opened the stairs door and went upstairs in the darkness. She had to talk to Clover while her courage lasted; tomorrow would be too late. There was a faint light under her door. Ramona tapped on it insistently and called her name in a hoarse whisper. Eventually Clover opened the door. By the light of her oil lamp she looked deathly white, as if she'd been frightened.

'What?' she asked curtly and sat on her bed.

'Clover – I'm so sorry. I should've told you about Tom and me.'

'Oh, why?' she answered indignantly. 'Did you think I didn't know?'

Ramona shrugged. 'Maybe you did. I presumed you didn't. Anyway, I came to explain. To try and spare your feelings. I don't want you to think too badly of me.'

'I think it's a bit late for that, Ramona. Why do

you think I've avoided you all these weeks? Or hadn't you the sense to see? Are you so wrapped up in yourself, trying to look good in everybody's eyes that you can't see what's going on around you? Is that it?'

'I'm not sure what you mean, Clover,' Ramona said defensively.

'Well, it's simple enough. I've known about you and Tom ever since I saw those disgusting photos he took of you. I must say you cut a fine figure. I suppose Tom thought so too.' There was a mountain of scorn in Clover's voice.

'It wasn't like that, Clover.'

'Fancy. Nor is it now, I suppose. I suppose your skirt was all up round your waist in the brewhouse tonight to get some fresh air to your legs.'

Ramona did not reply.

'Well, let me tell you, Ramona, now you've given me the opportunity, that I despise you,' she went on calmly. 'Tom and I had our ups and downs, but we were able to sort out our problems and, I'm fairly sure, we would have enjoyed a decent marriage when the time came, if we'd been allowed to. But now you've taken him from me.' Her voice began to crack. 'I always knew you had your eye on him – right from the start – but I never thought you would stoop so low as to even try to take him. Is that what stepsisters are supposed to do?' She tried to force back the tears that were welling up in her eyes. 'Well, whether or no, I hope you're pleased with yourself. I just hope you don't live to regret it ... I regret it, though ... I deeply regret it, because I still love him and I suppose I'll always love him.' She

340

paused, heaved a great sigh of despair as her bottom lip trembled. 'But what's done can't be undone, can it, Ramona? I just hope you can live with your conscience, because I'm damned sure I never could if I were in your shoes.' The tears would not be stemmed and she reached for the handkerchief lying on her bed.

'Clover, I never intended–'

'Go, Ramona...' She wiped her eyes, her despondency becoming more absolute with each second. 'Please go. Please leave me alone.'

'But you've got Ned Brisco now...'

'*Go!*' she screamed at the top of her voice. '*Go, before I kill you!*'

So distressed was Tom Doubleday at being caught in a compromising position with Ramona that on the Monday he wrote to Clover. He wanted, not to justify his actions, but to try and win her back with a sincere plea to her heart. She received his letter by the first post on Tuesday morning and she read it with tears in her eyes as she walked to work.

It read:

Dear Clover,

I am so sorry that you had to be embarrassed by the inappropriate behaviour of myself and Ramona last night. You are the last person in the world I would want to hurt or embarrass.

I have no excuse, except to say that, for the time being at any rate, Ramona helps overcome the terrible feeling of emptiness now you have gone. Please believe me when I say I miss you and long for you. I do not love Ramona, nor shall I ever, though no doubt you will consider me even more of a cad for admitting it. In any case, I truly believe she does not love me either. We have never spoken of love.

If you can see it in your heart to forgive me you will make me eternally happy. If you cannot, then I shall spend the rest of my life in misery, cursing myself for being the ultimate fool, for throwing away the best chance of happiness a man ever had.

Clover, please reconsider. Whatever you imagined going on between Ramona and me when you found out about those photos, I give you my word I was innocent of everything except pressing the shutter on the camera. Maybe I have not been so innocent since, as I have freely admitted, but that does not mean I do not love you with all my heart and soul. Please let us take up again where we left off. Our last reconciliation made me realise how much I really do love you and how wrong I was about you. To lose you again is a blow I cannot stand.

I wait to hear from you.

Yours etc.,

Tom

Clover slipped the letter in the pocket of her skirt to read again later. She wept quietly and dabbed her eyes dry. Oh, it was gratifying to know that he still loved her and, if he was to be believed, was using Ramona like he would a poultice, but it didn't alter her own resolve. What was done was done. Things had moved on from when she discovered the photos. She might well find it in her heart to forgive him at some time, but more recent events had changed things irrevocably. She had actually happened upon them, interrupted them in the consummation of sex, like you might happen on a dog and a bitch coupling in the street. But for Tom to involve himself with her stepsister... It was bad enough having an irreparable rift in the family already. Going back to him would only make matters worse. Oh, she loved Tom, she loved him so much it hurt, but she could not return to his arms. Not now. She needed time; more time than he would be prepared to wait. In consequence, her only wish was to fall asleep for a year or two and wake up to find that this profound ache in her heart had gone.

Tom received no reply to his letter. Every morning for nearly two weeks he checked his post, but every morning brought him no response. He contemplated his liaison with Ramona. She was all right in small doses. Of course, he was grateful for her sexual favours but that's as far as it went. They had been meeting regularly for seven weeks or so and the novelty had all but worn off. He did not invite her to his studio for love sessions as often as in the beginning. Oh, she was a personable girl, pleasant, but there was no great mental rapport between them, no magic. It concerned him that while he was tending to draw back from the relationship, she was coming on strong lately.

Maybe he should end it. They had no future

together; just in case she was developing ideas to the contrary. It was the only fair way. It would release her to find somebody else. Not that she was short of admirers. But he wanted Clover back. If he ended the affair with Ramona, maybe Clover would be more inclined to a reconciliation. It would be worth it just for the chance of being reunited with Clover.

He had arranged to meet Ramona that evening, a Sunday. The air was hot and humid, typical weather for the middle of August; ideal for a stroll to Buffery Park where they could sit and talk it through rationally.

They met at eight o'clock by the Fountain Inn on Dixon's Green. She was dressed in a light cotton skirt in cream with a matching blouse and looked tantalising. Her fair hair was a mass of bubbly curls and her blue eyes were wide, yet somehow lacking that sprightly sparkle he normally associated with her. She took his arm as they walked down Bean Road, passing comments on this and that, but dwelling on no particular subject. Across the barren field to their right they could see the steeple of Top Church and Ramona commented on what a lovely church it was.

'I'd have liked to have got married there,' she said.

'You might yet,' he responded innocently and she looked at him hopefully.

They crossed Blackacre Road and headed for the park entrance just a few yards away. Tom recalled his first evening with Clover, how they'd spent an hour in this tranquil place before attending Ned Brisco's celebration. It did not seem so long ago but it had been a year. Ironic that that visit marked the beginning of such a bewitching romance, when tonight would mark the end of another. Well, that was the way of the world; full of ironies. They walked past hot-houses and flowerbeds and Ramona commented how beautiful the geraniums were. Further on a group of boys were playing cricket, making the best of a sloping expanse of mown grass. Beyond them, out of sight, they found a bench and sat down.

'You seem ever so quiet tonight, Tom,' Ramona remarked. 'Is there something on your mind?'

He sighed. 'As a matter of fact there is something I want to talk to you about.'

'Hmm,' she murmured apprehensively. 'Go on, then. What d'you want to say?'

He had rehearsed in his head exactly what he wanted to say, but now the opportunity had come he could not recall his phrasing. He hesitated, trying to reformulate his words.

'Well? Were you going to ask me to marry you?' she teased.

He laughed self-consciously and looked into her eyes, suddenly serious. 'No. As a matter of fact, I was going to suggest that we call it a day.'

'Oh?... That's a pity,' she protested with a look of genuine disappointment. 'That's *such* a pity.'

He shrugged. 'Well, I don't suppose it will come as any great surprise, but the truth is, Ramona, I don't love you. Don't get me wrong, I like you a lot and I've enjoyed our times together, but that's not the same as being in love, is it? And I thought, best give you the chance to meet

345

somebody altogether more suitable – more appreciative – and find real happiness.' She stared at him attentively without interrupting. 'You're a lovely-looking girl, Ramona. I've seen the men eyeing you up and down very covetously. You'll have no trouble finding somebody else. But I also get the impression that you're not in love with me either. So I doubt it will be any great hardship.'

'Do you want to ditch me so's you can start courting Clover again?' she asked pointedly.

He shrugged. 'I don't think I've got any chance at all of getting Clover back.'

'But you would if you could?'

He hesitated a second. 'I suppose so... If everything was right. If it could be put right between us.'

'You still love her, don't you?'

He sat forward on the bench and nodded, his elbows on his thighs, looking at the ground. A troop of ants were industriously foraging the pathway near his feet. 'I think I'll always love her... It's no reflection on you, Ramona. It's just that...'

'That you don't love me...'

'Had you been the first I've no doubt I would have fallen in love with you... As I said, Ramona, you're a lovely-looking girl. Many a bloke would be glad of a girl as pretty... And you're no less pretty than Clover–'

'Now you're patronising me, Tom. Don't!'

He sighed, a deep, unhappy sigh. 'The truth is, Clover has spoilt me for anybody else... But it's not just down to looks. Looks aren't everything,

346

don't you see? Looks are not the be all and end all.'

'So even if Clover was ugly, you'd still love her?'

'Her looks drew me to her in the first place. That's nature's way with a man. But inside – beyond Clover's looks – I see somebody even more lovely... That's the person I love.'

'So, you'd like to be rid of me to pursue Clover again? That's the top and bottom of it, isn't it?'

'I can't pursue Clover, as you put it, while I'm still seeing you – while we're still lying together.'

'I see... Well, at least that's noble. Nobler than some people I know... So, if we split up, you and me, and you succeed in getting Clover back, how d'you think I'd respond to that?'

'With dignity, I hope. With grace. With understanding. I'd like you both to be friends again, if you can find it in your hearts to be friends. If I know Clover–'

She uttered a derisory little laugh.

'What's so funny?' he asked.

'Oh... While you're stepping out with Clover I'm just wondering how dignified I can be with a big lump on my belly... Come to think of it, I wonder how dignified she would be about it. How gracious. How understanding...'

He looked at her perplexed. 'What do you mean, Ramona, a big lump on your belly?'

'I would have thought it obvious, Tom.'

'Well, it's not quite obvious to me.' A deep shadow of alarm darkened his eyes. 'What are you suggesting?'

'Oh, I'm not *suggesting* anything, Tom ... I am *telling* you, though, that I'm pregnant...'

'Jesus Christ!' Astounded, he put his head in his hands. *'Jesus Christ!'*

They fell silent. Tom was at once preoccupied with this disastrous news. He watched the ants at work; they were scurrying about darting in and out of cracks in the tarmacadam pathway, carrying fragments of leaves and other debris many times bigger than themselves. Winged ants emerged from small holes near the edge, an increasing number, struggling to make use of their wings, then flying off to God alone knew where. What fate awaited those flying ants? Did time and events play the same malicious tricks on them as it had on him? Did it make an absurdity of all their hopes, their dreams, like it did with his? But what could he do about it? Ignore it and hope she would miscarry? No, that was not quite his style. His conscience would not allow him that luxury.

Ramona was watching him, witnessing the turmoil he was suddenly plunged into.

'It's cruel, I know, how life never gives us exactly what we want ... isn't it, Tom?'

'God! Are you reading my mind?' he breathed, looking up at her, his eyes drawn.

'After what you've just told me, it's not difficult.'

'No, I suppose not... Well, that's pissed on the chips good and proper, hasn't it? If you'll pardon my French... Damn! Damn and sodding blast!'

She shrugged as he looked at her again. 'Well, Tom, you're an equal partner in this. It's not just my doing.'

'And you're absolutely certain about it?'

348

'Oh, I'm certain all right. I've been sick every morning for best part of a month, my breasts are fuller – I'm surprised you haven't noticed – they're tender, my stomach's as hard as a rock now and my waist has started to disappear already. Do I need more proof?'

'I take it you've missed your monthly bleeding?'

'Oh, and my monthly bleeding! Twice I've missed. Sorry, I forgot to mention that.'

In his frustration, he stamped his foot on a selection of ants, squashing them, then looked into Ramona's eyes again.

'Damn it all, I'll not see a child of mine fatherless, whether or no. If this is what fate's thrown at us, we can make a go of it... We'll have to. We'll just have to knuckle down, make the best of it. With the right attitude of mind, we can be as happy as anybody else. Especially with our own child to bind us together ... I'll marry you, Ramona.'

Inwardly, she breathed a sigh of relief and smiled. 'Thank you, Tom. And God bless you. But you'll have to cast Clover from your mind.'

'That's going to be the hardest part, Ramona. But I'll do the best I can. At least you understand.'

Chapter Twenty

Tom Doubleday accepted his fate with resignation. He was to acquire a pretty wife; not the pretty wife he wanted, but a likeable enough girl. It had never crossed his mind that he would make Ramona pregnant; he had always been so conscientious about withdrawing just before the critical moment. But folk did say that the stuff seeped out before you even got to the agony strokes. Just his luck for that to have happened. Still, he was responsible and he must face the consequences. He would have given anything for it not to have been Ramona; he knew the strife it would cause within the Tandy household, not least between her and Clover, but Jake Tandy too would be singularly unimpressed.

He called on Jake Tandy next morning. Jake was drying glasses in the taproom with no other help, but already customers were sitting around, smoking, swearing and supping their drinks.

'All right, young Tom? What can I get you? You'm early this morning. Not like you to be here at this time, eh?'

So Ramona had evidently not prepared her father for what was to come.

'I'd like a word if possible, Mr Tandy,' Tom said solemnly.

'Certainly, Tom. What can I do for you?'

'In private, if it's all the same to you.'

350

'Mary Ann!' Jake yelled. A few seconds later, Mary Ann appeared from the scullery. 'Watch the taproom for me, Mary Ann. Young Tom here wants a word with me.'

Mary Ann glanced at Tom with her usual measure of scorn and turned to Jake. 'Be quick then. I got some chitterlings on the hob.'

They went out into the sunshine of George Street. Jake thrust his hands into his trouser pockets and pressed downwards, putting strain on his braces. 'What's up then, Tom?' He smiled affably, smoothed his great moustache and nodded a courteous good morning to Maisy Crowe and Araminta Marsh who were each pushing a hand-cart towards the coal yard.

Tom scratched the back of his neck nervously and waited till the women were out of earshot. 'It's, er... It's Ramona and me, Mr Tandy... We, er... Well, we want to get wed.'

'You want to wed our Ramona?' Jake queried with some surprise. He regarded Tom quizzically, half amused. 'Am yer sure you've got the right wench? It ain't bin that long since you got engaged to young Clover.'

Tom, in turn, looked up to the clear blue sky as if seeking both forgiveness and inspiration. 'I know... Funny how things change when you least expect it,' he replied inadequately.

He looked at Tom suspiciously now. 'It's a bit sudden, this, eh, Tom? I never even knew as you was a-courtin' her serious... Mind you, it answers one or two questions if you am...' The open rift between his daughter and his stepdaughter came immediately to mind. 'Am you sure as you'm a-doing the right thing, Tom?'

'In the circumstances, I can't see any alternative.'

'Circumstances? What circumstances? Christ! It'd pay yer not to have babbied the wench.'

Tom looked suitably remorseful. 'Well, she's pregnant, Mr Tandy. She's carrying my child.'

Jake bridled yet looked mortified. 'You *bastard!* ... I've a good mind I'd–'

Tom at once raised both hands in a gesture of submission. 'I'm not going to fight you, Mr Tandy. I can understand how you feel.'

'Understand how I feel? I'll be buggered if you can! You ain't got the first idea.'

'All I can say is, I'm sorry. But it seems to me that we should try and make the best of a bad job. If you can just accept what's happened, things will be so much simpler in the end. And there's the welfare of a child at stake here. As I see it, the sooner we get married the better. If you prefer that we don't...' He shrugged. If only Jake *would* forbid it...

Jake was visibly affected by all this news. He looked at Tom with both disbelief and anger in his eyes; disbelief that his one and only daughter could be seduced at all, anger that this ... this smart-suited *blackguard* standing before him had abused his poor, innocent little Ramona, seduced her, taken advantage of the most amenable, the most sensitive little angel God ever graced the earth with.

'You've made your bed, the pair of you, you can bloody well lie in it,' he said brusquely. 'So when do you intend getting married?'

'We thought about this coming Friday – by special licence...'

'By spec–'

'To get it over and done with – quick.'

'Oh, so folk won't cotton on, eh? So tongues won't wag. Well, think again, sonny!' He stood looking at the ground for some seconds, shaking his head as if he was looking into a grave. 'I don't admire you for what you've done, Tom,' he rasped. 'When I think of you taking advantage of my young daughter like that – me only daughter... And you think getting married as soon as you can will absolve you of the mortal sins of seduction and fornication afore marriage? Well, it won't and I hope you burn in hell. God! It's a pity you ever showed up here in the fust place. I rue the day I engaged you tek we photos when me and Mary Ann was wed.'

'That's all well and good, Mr Tandy,' Tom replied, feeling he'd got the worst out of the way. 'But you can't alter what's happened. And nobody knows that better than me.'

'So where d'you intend to live?'

'I intend to rent a house somewhere in Dudley. That'll take a week or two to organise, I know that. And we'll have to furnish it. Till then, we shall live with my folks in Stafford Street.'

'So why don't you wait a week or two and get wed in church, like normal, decent folk? Do it right and proper. Give yourselves time to find a house to move straight into.'

'Because that would entail having the banns read out for three weeks in two parishes. Ramona would like to get married straight away – quietly,

353

with no fuss and no attention drawn to the fact.'

Jake shook his head in despair. 'You know, I've always wanted the best for my daughter. I always imagined sending her off with a decent wedding – no expense spared. But then some puffed-up bastard like you comes along, puts her in the family way and buggers the lot up. Well, I hope you'm satisfied.'

'Well, we're not the first, Mr Tandy, and I don't suppose we'll be the last.'

'That's no consolation. It don't justify what you've done, neither. Men like you with little or no respect for young women should be bloody-well neutered.'

'Well, I suppose that's easy to say, Mr Tandy,' Tom replied calmly, though he was riled by such a comment which, coming from Jake, he knew to be hypocritical. 'I daresay your first wife's father felt exactly the same way when you told him you'd put his daughter in the family way... Eh, Mr Tandy?' He looked Jake in the eye.

'Why, you–'

The thrum of a motor car's engine reverberating off the terraced buildings on both sides of George Street drew their attention. The two men looked and saw Ned Brisco approaching.

'Christ, that's all we need,' Jake exclaimed angrily. 'Pontius bloody Pilot. All I need now is for him to tell me he's put Clover in the family way.'

Tom's heart lurched at the thought while Ned pulled up outside the Jolly Collier. He greeted Jake with a tentative grin as he put on the brake, but ignored Tom.

354

'How's this?' Jake enquired tartly. 'No work?'

'Holiday, Mr Tandy. It's such a lovely day I thought I'd call for Clover and take her for a ride into the country.' He glanced at Tom. 'She's having a few days' holiday as well. I presumed you knew.'

'Well, the women in this house don't tell me much,' he jibed and looked at Tom testily. 'But Clover's told me that. I'll let her know as you'm here.' Jake left the two men and went back inside the pub.

Ned alighted from his vehicle and tightened the radiator cap on the motor car. Still he ignored Tom.

It irked him. He said: 'I take it that you don't want to acknowledge me, Ned.'

Ned's eyes met Tom's with an icy glare. 'Not particularly.'

'No, well, I suppose this thing over Clover has poisoned your mind, eh?'

'Oh, my mind was poisoned about you long ago, Tom. Why she ever got mixed up with you in the first place I'll never know.'

'Ah! Do I detect some jealousy?' he goaded, his mood growing blacker by the minute. 'Well, let me tell you, Ned – if ever I get the chance to have Clover back I'll grasp it with both hands. So make no mistake–'

Ned, reddening, reached out with both hands and grabbed Tom by the lapels. 'Just so much as look at her again,' he hissed, his nose almost touching Tom's, 'and I'll break your bloody neck!'

Tom raised his arms and tried to shove Ned

away. 'Get your hands off me, you damned great twerp. Who the hell do you think you are?'

They overbalanced in their struggle and fell against the motor car. Passers-by stopped to witness this sudden scuffle between two grown men whom, they presumed, were sober at this time of day.

Ned swung a fist at Tom but he was off-balance and Tom parried it easily.

'Calm down you bloody idiot!' Tom bellowed. 'What purpose does it serve to fight like–'

Smack! Ned hit him in the mouth, stood still and straightened his jacket as he watched Tom reel from the blow. 'It gives me bloody *pleasure,* you crap ant,' he yelled at his adversary. 'Now sod off before I hit you again.'

Tom touched his mouth circumspectly, looked at his fingers and saw that Ned had drawn blood. He flicked his tongue around his teeth to make sure none were loosened.

'Not before I clout you...' Tom swung out and caught Ned who had remained still from utter amazement at what he'd done. He caught Ned under the eye. It felt good to release his pent-up feelings thus. Ned lurched after him, a swelling at once visible around his left eye. He flailed about, fists flying but going wildly astray in his uncontrolled anger.

They both heard footsteps.

'Stop it, you two!' It was Clover. She pushed herself hurriedly between them, tried to keep them from each other, arms outstretched with one hand clutching Ned, the other clutching Tom. 'God! Grown men! Stop it!' she shrieked.

356

'You're both hurt, look.'

'I'll kill him,' Ned howled. 'I'll kill him for the way he treated you.'

'Leave him be, Ned,' she decreed, and felt the intensity and rage drain away from both men at her timely appearance, for neither wanted to upset her more than they had already done. She looked penetratingly into Tom's eyes, but addressed the other man. 'I think you'll find, Ned, that Tom has already had his come-uppance.'

'Word soon gets around,' Tom said sardonically, still looking at Ned with a glare enough to shrivel him. 'I'm sorry, Clover. I'm so sorry...'

Clover stepped up onto the front passenger seat, trying to control her trembling. 'Let's get away from here, Ned,' she said as she watched Tom disappear irrevocably from her life, from her future.

'Suits me.' Ned ceased his posturing and jumped into the motor car.

'That's going to be a tidy black eye,' she commented. 'You ought to bathe it in cold water.'

He fingered it carefully. 'Mmm. It'll keep. To tell you the truth, it was worth it just to get a poke at Tom Doubleday.'

She did not reply.

'Do you still want to go out, Clover? You seem a bit upset. I'll understand if you don't.'

'I am upset. And not just at you two stupid idiots... Come on, let's get away from here.'

Ned jumped down again and cranked the engine. It fired into life, he took his seat once more and they were on their way. 'Where shall we go?'

'Anywhere. I don't care. Just get away from here... But don't go down Cross Guns. Tom's gone that way.'

'What did you mean when you said Tom has already had his comeuppance? ... Clover... What did you mean?'

She said nothing.

He looked at her and saw tears streaming down her face.

'Clover...'

She broke down in a turmoil of tears, sobbing, her chest heaving with distress.

'Clover, are you going to tell me?... Look, do you want me to stop?'

She shook her head. As they pressed forward, tears were being blown about her face by the oncoming wind. Never in her life had she felt so miserable. What she'd just heard was worse than being kicked in the belly. She had to get away from that house while the inevitable inquest was in progress.

'I'll drive to the top of Oakham, shall I? We'll go to the top of Rough Hill where we used to fly the *Gull*. I'll pull up there and you can tell me what's so wrong. All right?'

She nodded.

In a few minutes they had arrived. Ned drew his vehicle to a halt at the side of the lane, stopped the engine and got down. He went round to Clover's side and offered his hand. She held onto it with a shuddering sigh as she alighted.

'Come on, let's walk into the field and look at the view,' Ned said kindly. 'We can put this on the ground to sit on...' He picked up his car rug from the rear seat and they began walking.

Clover took out a handkerchief and mopped her eyes. He opened the gate and allowed her to go first and they walked in silence through the uncultivated field. He watched her apprehensively. At what he considered a suitable spot he stopped, placed the car rug on the grass and gestured for her to sit down. The sun was high in the sky and high cloud signalled settled weather.

'Now tell me what you meant, Clover,' he said gently as he sat down beside her.

With hazy eyes, she scanned the landscape below, seeing nothing. She looked at Ned. 'You've got a lovely black eye. I've never known such a pair of fools.'

'Never mind me and him, Clover. Tell me what you meant when you said he'd had his comeuppance.'

A blackbird landed, cocked his head to one side then tugged at a worm. Triumphantly, he flew away with it securely in his beak.

Clover sighed again and wiped her nose. The heat of the sun did not warm her, the sunshine did not lighten the darkness within her. 'He's marrying Ramona... On Friday... He's made her pregnant.'

'He's made—' Ned looked scandalised. 'Are you sure?'

'Oh, I'm sure. I wish to God it wasn't true, but it is. That's why he was there. To tell Jake.'

'I imagine Jake's none too pleased then?'

She sighed again. 'Nor my mother. You should have heard her. She screamed at Jake for being too soft, then called Ramona a dirty whore. She told her it's a good job she's moving out so soon else she'd throw her out. She says she wants nothing to do with her any more.'

'And what did Jake have to say?'

'When he could get a word in, he agreed with Mother. Oh, it was pandemonium, Ned. I just had to get out. I left them to it. I couldn't stand it.'

'So how do *you* feel about it?'

'How do you think I feel?' She sobbed again. 'I love Tom. He was going to marry me. But now he's marrying my stepsister. Oh, Ned, I'm so miserable, I wish I was dead...' Another flood of tears streamed down her face. Never in her life had she cried so much. Where were all the tears coming from? Her eyes were sore from so much crying.

The grief of losing Tom was taking its toll in other ways. She had lost her appetite, couldn't face food, and lost weight in consequence. Sometimes she felt faint. Her complexion was wan, despite the sunshine of these summer days. Her eyes, puffed up now with crying, were developing dark rings under them.

'Well, now you can see what he's truly like. He's a philanderer. That's all he is. You know it better than anybody. How can you love a man like that?'

'You're making him out to be a cad, Ned, and he's not.' She reached out and picked a daisy from amongst the grass. 'Believe me, he's not. I know him better than anybody. I know what he's like.'

'You *think* you know,' he said disdainfully. 'You see a knight in shining armour. I see him as nothing but a scoundrel.'

She sniffed and split the stem of the daisy with her nail, then picked another to thread through it. 'It makes no difference to me what you think, Ned. I can't help the way I feel. Maybe you should try to understand that.'

'I understand this, Clover. I'm in love with you and I always have been. I hate to see you suffering like this just because you've been taken for a fool ... by a fool. Someday you'll see things as they really are.'

'You think so, do you?'

'I know so. Anyway, what shall you wear for the wedding?'

She looked at him in wet-eyed disbelief. 'Are you kidding? Do you seriously think I'm going to see him marry *her*?'

The wedding took place as planned on Friday 21st August 1908 by special licence. The bride, who was anxious to be wed as soon as possible lest her groom changed his mind, wore a blue dress that complemented the colour of her hair, while he wore a navy-blue suit and white shirt with a thin navy stripe. His parents did not show up and neither did Mary Ann. Jake appeared as witness with Dorcas, while Elijah remained at work in the brewery. Afterwards, the couple returned to the groom's family home in Stafford Street.

Tom's parents resented the marriage as much as Mary Ann. The shame of having to get married carried a stigma that was hard to bear and, whilst they condescended to allow the couple to lodge with them until they could find a house to rent, they were not made welcome.

Having chosen this week as a time for holidays, Clover decided she would be relieved to get back to work on Monday. Every day she'd avoided staying in. She had no desire to see Ramona, nor to remain in the awful atmosphere that prevailed for those tense days before the wedding. Yet that oppressive atmosphere did improve after Jake returned from the civil ceremony that afternoon. He seemed relieved that it was over, that Ramona was no longer his responsibility. Mary Ann in turn, seemed to quickly react and became altogether less intense and more relaxed. Clover, too, felt more at ease when she knew Ramona was gone.

Elijah came in for tea and the four of them sat in the scullery that afternoon while Zillah Bache tended to customers in the taproom.

'Well, I hope they'll mek the best of it,' Jake remarked and wiped tea from his moustache with the back of his hand. 'But I would never have believed it of our Ramona, to be took advantage of by any bloke.'

'Nor me,' Elijah said, shaking his head, but in agreement. 'It just goes to show ... with women, you never can tell.'

'Well, let this be a lesson to thee, our Clover,' Mary Ann proclaimed. 'And be thankful. There but for the grace of God...'

Clover blushed and looked down, trying to hide her face.

'I always had me doubts about him,' Mary Ann continued. 'I reckon you had a lucky escape. Count your blessings as you never fell prey to his damned sinful ways.'

Clover picked up her cup and sipped her tea, keeping it in front of her face. She resented her mother's remarks but it was politic to make no comment.

'Course, Clover will have to work in the business now Ramona's gone,' Jake pronounced and Clover looked at him aghast. He returned her look steadily. 'So Monday, you can hand in your notice at Cook's ready to start work here. I see no sense in employing anybody else when me own stepdaughter can do the job standing on her head.'

'What if I don't want to work here?'

'You'll do as you'm bid, madam,' Mary Ann responded haughtily.

'I'm twenty-one, Mother, and I'll do as I please. I won't work here if I don't want to.'

'Oh? Then you'd best find another bed to sleep in, 'cause there'll be ne'er un here for thee.'

Clover, of course, capitulated. Where could she go? She thought about it long and hard but, in the end, decided that to work in the family brewing business was the only right thing to do. Besides, it was unfair to put yet more stress and strain on her mother and Jake so soon after all the trouble and anxiety over Ramona. They had had their fair share of troubles also. So, on

363

Monday morning, she handed the letter she had written to the manager of her department and waited for the reaction.

It was a long week and Clover was still suffering acutely the pains of love and the shock of Tom's marriage to Ramona. Her appetite began to improve, however, except that in a morning she could not face breakfast. To compensate, Mary Ann, to her credit, made a special effort to present some tasty and substantial dishes to the meal table. She had noticed Clover's listlessness and sallow complexion and realised she needed feeding up. 'You'll go to nothing if you don't perk up, werriting about that ne'er-do-well,' she said, but not unkindly.

Each night that week Clover served in the taproom and helped clear up after closing time, preparing herself for the new routine that was to be her lot. She made no arrangements to meet Ned Brisco although he appeared in the taproom for a drink one evening. But Clover was neither impressed nor pleased with him. He had only ill to say about Tom Doubleday. His constant bitching was wearing thin. She assumed it was designed to colour her view of Tom, when nothing could. So she avoided seeing Ned further.

Besides, people were already talking.

Chapter Twenty-One

It was on the very Monday morning that she officially began working in the family business that Clover Beckitt realised she was pregnant. Any fool would have known it sooner, but Clover, so preoccupied with her loss of Tom Doubleday, had put down all symptoms to that very preoccupation. Worry had inhibited her monthly bleeding, or so she thought. It had not been a great concern at first; worry had had a similar effect before and she'd read somewhere that your mental state could affect your monthly cycle. Pains in her stomach and tender, swollen breasts had been suggesting for a while that she was about to start bleeding, but she had not shown. Morning sickness and a belly so hard that it seemed there was a football tucked away in there were the later clues that ultimately made her realise.

Strangely, she was not concerned. The child could only be Tom's. So, although she had lost him forever, she would still have something of him to last her the rest of her life. She hoped she would have a boy, the image of Tom, and she began imagining the child. In her daydreams she would nuzzle him at her breast, looking down on his little baby head with all the love and protection a mother felt. She pictured herself playing little games with him, teaching him how

365

to do things, kissing better the scratches and grazes that hurt him when he tumbled.

But would it ever be so idyllic? The realities of life were somewhat harsher. Losing Tom to her stepsister, when she now had an equal claim on him, galled her. As the days passed the irony of it grew even more bitter. She could have married Tom herself. She *should* have married him. He was the father of her unborn child as well as Ramona's. If she'd realised beforehand and he'd been offered the choice, she knew whom he would have chosen, and let Ramona sort out her own salvation. If only she'd listened to him when he protested his innocence. If only she'd heeded his letter, swallowed her pride and gone to see him, talked things over. She should have given him the benefit of any doubt. She had driven him into the arms of Ramona as certainly as if she'd shepherded him there. Her misplaced pride, arrogance and overdone prudishness had done her more harm than good. She had sown the wind. Now she was reaping the whirlwind.

Of course, she had not forgotten another side to all this, which was yet to manifest itself; the social disgrace. Some folk would cross the street rather than nod a greeting and be seen associating with her. Her child would be labelled a bastard, she a fallen woman. And if her mother took it badly...

Just how long could she keep the knowledge of her condition from her mother?

She began to count back the weeks. Her last lovemaking with Tom had been the night of their reconciliation; 3rd June. She remembered the date as if it were her own birthday; it was a glorious night of love, the recommencing of the rest of their lives. If the tenderness and love they felt for each other that night was the pointer for their future, they would have been a contented couple indeed. If only she'd known how short-lived it was going to be. Assuming she had conceived on 3rd June, and she knew well enough that it must have been, her child would be born at the end of February or early March. It was now the end of August. Already she was nearly three months pregnant. She would have her child before Ramona had hers. When Tom knew he would realise the child was his. How would he feel about that?

The mirror provided little evidence of pregnancy yet; her stomach, though slightly more rounded, would look flat enough under her dresses. She might hide her condition for another couple of months. But sooner or later, depending on how the child inside her affected her shape, she would have to confess. The trouble was, she lacked the courage to confess anything, especially after the hostile reaction Ramona had experienced.

So she continued to work in the Jolly Collier and in the brewery. She never asked for help from Elijah or Jake when it came to moving barrels or lifting hop pockets lest they guess her secret, and she hoped that such strenuous exertion would not cause her to miscarry; she wanted Tom's child whatever else fortune might fling at her.

In September a new bottling line was installed and four women were employed to operate it.

The brewery was prospering. Elijah, who was mastering the brewer's art commendably, employed an able assistant who had worked at another brewery and output was increasing steadily along with sales. Jake, for his part, was proving an astute businessman.

With Ramona out of the way, Clover was enjoying working at home, despite the cloud that hung over her. The pain of lost love was becoming less intense and only the apprehension over the likely reaction to her condition continued to concern her. She renewed friendships with people she'd not seen much while working at Cook's and it was a pleasure to see Zillah Bache regularly again. In slacker moments they would gossip for ages but never once was Clover inclined to confess her secret, even though she knew she could talk to Zillah about such things.

Ned Brisco, meanwhile, had given up calling on her. Clover imagined he was tired of losing the battle to win her when she remained so obstinately in love with Tom, a love Ned could not understand, and probably never would.

Ned Brisco was having problems of his own, however. The continued failure of Star Engineering to design and manufacture a suitable engine for his *Gull* irked him beyond belief. Another test in August had failed to get the *Gull* airborne and he was becoming despondent. So much so that he decided to spell out his grievances to Edward Lisle and hang the consequences. He tapped on the door of Mr Lisle's office and was summoned inside.

'Ned, good morning. What can I do for you?'

Ned stood before Mr Lisle's desk feeling like a naughty schoolboy yet determined that he would not to be overawed. He straightened himself up and took a deep breath. 'I'm here to complain about our lack of progress on the aeroplane engine, Mr Lisle.'

'I see.' Edward Lisle pressed his fingers together in a peak as if he was about to pray and sat back in his chair. 'Sit down, Ned.'

'I'll stand, if it's all the same to you, Mr Lisle.' This was a new Ned, combatant, more confident in himself.

'I too am disappointed, Ned. I have my own ideas as to why we have failed so far. But I'd like to hear yours.'

'It's because nobody in this factory has got a clue what's needed to produce an aeroplane engine. I keep telling Bill Harris till I'm blue in the face that I need speed, not torque but I'm still getting no more revolutions out of his useless creation than I was the first time.'

'So... Do you have a remedy, Ned?'

'I'm not an engine designer, Mr Lisle, but I wish to God I was, 'cause I would've sorted this lot out long ago. But I've got an idea. Why don't we buy an *Antoinette* engine from France? We could strip it down and see why it's so much better than ours. We could learn from it. Then, we could develop our own engine, based on what we discover – even improve on it.'

Mr Lisle continued to lean back in his chair, his fingers still together in a peak. 'It's an interesting idea, Ned, I have to confess. So how much do you suppose an *Antoinette* would cost us?'

'I don't know for sure. I reckon maybe nine hundred, a thousand pounds...'

Mr Lisle shook his head. 'I'm not committing us to spend a thousand pounds when we surely must be so close to achieving success with our own design, Ned.'

'I'm not so sure that we are close, Mr Lisle. I'm sure it'd be cheaper in the long run.'

'You may be right. Even so ... I refuse to be beaten by French machinery–'

'With respect, Mr Lisle, we've already been beaten by French machinery. Did you hear that somebody called Leon Delagrange had set a new record by staying up in the air for half an hour on the 5th of September ... in France? But it's not just the French, is it? In America last week, Orville Wright even managed an hour and ten minutes. We haven't been able to get off the bloody ground yet. My *Gull* flies, Mr Lisle, but with your engine it doesn't! I'm getting pretty fed up. You promised me co-operation and a free hand to get this project running. I'm not getting it, Mr Lisle.'

Edward Lisle leaned forward and placed his hands on his desk, his fingers interlocked, and forced a smile. 'I understand your frustration, Ned, but currently we have other priorities. As you know we have the Briton project on hand, our new company that will produce the cheaper range of Briton motor cars. They have to be designed and tested, the new factory has to be built. We are developing the new four-cylinder fifteen-horsepower, a more expensive motor car to be made under the Star banner. These things consume manpower and money, Ned. I'm sorry, but we can spare nobody else to assist you in the aeroplane engine project – not yet at any rate. However, Bill Harris will help you when he can, I'm sure.'

Ned sighed discontentedly. 'So let me have an *Antoinette*.'

The other man hesitated. 'Let me think about it,' he said eventually. 'Let me put it to the Board. I understand your concern and I'm as keen as you are to build successful aeroplanes. There's going to be a big market out there for them. I'll cite your very arguments. Thank you, Ned.'

'Thank you, Mr Lisle.'

The following day, Ned bought his daily newspaper from the paper shop in George Street on his way to his tram and was astounded by a headline that jumped off the page. He read on:

'An American army officer was killed yesterday when an aircraft piloted by Orville Wright lost a propeller blade which unbalanced the diametrically opposed blade causing it to tear through the loose wires controlling the rudder outriggers on the wings. Orville Wright was also injured in the resulting crash but is expected to recover. He had been conducting trials for senior army officers to demonstrate how the aircraft met all War Department requirements. Trials, however, were set to continue.'

Ned sighed. There was clearly a military use for

aeroplanes if the American military thought so.

Four days later, Ned saw in his newspaper that Orville Wright's brother, Wilbur, had stayed aloft for more than an hour and half, covering a distance of 61 miles. On October 4th, Ned's newspaper blared that the same Wilbur Wright had set a record time for carrying a passenger with a flight of 55 minutes. All this aerial success by these people was occurring with a sickening monotony.

It was at this point that Ned Brisco realised his dream of catching up with and overtaking the French and American aviators would never be achieved, whether or not Mr Lisle sanctioned the acquisition of an *Antoinette* engine.

By the middle of October the weather changed for the worse. Summer had gone and all there was to look forward to was winter with its bitter cold and its choking fogs. That Monday, the 19th, was wet and dreary with a piercing chill you would normally associate with late November. Clover, who had been working in the brewery, had gone to the scullery to make the mid-morning pot of tea for the other workers. She carried a tray containing the fresh-filled teapot and an assortment of mugs over to the brewhouse. While it steeped she could have a chat with Zillah who was doing the weekly wash.

'Hello, Zillah,' she said brightly. 'What have you done to the weather?'

'Hello, Clover, my wench.' Zillah was wearing a thick, hand-knitted ganzy to keep out the cold. 'I've done sod-all to the weather but it'll bugger up the drying and no two ways.'

Clover laughed at her concern and put the tray on the top of the boiler while she gossiped. 'Don't worry, Zillah. I'll pull down the drying rack in the scullery. When I've taken the tea to Elijah and the others I'll come and help you with it.'

'God bless you,' Zillah said gratefully, turning the mangle to squeeze water from a towel. 'How is Elijah? Is married life suiting him?'

'I think so. He doesn't say much, but he seems keen enough to get back to Dorcas when he's finished work.'

'Has he said whether the wench is pregnant? Your mother swore as her'd got one up her when they was wed.'

'Well, I think mother's going to be disappointed ... I don't think Dorcas is pregnant after all.'

Zillah chuckled. 'Well, damn my hide. Just goes to show, eh? That'll learn her to jump to conclusions. Hast heard how young Ramona is?'

Clover shook her head and a shadow seemed to cloud her face.

Zillah, as perceptive as ever, noticed. 'I'm sorry, my wench. I shouldn't have mentioned Ramona, should I?'

'No, it was a bit tactless, Zillah, if you don't mind me saying so.'

'Still painful after all this time then, eh?'

'And things will get even more painful...' She looked into Zillah's eyes tellingly.

'Oh?' Zillah queried. 'D'you want to tell me why?'

'I don't particularly want to tell anybody, but

it'll be obvious soon enough, if it isn't already ... I'm pregnant as well, Zillah...'

She ceased her mangling and looked with alarm at Clover. 'D'you mean what I think you mean? That you'm carrying Ramona's husband's child? Tom's child?'

Clover nodded. 'Well, it's nobody else's. And that's a fact.'

'Oh, my God. And does he know?'

'No, and I don't want him to know. As far as he's concerned it's somebody else's – anybody's. So swear to me, Zillah, that you won't breathe a word that it's Tom's child. If he doesn't know, then at least him and Ramona have a chance together.'

'Me lips am sealed, Clover. But to think – you could've married him yourself. You must be as wicked as a wasp... Have you told your mother yet?'

Clover shook her head and shivered from the cold. 'I'm dreading it. Do I show yet, Zillah? Can you tell?' She twisted round to show herself in profile.

Zillah offered another towel to the mangle's wooden rollers and began to turn the wheel. 'Yes, you'm starting to show, Clover, if you want the truth... But I guessed you was pregnant above a month ago. You've got that look about you. Course, I said bugger-all. I mean, it's none o' my business. So what am you gunna do?'

Clover shrugged. 'I want to keep the child. I just hope Mother will accept things. If not... If not, I don't know what I'll do.'

'I can't see Mary Ann taking kindly to this

news, Clover. Her abhors that sort o' thing. Her could never hold her head up in St John's church again.'

'I know.'

'Well, you seem very calm about it, young Clover.'

'The lull before the storm... Like I said, I'm dreading telling her.'

'Clover, my wench, be ruled by me. Get on and tell her, for Lord's sake. The longer her has afore the babby's born the more her'll get used to the idea. Tell her today. Don't thee hivver-hover. Her might be vexed at fust but her'll come round. No woman can resist a grandchild.'

'D'you think so?'

'I know so.'

Clover lifted the cosy off the teapot, took off the lid and gave the pot a stir. Then she poured a mug of tea for Zillah and stirred it.

'Here. Try this. I've already sugared the mugs.'

'Ta, my babby.' She took the steaming mug and took her first sip. 'How *is* Mary Ann today?'

'A bit grumpy.'

'Grumpy? Her's always bloody grumpy. I don't know how you put up with her.' She placed her mug on the brick windowsill and folded her huge arms across her ample chest.

'Well,' Clover sighed, 'she'll be a sight grumpier after I've told her.'

By this time, Tom and Ramona had found a terraced house to rent in Edward Street, not far from Tom's parents' home in Stafford Street on the other side of town from Kates Hill. From the front, the house looked like a normal two-storey affair but, at the rear, it had three storeys, the decent-sized scullery taking up the bottom floor and overlooking a small garden which Tom intended to use for growing vegetables next summer.

To their neighbours they seemed like any ordinary young married couple and Ramona always had a pleasant smile for them as she stopped to pass the time of day and gossip about everyday things. She settled into the rhythm of married life easily. In bed, Tom found her accommodating but, as her belly began to expand and her waist started to thicken, the frequency of lovemaking rapidly diminished and they both would lie awake unspeaking, thinking their own thoughts.

Ramona had irreconcilably alienated her stepmother by bringing shame on her and Jake. Thus, she knew better than to visit them at the Jolly Collier and suffer the ignominy of a monumental snub. Jake, though, while condemning his daughter's obvious lack of virtue for the sake of peace and quiet at home with Mary Ann, made secret visits to Ramona at least once a week, to give her money and such moral support as he was able. He could no more disown his only daughter and shut her from his life than he could Mary Ann. The two women were integral to his very existence and he walked a narrow path trying to oblige both.

Ramona pondered her lot as she lay awake waiting for sleep to encompass her. She might be pregnant, but she was lucky – she had a husband.

She'd found a man she liked who had played the game nobly and sacrificed what might have been, for her and the child. Oh, she was under no illusions about whom he really loved, but at least his sense of fair play, his integrity, had rendered her position rock-solid. But she was determined that he should not regret his marrying her. So, she was attentive, sweet and affectionate. She kept a clean and tidy house and, whilst it was as yet sparsely furnished, she brightened it with vases of seasonal flowers and made some bright curtains from material she bought from the market. She ventured that sooner or later he couldn't fail to realise on which side his bread was buttered and, when that happened he would realise he loved only her. But Ramona, always honest with herself if with nobody else, knew that if ever Tom did confess finally that he loved her, she would have achieved her goal ... yet once that happened, she would inevitably lose interest in him.

Naturally, she wondered how Clover felt about the whole unsavoury business and there were times when she was racked with feelings of guilt at having stolen Tom from right under that pretty nose of hers. She had not played fair with Clover. She was acutely aware of it and not particularly proud of the fact. But her own need had been the greater. She was with child. She needed a husband. Her unborn child needed a father. They had been blessed with the finest.

Tom pondered his lot, too. He had little to complain about from a husband's point of view. He had a wife who turned heads wherever she went, with her mass of yellow curls and big brown eyes. To look at her you'd think butter wouldn't melt in her mouth though he knew different. She was sensuous and affectionate but he knew she had been sensuous and affectionate with at least one other man. There might have been others for all he knew, so he could only speculate; but since speculation was dangerous and unsettling he was not inclined to do it. Ramona was proving to be a worthy cook, an adept homemaker; their bed was changed weekly, she did the washing on a Monday like any self-respecting wife and her ironing was exemplary. There was never a speck of dust out of place and the windows gleamed. By the time he returned from his studio every evening she made certain she looked her best. She was a worthy young woman, canny beyond her years.

So why did he not love her? Well, maybe he would grow to love her in time. Maybe, if only he knew it, if only he could see over the sides of this hole he'd dug himself so deeply into, she was the best thing that had ever happened to him. The truth was, he missed Clover. He still loved Clover with all his being and coming to terms with a life without her was difficult. Of course, he tried to hide the fact. He did not go about with his chin on the floor. But Clover was seldom far from his thoughts. When making love to Ramona in those early days he felt pangs of guilt that he was being unfaithful to Clover, despite the fact that their relationship was at an end. He was both amazed and confused that he could relish making love to one woman when he was so much in love with another. Perhaps that was the hypocrisy of man. Perhaps it was even the inconsistency of man that worked both ways, allowing him to square up to his undoubted responsibilities to Ramona and become her lawful wedded husband, when he was pulled so strongly by his love for Clover.

Well, Clover was gone. She was out of his reach. She was out of bounds now. Still he could not help wondering what marriage to her might have been like. He could not help imagining how life might have developed with her, how they would have fallen into each other's ways, accepted each other's little habits and foibles and laughed at them. He could not help wondering how they would have borne life's inevitable disappointments, felt elation at life's triumphs. He could not help wondering what a child of theirs would be like.

If only he had made *her* pregnant instead...

Clover determined to tell her mother that night that she was pregnant but her courage failed her at the last. She trembled at the prospect and felt her legs go weak. She realised, just at the point of forming the words on her lips, that she could not face the torrent of abuse that Mary Ann would undoubtedly hurl at her in consequence. No, she could not face that tonight.

But things have a way of happening, circumstances have the knack of unwittingly wrenching from us our most intimate secrets when we least expect it. So it was after tea that same evening. Clover had gone to her room to change, to smarten herself up ready to serve in the taproom.

Her mother had gone upstairs as well with the same notion. In her room, Clover took off the frock and the shift she had been wearing all day and stood in her drawers as she looked briefly at herself in profile in the long mirror, inspecting the size of her belly. Next, she reached in her wardrobe for the blouse and skirt she intended wearing. When she had found them she pulled open the top drawer of her chest and found a clean shift. Her door was ajar and she did not know Mary Ann was watching from the landing.

Clover sat on her bed and felt the cold linoleum under her bare feet as she fingered a stray piece of cotton. She heard the creak of floorboards and looked up as the door opened. Mary Ann appeared, half dressed in her own white shift, looking like Marley's ghost, her greying hair loose about her shoulders. Her expression was one of horror, as if she herself had just encountered some hideous ghoul. Clover thought she looked like a mad woman. Then she realised that her mother had been watching her, had noticed her swollen midriff that her clothes concealed so well.

'You've put on some weight, our Clover. You'm getting quite a belly on you.'

She knew.

By God, she knew.

Mary Ann knew her daughter well. This was the opening lunge, although it did not promise to be a lengthy fencing match. Both women were inclined to be direct, but Mary Ann could be brutally so. Besides, she would know by Clover's reaction the truth of the matter.

Clover sighed. It was a critical moment. The opportunity to confess her condition and be done with it was suddenly upon her. It would be hard to shy away from such a crucial juncture, timely or not, only to have to contrive another one later.

'So what's up?' Mary Ann persisted.

'I'll give you one guess,' Clover answered resignedly, looking directly into her eyes. All fear, all apprehension was gone. Her mother could do nothing that could hurt her. She had already experienced the most savage hurt that events could inflict upon her. Nothing could pain her more, physical or mental.

'I hope to God as you'm not pregnant.' There was stony contempt in her voice.

'Well, you'll have to go on hoping, Mother,' Clover said quietly, 'because that's exactly what I am.'

'If it's the truth, you'm no daughter of mine.'

Clover shrugged and looked at her bare knees, unwilling to meet her mother's scathing eyes. It was exactly the sort of unsupportive reaction she had envisaged.

'So whose child is it?'

Clover shook her head and looked defiantly up at Mary Ann. 'If I'm no daughter of yours then it's none of your business.'

'Just you mind your mouth, you damn tart.' She glowered at Clover with narrowed eyes that promised hellfire and brimstone. 'Who d'you think you'm a-talking to? Is it that Tom Doubleday's child you'm a-carrying?'

'I don't know whose child it is,' Clover lied,

with conviction.

'I asked if it was Tom Doubleday's. Ramona's husband's.'

'No, it's not Tom Doubleday's, so you can rest easy. I told you, I don't know who the father is and that's the truth.'

'You don't know who the father is?' Mary Ann's scorn was like frosted granite. 'What kind of a trollop am yer?'

'Oh, the worst kind, I imagine. It could be one of ... of ten men.' She threw her head back haughtily. Might as well be vilified for having ten lovers as for one. Might as well plague her mother with the thought that her only daughter had slept with ten different men.

'My God!...' Mary Ann paused while she assimilated this information. She folded her arms disdainfully across her chest. 'I knew as wearing ne'er a corset would lead to this. I tried to warn you but you wouldn't listen. And that Ramona an' all. Well, I hope you'm ashamed of yourself. May the Lord forgive you for your sins, 'cause I'm buggered if I can. I can't abide such vile behaviour and I'll not harbour such a sinful woman under my roof, daughter or no. You'll have to go, Clover.' She sighed with anger and disappointment while Clover suffered her mother's icy resentment, her eyes fixed on her knees. 'What a damned mess!' Mary Ann went on, trawling new depths for revilement of indignation and disgust. 'First Ramona, then you. It was bad enough the shock of young Ramona. Jake'll never get over that. And now you. I thought you had a bit more about you than that. I don't know what's up with you young women today, by God I don't. You've got no morals, no virtue.'

'And no corsets,' Clover replied under her breath.

'Well, you deserve everything that's a-coming to you.'

This diatribe was really no more than Clover expected. 'All right, I'll go,' she said coolly. 'If you want me to, I'll go. Disown me. Throw me out. I couldn't care less.' Tears trembled on her long lashes and one trickled down her cheek. She wiped it away with the back of her hand.

'There's me cousin Jemima in Wellington...' It seemed Mary Ann might be relenting.

'If you think I'm going to Wellington just to be out of your hair, just to spare your blushes, you can think again,' Clover replied, defiant, shunning this new-found forbearance. 'If you don't want me here, if I'm too much of an embarrassment for you, just disown me. The last thing I want is for you to be embarrassed over me. You must never let your church cronies see that you could condone your only daughter getting pregnant out of wedlock by doing something as mad as supporting her. Well, I can make my own way. I don't need you to help me rear my child.'

'Contrary madam!' Mary Ann rasped. 'I could bloody throttle you. You'll see what'll happen. You'll either end up in the workhouse or the whorehouse. And serve you damned right. You must have the morals of a bitch on heat. And to think you'm my own flesh and blood. Well get your things together and bugger off. You'm no

383

daughter of mine.'

'All right,' she said, unrepentant. 'I'll go tonight.'

'Then go to him who made you pregnant. Whoever he is.'

'How the hell do I know where I'll go then?'

Chapter Twenty-Two

She was outside in the street. In one hand she carried a basket containing the only other two pairs of shoes she owned, apart from the pair she was wearing, and her purse. With her other hand she clutched the strings of a brown-paper carrier bag that held clean underclothes and stockings, a dress, a skirt, a blouse, a bar of soap and a toothbrush.

By the scant illumination from the street lamps she could see the smoke swirling from the line of chimneys that stood like soldiers on the roofs of the terraced houses, the blustery wind ravaging it as inexorably as her hopes and dreams had been ravaged. She turned away, pulled up the collar of her coat against the driving rain and, instinctively, headed for Cross Guns Street and Dixon's Green where the wealthy merchants and professional men of the town sat in front of their warm hearths on that cold, wet night. She had no idea where she was going, nor what she would do. Her head was awhirl with the sanctimonious reaction of her mother and her own terminal defiance of it. Over and over, the row with Mary Ann repeated itself unbidden in her mind, like the persistent re-enactment of some hideous stage play.

She did not make a conscious decision to cross Dixon's Green at the Fountain Inn and walk down Bean Road opposite, as she had done with Tom that first evening they spent together before Ned's celebration, but it seemed a perfectly natural thing to do. As she passed the Blue Coat School in the darkness a creature leapt stealthily right in front of her from the top of the wall that surrounded it. Clover let out a frightened gasp as her heart vaulted to her throat and back again. It was a cat; nothing more. She breathed easy and continued walking, side-stepping the melanite puddles that glinted between the cobbles.

She walked on, into Buffery Park.

There were no lights here. She could just make out the path in the blackness, and the hot-houses, so full of thriving plants in the summer, loomed against the feeble illumination thrown up from Selbourne Road and Park Hill Street. No flowers bloomed tonight, inside or outside. She heard something scuff against a tree and realised that a courting couple were pressed against it, making the most of the privacy that the twilight and the solitude afforded, even on this bitter, inclement night. She walked on, ignoring them, envying them and pitying them at the same time.

She came to a bench, the same bench she and Tom had sat on weaving their dreams. It seemed appropriate to sit on it now to relive those moments, those implied expressions of love.

Maybe she would stay here the night; she had nowhere else to go. She huddled inside her coat as she sat down on the hard, wet slats. If only Tom were with her now. What would his reaction be if he could see her now, looking like some drowned rat at the mercy of the wind and the rain, when she should be snuggled up in a warm bed? What would he think if he saw her tonight, flung out of house and home for the sin of carrying his child, with her only belongings and what little money she'd saved? He would be appalled; that, she knew. Oh, he would fight her corner with a vengeance and no doubt about it. The trouble was she could not tell him; she could never tell him. He must remain always oblivious to her and her predicament, because of his obligations now to Ramona.

Memories flooded back. That first evening together. She'd been on top of the world. Never had she felt so happy, triumphant at having won Tom when she'd truly believed he was only interested in Ramona. How cruelly ironic that he was now married to her. She relived every tender moment they spent together. She recalled the first time they made love, how he was as nervous as she was. He possessed neither the attitude nor the technique of a Casanova. She relived the times they went to the theatres in the town, the easy, comfortable times she spent with his mother and father, the unhurried summer strolls in this very park, the walks over Oakham and Penny Hill, picking bluebells in Bluebell Wood last spring. She recalled the joy and pride she felt when he said they should be married and later the excitement of choosing an engagement ring. Now all was gone. She was utterly desolated, her most precious dreams burst as if they had been nothing more than soap bubbles.

But at least she was having his child. It would be a burden, but a burden she welcomed with all her heart. It would restrict her but, from now on, she foresaw her only joy in being restricted to that child she loved already. She had no thoughts, no hopes of meeting another man when perhaps her heartache had been mollified by the passage of time. She could love no other man. Her child would see her through. In any case, this same child would inhibit the approaches of any other man worth having; but that was for the best.

The rain came even heavier, drumming on the autumn leaves of the trees around her. If only she'd thought to bring a brolly. But in her anxiety to leave... She pulled her hat harder on her head, adjusted her collar and nestled deeper inside her coat. The rain and the wind and the cold, like Mary Ann, could not hurt her. She would weather it, like she'd weathered the priggishness, the heartache. She could feel the damp driving through her clothes to her very skin and she felt cold and desperately unloved. But she would weather it.

Numbed by the cold, she fell asleep sitting up, her basket and her brown-paper carrier bag by her side. Her head lolled forward and water trickled down her neck from her hat as the rain fell remorselessly.

She did not know how long she had been asleep when she awoke, shivering, her teeth chattering.

At once she was conscious of another person sitting at the other end of the bench. She started, peering at him or her, trying to discern who it might be in the darkness. Her heart pounded, for she did not know whether she was in any danger.

A gruff voice, that of a man, said: 'Yo'm awake then.'

'Yes.'

'So what's a young madam like thee doing sitting out here on a night like this? Hast got no wum to goo to?'

'I was out for a walk. I fell asleep, that's all.'

'Oh,' he replied, and she heard the cynical disbelief in his voice. 'Listen. This is my bench. I sleep here.'

'Have it. I've no intention of robbing you of it.' She gathered her things together and stood up.

'No need to rush off. Yo' can stop. Sleep wi' me, if you've a mind. I'll look after thee. You on'y seem young. I'n had ne'er a woman since Adam was a pit boy.'

'Thanks for the offer, but no.' Frightened now, she turned and walked away, hoping the man would not follow her, would not molest her.

But she heard his footsteps behind her.

She ran.

He ran after her.

God, please let her get to Blackacre Road and the entrance to the park before he caught up. The bottom fell out of her brown-paper carrier bag that was sopping wet and her belongings trailed all over the muddy footpath. Let them go. Leave them. She couldn't stop to pick everything up; he'd have her. So she ran for her life and let go

388

the carrier bag, clutching her basket with her shoes and her purse. Behind her, she could hear the heavy, laboured breathing of her pursuer. At last she reached the entrance to the park. Thank God. She turned right, towards the top of Buffery Road. There would be some folk about that way; the Bush Inn was there, the street lamps were brighter. The man chasing her might be deterred. She could always plead for help, scream as a last resort.

She risked a glance behind her as she ran. The man had fallen back, lumbering in his efforts to chase her. She ran on, her breath coming in gulps. When she reached the Bush Inn she looked behind her again. The man, whoever he was, had turned back, returned to his park bench, very likely picking up her clothes and things along the way. Now she had nothing else to wear, no soap to wash herself with, no toothbrush to freshen her mouth.

This was ridiculous. She would give anything for a hot bath now and the luxury of a clean, comfortable bed. Where on earth did she think she was going when she left the Jolly Collier in such a huff of obstinacy? There was nowhere she could go. Nobody would have her. In any case, it would be unfair to ask anybody to. She stood awhile getting her breath back, peering into the dim shadows of Blackacre Road. But at least she was warmer now after her escape.

She wondered what time it was. Folk were still coming out of the Bush. Maybe it would be better if she went home and threw herself on the mercy of her mother and Jake. Well, maybe it would, but she was not about to. Another idea had come to her.

Zillah Bache.

She would go to Zillah. Zillah would be happy to put her up for the night. Tomorrow, she could find some lodgings, pay for them out of the money in her purse.

So she tramped to High Street where Zillah lived opposite the Loving Lamb. Carefully, she avoided George Street and hid her face from anybody who walked in her direction. She would not use the side streets after her scare with the strange tramp, but keep to the main road where folk were more likely to be, where the street lamps offered some protection. At last she came to Zillah's small terraced house. She walked up the entry and knocked on the back door.

But the house was in darkness. No candle flickered, no oil lamp burned.

Of course, Zillah would be in the Four Ways, supping beer with Annie Brown.

Clover went back down the entry and sat on the front door step. If only she knew the time she would know roughly how long she might expect to wait. The wind continued to blow the rain in her face so she stepped back into the entry for shelter.

After about three-quarters of an hour, Clover looked out and saw the unmistakable bulk of Zillah waddling along High Street from the direction of the Four Ways and the Bethel Chapel. So as not to scare her Clover stepped onto the footpath in plenty of time and greeted her.

390

'Why, it's Clover, as God's my judge,' Zillah exclaimed. 'What brings yer out on a filthy night like this?'

'I took your advice and told mother I was in trouble, Zillah. She threw me out.'

'Her threw yer out? On a night like this? Heartless bugger! Her wants hoss-whipping. Look at yer, you'm soaked through. Why, you'll catch yer jeth. Come on in and get warm and have a nice cup of cocoa or summat.'

Zillah fumbled in her pocket for her key as Clover followed her up the entry, never so glad of the offer of warmth and hospitality.

'Goo in, my wench,' Zillah said when she'd unlocked the door, 'while I light the lamp.' Still in her coat, she felt along the mantelpiece, found a spill and lit it from the glowing embers of the fire. From that, she lit an oil lamp and trimmed the wick to stop it smoking and placed it on the table that overlooked the window onto the back yard. 'Here, let me tek yer coat.'

Clover peeled off her wet coat and handed it to Zillah. 'Thanks, Zillah.'

'I bet your frock's all wet an' all, eh?'

'Yes, it's a bit damp but it'll soon dry out.'

The enamelled kettle was standing on the hob of the fire grate. Zillah lifted it to determine how much water remained and sat it in the embers of the fire, which shifted among a flurry of sparks that were drawn up the chimney.

'Dun yer want some cocoa?'

'Tea will be fine if you're making tea,' Clover replied.

'And we'll have a drap of whisky in it an' all, to

391

warm we up, eh?'

Clover smiled.

Zillah spooned tea in her teapot and rummaged through her cupboard at the side of the grate. She withdrew a half bottle of whisky with a look of triumph.

'Jake gi'd me that,' she said proudly. 'Yer mother knows nothing about it though.'

'Jake's all right,' Clover said. 'But what he ever saw in my mother, I'll never know.'

'An ailing business waiting to be nurtured, I 'spect. Money to be med. That's what Jake sid. That's what he wanted.'

Clover nodded. 'Serve her right if he left her, the miserable bitch.'

'So tell me what happened – what her said when you told her.'

Clover related everything. She told how she subsequently went to the park, how she got colder and wetter in the rain, how she fell asleep to find a vagrant watching her, how he chased her, how she lost her spare clothes.

'If I can just stay here tonight, Zillah, I'll find some lodgings tomorrow. Maybe the rain will've stopped by then.'

'Lodgings be buggered!' Zillah exclaimed. 'Yo'll stop here. Yo'll need looking after in your condition. Who d'you think's gunna keep thee?'

Clover smiled through her anguish. 'Well you can't keep me, Zillah.'

'Well, somebody has to, else it'll be the workhouse. Anyroad, yo've always bin that kind to me, young Clover. And I as good as reared thee, remember? I'll not see thee wanting.'

'Oh, Zillah...'

'Why, that Mary Ann, the evil sod,' she added contemptuously. 'I could crown her. Her need go to church. Wait till I see her in the morning. Her'll get a piece of my mind.'

Clover shook her head. 'No, Zillah. Don't get into trouble on my account. You know what she's like. She'll probably sack you as well.'

'Good. 'Cause I can get work anywhere, me. Why, at the Four Ways they'd have me there like a shot, I reckon. I got no fear of Mary bloody Ann.'

'Then let me pay you some rent,' Clover suggested, leaning over to reach her basket.

'There's no need,' Zillah protested.

'Yes, there is.' Clover smiled in thankfulness at Zillah's infinite kindness. She rummaged in her basket, past her shoes. 'Pass me the oil lamp, Zillah.'

Zillah handed it to her.

Clover held it over her basket, then looked up in disbelief. 'Zillah, my purse has gone. It had all the money in it that I've been able to save... That tramp must have had it while I was asleep on that bench. What shall I do now? I've got nothing at all.'

Clover stayed. Zillah's house was hardly the height of elegance and luxury but it was no worse than what she and Mary Ann had endured before Jake and Ramona came along. Zillah was bold enough to tell Mary Ann exactly what she thought of her for evicting Clover but, when Zillah admitted the girl was lodging in High

Street with her, Mary Ann evidently saw fit not to sack her for fear of hurting Clover more.

Zillah rummaged around and found a brass ring in one of her drawers. She polished it up and gave it to Clover, knowing that she was about to seek employment.

'Wear this, my flower,' she advised. 'Wear it like a wedding ring. They'll be more inclined to gi' thee a job if they think as yo'm wed.'

Clover smiled and thanked her as she slipped it on her finger.

She found a job; in Neal's Cake Shop in the town. She admitted she was pregnant and would only be able to work till the New Year.

By the beginning of November, Ned Brisco learnt that Clover was no longer living at the Jolly Collier and that she was working in a cake shop. Eventually, he found her and, leaving work early one afternoon, waited for her to come out at closing time.

'Ned! Fancy seeing you,' she exclaimed when she saw him.

'I heard you was working in a cake shop in Dudley town. It wasn't that hard to find you.'

'So how are you?'

'I'm all right. What about you, though? I heard you're not living at the Jolly Collier any more.'

'I'm pregnant, Ned,' she said flatly. 'Can't you tell? My mother doesn't take to daughters and stepdaughters that get pregnant out of wedlock.'

'I heard you was having a baby, Clover,' he admitted. 'I guessed that's why you left the Jolly Collier. Is it that swine's baby you're having? That Tom Doubleday's?'

'Are you going my way or not?' she replied, avoiding his question.

'Yes, I can give you a ride home.'

'Thanks. So how is your mother, Ned? Is she keeping well?'

'Yes, she's pretty well. And Father. Father was asking about you the other day... Look, there's the motor. Come on, I'll help you up.'

Dudley town was, as usual, teeming with folk on their way home from work. The trams disgorged one set of passengers and absorbed others. Christmas decorations were already on display in some shops and people jostled each other as they hurried along Hall Street's narrow confines by the light spilling from shop windows. When Ned, with Clover aboard, tried to negotiate his motor car along there as well he received howls of protest from those who had to scurry out of the way to allow him to pass.

'I haven't seen you for ages,' Clover commented when they were past the junction with King Street, away from the thick of the people.

'No, well ... I thought it best to leave you be.'

'Oh? But I value your friendship, Ned. I've always valued your friendship. You know that.'

'Maybe so... But it was getting on me nerves how you was always mooning over *him*. You could see no wrong in him. You wouldn't hear a word said against him.'

She shrugged and pulled her collar up. 'I still won't. I don't feel any different.'

'Then more fool you. I suppose it is his baby you're carrying? You never answered me.'

She looked at him with honest eyes. 'What do

you think, Ned?'

He turned to look at her as he drove, trying to catch her expression in the twilight. 'I suppose it must be then.'

'But Ned... Keep it to yourself – please. I don't want it to get back to him that I'm having his child. I don't want him to start feeling guilty over me. He'll have enough on his plate.'

'There you go again, Clover. You're too soft. But I wouldn't let him have the *satisfaction* of knowing. Sod him. So what are you going to do? I mean, you can't look after a baby and work. Shall you give it up? The baby, I mean. Shall you have it adopted or chuck it down a well or something?'

'Ned!' she shrieked contemptuously. 'What a terrible thing to say. You ought to be ashamed of yourself for thinking such a thing. Of course I'm going to keep the baby. I want this baby. I'll struggle through. I'll manage somehow. You don't have to worry about me... Chuck it down a well indeed! What a thing to say...'

They turned the corner from Waddams Pool into St John's Road.

He shrugged. 'Well, I didn't know how you felt about it.'

'Well you do now.'

They fell silent for a few seconds, listening to the harsh thrash of the motor car's engine.

'You'd better tell me where it is you're living.'

'At Zillah's. In High Street. Opposite the Loving Lamb.'

They turned into Brown Street and a dog thought twice about running in front of them, but desisted just in time.

'Are you happy there?' Ned asked.

'I'm grateful for Zillah's kindness, Ned. I don't think I'll be happy till I have my baby in my arms... Then I'll be happy.' She smiled to emphasise her point.

At the Bird in Hand, which faced the Bethel Chapel on one corner and the Four Ways on another, they turned left into High Street. Ned pulled up outside the Loving Lamb which itself looked peculiarly as if it stood in the back yard of the Bird in Hand.

'But then what are you going to do when you've got the baby? You can't expect Zillah to keep you. Nor a baby as well.'

She shrugged. What he said was true. Zillah, out of the kindness of her heart, might be prepared to look after her, but it was not really fair on her. Zillah had struggled enough during her long widowhood, trying to make ends meet, trying to fend for her own children. To volunteer to support two extra burdens now was beyond what could be reasonably expected.

'Marry me, Clover.'

She looked at him aghast. Nothing could have been further from her mind. 'Don't be stupid, Ned. You can't sacrifice yourself just to help me. I wouldn't hear of it.'

'Just think about it. Your problems would be solved. So would Zillah's. You'd have a husband. Your child would have a father. You could assume respectability – well, a sort of respectability... Especially if we moved away from Kates Hill...'

'You're mad, Ned,' she said with earnest disparagement. 'You're off your head. Anyway, I'd be no good for you. For a start, I don't love you.'

'I'm not asking you to love me. I don't expect you to love me. I just want to be your husband. At the same time I'll be a father to your child.'

She turned to him with a look of tenderness in her eyes. He evidently meant what he said. She had no option but to admire his stupid penchant for self-sacrifice. 'Ned,' she said gently. 'That would be no life for you. Don't you see? You don't want me, I'm a fallen woman. Around the next corner the ideal girl might be there, waiting for you. Somebody you could be happy with.'

'I'd be happy with you, Clover.'

'No, Ned. You'd never be happy with me. Not truly happy.'

'I'm prepared to take my chance.'

'But I have nothing to give in return... Nothing.'

'Just by being there with me–'

'No!... I'm sorry, Ned. I could never agree to it.'

'Never?'

'Never in a million years.'

Chapter Twenty-Three

Clover and Ned Brisco were married on Friday 5th March 1909 in a civil ceremony at Dudley Registry Office. She had held out till the last, after months of dogged persuasion, unwilling to let Ned sacrifice himself on her behalf. Over

Christmas he came bearing gifts – clothes and things, mostly for the baby – and once more spelled out the advantages for her if she deigned to marry him. In the finish, at the very beginning of March, his logic as well as his persistence prevailed. It was evident that, since Clover had given up work, it was too much of a financial struggle for Zillah to support her and Clover perceived that in any case it was not fair that she should. If her mother had helped by sending a few shillings now and again, a quarter-pound of tea occasionally, even a loaf of bread, then that might have made the difference. But nothing was forthcoming from the Jolly Collier. Not a sixpence, not a silver threepenny-bit, not a penny, not even so much as a grain of sugar. Besides, Ned argued, what did Zillah want with a screaming baby around her at her time of life? Well, he had a point there too. He told Clover again that he expected nothing from her; he accepted that she was not in love with him. He loved her, though. Enough for the two of them, he said. He had always loved her. It had always been his intention, one way or the other, to marry her. Now, she needed him more than he needed her and he was glad of it. Further refusal was madness.

'And, as far as anybody else is concerned,' he added, 'I'm the father of the child.'

At that she looked at him and nodded, slowly. It was her solemn consent at last.

'So you agree?'

'Yes, all right. I'll marry you. But I don't deserve you. And you don't deserve what you're about to get.'

He afforded himself a triumphal smile. 'Whether or no, we're cutting it a bit fine. You've only got a day or two to go, remember.'

'As if I needed reminding.'

'It'll have to be by special licence. I'll organise it tomorrow.'

Come the morning of 5th March, Zillah fussed around Clover like a mother hen.

'Come on, put this new frock on as you've med, my wench, and look sharp about it. That registrar won't wait for thee if you'm late. Then where will you be, eh? Up the creek with ne'er an oar to row theeself with.'

The frock was a necessary addition to her scant wardrobe now that nothing else would fit. It was like a tent, she said as she ran it up on Zillah's trusty treadle machine, her pride and joy.

Clover, her hair done up beautifully, pulled the frock over her head and arranged it over her nine-month belly. She peered at herself in the long mirror in Zillah's bedroom. So this was to be her wedding day. It was a far cry from the brilliant event she and Tom had planned in those heady days of their courtship. How fortune played some cruel tricks! The white bridal gown she'd always imagined herself to be wearing remained part of a roll of satin stashed away somewhere, never destined to be fashioned into an elegant dress to fit a slender bride with a mere twenty-four-inch waist. Never would it witness the romance and glory of a resplendent wedding in a church attended by countless friends, and relations coming from far and wide.

400

'Well, the registrar will only have to take one look at you to know why you ain't a-getting married in church,' Zillah commented, breaking Clover's daydream.

Clover chuckled at Zillah's irreverence. 'I didn't think I'd be getting married at all three days ago. D'you think Ned's daft?'

'Stark staring mad. To tek on another chap's child he must be. But he must've thought hard about it. For that you should be thankful, Clover. Even though he ain't the chap you wanted.'

Clover nodded, and more solemnly said: 'I know. The trouble is, he can't really afford it. He still owes a loan of two hundred. Did you know about that?'

'I seem to remember some talk of a loan.'

'Yes, somebody donated it through that reporter from the *Herald*, Julian Oakley. We neither of us know who it was. Well, it's got to be paid back and the sooner the better. But God knows how. We'll have to live in penury till it's paid back, I reckon. I shall look forward to the day when I can go to the *Herald* offices and say, "Here, Mr Oakley. Here's that loan repaid. Pass it on to whoever it was that was daft enough to lend it".'

They heard the noise of Ned's motor car as he arrived to collect them, with his mother and father as well.

'Ready?' Zillah asked.

'Yes, just about. What about you, Zillah?'

'Listen. Don't fret about me. I'm only your bloody witness, not your bridesmaid.'

This made Clover laugh again. They both

401

laughed more at the absurdity of their mutual struggle to negotiate the tight bend in the narrow staircase, one behind the other, neither able to look down and see the stairs beneath them for the size of their bellies. Outside, Zillah locked the door behind her and followed Clover down the entry. In the street, Ned was standing at the side of his motor car, waiting.

'Zillah, can you get in the back with Mother and Father?'

'Christ, but we'll all be squashed to jeth,' she replied.

Ned helped her up as Mr and Mrs Brisco hodged up to make room.

'Me stays am a-crippling me already,' Zillah complained, a look of agony on her big, kindly face. 'Thee'd best not goo too quick over them blasted pot-holes, Ned, else I'll be stabbed to jeth by me own whalebones.'

They all laughed and Ned handed Clover up into the passenger seat at the side of his.

'You look a picture, Clover,' he said as he put the vehicle into gear.

'Thank you, Ned. But see if you can tell me the same in a week or so.'

'A wik or so?' Florrie retorted. 'It'll be a mizzle to me if we ever get to the Registry Office afore you have this babby.' She turned to Zillah. 'I live in fears and dreads, Zillah, that her'll drop it afore they'm wed. Call this cutting it fine!'

'It's all right, Florrie,' Clover said, turning her head so she could be heard above the engine's racket. 'There's no signs of any labour pains yet. I reckon I'll get through the ceremony all right.'

'Why on earth he left it till the last minute to wed thee, Clover, I'll never know. Ned should've accepted his responsibilities sooner to mek an honest woman of thee. He'd took his pleasure, Clover – not as I blame thee – he should have faced the consequences sooner.'

And so Clover Beckitt became Mrs Edward Brisco in a civil service that seemed to be over as soon as it had begun. There was a small party afterwards at the Briscos' home in Watson Street where bride and groom went to live as part of an extended family, like so many other young couples starting out.

On the same day, Jake Tandy visited Ramona and broke the news that Clover had married Ned Brisco. As she lay in bed with Tom that night, Tom was trying to read a pamphlet by the light of their oil lamp on a new camera he was considering acquiring. Ramona, however, was determined to pass on the news, even though the baby was inordinately restless.

'Tom! Put your hand on me belly... Quick!... Can you feel him kicking? Me ribs'll be black and blue.'

'He's lively tonight.' His eyes and hand returned to the pamphlet.

She turned over, trying to get comfortable. Her belly was big and for some time she had realised what an encumbrance this later stage of pregnancy was, how it limited your movements.

'Father came today...'

'Oh? How is he?'

She turned onto her back now, a huge lump

403

under the bedclothes. 'He's all right.'

'Good.'

'He left five shillings. I think I'll put it towards a new table.'

'I wish he wouldn't keep leaving money. I find it demeaning. As if he doesn't think I'm capable of providing for you.'

'But he means well.'

'I'm sure he does. All the same...'

A pause...

'Tom?'

'What?' There was exasperation in his tone.

'Something I didn't tell you...'

'What?'

'Something I intended telling you a while ago. But I forgot ... Mary Ann threw Clover out of the Jolly Collier.'

He turned and looked at her at once, concern on his face. 'What?... Why?'

Well, now she had his attention.

'It turns out she'd got herself pregnant,' she reported casually. 'She and Ned Brisco got married today.'

'She's married *that* tosspot? I can scarcely believe she'd have anything to do with *him*. Certainly nothing like *that*.'

Ramona turned her head away from him and half smiled. 'I've told you before – women are a funny lot. There's no knowing what they might do. Especially on the rebound. But if she got pregnant by Ned Brisco, it's only right as she should marry him. Don't you agree?'

'Well, I suppose I do,' he agreed grudgingly. 'But I can still scarcely believe it. Clover Beckitt married to Ned Brisco?... Who the hell would have thought it?'

As she turned back to him to study his reaction she felt a pain in her stomach that made her wince.

'Jesus!...'

He looked at her with concern. 'Are you all right?'

'Yes, I think so. I just had an awful twinge. Not surprising the way he keeps kicking me.'

'Well, that's all it must be. You're not due. You've another month to go yet.'

'I know. More's the flipping pity. Anyway, he's not turned yet. I can't be ready. Can you dowt the lamp? We should get some sleep now.'

Tom put his pamphlet on his bedside table and blew out the lamp. 'Sleep tight,' he said with a sigh. 'See you in the morning.'

Neither went to sleep, but each believed the other had drifted off. Tom was wracked by emotions he thought he'd got over, thinking about Clover ... but with Ned Brisco... He imagined them making love and felt hot and angry at the thought. He felt trapped in his own situation, helpless. He could do nothing. Circumstances had certainly made a fool of him. Bitterness and anger welled up inside and the more he pondered everything, the less inclined he was to sleep.

After about an hour, tossing and turning, Ramona spoke.

'Tom?' she croaked. 'Are you awake?'

'No.'

'Yes, you are, you fibber ... Tom, I've had another couple of pains – strong pains. I think I must have started.'

It was entirely strange going to bed with Ned Brisco. Fortunately, he slept in a double bed, but his room was tiny with little room to manoeuvre around it. She guessed him or his mother had made an effort to tidy it up and clean it before she came to occupy it but there was still evidence of his preoccupation with aviation, totally unfeminine. Ned returned from the privy before he settled down for the night. He proceeded to watch Clover in the last throes of getting undressed.

'Please don't watch me, Ned.'

'Sorry.' He looked away. 'It's just that—'

'It won't be a pleasant sight, me with a nine-month belly.' She sat on the bed and turned her back on him as she pulled her shift over her head. Unlike many women she knew, she had not put on excessive weight during her pregnancy. Her legs and arms were as slender as before, her face was no rounder, her bottom was little wider; only her belly and her breasts were bigger. 'Besides, I feel embarrassed getting undressed in front of you. It's only natural that I should.' She reached for her long nightgown which lay beside her and pulled it over her head. That done, she stood up and removed her drawers as modestly as she could, careful not to show her legs. Then she pulled back the bedclothes and slid tentatively into bed beside him.

'Don't worry, Clover,' he whispered. 'I'm not going to roll on top of you and demand my conjugal rights,' he said.

406

The thought appalled her but she smiled gratefully. 'I reckon it'd be impossible anyway, the way I am.'

'I reckon so, too... Shall I blow the candle out?'

'Might as well.'

He leaned over and did it, then nestled down again, deliberately avoiding touching her, it seemed.

'Good night, Ned,' she said, thankful for his consideration.

'Good night, Clover ... Mrs Brisco.'

Mrs Brisco. Never in her life had she imagined she could be married to Ned Brisco. And here she was, lying next to him in his bed, apprehensive, a million miles away from sleep. At some point it was inevitable that they would touch and the thought of it set her teeth on edge. Even before she became pregnant, even before she knew Tom, she had never relished the prospect of Ned touching her. What if he put his arm around her? She liked him well enough, but not well enough for that. Time and events had not changed her. And yet she was deeply in his debt now for taking the responsibility of marrying her.

'Do you want to sleep in my lap?' he breathed.

'No, it's all right. It'll make me too warm. Besides, I get off better on my back.'

'All right... Can I just put my arm over you?'

Oh, Lord. He wanted to reconnoitre her body already. 'I'd rather you didn't. It'll be too uncomfortable.'

'All right.'

'Good night, Ned.'

'Good night, Clover...' He shuffled himself

407

comfortable, shaking the bed as he did so, still avoiding touching her without her consent. 'Yes, I suppose it'll be easier when you've had the baby.'

She cringed at the thought. 'I'm going to sleep now, Ned.'

Tom's first reaction was to run up Stafford Street and fetch his mother. She roused herself from sleep and dressed and they scurried off together, back to the house in Edward Street. Ramona complained that her pains were coming every twenty minutes and were more intense.

'We'll need plenty boiling water,' Amy Doubleday declared. 'Is there a fire lit?'

'I'll get one going,' Tom said.

'Light one under the wash boiler as well and fill it with clean water. Then fetch Nellie Kemp from Hellier Street. I'll stop here and keep an eye on madam.'

Tom lit his fires and filled every available vessel with water. He received instruction on which house in Hellier Street the midwife dwelt and ran to fetch her. Eventually, he made himself heard and Nellie Kemp, indignant at being woken from her beauty sleep which, evidently, she sorely needed, was shepherded to Ramona's bedside.

'Has your water broke?'

'Not yet.'

'Right. Let's have a look at you.' The midwife pulled back the bedclothes unceremoniously. 'Lift your nightgownd up.'

Ramona pulled up her nightgown.

Nellie kneaded and prodded Ramona's belly.

'This babby ain't turned or I'm never here. When did you last see your doctor?'

'I haven't seen the doctor. I've felt well all along. There seemed no need. Besides, I'm not due for another month yet.'

'Well, you've got a tidy belly on you for eight months. Prepare yourself for a hard night and a hard day tomorrer, my wench. We've got a breeched birth here to contend with unless I can turn it. Still, you'm on'y a kid yourself by the looks o' yer. You'll be all right.'

The next day proved to be a hard day, as Nellie promised. All day, Tom sat in his chair downstairs listening to Ramona's agonised screams. At times he covered his ears so as not to hear, but he could not help but hear. There must be something they could do to relieve the excruciating pain. Surely, no woman need endure this, no matter what the complications. As the day drew on, he noticed that Ramona's cries were becoming weaker. By six o'clock in the evening, she was still in labour and exhausted.

Nellie Kemp stood at the foot of the stairs, her hair straggled, her expression grave.

'Yo'd best fetch the doctor,' she said. 'This is a big child and her's such a small madam and her's absolutely buggered with all the pushing and a-shoving. I want the doctor here to see to her.'

'I'll fetch him straight away Mrs Kemp.'

'Be sure to tell him it's Nellie Kemp what's sent for him. Tell him it's a breeched presentation and I'm afeared for both of 'em. He'll know what to expect then.'

Tom pulled on his jacket and put on his cap. Like a hare sprung from a trap he ran to the home in Wolverhampton Street of the doctor he had known all his life, Dr Carter. He rapped loudly on the door and, when a maid answered, he gabbled on about his wife's breeched birth and that Nellie Kemp was worried. The maid asked him to hang on and she would see if the doctor would see him.

Of course, after Tom had explained, the doctor came. He took one look at Ramona, doffed his jacket, loosened his necktie and set to work.

'How long has she been in labour?'

'They fetched me at two o'clock this morning, Doctor. Her must have bin in labour afore that. It's a big babby I reckon, Doctor, and her's only a tiny madam.'

'Yes, I can see the difficulties, Mrs Kemp.' He opened his bag and looked inside. 'She's in some distress, Mrs Kemp,' he said quietly while Ramona squirmed, her hands raised behind her, her knuckles white as she gripped the brass bedrail in her anguish. 'I'm going to administer a small amount of morphine and scopolamine to reduce her pain.' He took out a hypodermic syringe, charged it and spoke to Ramona. 'This will induce you into what we call a twilight sleep, Mrs Doubleday. You'll feel very little pain once it takes effect...'

Within a short time, her distress diminished.

'Right, now let's get to work,' the doctor said.

Ramona's son was born at ten minutes past eight on the evening of 6th March. The child weighed nine pounds five ounces but was weak and bruised from the trauma of a complicated birth. Ramona suffered more than the child, however. She could not expel the afterbirth and, when artificially removed, she was seen to be hae-morrhaging, though Dr Carter believed he had stopped it. He spoke to Tom afterwards and said he didn't believe the child would survive, but he would find a wet nurse who could come and feed it in case it did, for Ramona was in no fit state.

Next morning Dr Carter returned and was surprised to find the baby still alive. Ramona, however, was still very poorly; the haemorrhaging had obviously not been stemmed and she was weak from loss of blood. By evening, she showed no signs of recovery. If anything, she was worse and the bed was a mess of blood. When the wet nurse, a girl called Miriam, called to feed the child, Tom set off for the doctor's house again and asked him to call. Dr Carter promised to attend within an hour.

When he arrived he examined his new patient thoroughly. The bleeding alarmed him.

'Leave me with her, Tom,' he said kindly. 'I have to try and stop this haemorrhaging somehow. Ideally she should be in a hospital but I fear she's too weak to move. I'll have to do what I can here. Do you have a rubber underlay?'

Tom shook his head, looking more and more perplexed.

'Pity. When I'm through, I want you to ask the girl to help you change the bed. Your wife will need clean sheets.'

411

'So what's the problem, Doctor. Why is she still bleeding?'

'Because the birth was protracted and difficult this has caused lacerations of the uterus. As you can imagine, inserting sutures is difficult enough, but under these circumstances ... I must try and reduce the bleeding somewhat so she might recover enough for us to get her to hospital. There's also the risk of infection, of course.'

'Is she going to be all right?'

'That I don't know,' he answered frankly.

'You mean...'

'Are you a praying man, Tom?'

'Not especially.'

'Then I'd start if I were you. Leave me be with her now...'

Tom left the doctor with Ramona and went downstairs. His mind was in turmoil. What if anything happened to Ramona? What if she died through having his child? He would never be able to forgive himself for making her pregnant in the first place. It would be because of his careless-ness, his casualness when they began their affair. Please, God, please make her better...

He sought Miriam in the scullery. If he could talk to somebody it might take his mind off things.

'How's the baby?'

'No different,' she replied. 'He's in his crib sleeping, look.'

'Has he taken any milk?'

'He vomited a while ago. All the rubbish he swallowed being born, I reckon. He took no feed when I tried him.'

He asked her about her own child and received a potted history of her family.

'So what if your own child gets hungry and you're not there?' he asked.

'My sister'll feed her. She's got a kid of her own.'

'Oh, I see.'

'How's your wife?'

'Poorly. Dr Carter's trying to do something for her now.'

'Think she'll be all right?'

'I hope so.'

'Would you like a cup of tea?'

'Tea? I'd *love* a bottle of whisky... Yes, thanks, Miriam. A cup of tea would be nice.'

'I'll make one.'

While Miriam made tea the doctor called down to him and Tom went up.

'How is she, Doctor?'

'Comfortable for now, but I want you to change her sheets when I've gone. You must try not to disturb her too much, though. Lift her very gently, pulling the soiled linen from under her and replacing with clean stuff in the same way. She could do with a clean nightgown as well.'

Tom nodded. 'I know what to do.'

'Give her plenty of boiled water to drink or lemonade. Try and get her to eat something if she'll have it. How's the wet nurse doing?'

'She's doing all she can.'

'While I'm here I'd best look at the child.' He smiled reassuringly. 'Have you decided what to call him?'

'We'd thought about Daniel.'

'Well, he's a plucky little blighter.'

They went downstairs to the scullery. The doctor asked if the baby had been fed and Miriam told the doctor what she'd already told Tom.

'Hmmm,' murmured the doctor. He examined the child again. 'Well, I hope to goodness we rear him, Tom. But it's touch and go, I fear.' He took Tom's arm gently, gesturing that they go back upstairs to the sitting-room.

'Step to the front door with me, Tom... Tell me, have you let your wife's family know the situation?'

'Not yet, Doctor. There's been no time.'

'I know it's been difficult. But your wife is seriously ill, as well as your child. I think you should solicit their help to look after her, you know. You're going to need it, my boy. And forewarn them that all is not well. I've done what I can to stop the bleeding. How successful it is we shan't know till morning. When you've cleaned her up I suggest you go and see her family while she is asleep and the wet nurse is with the child. I'll call again first thing in the morning...'

Jake Tandy came at once. He and Tom hurried through the town in their anxiety to be with Ramona. Tom left him in the bedroom watching over her with tears in his eyes while he himself went to see Miriam and his child. Jake stroked her face gently with the backs of his fingers. Her skin was clammy with sweat, yet felt cold. Never had he seen her looking so pale.

'My babby,' he breathed, wiping away a tear from his own eyes. 'What have they done to yer?'

Ramona slept on, oblivious to his loving attention. 'You'm little more than a child yourself. I knew no good would come of you having this child. Why couldn't men just leave you be another year or two?' He sniffed and a tear fell on the sheet as he leaned towards her. 'But we'll look after you. I'll get you back to the Jolly Collier to look after you if need be, and to hell with Mary Ann...'

When Miriam attempted to feed the child again, Tom left her and sat with father and daughter for more than an hour. Ramona hardly stirred. He watched as Jake tended her lovingly.

'What time shall you go home, Mr Tandy?'

'Oh, I won't go home, Tom. Not tonight. Maybe tomorrow, if she shapes up.'

'I could do with a cup of tea,' Tom said. 'I bet you could too, eh, Mr Tandy? I'll go downstairs and brew a pot.'

'Good idea. While you'm doing it, I'll try and give our Ramona something to drink, if I can get her to take it.'

Tom left the room and Jake tried to rouse Ramona. Eventually she opened her eyes and looked about her.

'Father,' she uttered, her voice weak.

'My flower... How do you feel now, eh?'

'Tired... So tired.' Her eyes closed again, overwhelmed by the urge to sleep, but she fought it.

'I want you to try and drink some of this.' He reached for the glass that was on the wash-stand. 'Here...' He helped raise her head so she could take a sip or two. 'That's good. A drop more in a little while, eh?'

'How long have you been here?'

'Two or three hours now, I daresay.'

'What time is it?'

'It's getting close to eleven, I reckon.'

'What time are you going back?'

'I'll stop here with you tonight, have no fear. Tom's seeing to the babby. There's a young woman here to help and to feed the bab.'

'How is the baby, Father? Is he all right? I haven't even seen him yet.'

'He's being well looked after,' Jake answered tactfully. 'Don't thee fret. You just rest and get better...'

Ramona drifted off into sleep again, then woke with a start. 'Father... My baby's going to die, isn't he?'

Jake wiped her brow with a flannel. 'Just rest, my flower.'

'Father, I just know he's going to die. I don't think I'm going to get better either... Am I?'

At once his eyes filled with tears. He brushed them away with the back of his hand. 'Course you'm going to get better, my angel. And the baby. But you both need rest.'

He watched her close her eyes, then open them again. Her pulse was visible at the soft part of her throat, beating fast, trying to compensate for the low blood pressure. She was fighting the urge to drift into unconsciousness also, fighting the soporific effects of loosing so much blood.

'Father, there's something–'

'Not now, Angel,' he said soothingly, concerned that she was getting too excited. 'Try and get some sleep.'

'In a minute.' He detected impatience in her tone, despite her weakness. 'First, promise me something...' Her eyes rolled uncontrollably under her lazy lids.

'Whatever you want. You know that.'

'Will you get a message to Clover for me?'

'To Clover?' he queried.

She nodded, almost imperceptibly.

'If that's what you want, my flower, course I will.'

'Ask her to come and see me. She won't want to, but I have to see her. There's something I want to say to her. Something she has to know... As soon as she can... You'll get rid of Tom for me before she comes ... won't you?'

'Yes, o' course. I'll tell her. I'll tell her in the morning.'

'Thanks, Father. Don't forget.' He stroked her hand. 'Don't worry, my angel. I won't forget. Now get some sleep.' She smiled with gratitude and drifted off once more into sleep.

Chapter Twenty-Four

On Monday morning Clover heard the unmistakable clop of a horse's hooves and the rattle of iron-rimmed cart wheels on the rough, stony surface of Watson Street. Seconds later she heard an urgent rapping on the front door. Rushing from the back yard where she was pegging out washing, she hurried through the house to answer it. Jake Tandy was standing there. He looked tired and racked with anxiety, his eyes red as if he had been weeping. He was unshaven, unkempt, far removed from his usual tidy appearance. Something was radically wrong.

'Pop!' she exclaimed, regarding him anxiously. 'Is it my mother?'

Jake shook his head. 'No, it's not your mother, Clover–'

'Thank God. Come in and tell me what's up.'

Solemnly he stepped inside.

'Florrie's in the brewhouse up to her elbows in soap suds.' She closed the door and led him into the scullery. 'We're doing the washing. Can I make you a cup of tea?'

He shook his head. 'I'm pressed for time, Clover, but thanks.'

'So what's wrong?'

'It's our Ramona. She had her child on Saturday. A boy.'

She looked at him anxiously. 'Are they not all right?'

'She had a hard time of it and ... well, it's touch and go whether either will come through it.'

'Oh, God, no.' She looked at him with all her sympathy in her eyes. She had not seen Jake since the night she left the Jolly Collier, the night she and her mother became estranged. Often she had wondered how they might react when they inevitably met again. Well, now the ice was broken, but she never imagined it would be under such sombre circumstances. 'And poor Tom. He must be at his wits' end.'

418

'He's taking it brave, Clover.' Jake's eyes flushed with tears. 'And look at you... Close to confinement as well, or I'm a monkey's uncle. I was surprised but pleased when Zillah said you'd got married after waiting so long... He's made an honest woman of you, after all. I don't know why it took him so long, eh?'

She smiled blandly, hoping he would not be so bright as to count back the months and associate her pregnancy with Tom. 'So what went wrong with Ramona?'

'Well...' He shook his head in despair. 'She wasn't due for another four weeks you know, but it come early. A big child, and all. Well she had a real hard time of it, like I say. Now the doctor can't stop her haemorrhaging. She's lost a lot of blood.'

'I am sorry, Jake...'

Jake acknowledged her obvious concern with a single nod. 'She's asked if you'll come and see her, Clover. There's summat she wants to tell you.'

Clover hesitated, wondering how best to refuse. 'I don't know, Pop...'

'Please... Look, it's touch and go with her. She's ever so poorly. Don't deny her this one wish, for all we know it might be her last.' His voice was thin with emotion. 'I know how it's been between you two since last summer, and I understand – believe me, I do. But put it aside, Clover. Ramona's willing to. I beg you. Come and listen to what she wants to tell you.'

'Do you know what it is?'

Jake shook his head. 'Not a clue. But it must be

419

important to her.'

'But Pop, I wouldn't want to see Tom. Besides, you can see how I am myself. I'm not even sure–'

'I've got one of the drays out in the street. I'll take you there meself. And anyroad, Ramona said as I'd got to get Tom out the way by the time you arrived. I think she realised you wouldn't want to see him. So he'll be out on an errand. I've already seen to that.'

'All right,' Clover said, but reluctantly. 'Let me take off my apron and put on my hat and coat.' She went outside and told Florrie she'd been called away and would explain later. Florrie muttered under her breath but Clover told her it couldn't be helped.

The prospect of the meeting filled her with dread. What was Ramona about to tell her? That giving birth was not the nicest thing that could happen to a girl? Just seeing her, if she was so ill, would put her off having her own child. It would make her fear her own labour. It was the last thing she wanted, as if she wasn't apprehensive enough.

Jake helped her up on to the passenger seat and drove steadily away in deference to her condition. It threatened rain but a weak sun tried to push its way through the film of grey, racing clouds and, for a few seconds, the dingy red-brick landscape brightened a little. At first they talked about generalities, skirting round the questions that should have been discussed; till Clover asked how her mother was.

'Same as ever,' Jake responded evenly. 'I know one thing – she misses you, Clover.'

Clover did not answer.

'Why don't you put aside your differences with your mother as well and come and see her? Life's too short to harbour ill-feeling.'

'If she's so anxious to forget what's happened why hasn't she been to see me? Why doesn't she come and apologise to me for throwing me out when I needed her support?'

'Because she's proud, your mother.'

'So am I, Pop,' Clover replied with finality.

'Giddup!' Jake flicked the reins and the horses broke into a trot. The road surface at Waddam's Pool was more even and did not shake Clover about too much. He asked how she was coping with married life and living with in-laws.

'I daresay I'll get used to it,' she said.

He turned to look at her but she gave nothing away in her expression.

'You don't sound too keen.'

She shrugged. 'Oh, they're decent enough folk...'

'I never thought you'd take up with Ned Brisco, you know, Clover. You've really surprised me.' She shrugged again. 'Still – as long as you're happy... Life's too short...' He told again of Ramona and spoke more of her baby and how poorly the little mite was. It was not long before they pulled up outside the house in Edward Street.

'You're sure Tom won't be here?' she asked, seeking reassurance.

'He won't be here. Don't fret.'

Jake let her in and Clover looked about her at the pretty curtains, the early daffodils that were wilting now in their vases as if in sympathy for Ramona. It was a cheery, homely place and Clover, as well as being surprised, was envious. Ramona had tried to make a comfortable home for Tom. Even if she and Ned had a house of their own Clover doubted whether she would have the enthusiasm to do for Ned what Ramona had done for Tom.

'This way,' Jake said.

She followed him upstairs, full of apprehension. Her head was filled with memories of all the heartbreaking events that had led to this absurd situation. She had felt anger, bitterness, hatred for Ramona. But, when she saw her, she was visibly shaken. Her heart went out to her stepsister. The girl that had always looked so pretty, so zestful, so spirited, looked like death, lying pale and sickly and helpless in that brass bed. Her face was lined, she looked twenty years older than last time she saw her. When she opened her eyes Clover saw at once their dullness, lacking the sparkle she'd always associated with her.

'Oh, Clover, hello... Thank you for coming...' Her voice was weak and her breathing was laboured, but it was obvious she was determined to fight her fatigue. But then she'd always been dauntless.

Clover went to her and took her hand, putting behind her at once all the animosity, all the prejudice she'd harboured these last months. 'Ramona, I'm ... I'm so sorry you've had such a rough time of ... of your confinement. How are you feeling now?'

'Oh, so tired, Clover... So weak–'

Jake butted in. 'I'll leave you to it,' he said quietly to Clover. 'I'll be downstairs. Call me if you need me.'

Clover smiled her thanks and turned to Ramona again. 'Let me give you a drink. Is this lemonade?'

Ramona nodded. Clover took the glass and raised her stepsister as best as she could from her pillow, enabling her to sip from it. She seemed so light and so frail.

'Thank you...' Ramona wiped her lips with the back of her hand. 'We sort of lost contact with each other, didn't we, Clover?'

Clover smiled forgivingly. 'I think circumstances got in the way a bit.'

'And since last time I saw you I've had plenty time to think it over... And there's something I want you to know.'

'No, you don't have to say anything, Ramona, believe me. You were just as entitled–'

'No, Clover...' Ramona shook her head and it seemed to take a great effort. 'I have to tell you this. It might be my one and only chance to make amends before I meet my Maker–'

'Don't say that, Ramona.'

'If I don't tell you I'll never rest in peace...' The hazy sun managed to break free of the grey clouds that had been smothering it, lending a suffused, eerie glow to that bedroom through the net curtains. Ramona sighed profoundly. 'My baby, Clover... Have you seen him yet?'

'Not yet. Later. When I've seen you. Who's he like?'

'I don't know. But I hope to God he's not like his father...'

'Not?' Clover was taken aback.

'No...' She shook her head again. 'I can't tell anybody else this... But, you see, Clover, it's not Tom's child ... Tom's not the father. Oh, I thought he was. I want him to be, more than anything. But see, he can't be. It's another man's child...'

Clover closed her eyes in anguish at hearing this astonishing confession. She felt herself begin to tremble and wilfully tried to check it. She tried not to show the new and totally unexpected twist of pain from the grief that suddenly rent her heart more cruelly than any spear could. Thoughts of what might have been flashed through her mind in little more than the time it took to blink. So many missed opportunities to rectify her rift with Tom had passed her by and she had nobody to blame but herself. Yet there was also bitter-sweet relief drifting around somewhere in her tortured mind; it was the relief of learning that Tom, after all, was not responsible for making Ramona pregnant.

'So do you want to tell me who the father is?' she asked, overcoming the torpor of shock by force of will.

'No, Clover ... I don't want to tell you, 'cause I'm ashamed... Really ashamed... But I'm going to tell you anyway, 'cause I want you to be under no illusion about me...'

She paused and Clover did not know whether she was trying to summon up the courage or muster the physical strength to finally name the mystery man. Clover tensed, conscious that her fingernails were pressing into the palms of her hands.

'My Uncle Elijah is the father...'

It took a couple of seconds for this further, electrifying revelation to register. When it did, Clover gasped. For a few seconds she could think of nothing to say. No suitable words would lend themselves. Eventually, it dawned on her what must have happened. 'You mean he raped you?' she suggested with abhorrence.

'No, I mean we had a thing going – an affair. Oh, for months.'

'Good God! But... Your own uncle?'

'I know,' Ramona said, her voice tailing off in resignation. 'I think that's why he got married to Dorcas all in a rush ... so as he was out of reach, sort of thing, 'cause I wanted him to give her up and just have me ... I think he might have feared he'd put me in the family way as well ... I was in love with him, Clover... Anyway, at about the same time, you and Tom had stopped courting, and I... Well, we started meeting, Tom and me ... and ... Well, we were both upset... Both on the rebound, I suppose... But I really thought it was Tom's child I was carrying.'

'So what made you realise it wasn't?'

Ramona moistened her lips that were blue from loss of blood and she shivered. 'When I started in labour and Tom went for the midwife, I found me diary from last year. I looked for the last time I'd started me bleeding. I had to go back to the beginning of May to find it. I was never that regular, Clover. Sometimes I'd go six weeks ...

more sometimes. The last time me and Elijah had it was the fifth of June. Then I looked for where I knew I'd written down the first time me and Tom had it. It was a Thursday. The twenty-fifth of June. Three weeks later. So I worked it out – if the child was Tom's it would be no more than an eight-month baby by this time. But he's big, Clover. He's gone full term. He might even have gone over his time and be late if I got caught sometime in May. It has to be Elijah's baby. Don't you see?'

'Yes, I do see, Ramona...'

There followed a long silence while Clover digested this news. If only she had known this before. If only she had had an inkling about Elijah. Things would have been so different. Even now, she might be married to Tom herself, perhaps living in this very house with him. Oh, she would have been so content. She would have been so happy. But fate had not ordained that she should be so fortunate.

Ramona, meanwhile, was glad of the few moments' rest; she was exhausted. She closed her eyes and tried to ease her physical discomfort by shuffling, a look of intense tiredness on her ashen face. Eventually, she opened her eyes and looked at Clover. 'I'm so sorry, Clover,' she whispered, seeing her stepsister so visibly troubled. 'I feel so guilty that I sort of stole Tom right from under your very nose ... specially because I realise that the child you're carrying *must be* Tom's.'

'Of course it is,' Clover said quietly.

'But knowing you, I suppose you wanted to hide it from him anyway, eh?'

Clover nodded. 'I didn't realise I was pregnant till after you were married. If I'd known, I would have gone to him.'

'And by rights, you should be married to Tom... Not me ... I deserve to be in the workhouse.'

Clover sighed. Inside she was trembling. She felt like screaming, like tearing down the pretty curtains at the window of this, Tom's home... So this was how she'd been robbed of the man she loved. Somehow she was not surprised. Always she'd had the feeling she'd been cheated. But not like this. Never like this.

'Oh, Ramona,' she lamented mournfully. 'What fools we've both been. What troubles we make for ourselves.'

And poor Tom. A cuckoo's egg had been laid in his nest and no mistake. He was the one who had been used, taken advantage of, wittingly or unwittingly. He was nowhere near as bad as Ned made him out to be. And he'd been noble; typically, he'd done his duty by Ramona as he saw fit, sacrificed himself, unaware she was carrying another man's child.

'My baby's going to die with me, Clover... Will you tell Tom for me what I've just told you? Will you tell him the child wasn't his? I haven't got the courage anymore... Nor the strength.'

'But Ramona, how can you tell that to a man?' Clover queried, wiping an errant tear from her cheek.

'Sometime ... I want him to know... Sometime... To release him from any guilt he's bound to feel when I'm dead and gone. He'll think it was his fault I died – having *his* child... Don't you see? I'd like him to know how sorry I am ... how much I appreciated his standing by me... He never loved me, you know, Clover. He only ever loved you. The very night I told him I was pregnant he'd told me just before that he was giving me up ... so as he could win you back...'

Clover heaved a great, gushing sob. 'Oh, Ramona, stop it! You're breaking my heart...' She took a handkerchief from her pocket and wiped the flood of tears. 'Don't tell me any more ... I can't stand it.'

Ramona reached out to place her hand on Clover's. 'Hear me out, please...' She went on in barely a whisper, her voice distinctly weaker now than when she started. 'I didn't love Tom at first either... But I was determined to make him fall in love with me ... I didn't succeed, Clover ... I know I didn't... But I did succeed in one thing...'

'What was that?'

'In falling in love with him myself.' Tears filled Ramona's eyes and her colourless face contorted as her bottom lip began to quiver. 'He's the most–'

'Oh, look at you,' Clover reprimanded gently, her own eyes streaming. 'See how you're upsetting yourself.' Typically selfless, she put her handkerchief to Ramona's cheeks and eyes, and gently patted them dry.

'Oh, I've been such a fool, Clover...' She paused, plumbing depths of her reserves for the extra strength to finish saying what she was bent on saying. 'I've lied and cheated and – oh, you've no idea what a whore I've been...'

'That's enough,' Clover answered gently. 'I

don't want to hear any more of your confessions. I've been fool enough for both of us as well. Why don't you get some rest now?'

Ramona nodded weakly. 'I will. But first promise me that you'll tell Tom for me? Promise?'

'All right,' Clover replied. 'I'll tell him. If you think it will ease his conscience.'

A faint smile formed on Ramona's lips. 'Thank you.' She closed her eyes and drifted off into sleep.

Ramona passed away peacefully that afternoon. Tom sat staring at her for a long time afterwards. Motes of dust played in the diffused beams of weak sunlight that entered the room obliquely in that cold March afternoon. He watched as the extremity of one of those indistinct shafts of light moved slowly, poignantly across the pale, slender fingers of her left hand, one of which bore his wedding ring.

He had held that hand while she was dying, after Dr Carter had visited her again and told him there was no hope. As the end approached, she had opened her lack-lustre eyes and tried to smile at him through cold, parched lips. Then, faintly, he'd felt her feebly squeeze his hand as she'd mouthed something which he believed were the words 'I love you'. Then he held her hand more tightly as if, by so doing, he could stop her going, prevent her from leaving this imperfect world of theirs, for it was infinitely better than a cold, dank grave. Well, now she was gone. Ramona. Nineteen years old. A princess of a girl. Plucky. Wily.

It was a sin.

It was a sin that God should take one so young, one so full of vitality.

With tears in his eyes he looked around him. On the mantelpiece, over the small fireplace where a fire still flickered, stood a clock and two candles that had afforded the only light by which Dr Carter, uncomplaining, had worked so hard to try and save her. In front of the fire lay her slippers, where she had left them. Just two days ago she had been padding about in them. How much can happen in just two days. On the wash-stand stood the bowl and ewer and close to it a towel, a feeding bottle in case they could not find a woman who was lactating to feed the baby. Next to that was a jug of lemonade, a glass half full, half consumed. On the second-hand dressing table lay her gold necklace and a pair of gold earrings – gifts from Jake.

Death had erased the ominous lines of pain, suffering and fatigue. Her hair remained abundant and unruly in death as it had in life, golden curls caressing that pale, girlish face that had lured so many admirers. It was a face always so full of expression, now devoid of any. And yet he could still imagine that any moment she might open those eyes and smile at him again.

Tom sighed, feeling guilty that he had never loved his poor wife who had made the supreme sacrifice in bearing his child. A tear rolled down his cheek and dripped onto the counterpane that covered her. Ramona. Young, sparkling Ramona, never fazed, never afraid, never loved – well not by him. 'I'm so sorry, Ramona,' he mouthed in his anguish as he stroked her hand. 'I'm so sorry, my poor love. You deserved better than this. You deserved so much better than I could give you.' He let go her hand. 'Goodbye, Ramona... Goodbye...' He leaned over and placed a kiss on her cold cheek, stood up and pulled the counterpane gently over her head.

He dried his eyes, thinking what best to do next. Pull the curtains to. Shut out that intrusive, pallid sunlight. Quietly he went downstairs, straight down to the scullery. Miriam had the child at her breast.

'He's feeding, Mr Doubleday,' she said with a smile of triumph on her round face. 'See, he's sucking away like mad. He's hungry. I think we'll rear him yet.'

Tom smiled. 'Thank God.' It was some good news amid the sadness.

'How's Mrs Doubleday now?'

'She passed away about twenty minutes ago, Miriam.'

'Oh, no. I'm so sorry, Mr Doubleday. Oh, wait till Mr Tandy knows...'

Clover reckoned it was the ride on Jake's dray that started her off in labour that afternoon. By the time Ned returned from work she was experiencing the first contractions. Immediately he went to fetch Annie Soap, the local midwife. There was pandemonium in the Brisco household from then on. Florrie started running round like a cat scalded by the gallons of water she was putting to boil. She swabbed down the table, the

431

furniture – anything with a hard surface – with caustic soda so that it was clean and free from germs. She sent Clover to bed and fussed over her until she was content that her daughter-in-law was as comfortable as she could be. She fetched a shawl she had washed and ironed specially to wrap Ned's child in when it was born, and put it on top of the tallboy, ready. It was the same shawl Ned had been swaddled in.

The baby, a girl weighing seven pounds eight ounces, was born at ten minutes past two next morning, Tuesday 9th March. It was a straightforward birth; no complications, and Clover met her new daughter with a surge of happiness the likes of which she had not known since the child's conception. She decided to name her Josephine.

Her joy was marred by the news later that morning when Jake called to tell her that Ramona had died. Ramona's son, to be christened Daniel, seemed to be on the mend, however.

Ramona was buried in St Thomas's churchyard on the Friday. Clover could not attend the funeral because of her confinement but Ned represented her, though he kept a low profile. Most of the mourners retired to the Jolly Collier afterwards, although Ned did not; he did not wish to remain where Tom Doubleday was, even though he felt sorry for his old rival. Too vividly he recalled the fight they'd had outside the Jolly Collier all those months ago; sheepishly, he recalled his own occasional evenings out with Ramona. Instead, he went to register the birth of Clover's daughter.

Chapter Twenty-Five

Motherhood came naturally to Clover. She idolised her child and watched her bloom into a healthy, contented baby. Little Josephine tended to take her mind off the marriage that, increasingly, she was regarding as utter folly. More and more, she saw herself as having been both foolish and reckless in marrying Ned. Just think – if she'd waited just a few more days she would have remained unmarried, free to wed Tom in his widowhood. Why hadn't she waited? Couldn't Fate for once have been kind and prompted her somehow, given her a sign? All right, she would have had Josephine out of wedlock but then she would have let Tom know her child was his. He was sure to have married her after a suitable delay; she would have waited.

Additionally, Clover saw Florrie, her mother-in-law, as interfering and domineering, although she knew she meant well. Clover wanted to raise her daughter her own way, without some of the old-fashioned notions that Florrie propounded. Clover was horrified when one day Florrie suggested they have the baby's ears pierced and they place studs in them. 'She might not thank me for that when she gets older,' Clover explained. 'Besides, it would hurt and I'm not going to hurt her.' For a while afterwards she was afraid to leave the child with Florrie, lest she carry out her

433

intention anyway.

She had not expected Ned to show the same interest in Josephine that a natural father would. However, he was totally disinterested in the child. He never offered to do anything for her and seldom held her in his arms. His attitude was a disappointment but, after all, the child was not his so she did not censure him. At least he had given her his name and the money he turned up every week meant that he kept her as well. Ned, however, was beginning to expect favours in return.

Clover's figure returned to its former slenderness. While she carried no excess fat, her curves were utterly feminine. Her pregnancy had left no stretch marks and her stomach had returned to its former youthful shape. Her breasts, though, were round and alluring as she fed her child. Ned watched her every night as she gave Josephine her last feed before going to sleep. With lust in his eyes and resentment in his heart that so far, his attentions had been successfully fended off, he lay in bed beside her, his hands behind his head, enjoying the sight one Sunday evening in June.

Through the bedroom window they could see the last slanting rays of the swollen sun skimming the chimney-pots of Hill Street. It had been a hot day and, anticipating a warm night, Clover wore a sleeveless cotton nightdress that buttoned down the front. Florrie and Old Man Brisco had gone out for their Sunday evening constitutional at the Dog and Partridge in Cromwell Street, so they had the house to themselves.

Ned looked on. The smoothness and plumpness of Clover's breasts looked so inviting. Momentarily, the baby stopped sucking and lost the nipple. He saw it glistening with wetness, hard, and he felt a potent stirring below. He felt jealous of the child, for the child had access to that alluring part of Clover that was as yet denied him.

Clover guided her nipple to Josephine's searching mouth once more and Ned watched the child resume feeding. Clover was sitting up next to him in his bed and, in his mind's eye he tried to visualise her nakedness beneath her nightgown. She was so close – almost touching – and yet she was so far from him. Every night in bed he felt the luxurious warmth of her desirable femininity radiating towards him, he wallowed in the sweet, warm scent of her, relished the brushes with her skin that he made, hoping they would appear accidental. In a morning, when he awoke and threw the bedclothes off, he looked to see if her nightdress had crept up in the night to afford him a glimpse of her creamy, unblemished thighs. This enforced celibacy, while lying next to the woman he desired so earnestly, the one woman he had always desired, was driving him mad.

He longed to take a good handful of Clover's breast and gently knead it between his fingers. He wanted to run his tongue over those soft, smooth contours and feel her body writhing ecstatically under his. He wanted to taste her milk in the same way the baby was doing right now. He longed to explore the soft hair between her legs that so far only his arch-rival, Tom Doubleday, had had the pleasure of knowing.

435

What was it that Tom possessed that he lacked himself? What was it that Clover loved in Tom that she had failed to recognise in himself? It was driving him mad not being allowed to touch her.

Clover looked up and saw his frown. 'A penny for your thoughts.'

He shrugged like somebody hard done by. 'I was just wondering when we might actually be man and wife – in the real sense, I mean. You can't put me off for ever.'

'My body's not ready yet, Ned. It's been barely three months since Josephine was born. A woman's body takes time to heal after having a baby.'

'So you keep telling me. I've been talking to the blokes at work. One of 'em even had it with his wife two days after their kid was born.'

'Oh, that's disgusting,' she said with disdain. 'It can't have done her any good.'

'At least he's happy.'

She turned to face him. 'Oh, *he's* happy?' she repeated indignantly. 'But is his wife happy? Did you ask him that? I don't suppose he cares too much whether she's happy or not.'

'But three months, Clover. Some women are pregnant again within three months of the first.'

'Do I glean from that then, that you want to make me pregnant?'

'Josephine isn't mine. You know that. I'd like to father a child of my own – by you.'

'If you paid a bit more attention to the child we already have I might be more inclined to consider it.'

That struck a chord, she could tell. He didn't

436

answer straight away and there was a pause while she looked down at the child sucking contentedly.

'In any case,' she said eventually, 'you remember what we agreed.'

'Look, I gave you my name. I also gave your bastard my name.'

That hurt and Clover visibly flinched at his harsh words. It was the first time he had been so obtuse about Josephine and never would she have believed he could be so unfeeling. 'I don't think there's any need for you to call Josephine that. Let's face it, *she's* not to blame. Anyway, you were keen enough to take us on. It was all your idea. I wasn't bothered.'

'Whether or no, it's me that keeps you both. I think I deserve something in return. You owe me, Clover. I agreed to marry you when you were in *trouble*. I gave you respectability.'

'And at the time, if I remember correctly, I told you to expect nothing in return. I told you I had nothing to give you back. That hasn't changed. It didn't change your mind then. Why should it now?'

'Because I want you. I always assumed, when you'd had the baby, that we'd be like any other man and wife.'

'Whereas I thought I'd made it plain we wouldn't be.' The child stopped feeding, evidently sated. Clover wiped the wetness from her breast with a cloth and covered herself up, then she put the baby against her shoulder and gently rubbed her back. 'I didn't make you any promises I haven't kept, Ned. It might pay you to

437

remember that.'

'Well I can't go on like this. I demand my rights as a husband... Otherwise...'

'Otherwise what?'

'Otherwise...' He was going to say otherwise he would turn her out of the house. But of course, if he did that, she would almost certainly run to Tom Doubleday now he was free. There was always Tom Doubleday lurking in the background, damn his hide.

'Otherwise what?' Clover urged, aware of his dilemma.

He had no threat strong enough. And, short of rape, which was not an option, he was not going to get his way. Not yet at any rate. If he was ever going to have his way, he was going to have to earn it.

'Oh, I'm sorry, Ned.' She cradled the baby in her arms. 'In any case, I could never feel relaxed enough to do it in this house, with your mother and father listening to every squeak of the bedsprings. The walls are paper-thin.'

The comment was not intended as encouragement; Clover was unhappy about Florrie's interference. She would do anything to escape her influence.

Ned, however, was encouraged. 'So if we moved to a rented house somewhere, would that make it all the more likely to happen?'

'I'd be happier somewhere else,' she answered ambiguously.

Rented unfurnished accommodation was plentiful and they found they could take their pick.

Within a month they had moved into a small terraced house in Hill Street, just around the corner from Florrie and Old Man Brisco. The back yard, although separated by a high wall, backed on to the Briscos' back yard while the privies stood almost back to back. Indeed, an exchange of gossip would not have been impossible, albeit in a raised voice, had visits to their respective lavatories occurred simultaneously. The house itself had two bedrooms and a box-room. You went up the narrow, twisting staircase by opening the door at the side of the fire grate and descended to the cellar using the door next to that. The only entrance from the street was via the front room that had a decent fireplace with useful cupboards on either side. The sash window, however, was seized up solid from layer upon layer of ancient paint and varnish. The place needed decorating so, while Ned was at work, Clover knuckled down to some serious paper-hanging when Josephine's needs had been tended to.

Since she was a stickler for cleanliness she cleaned and scrubbed and wiped down all the paintwork. She hunted for woodlice that hid in the cracks of the window-frames and the silverfish that emerged from behind the skirting-boards and popped up from under the linoleum. Once she spotted a mouse poke its tiny head from a hole at the side of the grate and stood for ages waiting for it to pop out again, hovering with a kettle of boiling water to pour over the poor mite. She suggested to Ned that they get a cat, for there was sure to be a nest.

But she could summon little enthusiasm for homemaking, leastwise with Ned. She recalled how attractive Ramona had made Tom's home and knew that she could not apply herself with anything like the same zeal – not for Ned. She had little interest in the house and even less interest in him. She still thought about Tom a great deal; she still loved him dearly. The last she heard, the baby Daniel had survived and was doing well. Zillah kept her informed of any developments but nothing had been reported since. Clover didn't even know whether Tom kept in touch with Jake. She presumed he did, since Daniel was Jake's only grandchild, and she could not conceive of Tom wilfully withholding access.

How was Tom coping? Did he have any inkling at all that the child he was committed to rearing was not his? Her heart went out to him when she thought of the sacrifices he must be making to bring up Elijah Tandy's illegitimate son, believing it to be his own. And she had promised to reveal the truth. She had promised to confess on Ramona's behalf Ramona's misdeeds. Fortunately, there was no rush; she would do it sometime. But when would she ever be able to pluck up the courage to impart that sort of information? Would it be fair on the child? How might such a revelation affect the relationship between Tom and the child? It was not a promise she relished fulfilling. Oh, she would love to see Tom again and no two ways, just the two of them, without either of the children present. She yearned to be close to him again, wondered whether that spark of love for her still existed within him. However, the prospect of meeting him, with the sole purpose of revealing what Ramona had asked her to reveal, filled her with dread. Had little Daniel not survived, that might have been different. But little Daniel had survived. And that made all the difference.

Although Clover and Ned were at least on their own with Josephine, their fragile marriage was still in crisis over the ceaseless demands for conjugal rights which she continued to withhold, unrelenting, despite the move to Hill Street. Ned was bitterly disappointed, particularly because he thought he'd done enough to justify his rewards.

'If you want that, why don't you find yourself a mistress?' Clover suggested huffily one night as they lay in the darkness of their bedroom. She had been woken up from her sleep feeling his hand probing between her legs, surreptitiously seeking her most sacred place. She brushed him away, thoroughly indignant.

Ned sighed with exasperation. 'I don't think you're being very fair with me.'

She turned her back on him, roughed up her pillow and let her head fall back on it exaggeratedly to demonstrate her annoyance. He knew exactly where he stood. 'Look, find yourself a mistress, for God's sake. I won't mind. Pay for it if you have to.' She closed her eyes and knew that Ned had sulkily turned his back on her too. She sighed theatrically. 'Oh, and if you do decide to go out and pay for your pleasure, just remember there's a loan still hanging over your head that has to be paid back at some time.'

'The loan isn't your concern,' he muttered.

441

Next day, when he returned from work he felt in his pocket and withdrew a black-and-white kitten.

'You said we needed a good mouser.'

Her face lit up and she held her hands out to receive the irresistible bundle of fluff and large eyes. 'Oh, he's beautiful,' she drooled, stroking its soft, warm fur. 'Look, Josie, Daddy's bought us a pussycat to catch the mice.'

The child watched with wide-eyed curiosity, too young to know whether the moment was auspicious or not. She waved her arms in front of her, emitted an appealing gurgle and turned her attention back to the clothes-peg she'd been playing with.

'Where did you get it?' Clover asked.

'One of the lads at work. His mother's cat had had kittens. It seemed a pity to drown 'em all.'

She continued to stroke the kitten as it lay in her arms. 'What shall we call it? Any ideas?'

'How about Tom?' he suggested sarcastically.

She looked at him askance but made no comment. 'Let's call it something daft. How about Liquorice?'

'You daft bugger!'

Ned felt he had earned some more points in his battle to win Clover's favours. Despite her continued resistance, he realised that the move away from his mother had been a good move. The cat could only enhance his standing. Over the weeks and months Ned became very attached to Liquorice. He would sit at night with it draped around his shoulders as he read the evening newspaper, or on his lap as he snoozed. In fact, he paid far more attention to the cat than he paid to Josephine. He would tickle its belly and Liquorice would lie in ecstasy, he would offer it morsels of food from his dinner-plate as it sat looking up at him expectantly. Certainly, Liquorice and Ned enjoyed a mutual affection. It seemed that the cat was his substitute for the warm relationship that he sought but failed to attain with Clover.

In her heart Clover felt sorry for Ned. She understood what he was going through. But feeling sorry for somebody did not constitute strong abiding love where sex should necessarily be an integral part of it. Besides, their marriage was his idea. She loved him no more now than the day they were wed. She could never love him. In fact, the longer she lived with him, the more his negative side was revealed and the less she was inclined towards him. No, she yearned for Tom. Her heart had never stopped aching for want of Tom. To hold Tom in her arms again, just once, would brighten her life no end. But it could never be. She was trapped in a loveless marriage. Worst of all, had she side-stepped marriage for just a few more days, she would have known not to commit herself to it.

But such was her luck; such was her fate.

Yet all was not misery and unhappiness. She had Josephine. Josephine was the absolute light of her life and such a pleasant child. So contented was she that, if she cried, you knew it was because she was hungry or in discomfort. She was endowing everybody with her first bewitching smiles and Clover seemed to spend half her life now trying to induce them the more for the pleasure they brought her. She seldom stopped talking to Josephine. They played baby games and she spoke baby talk and their lives were filled with each other. When Ned returned from work Clover began to regard him as an intruder and was perfectly content to watch him tend to Liquorice. She was perfectly happy to watch him pour out all his affection on the cat.

It was in March 1910 that Ned was called into the office of Mr Edward Lisle for a rare interview.

'Ned,' Mr Lisle greeted when he stepped over the threshold. 'Please sit down. I need to have a chat with you.'

Ned duly sat down on a high-backed chair facing Mr Lisle.

'Ned, the time has come for me to turn my full attention to the question of developing an aeroplane.'

'You mean unhindered development?' Ned suggested with a hint of sarcasm.

Mr Lisle ignored the jibe. 'We had Bleriot crossing the Channel last July, we had the first international air race last August, and we've seen the Wright Brothers take an aeroplane to a height of sixteen hundred feet. All this has captured the public's imagination, Ned.'

'Yes, I know. But nothing's changed here at Star, Mr Lisle. We still don't have a suitable engine.'

'Ah... Well, for the past couple of months I've been in talks with a Mr Granville Bradshaw, a fine engineer. He has some proposals for a new engine and for two new aeroplane designs. I am engaging him as a designer. His designs are already well-advanced.'

Ned looked horrified. 'I take it then that you don't need me any longer.'

'Oh, on the contrary, Ned. I would like you to work closely alongside Mr Bradshaw.'

'And if we don't see eye to eye?'

'Oh, I'm confident you will. You could learn a great deal from such a gifted engineer.'

Granville Bradshaw duly entered the firm. He brought with him proposals to manufacture a lightweight engine featuring weight-saving water jackets fabricated from copper instead of being cast from iron. Ned saw the potential in such an engine and was encouraged. Maybe Bradshaw was gifted. However, Bradshaw had also designed two new aircraft, as Mr Lisle had intimated. One was a biplane configuration with a pusher propeller, the other was a monoplane. The latter was unusual in that the control surfaces were incorporated only in the tail.

'I can tell you straight, Mr Bradshaw, it'll never fly,' Ned advised when he saw the drawings.

'Of course it'll fly,' Bradshaw argued. 'It's not a million miles from Levavasseur's *Antoinette VII* and that flies. The only difference is I'm using the tailplane only for control.'

Ned shrugged resentfully. 'Even if it does fly, you'll never be able to control it.'

By July, Ned was proved right.

'I have a perfectly airworthy biplane already built, just waiting for an engine, Mr Bradshaw,' Ned informed him. 'You have the engine, I have

445

the aeroplane. Let's just pool our resources and get on with it.'

'I already have two designs, as you know, Ned,' Bradshaw responded, too contemptuously for Ned's liking. 'I also have Mr Lisle's permission – indeed, his specific instruction – that we give *them* priority.'

Ned realised he was wasting his time and his talent. By August, he had left the Star Aeroplane Company Limited, as it was by that time called, and was unemployed.

Yet another dream was shattered.

'So what do you intend to do?' Clover asked when he returned home from Star for the last time.

'I'll find another job.'

'Times are hard, Ned. Jobs are not that easy to come by. It might be ages before you find another job.'

He sat down and Liquorice leapt up onto his lap. 'Times *are* hard, Clover, I agree. But I shall start looking tomorrow for work. I'm a good moulder. I could get a job moulding. Trouble is, I don't fancy going back to foundry work.'

Clover shuddered at the thought. 'In the meantime, you'd better sell your motor car. That should raise enough to keep us going. It's a bit of an extravagance anyway for a family like us. I mean, it's not as if we need a motor car. We can walk and catch trams, same as everybody else.'

He nodded. He was not so unreasonable that he would not see that her words made sense. 'I'll see about it tomorrow.'

Ned sold his motor car within a week and it realised over a hundred pounds. He tossed a bag of gold sovereigns towards Clover with a look of triumph.

'You take care of it, Clover. I know you'll be thrifty. I know you won't waste the money.' This action and all it implied would earn him more points.

She smiled at him in acknowledgement of his high opinion of her. 'Maybe I could splash out on some new clothes for Josie,' she suggested tentatively, appealing to his generosity. 'She desperately needs new things.'

'As long as you don't go overboard.'

'I won't. Don't worry.'

Clover had her own idea of what to do with the money. She decided to use as little as she could. Whatever was left by the time Ned found other work she would put towards paying off that loan that was hanging over them. To her, it was like a big, black cloud forever looming. Until they were free of it she could hardly be extravagant. It was worrying her, although it hardly seemed to bother Ned. He, however, had received the money and it had to be paid back. There were no two ways about it. Whoever had been daft enough to stump up all that money in the first place, and trust Ned to use it wisely, obviously didn't know him very well.

By September, Josephine was thriving. At eighteen months, she was the apple of her mother's eye, as well as Florrie Brisco's. Over the months her name had evolved from Josephine to Josie, and then to Josy-Posy, only to be shortened further to Posy. Posy seemed to suit her and it looked as if it was going to stick. She was bright and intelligent, and possessed a sunny disposition that was utterly disarming. Not only that, everybody said she was the image of her mother. Clover, however, could only see Tom in her.

Come October, and a workmate of Ned's from Star who had changed his allegiance to the Sunbeam Motor Company in Wolverhampton, let it be known that Ned Brisco, a talented aeronautical engineer, was available for work. Sunbeam needed somebody with his natural flair and instinct and they approached him. They offered him a job at their works in Villiers Street where they, too, were developing aeroplanes and aeroplane engines. It was another feather in Ned's cap as far as Clover was concerned.

After more than a year and a half of marriage and sleeping in the same bed as her husband, Clover had got used to his foibles and quirks. Lately, he had been more affable, more relaxed about their relationship. Unemployment and the threat of mutual hardship ensured they forged a bond that had been absent before. She noticed that they were beginning to laugh together and his landing the job at Sunbeam relieved the pressure further. But the bond remained. Maybe she was learning to love him after all.

Ned was no more inclined to fuss Posy but when, toddling now, she tugged at his trouser-leg for attention with her disarming smile, she normally got it and he would pick her up and walk with her up the back yard and show her the pretty flowers he'd been growing in a bed alongside a wall, as if she understood everything about them. Even Ned was becoming ultimately susceptible to Posy's charms, Clover realised.

Clover was also beginning to understand that, with this growing esteem, maybe she was being grossly unfair in prohibiting further the possibility of his fathering a child. She didn't relish the thought of physical union with Ned – nothing had changed there – but, doubtless, she could quiescently suffer it and think of something else – or even *somebody* else. It would be no good making believe it was Tom because whenever Tom touched her she'd simply melted. Thus, any such fantasising would only highlight Ned's inadequacy and very likely incline her to shun him the more. But maybe he should father a child of his own. Maybe, at some time, she should allow him that. It might predispose him to become more involved with Posy, combine them more securely as a family.

By Easter Sunday in 1911, Ned had endured two years of celibacy. Lying every night next to his lissom young wife, feeling the warmth of her body close to his but not being allowed to touch, had been purgatory. That morning he awoke to find her lying in his lap. His arm remained around her waist – a surprising turn, since usually she would have removed it by such as this time. Most mornings he awoke with an erection and this morning was no exception. It pulsed insubordinately against her bottom.

'By the feel of it, Jesus isn't the only entity to

have arisen this morning,' Clover quipped. She had been awake a while, inordinately conscious of the disturbing protuberance hot in his pyjama trousers, but too cosy and warm in his lap to turn over. Besides, it was not an unpleasant sensation and she began to feel a warm glow of desire. It reminded her what a long time it had been since she had last enjoyed a sexual encounter, how long since Tom had exhibited similar excitement for her. Of course, that last time she also conceived, she was certain it was then. And in the ensuing two and three-quarter years she had grown used to celibacy, celibacy she would now give up reluctantly. But maybe it was time. To be fair to Ned, maybe it was time.

She turned over, smiling at him with some of her erstwhile mateyness. 'What do you think you're going to do with *that?*'

'I know what I want to do with it.'

'I bet you do,' she replied unflinching, her arm still propping up her head on the pillow.

'You know, Clover,' he said softly, 'when you used to come around to the old stables at Joseph Mantle's and help me build the *Gull,* we never said a lot...' She nodded, acknowledging the fact; she'd often commented on it. 'Well, while I worked, I used to daydream about us as a married couple. I used to imagine us in our own little house – like this one – with two or three kids around us, you mothering them just like you mother Posy. We were that contented...' He shook his head as if to dislodge the dream and be left with the appetising reality. 'All I ever wanted was to fly my *Gull* and make you my wife. Well,

450

I've done both, I suppose, but only to a limited degree. I've flown the *Gull* but had nothing to drive it forward, and I've married you, but had nothing to drive that forward either – if you get my meaning.'

She regarded him with a tenderness that had been lacking too long. 'I know,' she whispered. 'And I'm sorry...'

There was a pause while Ned, thrown, considered this unusual reaction.

'You mean?...' He looked into her eyes earnestly. 'You mean, you don't mind if we...?'

She shrugged awkwardly as she lay on her side, facing him and smiled again. 'Maybe it's time you tried your luck.'

His arms went about her in a frenzy of devotion. First, he kissed the soft part of her neck near her throat, nuzzling his lips against her slightly damp, warm skin. With fumbling fingers he managed to undo the top buttons of her nightdress and he inclined his head to more easily experience the smooth softness of her breasts against his eagerly exploring mouth. Oh, he'd yearned for these moments, for this opportunity. His free hand went to her bottom and he cupped her left cheek with his right hand. Encouraged by the distinct lack of resistance, the same hand found its way under the hem of her nightdress and glided lingeringly over the sleek tract of her thigh before cupping again the same warm left cheek, but in the flesh this time.

'Oh, Clover,' he sighed emotionally, unable to believe his luck, 'I've been dying for this moment.'

His hand went to her bare waist, advanced investigatively across her smooth belly. From there it journeyed up to her breasts and kneaded them to appreciate how they yielded to his touch like incredibly smooth sponges that magically resumed their true shape when he moved on.

But Clover was not relishing his ardent scrutiny at all. His hands were hard and rough, his caresses were inept and clumsy. He touched that sanctified place between her legs and hurt her when he started bodging his fingers into her too soon. She felt her flesh creep with distaste. Then his face hovered about hers as he tried to kiss her on the lips and she caught a whiff of his stale, morning breath that turned her stomach.

'Please, Ned...' She turned her face away from him.

'What?' he muttered apprehensively.

'I can't ... I'm so sorry.'

'Hell! What's the matter now?' He sounded exasperated.

'I need to go up the yard, Ned.'

'Jesus Christ! Use the bloody chamber pot.'

'I can't. I'm going up the yard.'

'Hurry up then. For God's sake!'

He lay back in the bed alone with his erection and waited for her to return.

But Clover did not return. At least, not till Posy woke up.

Chapter Twenty-Six

A Frenchman called Louis Coatalen was the inspiration and the intellect behind a range of aeroplane engines being developed by the Sunbeam Motor Car Company of Wolverhampton. M Coatalen joined the firm in 1909 as chief engineer and a succession of fine motor cars emerged from the Sunbeam factory thereafter. Using Coatalen's French connections, Ned Brisco and his team were able to acquire a Farman biplane from France and Ned, the only employee with any experience at all in aviation, was allowed to test-fly it once the eight-cylinder, liquid-cooled, Coatalen-designed engine had been installed. The local authority was duly notified that test-flying was about to take place. By this time Ned had given up the idea that his own *Gull* might be used for such trials.

This first engine was a moderate success. In the sense that Ned achieved powered flight, it was an undoubted triumph. The flight was not long; he was airborne for no more than a hundred and fifty yards or so but, at least there was power enough to get the small aeroplane off the ground. Ned felt he could have gone further but the engine vibrated appallingly and Ned was scared that it might shake loose from its mountings and cause a fatal accident. Neither was he used to the controls of the Farman, which relied on wing-warping, as did the Wright Brothers' aircraft. He decided that initial caution was preferable to heroics until he'd got some hours of practice behind him. Clearly, more work was needed, but the early signs were very encouraging.

Consequently, Ned felt uplifted for the first time in ages. He had flown an aeroplane under power for the very first time and it had been an exhilarating experience. Further, he had been chosen as test pilot for this and all foreseeable future projects, with licence to test whenever he deemed it necessary and when staff were available to help.

Work refining the Coatalen engine continued and each improvement that was made saw Ned, wrapped up warm against the cold, climbing into the Farman at a flat area of open countryside just outside Wolverhampton called Pendeford. Normally, he was accompanied by at least two or three other people. Understanding the principles of powered flight intimately, he soon became used to the controls and the quirks and peculiarities of the Farman biplane. The engine began to benefit from the many modifications but, after some months and into the early summer of 1911, it still vibrated harshly but not sufficiently to deter Ned from achieving flights of several miles, circling triumphantly over Codsall, Coven and even as far north as Penkridge.

Ned, at last, had achieved one ambition, although not in his own *Gull*. When he was wheeling around the skies he forgot his frustrations. He learned to throw the plane all over the sky in loops, testing the little Farman to the limit. He performed stalls, spins, slow rolls, dives and everything else he dared to do. He frightened himself at times but his confidence in handling the machine increased along with his enthusiasm. And it was wonderful to see the countryside whizzing by below. It was astonishing to see into the vast gardens of some of the fine houses in the area, to see just how many lakes there were, how many finely manicured lawns.

Meanwhile, development of the Coatalen engine continued. Plans were made for a new twelve-cylinder and even an eighteen-cylinder version. This would mean more and more testing, more and more flying. Ned had the best job in the world and Sunbeam intended to be the leader in British aircraft engine production.

The coronation of George V on 23rd June 1911, whilst hardly a holiday for the king who was obliged to endure seven hours of kingly ceremonial glory, was reason enough for the nation to enjoy a day's holiday. Tom Doubleday awoke at his usual time, seven o'clock and, since he was not due to open his studio that day, stretched and yawned and arose from his bed with a leisureliness that was strange to him. He quietly stepped into Daniel's room and looked down on him. His fair-haired son looked so angelic and so appealing as he lay silently sleeping. Such innocence, such lack of guile brought a lump to his throat. Tom watched him for a while, his heart overflowing with love and devotion before he went down to the scullery to make himself a pot of tea.

As he drank it he pondered his son and his thoughts turned to Ramona and then, inevitably, to death. The necessity for a coronation today was because of death; the death, more than a year earlier, of Edward VII. Tom recalled reading about the funeral in the newspaper the day after it occurred; a day of national high drama and great sadness. That death seemed to have been the precursor to so many other tragic events, attributable by some to the proximity of Halley's Comet, which was spectacular at the time in the night sky. All these deaths depressed Tom. Last August, Florence Nightingale died, heroine of the Scutari hospital in the Crimean War. In Japan, eight hundred souls perished in severe flooding. The death toll from cholera in Russia topped sixty thousand. Last September a hundred thousand folk, all frightened of death, fled Naples as cholera broke out there too and, a month later, as if that wasn't bad enough, a tidal wave lashed the Bay of Naples, causing a thousand more deaths. In October, Dr Crippen was sentenced to death, which actually served him right and, in November, Leo Tolstoy passed away. Christmas was spoilt when three hundred and fifty men and boys met their deaths in an underground explosion at a pit near Bolton in Lancashire. All this waste of human life. All these deaths. As if one death – Ramona's – was not enough.

He sighed as he thought of Ramona. Although he had never loved her, she did not deserve to die so young and he still suffered pangs of guilt that she so tragically had, bearing his son. It seemed this sense of guilt would never leave him. He was reminded of it every time he looked at Daniel with his unruly mop of pale yellow, curly hair, just like his mother's. Somehow it seemed he had swapped one person for the other; a wife not relished but not disliked, for a cherished son. Maybe it was a fair swap, all things considered. He loved his son so fiercely, so protectively, that its very intensity surprised him sometimes. Oh, he knew he was eminently capable of strong, steadfast love; he still loved Clover Beckitt with all his heart and suspected he always would, although he wished he didn't, for it was sometimes too painful to bear. But the love for his son was different.

He trudged back up two flights of stairs, went into Daniel's room and opened the curtains. Daniel roused and rubbed his eyes at the invading light.

'Time to get up if we're going to see all the fun going on in the town,' Tom chirped brightly. 'Remember I told you last night before I read you your story?'

Daniel rolled over and pretended to go back to sleep.

'Have I got to tickle you?' A smile appeared on the boy's cherubic face as he rolled onto his back. 'I'm coming... There...' Daniel shrieked with chuckles and Tom thought that's how bubbles would sound if you could hear them. 'I told you I'd tickle you.'

'Do it again.'

'No. It's time you were up. Do you want to sit on your pot?'

'I fink I want a wee.'

'All right, I'll lift you out and you can have a wee.'

Daniel still slept in a cot with tall sides but Tom felt he was at an age now when he could buy a proper bed for him. It was time he organised it. That would make the child feel more grown-up. He lifted his son out and withdrew the chamber pot from under the cot, whereupon Daniel lifted up his nightshirt and peed into it, thrusting his pelvis forward in an exaggerated movement.

After Tom had filled the washbowl with cold water from the ewer, just like the ones grown-ups have, he observed with pride as the boy washed his face and neck and ears, then took a towel and dried himself. It was a good thing to teach him these things that a mother might still be doing for him at this age – if he still had a mother. Tom never ceased to be amazed at the quickness with which Daniel learnt to do these things. Normally, Tom only had to show him once.

'When you're dressed, Daniel, I'm going to do us a boiled egg each for our breakfasts.'

The boy nodded.

'Here are your clothes. Show me again how you can dress yourself.'

Tiny hands fumbled through the neat pile of garments. Awkwardly, the child began to put on his clothes, helped by Tom when he got stuck or confused. Little buttons are difficult for little hands to fasten and Tom helped there too, all the time talking to him, offering gentle and very patient encouragement.

As they descended the stairs slowly, Tom held

Daniel's hand to steady him and they went into the scullery. Daniel ran outside to try and find the hedgehog he'd seen the day before in the back yard. While the eggs were boiling Tom followed.

'Where's he gone, Daddy?'

'I don't know, son.' He bent down, trying to attain Daniel's diminutiveness. 'But don't worry, he'll be back. We'll leave him some bread for his dinner and have another look for him when we get back from Gran's later, eh?'

Daniel nodded his firm agreement.

Back inside, Tom sat him at the table on a chair with a pile of cushions on it. The child scribbled on a sheet of paper with a blacklead while Tom sliced and buttered some bread and delivered their breakfasts to the table. Tom cut off the top of the egg for Daniel and watched him poke 'soldiers', strips of bread, into the yolk, just like he'd taught him. He handled food well for a child not yet two and a half. And for his age, he was eminently sensible. Tom was so proud of his son. His days revolved entirely around him.

It was not a sunny day so far, rather it was overcast but, as long as it remained dry for the street parties that were due to take place later, nobody would complain.

When they arrived in the town, Dudley was a picture of festivity. Bunting flapped across the streets from practically every building. Union Jacks flew from upstairs windows and regal plaster crowns, coated in gilt paint, adorned shop windows along with photographs of King George and Queen Mary. Daniel looked at it all with

wonder and delight and Tom smiled affectionately at his son's excitement. In the Market Place
in front of the great marble fountain that spurted
water exotically, a man with a hurdy-gurdy had
people laughing and joining hands to dance to its
mechanical music. From the immense height of
his daddy's arms Daniel watched and listened to
the instrument, fascinated. His face lit up when
the man took to them his monkey that was
holding a tin cup to collect coins. He looked at
his father beseechingly for a penny to give to the
monkey.

Tom handed over a few halfpennies to Daniel.
Tentatively, Daniel stretched out his hand and
dropped the coins into the tin cup the monkey
was proffering, immediately drawing away. 'He's
all right, sonny,' the hurdy-gurdy man said. 'He
won't bite yer.' Daniel smiled uncertainly at his
daddy while the hurdy-gurdy man and the
monkey passed on to the next folk, rattling their
cup.

A man rode in front of them on a one-wheeled
cycle waving bunting and performing impossible
twists and turns. Another man rode a gigantic
ball, controlling it cleverly with his feet, dancing
on it. The romantic sound of a barbershop
quartet, harmonising like divine songsters from
another world, drifted over from the other end of
the market while Tom and Daniel watched a
dance troupe with bells on their toes. They went
to move on.

Somebody behind him spoke.

'Hello, Tom.'

It was a woman's voice; such a heartbreakingly

familiar voice.

Tom looked around. 'Clover!... Lord above!'

She smiled at him hesitantly. 'Is this your little boy?'

Tom, for a second or two, was dumbstruck and his heart seemed to stop beating altogether. When he found his voice he said: 'Yes, this is Daniel. Daniel, say hello to ... to Mrs ... er ... Brisco.'

Daniel politely said hello.

'He's the image of his mother,' Clover said, recognising the child as a Tandy through and through. 'What a beautiful crop of fair hair he's got. Just like Ramona.'

Tom found himself smiling. Seeing Clover after so long was a surprise he hadn't reckoned on. He'd often wondered whether it would be a cordial exchange if they ever ran into each other again after they'd parted in an argument. 'So how are you, Clover? It's been a long time.'

Clover was smiling too. 'I'm fine, thank you.' As soon as she had spotted him Clover couldn't help herself; she had to go over and speak to him. Her heart was beating so fast and she hoped it didn't show.

'And this is your daughter? I heard you'd had a daughter.'

'Say hello, Posy.' She almost said, *say hello to your father*, but managed to stop herself. 'Say hello to Mr Doubleday.'

'Hello, Mr Doubledouble,' Posy managed to utter.

They both laughed.

'It is a bit of a mouthful, my name,' Tom said

461

cheerfully to Posy. 'I can forgive you for not getting it right, little lady.' He looked at Clover and their eyes met and held for a moment. 'She's the image of you, Clover. She's beautiful. Nothing like Ned.'

He really believes Ned is her father, Clover deduced from that comment.

'Is Ned with you?'

'He's listening to the barbershop quartet over there.' She inclined her head in that direction. 'With his mother and father.'

'Oh. Family day out then?' He smiled openly.

She nodded. 'And you? Just the two of you?'

'For now. We're going back to Mother's after. There's a street party in Stafford Street this afternoon and another in Edward Street tonight. I've been promising to bring Daniel here this morning to see all the fun. He's been looking forward to it, haven't you, me old mate?'

Daniel nodded on cue.

Posy meanwhile looked suspiciously at Daniel and tugged at her mother's hand. 'Come on, Mommy.'

Clover tugged back admonishingly; she did not want to be rushed. 'Wait. And just behave.' She found Tom's eyes again. 'I was so sorry about Ramona, Tom... It must have been awful for you.'

He nodded, his mouth tightening. 'Thank you, Clover. It was ... difficult. But, thankfully, Daniel pulled through. To look at him now you'd never know it was touch and go with him as well. I don't know what I'd do without him now.' He shifted the boy's weight to his other arm. 'He's no

462

trouble, you know, Clover... Are you, old mate?'

'So how do you get on with him during the day while you're at work?'

'Mother takes care of him, bless her. I drop him there on my way past and pick him up on my way back. She loves having him.'

'He's very well behaved,' she commented.

'Takes after his father.' Tom smiled, feigning smugness.

Let's hope not, Clover thought, reminded of Elijah Tandy. She glanced around nervously for sight of Ned. She did not want Ned to see her talking to Tom; all hell would be let loose.

'I'd better get back to Ned,' she said apologetically. 'He'll be wondering where we've got to. It's lovely to see you again, Tom. Such a pleasant surprise.' She didn't want to leave him. There was so much to say, so much ground to cover. Damn Ned for being around. Damn Florrie. Damn Old Man Brisco. Damn them all. 'It's nice to see you looking so well.'

'You, too, Clover. You don't look any different to how you did before. Marriage evidently suits you.'

She looked tellingly into his eyes and shook her head.

'No?'

'No. Leastwise not with...' She inclined her head again in the direction of the barbershop quartet and Ned.

The sudden silence between them was noticeable. Tom felt he should respond but could not think of anything relevant to say. He was also inhibited from saying anything in front of

Clover's daughter. Till an idea struck him.

'Why don't you bring Posy along to the studio to have her photo taken?'

Clover smiled delightedly. What a brilliant idea. 'Yes, why don't I? When could I?'

Tom shrugged, his eyes dancing with expectation. 'Whenever you want. Whenever you can. Afternoon's best. As you know, I tend to be quieter late afternoon.' He gave her a look that suggested he still felt something for her and her heart pounded once more.

At first, Clover could hardly believe she'd met Tom Doubleday again after three years of studiously avoiding him. In the days that followed the meeting her head was full of him. Over and over, their conversation ran through her mind. Each time, she analysed his words and the images she carried of his expressions, trying to recall whether she'd left out any bits, trying to glean whether he still loved her. She had the feeling that he did and it gladdened her heart; not that it could do her much good; she was, after all, a married woman, albeit married to the wrong man.

The thing that really convinced her of his love was his suggestion that she take Posy to his studio for some photographs. Of course, she would love to, but there was the distinct possibility that all those painful memories would be churned up along with her long-stifled emotions and she would not be able to sleep at night for thinking about him. Because, sadly, her marriage precluded any hope of them ever

464

being together.

So she avoided going. Rather, she avoided going till her bursting heart dictated that she could put it off no longer. Besides, it was a shame not to have any photos of Posy at age two and a half to look back on, when she was such a joy and so pretty to behold. So, in the late afternoon of a warm September day, she finally plucked up the courage to make the most of herself, dress Posy in her best dress and visit Tom Doubleday's studio.

As she stood in the foyer with Posy clutching her hand, the memories of the wonderfully romantic and emotional hours they'd spent there together came flooding back. It had been more than three years and yet it could have been yesterday. Little had changed materially. There were still some photos of her displayed on the wall and, she noticed, some newer ones – of Daniel. She wallowed in the memories and the ambience for a little while before she rang the bell. This place had brought her such contentment during those precious hours she'd shared it with Tom; precious hours when she had never known such happiness. In those days she would have wagered any money that nothing could ever happen to cause them to part, so certain was she of their future together.

The inner door opened and Tom appeared. His face lit up like a lamp.

'Clover.'

'Hello, Tom. I brought Posy to have her photo done,' she explained superfluously. 'Is it convenient?'

'Course it is,' he answered warmly. 'Come on through.' He lifted the counter top that concealed the half-door that gave her access and she followed him into the studio. She looked around. It was exactly the same as she remembered. Everything was there that had been there before, including the bearskin rug. Images of them rolling around on it naked flashed into her mind and the blood coursed through her veins at the memory.

'I'm glad you came at last,' he said. 'I'd given up hope of you coming at all.'

'It was a question of finding the right moment, Tom,' she fibbed. 'I always intended to come. I always intended Posy should have her photo done, once you'd mentioned it.'

Tom stooped down and took Posy's hand. 'You're just like your mommy,' he said gently. 'Has anybody else told you that?'

Posy smiled bashfully and looked to her mother for help.

'One or two have said the same thing,' Clover said. 'Haven't they, sweetheart?'

The child nodded coyly.

'I think you're a very lucky girl to be so much like your mommy. Your mommy's beautiful as well, isn't she?'

Posy smiled and nodded once more.

'So we're going to take a picture of you to show all your friends. And when you're a lady you'll be able to show it to all your men friends and say, "Look, this is me when I was just a little girl".' He let go the girl's hand and stood up. To Clover, he said: 'She's so pleasant, Clover. We'll get some

466

lovely photos.'

'How's Daniel? Is he all right?'

'Oh, he's fine. The apple of my eye.'

She smiled. 'I'm pleased. It's good to know you've taken so well to fatherhood.'

'Life has changed so much, Clover, but I wouldn't be without him.'

Clover sighed. It was going to be so difficult to tell him Ramona's secret.

'Well, let's get cracking,' Tom said. 'I'll just get some plates for my camera.'

'That's a different camera,' Clover observed. 'You've changed it.'

'You noticed.' He smiled with pleasure at her remembering. 'I've had this one about two years. It's more modern than the old one and it's got a better lens with more shutter speeds.' He put a plate in the camera. 'How do you want her? Any ideas?'

Clover shrugged. 'How do little girls normally pose?'

He asked Posy to sit on the piano stool with her hands resting on it at her sides. He asked her to smile and remain still. She obliged appealingly and he clicked the shutter. Next he asked her to stand beside a whatnot that supported the shiny-leafed aspidistra in its brass pot. Again, she delivered a shy smile on request.

'One more,' he said kindly.

Posy pointed to the bearskin rug, its fur appealing to her. 'On there,' she said.

Clover and Tom looked at each other and laughed.

'Oh, you're *just* like your mother,' he could not

resist saying.

Clover giggled, blushed and said, 'Tom, I really don't know what you mean.'

So Posy sat on the rug and made herself comfortable while Tom lowered his tripod and moved in closer.

When he had taken the picture, he said: 'Let me take a photo of both of you together.'

'Oh, you don't want me on a photo,' Clover declared. 'I'm not dressed up for it. And look at my hair.'

'Your hair's fine,' he answered. 'So is your dress. The thing about you, Clover, is you look ravishing in anything. Even when you're untidy you look bloody marvellous.'

'No, I don't,' she said, feigning embarrassment, but delighted at his comment.

'Remember when you used to come in to the Jolly Collier from the foundry and hide so as I shouldn't see you?' She nodded and laughed. 'You looked beautiful even then. Leastwise, seeing you like that never put me off.'

'Oh, you're a fancy talker and no two ways, Tom Doubleday.'

'But it's true. So sit on the *chaise-longue* and have Posy on your lap.'

She did as he asked with pleasure and he readjusted his camera after refuelling it with another plate.

From beneath the black cover at the rear of the camera he said: 'Ready? Smile, keep very still and watch the birdie.' He clicked the shutter and removed the plate.

'Thank you, Tom...'

'My pleasure...'

He looked into her eyes, a look she could not hold lest he see right into her mind and read her thoughts which, by this time, were not entirely proper for a married woman. But the look she saw in his eyes during that brief glance hinted that he was still interested in her.

'It's so good to see you again, Clover,' he said softly. 'I'm so glad you could come. Ever since I saw you on Coronation day I've thought of little else.'

'Me, too,' she admitted with a sigh. 'For all the good it'll do.'

'So what's wrong between you and Ned? You gave me the distinct impression that you weren't happy.'

'I'm not happy.'

'Do you want to talk about it?'

She shook her head. 'Not now. Not in front of madam. She picks up conversations like stones and drops them out at the most embarrassing times.'

'Some other time, maybe.'

'Yes, maybe some other time... When will the photos be ready?'

'Oh, tomorrow, with any luck.'

'Do you still open Saturday mornings?'

He nodded. 'Till one.'

'I'll come sometime between twelve and one, shall I? I daresay I'll have to go to the town for some shopping.'

He smiled optimistically. 'I'll look forward to it.'

On the way home, Clover said to Posy: 'We

469

won't tell daddy we've had our photos taken. We'll let it be a surprise, eh?'

Posy nodded. It was a solemn promise.

Chapter Twenty-Seven

Clover was filled with anticipation and apprehension as she approached the front door of Tom's studio on Saturday. The assembled butterflies in her stomach, she was sure, were dancing a military two-step. It was a quarter past twelve and she had been to the town, as she often did on a Saturday but, significantly this time, she had not called for Florrie Brisco to accompany her. She entered the foyer and, after smoothing out her skirt and nervously tucking an errant strand of hair up, she rang the bell.

Tom answered at once and smiled amicably, making all her nervousness disappear. 'Ah, it's you. Good. Come on through.'

'Have the photos turned out all right?'

He held the counter top open for her. 'Brilliant,' he enthused. 'She's so photogenic, your daughter.'

Clover smiled. 'I can't wait to see them.'

Inside the studio Tom took the pictures from his work table and handed them to her. She stood close to him at the table, her thighs pressed against its edge, and he watched as she flipped through the pictures, quickly at first, then more studiously. He was enchanted still by the girlish

470

set of her head as she looked down, by her exquisite nose that, from the outset, he had adored and unwittingly made her self-conscious of.

'Oh, look at her here,' Clover said delightedly. 'She's such a cheeky little madam sometimes. Look at her expression... And this one...'

'It's a good one of you, as well,' he commented.

She lingered over it for few seconds, her eyes dwelling on Posy, not herself. 'It's been ages since I last had my photo taken. You should know. You took it.' He was in his shirtsleeves and his arm was touching hers. The agreeable warmth that emanated from it was simultaneously enervating and unsettling.

'How much do I owe you, Tom?'

'Oh, nothing. The photos are on me. It was a pleasure to do them. It was such a pleasure to see the prints for the first time.'

'If you're sure. But I'd rather pay for them.'

'No. My treat, Clover. I owe you that much and more.'

Their eyes met. 'You owe me nothing. In fact, I owe you.'

'Oh? So how do you work that out?'

There was an awkward silence. Clover was suddenly aware that this could be a critical moment in her life, in his life, too. She could either politely thank him for his kindness, say her goodbyes, and draw a line under the saga of Tom Doubleday and herself for ever. Or she could stay and explain what she meant, become emotional and be sure to end up in his arms. The latter seemed entirely preferable.

'Because I've been a fool, Tom,' she responded with a deep sigh. 'I look back over the last three years or so and I can see just how big a fool I've been. I loved you with all my heart and I let you go, out of stupid pride and pig-headedness, when all the time I was aching for you...' A tear trembled on her long eyelashes and Tom watched, encouraged, as it trickled down her cheek. He wanted to lick it off, to taste the sweet, salty liquid that had emerged from inside her emotional as well as her physical self. 'I drove you into Ramona's arms as sure as I'm standing here. As sure as night follows day.'

'Well... That's an interesting analogy, Clover.' he answered softly. 'After we split up, you and me, it was like a dark, moonless night following a bright sunny day. A night so dark I couldn't see where I was going or what I was doing.'

'Even with Ramona to keep you company?'

'Even with Ramona to keep me company, God rest her soul. All I ever wanted was you back in my arms. We were engaged to be married, for Christ's sake. What went wrong?'

She wiped the wayward tear from her cheek. 'You know what went wrong. Madness seized you. For some reason I'll never understand, you thought I was having an affair with Elijah Tandy when nothing could have been further from the truth. I wasn't, Tom. I swear to God... But you know I wasn't.'

'It was Ramona that told me you were in the first place.'

'Ramona?' She rolled her eyes in resignation. 'Like the time she told you I was courting Ned

472

Brisco, when I wasn't?'

'She said she'd seen you and Elijah in the yard at the Jolly Collier one night with your arms around each other.'

'Me? And Elijah? God, what an imagination she'd got.' And then a thought struck her. She remembered something. 'Wait a bit... There was a time when Elijah helped me to lay the fire in the boiler in the brewhouse ready for Zillah's wash the next day. When we came out I tripped ... Elijah caught me in his arms ... and we laughed. I thought nothing more of it. But surely Ramona could never have interpreted that as evidence of an affair, even if that's what she'd witnessed.'

Tom shrugged. 'Perhaps that's exactly what she did see, and how she interpreted it.'

'But it's inconceivable, Tom. In any case, Elijah was... Well, he was courting Dorcas. He married her, if you recall.'

'I know. And I also know I was completely wrong in taking Ramona's word as gospel. Even if *she* believed it, it was no reason for me to. Deep down, I knew well enough I could trust you.'

'But then you took those scandalous photos of Ramona. What was I to think when I found out?'

Tom sighed. 'I was at fault again, I admit it.' He threw his hands up as an admission of his error. 'When Ramona asked me to do them I should have refused. I should have foreseen that if they came to light it would reflect badly on both of us and cause ructions between you and me. I still can't believe I was so naïve. Can you ever forgive me, Clover?'

473

'Oh, I already have. I can't nurture a grudge. I have to let go of it or it makes me too miserable. I forgave Ramona as well. The question is, can you forgive me?'

'There's nothing to forgive.'

They fell silent again for a few seconds, reflecting on what each had said to the other.

'Ramona thought you didn't love her,' Clover said experimentally, trying to elicit confirmation. 'She told me you wanted to give her up to get back with me – just before she told you she was pregnant.'

'She told you? When?'

'Just before she died. Didn't you know that? Didn't you know Jake fetched me to see her?'

'No. I didn't know. I'm flabbergasted.'

'I think there were some things she wanted to get off her chest. She wanted us to make up and be friends again before she passed on.'

'What else did she tell you?'

There was a second's hesitation in her response. 'Oh, nothing very much. Things just between her and me. They wouldn't interest you.' It had been an ideal opportunity to fulfil Ramona's wish that she tell him about Daniel, but she could not do it. She just could not bring herself to do it. 'So just think,' she went on, '*if* Ramona had never lied about Elijah Tandy and me, you and I might be married to each other now...' Tears welled up in her eyes again.

'*If...*' He uttered a sardonic little laugh. 'It's a big word, *if...* But how I *wish*, Clover.' He closed his eyes and looked up. 'How I wish we'd married...'

'How I wish it as well...'

'God, what a mess!' He shook his head slowly as if in disbelief of everything that had transpired. 'I still love you, you know, Clover... As much as ever I did.'

She thought her legs were going to give way under her. She clutched the edge of the table tight to hold herself steady. 'Oh, Tom! I think you shouldn't have told me that.'

'On the contrary, I think I should. I want you to know. I'd fully intended telling you today. And you're not happy with Ned. You've admitted as much.'

'But I'm married to him...'

During this discussion they'd been standing side by side at the table. Now he turned towards her, took her hand and she swung round slowly to face him, to face the inevitable. They looked into each other's eyes. Already there was no way back, there was no exit from what was happening. Each knew that they could not help themselves, that their love was too potent to avoid. She fell into his arms submissively and a flood of tears soaked the front of his shirt. He held her tight while she felt an unspeakable sadness that they had missed each other through other people meddling. Oh, they would embark on an affair and try to make up their lost years together. Not only did they owe it to each other, they could hardly escape it. But if only they could have been wed...

The two lovers held each other silently for a while. More words seemed strangely superfluous. Tears began to flow from Tom's eyes too and he sniffed to try and stop his nose running. He closed his eyes, trying vainly to stem the tears, trying to imagine that everything that had passed had been a malicious dream and they were married after all. He wanted to alter the past by power of will, so that their respective children were by each other and only this – this ardent, *ardent* desire – was the true reality. He felt in his pocket and withdrew a handkerchief. As he wiped his eyes Clover looked up at him, her own eyes red and watery.

'What a pair of fools,' she sobbed.

'Promise me you'll always love me.'

'I don't need to promise,' she replied, trying to laugh at how they must appear. 'It's a fact of life. I'll always love you. I always have. I can't help it.' She sniffed and tried to laugh again. 'God! Look at your shirt.' She let go of him and stepped back. 'Let me dry my tears and wipe my nose. There's a handkerchief in my bag.' She reached down to where she had placed it on the floor, found the handkerchief and wiped her eyes and blew her nose. 'Well ... here we are again,' she said, and heaved a residual sob. 'Back where we started.'

'We'll have to work out how we can meet.'

'I know...' She went back to his arms. 'But we both have kids to work around this time. Maybe I could come here sometimes – like we used to.'

'Yes... And if you can get out at night you could come to my house. Daniel would be fast asleep in bed.'

'I've already thought of that,' she said. 'But I don't know if I want to–'

'You mean because it was Ramona's home and all that.'

'And Ramona's bed ... I want to lie with you again, Tom. But not in Ramona's bed. Not the bed she died in.'

'I understand.' He squeezed her tight. 'I'll move. I'll find another house.' His face lit up into a smile, creasing his eyes that were still moist with tears. 'You can help choose the furnishings and all that.'

She laughed more easily now. 'I hope to God I'll make a better job of it than the one I already had a hand in.'

'We can pretend we're married after all. You'll be called a scarlet woman... Calling on a man, a known widower, at his house, unchaperoned.'

'I've been called worse. But I can stand it. My skin's thick after what we've been through.'

'Kiss me, Clover.'

'I thought you'd never suggest it.'

Clover hid the photographs. There was no point in showing them to Ned because he would know she'd seen Tom. Naturally, he would fear the worst and God knows what he might do. He was not a violent man but he was extremely jealous, and jealousy could prompt him to be devious and possibly cruel in other ways. There was no sense in inviting trouble. Now, more than anything, she wanted her freedom. She needed to be free to come and go as she pleased within the constraints that having a young dependent daughter imposed upon her.

And for a time, discreetly, she called at Tom's

studio two or three afternoons a week, leaving Posy with Florrie Brisco who was happy to have her, giving any excuse that seemed plausible. When Tom knew she was due to arrive he would usher out any customers who were predisposed to linger and chat, then anxiously wait for her, hoping Ned had not cottoned on and forbidden her to leave the house – or worse. And when she turned up, breathless, her eyes sparkling, he would know all was well and welcome her into his arms. Of course, they made love on the bearskin rug and these encounters elicited more emotion, more passion, more tenderness and more pleasure than ever either of them could recall. Sometimes, in the frenzy of orgasm, she would weep and call out his name and cling to him and wonder how she ever managed to survive without him. And he would ponder exactly the same thing from his viewpoint.

He moved house, as he said he would, to a small terraced house in Salop Street at Eve Hill, far enough away from his mother to inhibit her visiting him at inopportune moments. Clover helped him choose furnishings, curtains, rugs, linoleum, as she promised she would, all the time conscious of what Ramona had achieved at the house in Edward Street. He never complained about the cost but happily dipped into his pocket and, before she knew it, the house had become a comfortable home for Tom and Daniel. Clover was pleased with her home-making efforts that she had approached with care and enthusiasm. Although it was not her own home, nor could it ever be, she felt a part of it and loved being there whenever she could steal away from Hill Street. On those occasions, she got to know Daniel and realised how bright and intelligent and how likeable he was. On Saturdays, when Tom had left for work she would go there, let herself in and pretend she was the lady of the house. She would clean and dust, polish and change the beds. She would make sure they had sufficient food in the pantry and leave Tom a note telling him of anything he was running short of.

It was a tram ride back to the town centre for Clover on a Saturday afternoon, when she would commence shopping for her other home, the one she and Posy shared so reluctantly nowadays with Ned. If only she could wave a magic wand and abandon this mock home and this farcical marriage. She had a strong sense of belonging in that house in Salop Street with Tom. In consequence, she resented more than ever the constriction that marriage to Ned had imposed. If only she had the courage to let him know what was going on; he could divorce her, or even just let her go.

At about this time, Ned was noticing subtle changes in his wife's demeanour. She was unusually nice and affable towards him, smiling and letting him get away with things that previously she would have pulled him up over. She went out of her way to do things for him. There was a sparkle in her eyes as well these days, and she seemed less tense and much more content than he had ever known her in all their married life. Although he knew she was putting as much money away each week as they could afford, to pay back that lingering anonymous loan, she managed to afford some smart new clothes now, and he'd noticed that some very pretty underwear had appeared as well. She was taking extra care with her hair and in her whole appearance. Most days and nights latterly she looked serenely beautiful and he was delighted to see it. She told him she had made friends with another girl called Rose who had a son the same age as Posy, and they'd joined the Mother's Union at St John's church and went to meetings on Tuesday nights. St James's church at Eve Hill, Rose's parish, had started a Young Wives section and she and Rose had joined that as well, she said; they met on a Thursday night. But she was never late back and Ned had no reason at all to disbelieve her. Nor did he ask if they competed for prettiest underwear at those meetings, for those were the times when she seemed to wear all that stuff. He never asked if she went out while he was at work because it never crossed his mind. Adding two and two together in the game of life was never Ned's strong point. He had not been allowed any sexual liberties from the beginning, so he was not aware of any change in her attitude in that respect.

Clover's affair had been burgeoning for about a year when, in the warm September of 1912, Ned damaged the Farman biplane which he piloted to test the latest Sunbeam Coatalen engines. The damage was superficial but it meant the aeroplane was out of action while spare parts could be manufactured to repair it and restore the wing-warping to full working order. Ned commended his *Gull,* still stored in Fred Woodall's barn at Bobbington. If they could install the engine in that, he would finally achieve the ambition he had first set himself as well as expediting engine development. So he and a small party of helpers took a couple of steam lorries to Fred Woodall's farm and disassembled the *Gull.* They transported it back to Sunbeam, reassembled it and set about making the necessary alterations to the engine mountings so it could accommodate the Coatalen engine, and a few other control improvements. Ned was happy to receive the praise and kind comments about the *Gull* that were heaped upon him and even Louis Coatalen himself came into the shop to inspect the machine.

Prior to installing the engine, Ned recalled having made some notes and calculations of ideas he'd had long before, when he was working at Star; he wanted to go over them first. The details he could not recall exactly but they were vital to safety, containing some rough calculations for stresses on the fuselage, conditional on engine weight, torque and so on. He did not know where they were. He might have left them at his mother's house. So, on his way home from work he stopped by to have a look for them.

'Clover ain't long gone,' his mother informed him.

'Oh?'

'She came to pick Posy up.'

'Oh? But why did she leave her here?'

'Am yow living in cloud-cuckoo-land or what?'

Florrie asked pointedly. 'Her leaves the babby here regular while her goz down the town.'

'She's never said.'

'Maybe you should pay her a bit more attention.'

He nodded his head, preoccupied with his search.

'Wha'n yer looking for?'

'Oh, just some notes with some calculations on the *Gull*.'

'There's no notes here. Everything to do with your flying machine you've had.'

'I reckon you're right, Mother. There's no sign of 'em here.'

So he went home. A wonderful aroma welcomed him as he ambled in; the unsurpassed aroma of home cooking.

He sniffed the air expectantly. 'What's for tea, Clover.'

'I've done you some pork chops. They look lovely and meaty.'

'They smell nice. Mother says you've just been there to pick Posy up.'

'Yes, I went to the town.'

'Well you don't need to take her to Mother's do you? Why can't you take her with you?'

Clover shrugged and felt herself go hot. 'She's such a weight to carry now.'

'She can walk. Let her walk. It'll do her good. You're making her too soft.'

Clover readily agreed, to save an argument, to avoid discussing it further.

'How long will tea be?' he asked.

'Twenty minutes.'

'Right. I've got to find some notes I made ages ago. We're going to fly the *Gull* and I need to check on some things.'

'You're flying the *Gull?*' She sounded pleased.

Clover placed a saucepan containing water and potatoes over the coals of the fire grate. Some spilled over the side, hissing and spitting in the flames. She moved away from the stairs door as he opened it and went upstairs.

He searched through all the drawers in the old second-hand dressing table they'd bought when they moved, in the wardrobe as well but found nothing. The boxroom, as yet unfurnished, housed a large cardboard box and a storage chest given to them by Florrie Brisco. The chest looked promising so he opened it. At once evident were some of his old drawings folded up, piles of newspapers, cuttings and ancient magazines. He rummaged through avidly, excited at the prospect of flying his precious *Gull* at last. He would know the paper he was looking for as soon as he saw it. But he saw no sign. Maybe he, or even Clover, had packed it with other papers into one of the large envelopes or folders he could see. He withdrew one and opened it up. Childhood scribble, his own, sentimentally accumulated and saved for years by his mother who apparently thought he should have them. He cast it aside and took out another, opened it up and peered inside.

Photographs...

Of Posy...

Photographs of Posy? Strange...

He pulled them out of the envelope. Why had

Clover not shown him these? There was one with Clover on as well, posing wide-eyed and sporting a very self-conscious smile, taken about a year ago judging by Posy and the clothes she was wearing. In the bottom right-hand corner of each was embossed the words 'Doubleday of Dudley'. So that's why he hadn't seen them before. Because Tom Doubleday had taken them. She'd been to see Tom Doubleday. She just could not keep away.

It all started falling into place.

The changes. Her being strangely nice, either to divert him from any suspicion or to assuage her guilt. The extra care and attention she was paying to her appearance, the new clothes and, dammit, the new underwear. New underwear for that swine to admire. And what had his mother told him only an hour earlier? She was leaving Posy there regularly. Why? Where was she going?

Well, he could guess.

In a flash his world utterly collapsed. He felt entirely devastated, cheated. Life had cruelly dropped into his lap a calamity that, stupidly, he had not anticipated. Oh, he knew his marriage was far from perfect. In fact, it was the strangest marriage he'd ever heard of. What other poor, maligned sod, breadwinner and provider of everything, was daft enough to tolerate never being allowed sexual access to his own wife, apart from one embarrassing, abortive attempt? What other stupid bugger was demented enough to take on a woman nine months pregnant with another man's child, even loony enough to plead for the privilege? What other bloody idiot could

484

overlook for so long the needs of a healthy young woman like Clover, for the pleasure and release that love-making brought, especially when she was not getting it from her husband?

Bloody Tom Doubleday. Advantage-taker. Toss-pot. Seducer. Adulterer.

He might have known this would happen. Why should it be any great surprise? He should have foreseen that those two would get together sooner or later and resume their dirty goings-on. In a way it served him right. He had been blind, naïve, soft. More; he had been unutterably stupid. Maybe a man gets what he deserves. But it angered him beyond measure just the same.

He held on to the photographs and went downstairs. Posy was sitting quietly in the clothes basket in front of the middle door, tugging diligently at the woollen hair of her rag doll. Liquorice the cat was under the table. Clover was stooping at the oven at the side of the grate, withdrawing the meat tin in which the pork chops were cooking. She turned and smiled affably as she placed them on the table with the intention of using the fat to make some tasty gravy.

'I found these.' He waved the photographs in front of her face indignantly. She coloured up and her mouth suddenly went dry. 'Why didn't you show me?' There was a mean glint in his eye, anger, hurt, resentment.

'Because I knew if I showed them to you, you'd know I'd seen Tom.' She answered honestly, trying to remain calm.

'And obviously, you're still seeing him.'

485

'Yes.'

The back of his right hand cracked viciously across her cheek, sending her crashing into the grate. As she fell, she knocked the pan of potatoes, boiling by now, into the fire. She screamed, trying to regain her balance and get out of the way of the boiling water as it hissed and spluttered over the coals and the hearth in angry clouds of steam. The pan crashed to the hearth with a clatter, splashing the residue over her long skirt. She put her hand out to steady herself only to find the scorching hob. She shrieked with the pain of it while the cat howled and leapt out by the back door in a blur of black-and-white fur. Posy was squealing too, and Clover, forgetting her own pain completely, instinctively rushed to her and picked her up.

'Oh, my precious, are you hurt, are you hurt?' she blurted, terrified that the boiling water had splashed over the child and scalded her. She hugged her and ran her fingers through Posy's hair consolingly, ignoring the searing pain in her own hand.

'He fwighkened me, Mommy,' the child blubbered. 'Daddy fwighkened me. The cwash frighkened me.'

'Let me look at you.' Hot water was flowing across the linoleum towards the clothes basket, some of it soaking into the hearth-rug. She stepped over the hot puddles, grabbed Posy and sat her on the table in the front room to inspect her carefully. Relief swept over her as she realised she was physically none the worse, untouched, just scared by the sudden violence of the incident. 'You're all right, Posy, thank God.' She gave Ned a look of utter contempt and held her daughter protectively. 'But it's no thanks to your daddy.'

'I'm not her *daddy*,' Ned protested vehemently.

'Yes, you are my daddy and you fwighkened me,' the child shrilled defiantly, not understanding the gist of the argument at all.

'All right. Let's all calm down,' Clover said and looked at her hand that was causing her so much pain. A huge blister had appeared in the palm of her hand at the base of her thumb. She went to the tap and ran cold water over it. 'Well, I hope you're satisfied with your little outburst,' she said coldly to Ned. 'We could have scalded poor Posy. Disfigured her for life.'

'I didn't mean to hurt the child. Only you.'

'Well, you succeeded in that all right.' There was a mirror hanging on a nail tapped into the window-frame over the sink. She peered into it to look at her cheek where he had struck her. A blue and red bruise was already showing through. With her dry hand she rubbed it gently. 'I hope you're proud of yourself. You've shown me what a real man you are.'

'And you've shown yourself to be what you really are,' he hissed scornfully. 'A whore. Tom Doubleday's bloody whore. Well you'd better not bring another of his bastards into this house.'

Clover sighed. Of course, it was irrational to expect that she'd never be found out. Yet she felt no guilt. Why should she? She had never declared any love for Ned. He had always known where her true emotions lay. She had never made any

487

secret of it. Oh well, it was certainly out in the open now.

'So where do we go from here?' she asked. 'Are you going to divorce me?'

'What, and make it easy for you to marry him? Do you think I'm going to reward you with a divorce? Never. You can stick it out, like I've had to stick it out.'

'I won't stop seeing him, Ned.'

'Oh yes you will.'

She shook her head resolutely. 'Never,' she said and she meant it. 'I lost him once before. I'm never going to lose him again. Scheme and contrive how you will if you must, you'll never stop me seeing him. So why not let me go?'

Ned slumped to the chair that was behind him. His head went in his hands and his shoulders started shaking. He looked up at her, sobbing, his eyes wet with tears, his face contorted in his absolute misery.

'Because I love you, Clover,' he wailed. 'I've always loved you, though Christ knows why.' He fumbled in his trouser pocket for a handkerchief, pulled it out and blew his nose. 'Why should I be afflicted with a love that could never be returned? Do you know what that's like, Clover? Have you any idea of how miserable it makes life?'

'Yes,' she answered softly, continuing to run her hand under the cold tap. 'I know very well how it feels.'

Chapter Twenty-Eight

Ned turned up at work next day brooding. When his workmates, nudging each other covertly, asked him what was wrong he declined to answer. During his time at Sunbeam, little comments he had made about his life and habits, although insignificant by themselves, together painted a picture of strange irregularities in his marriage. They would laugh behind his back at his incredible naïvety, married to a girl who was rumoured to be unsettled, unfeeling, quite a bobby-dazzler and beyond his aspirations to satisfy. They would make openly sarcastic and also very cryptic allusions to his sex life that passed over him unfathomed, amusing his workmates the more. To perceive he was the butt of their ribaldry grieved him, he could not understand why they would burst out laughing at his expense, and even that showed up as one of his quirks; he had no sense of humour. In other things he was not so dumb, they knew. His flair for his job proved that. Certainly, they respected his knowledge and instinct when it came to trimming and flying aeroplanes. He would show them. He would show them he wasn't half the fool they thought he was.

Ned did not find the notes he'd sought about the fuselage of the *Gull,* but they pressed ahead anyway and installed the latest version of the

Coatalen engine. If Ned's report on its behaviour was favourable the engine was scheduled to go into production. Already potential customers had been informed of its impending introduction and there was significant interest, not least from the Army.

So, a couple of lorries delivered the *Gull*, complete with engine and propeller, to the flat fields of Pendeford and the job of reassembling the old flying machine began. When it was ready, Ned sat on his seat like a distrustful king on a rickety throne, his mind awhirl with an unnatural fusion of profound despondency over Clover, and excitement at the imminent likelihood of taking to the skies in his beloved *Gull*. At his signal one of them cranked the engine and it fired into life, spluttering and backfiring at first, till it found its harsh but steady mechanical rhythm. Ned opened the throttle a little and felt the *Gull's* urge to go. He pulled his goggles over his eyes, allowed himself a half smile and thrust his chin out in defiant resolve. He was about to fulfil a long-cherished dream on this, the most confusing day of his life.

He would certainly show them. He would show everybody he was nobody's fool.

He nosed the *Gull* into the wind and taxied forward, then opened the throttle fully and waited for the surge of power that would haul him into the blue. It did not disappoint. The more he flew, the more he was surprised at how quickly the ground beneath you stretched away. He peered over the side as he banked. His colleagues, getting smaller, waved frantically and he waved back. The engine seemed to be performing well. Vibration was still there, possibly amplified through the frame of the *Gull* which had not been tuned to handle it like the Farman, but it was not as harsh as before.

Ned scanned the landscape sliding away underneath him for landmarks. A canal, the Staffordshire and Worcestershire, lay below him, glinting like a length of shiny bent wire as it disappeared into the hazy southern distance.

Follow it.

It was such a pleasure to be perched up here, flying free with the birds, although the birds scattered in all directions at the raucous sound of his engine. Up here he could watch the world and all its troubles go by and be untouched by it. Up here, he was not a part of the world; he was insulated from the traumas and strife of a mundane and largely disappointing earthly existence. Up here, he was in charge, his beloved *Gull* did his bidding, not like the wayward, wilful wife below who resented and avoided him, who deceived and made a cuckold of him as if he were the biggest fool ever to pull on a pair of trousers. Up here, the clean, fresh wind in his face, he was above all that, in every sense. Up here, he escaped into his own preferred world.

It was time to turn back. The crew would be waiting for him. He would be out of their sights now, out of earshot. But it was much too intoxicating up here to turn back yet. He was in his *Gull. His Gull.* He had waited too long to ride it, too long to return after a mere couple of minutes flying. And how well it handled. How skilfully he had designed and built it. So he flew on proudly, following the canal, exhilarated, making the most of his elation, his spiritual freedom for, by the very nature of it, it would be short-lived.

He tailed the smooth bends for some time, over countryside patched with gold and yellow and green, lush with trees. To his left he saw a stately home in magnificent grounds, with a shimmering lake. Himley Hall. Beyond it lay Baggeridge Wood where he had taken Clover in the first throes of heartbreak over that out-and-out swine Tom Doubleday. Running west to east alongside the grounds of Himley Hall stretched the Himley Road that led to Dudley. Damn it, he would follow it. He would show them. He would show them all.

Through the haze, the spire of Top Church in Dudley came into view, then the old grey castle. Good markers. He headed for them. After a few minutes he flew over the castle so close that he almost grazed the castellated Norman keep. Beyond he could see the dismal Coneygree Colliery and the Coneygree Foundry where he used to work and flew towards them. He would show them too. He would zoom low over the foundry, let them see he was not such an idiot, let them know he had achieved his main ambition, let them witness it. For all they knew there, he had achieved two ambitions, for he had married Clover also. They weren't to know the antagonism he had to contend with. So he swooped low over the roof of the moulding-shop, the Coatalen engine roaring so loud that nobody could have failed to hear, and dipped his wings in a salute.

They would know who it was. Of course they would know.

He banked to the right, and started to climb, circling the red brick hulk of St Michael's church in Tividale. A little further on at Burnt Tree he spied the bottom of Bunns Lane and headed for it, followed it. How many times had he walked that route on his way home from the foundry, generally with Clover? If only he had known then what he knew now... The *Gull* climbed effortlessly towards the top of Kates Hill, the engine growling gratifyingly as he followed the upward contours of the landscape. He banked to the left over the brick works in an aerial swagger, over the slag heaps of Springfield Pit then to the right, to approach Hill Street from the top. Deftly, he skimmed the staggered rooftops, still climbing. He looked down to see if there was any sign of Clover. He would show her. He might not be the most commanding man when marital considerations were uppermost but by God, he was commanding the sky right now. Joseph Mantle's house came into view and, as he flew over it, it struck him again that Mr Mantle must have been the anonymous benefactor to whom he still owed two hundred pounds. Well, there was some saved towards it now. Despite her other faults, Clover could be thrifty. Below him now was Oakham Lodge with its fine ornamental pond, the garden incongruous to the ravaged landscape of the quarries and mines so close by.

He banked round in a loop to come back the other way and do a 'downhill' run. Everybody would know who Ned Brisco was by the time he had finished this memorable exhibition of aeronautics. As he swept low again, everybody in his path left their homes wondering what outlandish creation was responsible for the thunderous racket above that was causing the roof slates to rattle, the houses to shake and the dogs to bark. He peered down and waved his arms in a signal of triumph, then banked round to enjoy yet another lap, heading again for Oakham Lodge, his chosen marker.

The Coatalen engine spluttered.

He pulled on the throttle to increase the speed and clear whatever it was that was causing the misfire. The engine faltered again, spitting and sputtering, then began running smoothly once more and he started to climb, to clear the tall trees of Tansley Hill Road that were *en route*.

Again the engine stuttered, backfired ... and died... Oh, shit!

Petrol.

Nobody had thought to check the tank. In his earlier elation he'd overlooked how much fuel he might have to enable him to fly this long. There were no fields within reach that he knew to be smooth enough. If he came down now he would have to land in the street or crash into the side of a slag heap – or mess up somebody's allotment.

He could glide for a little while. He could glide even further if he had greater height. But the weight of the engine made a terrific difference to the way the *Gull* handled in a glide. He trimmed the wings and the tail flaps to flatten out his descent and avoid the tree tops. The flat stretch of Hill Street would have to do as a landing strip.

It was wide enough there. If he could just keep aloft that long... He skimmed the trees then allowed the biplane to drop dramatically, making his stomach churn. Once again Joseph Mantle's house was just below. What a bloody irony if he crashed into the house after the man, out of the kindness of his heart, had lent him all that money.

Down, down... Steady now...

He landed, heard the creak of the frame, and felt the impact of the old bicycle wheels that formed the undercarriage, as they hit the ground and rolled forward, urged on by the sheer impetus of forward flight. He prayed he would stop soon, pulled hard on the lever that lowered the flaps as an air brake. Brakes on the wheels had been the last thing to consider installing on a craft like this. Onward the *Gull* rolled. They reached the end of the flat stretch, only fifty yards from where he had landed. Hill Street, by no means misnamed, fell away from that point with a steady and sustained descent. There was no way he would be able to stop once it was rolling down there.

As the *Gull* wheeled over the crown of the hill he saw children playing ahead of him. He yelled at the top of his voice and waved his arms. It was not just children. The street was alive with folk who had left their white-washed sculleries and the malodorous sanctity of their earth privies to witness the commotion that his deafening flight had created. He tried to steer a straight course with the aid of a rudder that was ineffectual on terra firma. People saw his plight and hid in their entries to avoid being hit. The *Gull* rolled downhill uncontrollably. The last time anybody had witnessed anything like this was when a horse bolted dragging behind it a cart that bounced and crashed off the walls of the houses and railings as it hurtled recklessly through the inclined streets.

The *Gull* rattled on, bumping over the potholes that perforated the surface. He caught sight of Clover, holding Posy in her arms, watching, looking incredulously at his unforgivable antics. Yet another incident to commend him this was turning out to be. He was gathering speed. Perhaps he might even take off again. But no, the weight of the dead engine was too much of a handicap. He whizzed past the corner shop, past the Junction, onlookers gawping with open-mouthed incredulity. A line of wrought-iron railings loomed, fronting the little ivy-clad cottage that was directly in his path, precisely at the bend where Watsons Green Road joined and the hill fell away alarmingly.

There was a crash and Ned was suddenly conscious of flying through the air quite independently of the *Gull*. He closed his eyes and braced himself. He made abrupt contact with the soft earth of a flowerbed, was scratched alarmingly by some unsympathetic rose trees as he hurtled through them, and sensed that he was rolling over and over. Then, he felt a sickening thud as his shoulder struck something solid.

Clover, of course, saw everything that happened. Still with Posy in her arms she rushed to the bottom of the street where the *Gull* had ploughed through the railings of the little Ivy Cottage with its pretty foregarden. Other people joined her, anxious to help, anxious for the details of an incredible tale that they would have honed to perfection, ready to relate to their loved ones by the time they returned home.

'Damn fool!' Clover remarked scornfully to one of her neighbours as they ran together.

There was a moment of confusion. At what had been the front wrought-iron gate of the ivy-clad cottage, a startled woman was standing. 'And who's gunna pay for this?' she asked anybody and everybody. Other people arrived and looked around at each other incredulously, seeking a lead from somebody. A groan emanated from where Ned lay randomly folded in a heap.

Clover put Posy on her feet and addressed the woman. 'That's my husband.' She sounded both apologetic and defiant as she brushed past, ducking the loose wires and struts and torn sailcloth of the *Gull's* wings, and ran to Ned.

'What's he doing in my garden?'

'When he comes round you can ask him,' she replied pointedly, displaying no sympathy for either the woman or the unfortunate aviator.

'Oh ar? And will he bruise my cheek like he has yours?'

Ned opened his eyes and looked around him. He felt a nauseating pain in his shoulder and couldn't feel his right hand. He saw Clover stooping beside him looking decidedly displeased and wondered for a moment if she was an angel at the gate of St Peter frowning on him for having arrived unscheduled.

'You damn fool,' she rasped. 'What the hell did you think you were doing?'

'I crashed,' he bleated meekly. 'I'm hurt.'

'Serves you damn-well right. I suppose you did this on purpose?'

He winced at her accusation and protested: 'I ran out of fuel, Clover.'

'Huh!' she exclaimed. 'On purpose.'

'He needs to be got to a doctor,' somebody said.

'We'n gorra wheelbarrow,' his mother said, arriving horrified on the scene. 'I'll goo back and fetch it.'

So Ned suffered the indignity of being wheeled to the doctor's surgery in a wheelbarrow to add to his general humiliation. The doctor said he'd broken his collar bone and his right wrist on the impact with the cottage. He set his arm in plaster, tied a sling under it and around his neck and told him to rest completely. Work was out of the question till he was mended, especially low flying.

The up-ended biplane, its tail high, its propeller meshed intricately and artistically with the wrought-iron railings of the ivy-clad cottage, was quite an attraction for the rest of that day and night. Word spread fast that a mad aviator had deliberately crashed his biplane into a little house opposite the Junction and the crowds duly gathered to see the wreckage. Clover managed to get a message to Sunbeam giving news of the incident and next day two steam lorries and four people appeared in Cromwell Street to collect it.

The *Gull* was duly disentangled from its snare, disassembled, strapped on to the lorries and taken away.

'And who's gunna pay for this?' the occupant of the little cottage asked again before they disappeared, pointing to her demolished railings.

Ned was incapacitated and in some pain. He took to his bed, the intention being to make Clover feel sorry for him and render himself totally dependent on her. Because his right wrist was broken and he was right-handed, he could do little for himself, and it was obvious she would even have to cut his meat prior to serving his meal so he could eat it. He believed she would wash him and shave him but, with her own hand damaged and bandaged up, she refused, deciding he would have to do these things himself, and serve him right.

'And if you think I'm going to the privy with you to wipe your bum, you can think again,' she informed him decisively. 'Learn to do it left-handed.'

The accident threatened to interfere seriously with Clover's affair. That same afternoon she wrote Tom a note and ran down the street to post it, knowing he would receive it by first delivery tomorrow. She explained briefly that Ned had found out about their affair and had crashed his aeroplane. Whether the two events were connected, however, she wasn't sure, she said, and neither did she care. But, because he was injured, she was obliged to look after him. He was not to worry though. She was well, missing him and would see him as soon as it was possible, and was ever likely to bring Posy with her.

A few days' grace would not be so bad, she realised. It would give the bruise on her cheek time to fade and the great blister on the base of her thumb time to heal. She knew that if Tom saw either injury and she confessed the truth, he would want to confront Ned, and already there had been trouble enough.

Ned had been in bed a week, feeling abundantly sorry for himself, when Clover went to his room and sat on his bed.

'I'm going to see Tom tonight,' she announced. 'I'll try and be back by ten.'

'Oh?' he muttered, irked. 'And what if I say as you can't go.'

'You can say what you like, Ned Brisco, but I shall go anyway.'

'And what about Posy? You surely can't expect me to look after her in my condition?'

'I wouldn't inflict you on Posy,' she said, implying that he was the burden. 'I shall take her with me.'

'So you're dragging the poor innocent child into your vile shenanigans now then?'

'Tom is her father – if you recall.'

'Oh, so he knows then?'

'No, he doesn't know, as it happens. So you can rest easy.'

Ned, after a week, had grown more used to the idea of his wife's affair although, after his accident, he had cherished the forlorn hope that she might have realised her folly, felt sufficiently sorry for him to induce her to fall deeply in love with him in consequence, and give up Tom. After this conversation, though, he knew there was no chance of it ever happening. Anyway, if she was taking Posy along with her, the child's very presence would preclude them from lying together; his main concern.

Ned's incapacity created a further problem; he would not be paid his full wages, which would mean dipping into the money Clover had reserved to pay off his loan. Already she had more than a hundred pounds saved, most of it the proceeds of the sale of his motor car, but she had added to it conscientiously, a little at a time.

Many of Ned's workmates called to see him and to get a first-hand account of what went wrong on his fateful flight in the *Gull*. They seemed to regard Clover with interest as she welcomed them pleasantly with cups of tea, slices of apple pie and home-made fruitcake, and they wondered what had ever possessed her to marry a fruitcake like Ned.

Louis Coatalen called, specifically to get Ned's impression of the modifications to the engine, which were favourable. 'I am 'appy to see zat your appetite for zee flying 'as not been suppressed by zees leetle incident,' Monsieur Coatalen remarked dryly.

Indeed, it had not. Ned looked forward to his next flight with zeal, determined that in future he would always check and double-check the fuel in his tank.

'In zee meantime, I myself will 'ave to be zee test pilot. As eef I 'aven't enough to do testing zee racing cars.'

As Ned improved, he whiled away his time dreaming of new aircraft designs and, in November, read in his newspaper that two Frenchmen had made the first flight in an aeroplane constructed entirely of metal. At once his mind started working overtime and he sent a letter to Louis Coatalen asking if he could obtain more details. Such news on aviation was welcome and things were happening at such a pace these days.

Ned returned to work on 18th November, fit and recovered, and raring to fly again.

The Balkan war had dominated the headlines recently. The Bulgarians and the Serbs had mobilised troops in October, as had the Greeks, ready for war with Turkey if Macedonian autonomy from the Ottoman Empire was not granted. Fearing they would be provoked into intervening by virtue of their ties with Serbia, the Russians duly mobilised a quarter of a million troops. Austria, too, stood ready to join the fray.

With the Turks coming off worst they concluded an armistice with all Balkan allies except Greece, which refused to sign, and in December a peace conference opened in London. In January 1913, Turkey breached this agreement by attacking Bulgaria and, later that month, it was reported that Serbian troops were indulging godlessly in the wholesale slaughter of non-combatant Moslems. In February, the Turks lost five thousand soldiers at Gallipoli and in March thirty-two thousand were captured by the Greeks when they took Janina. In April, eight thousand died as Scutari fell to the Montenegrins. June witnessed the break-up of the Balkan Alliance when Greece and Serbia fell out with Bulgaria over a border dispute. Bulgaria in turn attacked them and Rumania mobilised her army.

But the Balkans were not the only place trouble was brewing. Enough was fermenting at home to keep Herbert Asquith and his Liberal government well-occupied. Industrial unrest was at a level never before seen with strikes by miners, dockers and railway workers by the tens of thousands. The Suffragettes were becoming ever more militant, ever more a nuisance, and had embarked on a policy of guerrilla warfare that appeared, to society in general, to be aimed at society in general. Ulster teetered on the brink of civil war, rejecting violently Asquith's bill giving Home Rule to Ireland, and an arms race between the military powers of Europe was escalating wildly. War seemed inevitable, else why would they do it?

Of the money the government spent on arms, an increasing amount was committed to aircraft. The aeroplane was being regarded as less of an eccentricity and more of an aid to prosecuting a successful war, if and when war came. It was thus being conscripted as an instrument of war.

The previous couple of years had seen tremendous advances in the design and performance of aircraft. Speeds of up to 100 miles per hour were achieved, heights of 10,000 feet, distances of over 200 miles. Farnborough had mysteriously become the foremost of the world's aeronautical research establishments, developing both aircraft and aero-engines. After centuries when flight had been the wild dream of cranks, the few years between 1903 and 1913 had seen aeroplanes become almost commonplace.

The introduction of the Avro 504 biplane in 1913, earmarked as an important military machine, was significant for Ned Brisco, since a licence to build it was granted to Sunbeam. It fell to Ned to perform test-flights.

Meanwhile, trouble continued to flare in the Balkans and reached fever-pitch when the heir to the Austro-Hungarian throne, the Archduke Franz Ferdinand, was assassinated touring the streets of Sarajevo in Bosnia on 28th June. The Austrians alleged that Serbia was implicated. A month later, they declared war on Serbia. Germany subsequently declared war on Russia and then, to underline that they really meant it, on Russia's ally, France. The British government responded by telling the Germans that the United Kingdom would stand by the 1839 Treaty of London guaranteeing Belgian neutrality, and would protect French coasts. The Kaiser arrogantly dismissed the treaty as a mere scrap of paper and, the following day, 4th August, Germany invaded Belgium on their way to France. Britain was thus irrevocably involved. Two days after that, Austria declared war on Russia and Serbia declared war on Germany.

Chapter Twenty-Nine

'I think the world's gone bloody mad,' Urban Tranter declared from his wooden stool in the taproom of the Jolly Collier. He picked up his pint pot, swigged the contents entirely and wiped his lush, grey moustache with the back of his hand. 'Wha'n yow say, Mary Ann?'

'I say the world's been going mad since the year dot,' Mary Ann replied from beside her beer pumps. It was quiet and she had only two customers at that moment, those two stalwarts, Urban Tranter and Noah Fairfax. 'This lot's been a-coming years. Pray to the Lord as it's over afore Christmas.'

'Not according to Kitchener it won't be,' Noah said solemnly, his back to the fire as he sat opposite Urban. 'They reckon the Kaiser's already got one and a half million men across the Rhine, ready to invade France.'

'Lord help we. The Kaiser could do with one a half million boots up his arse, mine among 'em,' Urban said earnestly. 'He's bin squaring up for a fight for donkey's years, building new Dreadnoughts, them new tanks, making new guns ... you name it.'

Jake came in carrying a bucket of coal and placed it by the fireplace. 'This'll be scarce, coal.'

'Coal's always bloody scarce,' Noah complained. 'At least this war might keep the miners

505

at work. We might even be blessed with more of the damned stuff than we can burn.'

'We'll have a sight less here, if that Jacob keeps a-burning it while it's August,' Mary Ann protested. 'We don't need e'er a fire in here with the weather so damned warm.'

'I like to see a fire, Mary Ann. It's homely.'

'It's damned expensive an' all.'

'Food'll be expensive,' Urban predicted. 'It'll be scarce. Prices'll be scandalous.'

'And beer. They'll put the duty up on beer to help pay for the war.'

'Yes, Noah,' Urban agreed, 'But 'tis to hoped it ain't gone up too much by the time you get your hand in your pocket for the next round.'

He turned to Mary Ann. 'Pull us another couple, Mary Ann, wut?' Noah dug in his pocket for some change. 'And have one theeself while you'm at it.'

'Damn my hide!' Mary Ann said, feigning surprise. 'And everybody reckons a beer off Noah Fairfax is scarcer than coal.'

'Gerroff with yer. Anybody'd think I was tight. Put one in for Jake an' all.'

Jake looked up from where he was placing lumps of coal on the fire. 'That's very decent of you, Noah, thank you.'

'I went down the town yesterday,' Urban said. 'There was a queue a mile long at that recruiting office they've set up.'

'I might sign up meself yet,' Noah chuckled. 'Can you think of e'er a better way of getting out the road of my missus?'

'They'd have to be bloody hard-up to take the

likes of you, Noah,' Mary Ann chimed, typically poker-faced.

'Listen, Kitchener wants every man he can get,' Noah said.

'I know. Fighting men, not boozing men.' She placed two more pints on the table in front of the two men and held her hand out for the money in an exaggerated fashion.

'You'm glad enough of we any other time,' Noah protested good-naturedly, handing her a florin.

'I wonder if that son-a-law o'yourn is gunna join up, Jake?' Urban queried.

'Who? Tom Doubleday? How *can* he? He's got a young son to look after.'

'No, Jake, but t'other one might. That Ned. Him as married Clover. Him as crashed his flying machine into the railings o' that cottage.'

'Saft bugger,' Mary Ann muttered. 'He should have bin looking where he was going. I bet he was a-watching the women,' she said, not comprehending the nature of flying. 'I got no sympathy. And he never offered a penny to her as lives there to get the railings mended – by all accounts.'

'I don't suppose he's got any money, has he?' Urban speculated. 'He was out of work and had to sell that hossless carriage of his so as they could afford to live, so his mother said. They hadn't got two ha'pennies to scratch their arses with.'

'Well, remember that loan he had, Urban?' Noah said.

'Blimey, ar. I do remember summat about it

now you mention it.'

'What was that, then?' Mary Ann queried.

'Somebody lent him some money – two hundred quid, I heard – I'm certain it was Zillah what told me – to buy an engine for that flying machine of his. But just as soon as he'd had it, he got a job at Star in Wolverhampton and they was building engines any road, so he never needed the money. I heard as he's never paid it back neither. P'raps he couldn't afford to.'

'What fool was saft enough to lend him that much?' Mary Ann asked.

'Nobody ever knew. It was amon – anom – anomol –... Whoever lent the money wunt let on who it was.'

'Anonymous,' Jake prompted, laughing. 'That's the word you'm scratting round for.'

'Ar, that's the word, Jake. I always talk with a limp when I'n had a pint or two.'

'Limp?' Urban queried with a wry smile. 'You stumbled arse over bollocks with that un. Good and proper.'

'Well, anyroad, like I was a-saying, Mary Ann – whoever lent him the money passed it through that reporter from the *Dudley Herald* who did that harticle on Ned when he had his picture in the paper. Remember? Anyroad, maybe they'm a bit better off now he's in work again, flying for a living.'

'I wouldn't know,' Mary Ann commented affecting contempt. 'I don't suppose she'd come to me for help anyroad. She's too proud, our Clover, too independent. I ain't caught sight of her since that night she walked out of here. Zillah tells me as how that little daughter of hers is beautiful, but I've never clapped eyes on her.'

'It don't do for families to fall out, does it Jake?' Urban said seriously. 'Life's too short.'

'Life is too short,' Jake agreed sincerely. 'I've told her as much meself. Look what happened to our Ramona ... and her mother before her.'

Mary Ann turned away, trying to conceal her innate disdain for a mother and daughter who were both too weak to resist the advances of lecherous, demanding men, and who had duly paid the price. It had happened to Clover, her own daughter. But after all this time she still missed Clover, and that same innate disdain was too expensive a price to pay. Such innate disdain was not making Mary Ann happy and content. Rather it made her sad; she had suffered the loss of a daughter, enduring grief as bitter as any bereavement because of it. She regretted that horrible evening they argued, when she felt obliged to disown her. If only she could put back the clock. Clover had been right, Mary Ann had admitted to herself finally. Clover needed the willing support of her mother during the most difficult time of her life. She only had to imagine herself in Clover's position to realise it. Mary Ann knew full well her daughter had been carrying Tom Doubleday's child and did not admire her for it but, because Ramona had already married him, and because Mary Ann didn't want to cause any rift or dissension with Jake, she kept the knowledge strictly to herself. She realised now, too, that Clover had married Ned, not out of free choice, but because once offered it she had no choice; partly because of Mary Ann's own failings as a mother. The girl was having to tolerate the consequences of that, however objectionable those consequences might be. Besides, now she had a little granddaughter, a gem by all accounts, and she would love to know the child. Even if it was illegitimate, it was not the child's fault. Why should she miss out on her only grandchild for the sake of a principle it was now too painful to support?

'But what I'm saying,' Noah continued, determined not to be side-tracked. 'It wunt surprise me if that Ned Brisco does join up. The Royal Flying Corps am clamouring for chaps what can fly aeroplanes for this war.'

'Then let's hope he does,' Mary Ann declared, and the others looked at her, surprised she should want such a thing.

Clover had long given up the pretence of meeting her imaginary friend Rose when she went to see Tom. Nowadays, she was open with Ned about her affair and, when she was going out, she told him where she was going. Ned accepted it without comment. He had long ago conceded that he could never make her interested in himself. When they had eventually discussed it rationally he agreed that their marriage had not been the brilliant success he hoped it might be. It had not produced the results he desired, and he knew it never would.

So it was one evening in mid-September in 1914. Clover left the house at half past seven, having put Posy to bed and ensured she was no trouble to Ned who was content to sit at the table all night and draw plans of bombers, while Liquorice lay contentedly curled up on his lap. She arrived at five to eight having caught the ten to eight tram. It dropped her outside a public house called the British Oak and she crossed the street to Tom's house. She let herself in and took off her hat and coat.

'Is Daniel in bed?' she asked quietly, lest her arrival disturb him.

Tom nodded. 'Nearly an hour ago.'

Daniel had taken mightily to Clover and, if he suspected she was about to visit, he insisted on staying up to see her. Tom, as a result, found himself denying that Clover was expected any night, in order to get him off to sleep by the time she arrived.

'Is there anything that wants doing?' she asked. 'Ironing? Washing? Dusting?'

'No,' he said with a smile. 'You do enough. Come and sit down by me and take it easy.'

She smiled back and sat by him on his sofa. 'Did you get a paper tonight? I wondered what news there was.'

'It's depressing, this war. The British Expeditionary Force they sent out has been having a hard time of it. The Germans swept over most of Belgium and last I heard they were well within striking distance of Paris. Paris is sure to fall. Reims has already been taken. Ghent and Lille will be next.'

'I heard we were suffering heavy casualties, Tom, but some men saw a vision of an angel shining brightly, that actually stopped the battle

511

at Mons for a while.'

'And you believe that?'

'Too many witnessed it just to dismiss it.'

'Pity it's not about all the time then,' he commented sadly. 'The Russians have been routed as well on the Eastern Front. They're courageous and no two ways, but they say the Germans are just too well-organised.'

'What do you think will happen, Tom?'

'God knows, sweetheart,' he said, his heart heavy. 'They're not going to be the walkover everybody thought they would be. I suppose we'll recruit more men and have a good go back at 'em. We won't give in, that's for certain.'

'Promise me you won't join up.' She looked into his eyes earnestly.

'I can't join up. Daniel is my priority. It'd be irresponsible of me to leave him here with my mother, then go and get killed. I don't want him growing up without his father. Besides, I'm thirty-one now. They probably wouldn't have me.'

'I imagine they'd be glad of anybody who's fit and well,' she said, and nestled her head on his chest as his arm went around her shoulders.

'It's not that I'm a coward, or unpatriotic, Clover. I would go if I could. I feel I ought, like any decent Englishman. But–'

'Oh, *promise* me you won't go,' she pleaded anxiously. 'I couldn't stand to lose you again.'

'Oh, Clover,' he sighed. 'Have no fear...' He was touched by her obvious concern. 'Kiss me...'

She kissed him, lingering at the taste and feel of his lips on hers.

'Do you think for a minute I could give up your

kisses?' he whispered softly when they'd broken off their embrace. 'Do you honestly believe I could go away and maybe never have the pleasure of lying with you again?'

She shuddered. 'The thought is too horrible to contemplate...'

Both contemplated it...

'Take me to bed, Tom.'

He stood up, held out his hand to her and she took it. When he'd pulled her up he opened the stairs door quietly and they tiptoed up the bent staircase. They stood at the side of Tom's bed and turned to face each other. She rested her head against his chest, then he lifted her face to his and kissed her again, so sweetly, so lovingly. Dusk was neutralising the colour of everything, but its sub-dued greyness managed to send enough illumination through the sash window for them to see each other's expressions clearly. Looking deeply into her eyes, he unbuttoned the front of her blouse and, when it opened, he pushed it back over her shoulders and down her arms and it fell whispering to the floor. He unfastened the waistband of her skirt and allowed that as well to fall around her feet.

'I'll do the rest,' she whispered with a smile. 'Otherwise we'll be here all night.'

'I know,' he sighed. 'Women's underwear is much too complicated for me.'

As she divested herself of the rest of her clothes he too got undressed. Naked, she shivered at the cool evening air of September and jumped into bed first, snuggling under the layers of blankets and sheets for warmth. He slid in beside her.

'Hold me,' she whispered. 'I'm cold.'

'I'll soon warm you.'

'That's what I'm counting on.'

The warmth from his body was irresistible. It was almost as familiar to her as her own by now, yet she never tired of the feel of him against her own skin. His body was smooth, firm. In the darkness it felt shiny to her touch and she caressed it, sensually brushing her lips over his shoulders and his neck. He pushed himself against her and she held him there, her hand cupped around his firm right buttock. She felt him hard and ready against her thigh; such a welcome sensation. As she rolled onto her back submissively his hands gently stroked her stomach.

'To say you've had a child, your belly's like it always used to be – smooth and flat.'

She smiled contentedly. 'I'm glad you approve.'

'Oh, I do.' He felt her right breast and squeezed it gently. 'These too. As firm as ever they were. I always thought breast-feeding made them soft and pappy.'

'Maybe it does if you keep it up for months and months. Or after lots of babies.'

They kissed again and she found she was getting warmer.

'I wonder what a child of ours would look like?' he remarked, his fingers gently fondling the soft, warm place between her legs and making her squirm with pleasure.

She sighed, not certain how to answer. 'It would be beautiful,' she breathed, after due consideration. 'They say any child conceived in love

514

is beautiful.'

'Then ours would be the most beautiful child in the world.'

'Without doubt... But, if you don't mind, Tom, we'll try and avoid one as usual this time. I'm a married woman remember.'

'You know, that's the only thing I've got against you, Clover,' he said teasingly. 'You've already got a husband.'

'Don't remind me. Just shut up and kiss me again.'

He kissed her ardently. His skilful touch and his smooth skin pressing against her lit her up like a beacon, as it always did. Sensuously, she manoeuvred herself underneath him. When he rolled onto her she let out a little sigh of anticipation, then a gasp of pleasure as she felt him, as eager as she was, slip silkily inside her.

When she returned home Ned was sitting in the old second-hand armchair they'd bought when they moved into the house. He was reading the Wolverhampton *Express and Star* and looked up as she opened the door.

'Has Posy been all right?'

'I haven't heard a murmur from her.'

'Good. Thank you for looking after her, Ned. I'll put the kettle on, then I'll go up and have a look at her. Do you want a cup of tea?'

'Might as well.' He sounded depressed.

She went to move into the scullery, venturing no further conversation.

'Clover...'

'Yes?' She already had her fingers on the door

latch. She turned to face him.

'I've been reading the newspapers these last few weeks... Did you know it was a flyer on a reconnaissance mission at Mons that first saw von Kluck's army starting to surround the British Expeditionary Force?'

'I heard we'd been taking a bashing.'

'Well, when he reported it, the High Command knew they would have to retreat. I daresay it injured their pride but there's no doubt that the information saved our army. Then, at the end of August some French flyers observed the German army on the move again, which meant the British and French ought to change their positions – which they did. It brought about our victory at the Battle of the Marne, and so Paris was saved...' He paused to let this information sink in. 'That's what I want to do, Clover – reconnaissance... So tomorrow I'm going to the recruiting office to volunteer for the Royal Flying Corps. The country needs flyers like me. I can be of more use in France than I am here. It's not as if you want me around. It's not as if you're bothered about me. Besides, if I go, that'll leave you free to get on with your love affair. You will anyway, whether I'm around or not.'

'Always presuming he doesn't volunteer as well.'

'Is he likely to?'

'Who knows? At least he's got his son to keep him at home. He wouldn't want to leave the child fatherless. That much I know. But they might introduce conscription.'

He nodded his understanding. Since his acci-

516

dent he *had* been more understanding. He was easier to live with, he tolerated her affair well. He was maturing at last.

'But, Ned,' she said with genuine concern. 'I don't want you to volunteer on my account. That would be stupid. You could go and get yourself killed and I'd feel as guilty as hell.'

He smiled up at her. 'That would be a change.' He stood up, stretched his braces and then his arms. 'No, I've made my mind up, Clover. It's what I want to do. For as long as I can remember I've dreamed of being able to fly. Well, I'm going to do it. Test-flying Farmans and Avro 504s around Wolverhampton is all well and good, but not really that exciting. I want to go and do some real flying, flying with a definite purpose, with some excitement attached to it. I want to pit my wits and my skill against other flyers and know I'm the best.'

'And would you be able to fly straight away?'

'You're supposed to have an aviator's certificate to fly army aeroplanes. Nobody ever thought to let me qualify for one but I daresay they'll give me one once I get there. Flying's not that difficult. It's no more difficult than driving a motor car, whatever plane you're in. Folk just think it is.'

'If that's what you really want to do, Ned...'

'It is.'

She smiled sympathetically. He might as well do it. He had no life at home. She did not make him happy, nor could she. He might just as well exercise his God-given talent and be content in doing that, rather than staying home frustrated.

517

Who knows, he might even meet a nice young French lady who would fall in love with him and make his miserable life bearable again. That would be the ideal outcome.

So, as he promised he would, Ned went to the recruiting office next day, Friday 18th September. On Sunday morning Clover said good-bye to him. He touched her hand respectfully, bent down to kiss Posy on the head, stroked Liquorice a last time, and he was gone.

Clover watched him go, not closing the door till he was round the corner by the Junction Inn. Posy, now five years old, had her arms flung around Clover's legs, her face buried in her skirts so that she should not see him go. She did not understand the significance of the man she knew as her daddy going away to fight in the war. She was not even certain what war was. But she picked up the mixed emotions of her mother and sensed that whatever was happening her life was about to change; this man was not going to figure in it for some time at least.

Clover felt glad and sad and guilty all at the same time to see him go. She was glad because his absence would free her to spend more time with Tom, as Ned had anticipated she would. But because she could never be what he wanted her to be, the circumstances by which Ned had asked her to marry him, indeed insisted she marry him and offer himself for sacrifice in the process, made her sad. It was the possibility that he might never come back that made her feel guilty. But what if he did come back and she was prevented further from spending her life with Tom, which was, after all, the life she craved? What on earth did the future have in store for her?

Ned was a fool and always had been. He was one of those people blessed with a gift, a flair – maybe even genius – held back only by a lack of money but never ideas. Yet he lacked that most precious of gifts: common sense. Ask him to tell you why he needed a wing area of so-and-so square feet and he would tell you, but ask him to fetch some coal up from the cellar and he would bring enough only for one fire and never fill the scuttle... Why?...

Tom, on the other hand ... was also a fool. Ordinarily, he was blessed with the common sense that Ned lacked. However, he was fool enough never to have worked out that the son he adored was by somebody else, that the woman he married had used him to effect her own salvation. The difference between the two men in that respect was that Ned knew he was taking on another man's child.

So which of the two was the bigger fool?

The question needed no answer. It was irrelevant. Both were fools enough. *Her* fools. But she loved one more dearly than life itself and resented the other for having married her in the first place. The important question now was how to see more of Tom, without appearing to her neighbours and his that she was kicking her feet up and generally becoming unworthy of their respect while her husband was risking his life, fighting ultimately for her freedom.

Clover shut the front door, uncurled Posy from

around her legs and took her hand. Back in the scullery she sat at the table and Posy sat on her lap.

'When will me daddy come back, Mommy.' Posy asked.

'I don't know, Petal. He might not come back for a long time. It depends how long the war lasts... It depends on a lot of things.'

'Is he going to fly his aeroplane?'

Clover nodded.

'Then he'll be able to fly home and see us, I'spect.'

'No, he'll be too far away, love. Across the sea in another country called France. Aeroplanes can't fly that far.'

'Will he bring me a present when he does come?'

'Oh, I expect so...'

'Do all daddies have to fly their aeroplanes in the war?'

'Not all daddies have an aeroplane, sweetheart. But a lot of daddies will have to leave their wives and children and fight the Germans. Now what would you like for your breakfast? Would you like some French toast with some jam on?'

Posy nodded, slid down off Clover's lap and sat on the seat opposite her mother. Only her cherubic face was visible above the table.

Clover cut a slice of bread from the loaf that was upturned on the bread board, buttered one side and began toasting the dry side in front of the fire using a toasting-fork. 'This afternoon we'll meet Uncle Tom and Daniel and go to the Castle grounds for a walk,' she said, leaning forward to hold the slice of bread in front of the fire. 'Would you like that?'

Posy nodded again and smiled her approval. 'Shall I have an ice cream?'

'If we see an ice cream cart.'

The child looked pensive for a few seconds. 'Will Uncle Tom have to go and fight the Germans as well?'

'I hope not. Don't you?'

'But he's a daddy,' she reasoned. 'He's Daniel's daddy.'

'I know he is, but I hope he doesn't have to go as well. He has Daniel to look after.'

'I know...' She paused, thinking little girls' thoughts as she watched the slice of bread toasting. 'Why did Daniel's mommy die?'

'Because she was very poorly – after Daniel was born.'

'Did you know his mommy?'

'Yes, she was my stepsister.'

'What's a stepsister?'

Clover did her best to explain in simple terms.

'Was she nice, his mommy?'

'She was very nice. She was very pretty with curly, yellow hair – just like Daniel.' Clover withdrew the toast from in front of the fire, melted butter dripping from it. She put it on a plate and spread some blackberry jam over it. 'Here you are, sweetheart.'

Posy took it and put the toast to her mouth. 'When I grow up I'm going to marry Daniel, Mommy,' she declared, then took a bite.

'Mmm,' Clover mused. 'I hope it's that simple for you...'

They met, that afternoon. While Clover and Tom ambled up the steep, winding paths through the trees of Dudley's old, derelict castle, the children ran on boisterously in their best Sunday clothes, playing hide and seek, tick and other games that involved chasing each other about. She took Tom's arm, like any wife would take her husband's and relished the newly sanctioned freedom to pursue this course. She looked into his eyes lovingly.

'So how do you feel now he's gone?' Tom asked.

She told him how she felt when she watched Ned walk down the street with an old cardboard suitcase he'd borrowed from his father, explaining honestly her mixed emotions.

'At least you'll be able to come and go as you please,' he remarked. 'Within reason.'

'Already your neighbours must think I'm a fallen woman seeing me appear and disappear at odd hours,' she said.

'Mrs Jeavons next door believes you're a widow.'

She looked up at him and smiled. 'You told her that?'

'No. She just assumes. She's a widow herself. I think she envies you your brazenness.'

'Sees me as brazen, does she? If only she knew the truth, she'd think I was a whore.'

Through the trees they could see Dudley Station in the valley below. A locomotive, shunting wagons, huffed and clanked, sending volleys of steam and smoke into the late summer air. Beyond the station lay the tram depot and, beyond that, the headgear of the Coneygree Colliery loomed dismally over its grotesque slag heaps, the marl-hole of the adjacent brick works and the cupolas of the foundry where she used to work making cores.

'It wouldn't do for me to be seen calling on you at Hill Street,' Tom said.

'Course not,' she replied.

'You have your reputation there to protect.'

She laughed. 'Such as it is. If only I could come and live with you at Salop Street ... If only convention would allow it–'

'But it doesn't,' he stated firmly.

She looked at him, surprised and a little disappointed at this sudden propriety that she thought he might have defied. Maybe she did not know him as well as she thought she did.

He caught her glance, recognised her disillusionment. 'I'm only concerned for your honour, Clover. But there's another consideration...'

'Which is?'

'If we lived together, people would see you and assume we were wed. If you suddenly left me when Ned came home, what would they think then? What would *I* think?'

'Since when have you been so concerned about what other people might think, Tom? What we do is nothing to do with anybody but ourselves. Anyway, let me make one thing clear – if I do decide to fly in the face of convention, and Posy and I come and live with you – if you allow it, that is,' she added with a hint of sarcasm, 'I would not leave you even when Ned does come home. I couldn't go back to him.'

'You mean, you'd rob him of his daughter?'

She was tempted to scream out that Posy was not Ned's daughter, that she was his. But she stopped herself. Instead, she said: 'For you, I would do that.'

'I don't desire that of you,' he proclaimed, and she thought how strangely pious he sounded.

She sighed with frustration. 'But, Tom, he doesn't regard Posy in the same way you regard Daniel. He's never been a father to her in the same way you've been to Daniel.'

'All the same.'

Chapter Thirty

Next morning Clover arose early. It was washing day and, as usual, she would take her basket of dirty washing round to Florrie Brisco's and spend the morning in the brewhouse, up to her elbows in soap suds and steam while Posy was at school. She stretched herself and pondered again the conversation with Tom that had put a damper on her spirits. His words, his reasons not to go and live with him, hurt and disappointed her for they were incongruent with how she believed he felt about her. Something was holding him back, some doubt, some misgiving, and she had no idea what it was. Could he be afraid of commitment? She thought not. He had not been afraid to commit himself to Ramona; he had not been afraid to commit himself to Daniel. She could only presume it was because he would not be able to tolerate the heartache of losing her when Ned came home. Indeed, that made sense and Clover would have been content to believe that. But another thought, a fear, was lurking: what if he was considering volunteering for service? What if he was considering leaving Daniel with her for the duration of the war?

She roused Posy and together, they washed and dressed and breakfasted. This is like being a widow, she told herself, without Ned around. She brushed Posy's lush dark hair, they donned their hats and coats and Clover picked up the basket of laundry. On the way to school she deposited it at Florrie Brisco's and told her she'd be back in ten minutes when she'd delivered Posy.

During the morning, the two women discussed Ned's volunteering for service and the war. Florrie had many strange ideas and remedies on how to deal with the Kaiser, some of which made Clover laugh, some she knew were plain ignorant and stupid. When the washing had been pegged out, Clover collected Posy from school and they returned to Granny and Granddad Brisco's to eat bubble-and-squeak, the fried-up leftovers from yesterday's dinner. After she'd taken Posy back to school for the afternoon session, Clover made her way to the post office in St John's Road. On her way she met Zillah Bache and the two women greeted each other warmly.

'Ned's volunteered for the Royal Flying Corps,' Clover told Zillah. 'I'm on my way to the post office to see about my allowance now he's not picking up any wages.'

'Shall you be able to manage all right?' Zillah asked.

'I've got no choice. Posy gets through clothes and shoes like nobody's business but that can't be helped. I shall have to cut down on other things. I shan't be able to put any more money towards paying off that stupid loan till he gets back and goes back to work. If only I knew who the money was owed to I could apologise and try to reassure them I'm saving up to pay it off when I can afford to.'

'It's never bin paid off?' Zillah queried.

'Never. If Ned wasn't such a nincompoop he'd have paid it off long before he married me. Now I'm stuck with it. It's all I can do to manage as things are, without that hanging over me.'

'He's a clot, that Ned.'

'Clot? Listen, you're preaching to the choir here, Zillah. *I* know it better than anybody.'

'You'd have bin best off without him, if you ask me. What about the time he crashed that contraption of his into Maisie Winwood's railings?'

Zillah started to laugh at the memory and Clover laughed too. In fact, the whole of Kates Hill had never really stopped laughing. It was mentioned most nights in some pub or other and everybody would guffaw and make disparaging comments. It would take a long time for Kates Hill folk to forget that episode.

'It's a wonder nobody was killed, Clover.'

'Damn fool! I still can't get over it... Talking about fools – how's my mother?'

'Mellowing nicely,' Zillah replied with a certain

amount of satisfaction.

'Mellowing? Stone-faced old Mary Ann?'

'Nice as pie her is to me nowadays, Clover, my wench. Talks to me, her does – not *at* me, like her used to.'

'Struth!'

'I think her misses you, you know. Her generally asks me if I've seen yer. I generally tell her as I haven't, though, 'cause her'd only pump me for information. I only tell her what I want her to know, Clover.'

'Oh, you can tell her you've seen me today if you like. Tell her I've never felt better and that her granddaughter's beautiful. Tell her I would've taken Posy to see her if only she'd never thrown me out in the first place – I'll never forgive her for that... No. On second thoughts, don't tell her that at all, Zillah. She'll think I've been telling tales. She'd hate that. But tell her I hope she's keeping well – and Jake of course.'

Zillah smiled, her black eyes alight with satisfaction over her fat jowls. 'I'll tell her. Her'll be really happy to hear it. It'll mek her day. Yo'm mellowing nicely yourself, Clover.'

'God, and I'm only twenty-six!'

Ned was immediately drafted into 14 Squadron of the Royal Flying Corps. Because he had years of experience flying Farmans and, more latterly, Avros, he was given a mandatory test and immediately received an aviation certificate. Based for a few weeks in Hampshire learning military flying techniques, he quickly discovered that airmen were perceived as heroes and were

527

invited to lavish parties at big country houses where they met the county set. Suddenly, he was surrounded by beautiful, sophisticated women, many of whom seemed interested and impressed with him. He affirmed that he was married to a beautiful girl who was waiting anxiously for his return, but it only seemed to make the women even more interested. He told them he had a beautiful, blue-eyed daughter and that didn't deter them either. He received invitations to tea, to dinner and to more parties, all of which he accepted. When he was eventually posted to France in November, he was sorry to have to leave.

Ned's squadron flew Farnborough BE2c two-seater reconnaissance biplanes. The BE2c had staggered wings, giving a good view up and down, a wingspan of 37 feet and a maximum speed of 75 miles per hour. Ned loved it. On sorties into enemy territory, he and his observer, Jack Smedley, a lad eleven years his junior, defended themselves with a rifle or a hand-gun which Jack wielded in the forward seat. Sometimes they were asked to lob hand grenades onto enemy gun positions over the side of the aeroplane, and this they did with a spirit of keen aggression that grabbed all flyers. It took a great deal of courage to fly in the face of anti-aircraft fire and deal with enemy aircraft as they intercepted them.

On 15th December 1914, in appalling weather, Ned and Jack and two other aircraft were involved in a scrap with a German aeroplane that was intent on running them out of their back yard. The three British aeroplanes succeeded in forcing the German to land in Allied territory, whereupon its crew abandoned their aeroplane and escaped. But it was a victory and Ned's first significant one. With the others, he had proved himself and celebrated it handsomely with the rest of the squadron.

He adjusted to his new life quickly. Discipline was slack in the scout squadrons. Nobody really bothered what you did in your free time and, once in the air, they didn't know what you were up to anyway, since there was no two-way wireless communication to give orders. You were given a task and you got on with it. When you'd completed it, if you wanted to push your luck and go marauding, looking for a stray Hun to shoot down, then so be it. Ned never considered the inherent dangers, he merely enjoyed the camaraderie and back-slapping of his fellow flyers and was always happy to pull on his coat, his helmet and his goggles ready for another sortie behind enemy lines to see what they were up to. Anything to rove the skies in his BE2c.

Development of aircraft was rapid and it soon became evident that the sort of reconnaissance aeroplanes that Ned and his fellow pilots were using, needed to defend themselves and also deny the enemy a look behind your own lines. A machine-gun was needed, ideally mounted centrally on the fuselage, so that the pilot could aim his whole aircraft at his target and fire when attacked. The problem was, such a machine-gun, when firing, needed some sort of interrupter gear, synchronised to shoot through the propeller without shooting the blades off.

The first Allied aeroplane so fitted, sporting a Hotchkiss machine-gun, was monumentally successful, killing many enemy aircraft in its first few days of operation; until it was downed by anti-aircraft fire over German territory and the wreckage salvaged and inspected by Fokker engineers.

In the middle of July in 1915 Ned and Jack were given the task of taking photographs of German positions around Champagne. Ned looked up to the sky as they approached the BE2c.

'It's a clear day for it, Jack,' he commented, keen to be airborne.

As they reached the little biplane Ned tossed the camera nonchalantly to the flight sergeant who had been working on the craft with a team of mechanics. 'How'd you like to fix that on for us?' he said.

'Yes, sir,' replied the NCO, and set to attaching the camera to the underside while the two flyers routinely checked the struts, wires and ailerons.

'Have you topped her up with plenty of juice?' Ned queried, recalling his antics caused by lack of it over Kates Hill a couple of years earlier.

'Tank's full, sir, as you ordered,' came the reply.

They climbed aboard. Ned knew he would need a full tank of petrol to enable them to keep aloft for two and a half hours, even though its weight would limit their speed and rate of climb. He switched on his ignition and nodded to the flight sergeant who gave the propeller a sharp yank to start the engine. They let it warm up for a minute or two, Ned waved the chocks away and they tootled across the tarmac till they began to rise. At ten thousand feet about forty-five minutes later they levelled off. It was cool at this altitude and he was thankful for his flying jacket. In another thirty minutes or so they reached their designated area and began their beat, flying first one way then the other to capture every inch of ground on overlapping film.

'Quiet day today,' Ned yelled over the noise of the engine, and Jack nodded.

Indeed it was quiet; unnervingly so. They had seen little activity from enemy aircraft. Certainly no Hun had tried to intercept them but, on a day like this, they must be clearly visible both from the ground and from aircraft that were capable of flying higher. Ned raised his goggles and scanned the sky ahead, above and to either side of him. In the very far distance, possibly five miles away at about twelve thousand feet, he saw a tiny dark spot, ominous in the eastern sky.

Time to take evasive action. No sense in being a target over enemy lines. He banked the aircraft round sharply to the left to maintain a sensible distance between himself and his pursuer. The BE2c fell in a spectacular dive, designed to increase speed and Ned opened the throttle. The steep, sudden descent brought Jack's stomach into his mouth, but he merely turned round to Ned and grinned. Ned signalled with his thumb that there was an enemy aeroplane heading towards them. At eight thousand feet, they levelled off. Jack lugged up the heavy Hotchkiss machine-gun they now carried to protect themselves and peered into the skies about him.

531

He saw two other aircraft converging on them from below.

Jack gave Ned the signal and they dived again. The danger was that if an enemy aeroplane managed to get behind you and beneath you there was little you could do to defend yourself. If Ned could effect a quick turn and place his BE2c to the right or left of an assailant Jack could open fire with the machine-gun and there was a fair chance of scoring a hit. He turned sharply and two German Aviatiks passed above them going in the opposite direction. Ned saw them turn so they could follow and drive him away from home. He would have to disable both machines in order to escape. He turned again and the first Aviatik was at about the same height as himself. Jack took aim with the machine-gun. A hail of bullets strafed through the Aviatik and one evidently found the observer, for he slumped forward. Another rain of bullets, and they saw the enemy plane suddenly light up with flames flaring around it. With its engine spluttering it quickly fell away in a spectacular nose-dive.

Ned was exhilarated at their success. He was the better aviator, he'd proved it; Jack was a better gunner. The second Aviatik appeared, coming at them from the starboard side, the observer firing directly at them. Jack took aim again and raked a row of perforations along the side of the aircraft. This time the pilot's head went back and Jack guessed it was his instant reaction to the pain of a bullet in the leg. That Aviatik, too, headed downwards with the observer struggling to get a hold of the controls.

Ned tapped Jack on the shoulder again and, with a wide grin, gave him the thumbs-up sign. They both leaned over, watching the killed Aviatik's rapid descent. What neither of them saw was the first aeroplane they'd spotted at five miles distance, the aircraft that had induced Ned to head home in the first place. It suddenly appeared from the rear and above them, then dived at a tremendous speed in front of them, having overtaken them. Ned could see that it had a machine-gun mounted on top of the engine nacelle, so had the ability to fire through the propeller. He was aware that such developments were in hand and had heard rumours that the Germans might already be using them. Instinct told him that the pilot would next climb steeply, get behind them and machine-gun them from the rear. He had to prevent that at all costs.

Buoyed up by the success of two victories in succession, and in as many minutes, he was brimming with confidence and felt invincible. At once he side-slipped the aeroplane, falling away rapidly as the enemy aircraft, a Fokker M5K monoplane, obviously modified, sped away in the opposite direction. Ned turned and followed it, but it was out of range of Jack's machine-gun. He caught up, not realising that the German ace had allowed him to, and was flying below the Fokker with the intention of machine-gunning it from underneath its tail. Jack lifted the machine-gun, steadied it, and Ned inched the BE2c to get within range.

But suddenly, the Fokker went into a steep climb and Ned, in his fear and excitement, made the instinctive mistake of following him to try and maintain his proximity, exactly as his opponent had intended. But his BE2c had neither the same manoeuvrability nor power and he struggled to keep up, having to abort his own steep climb to save stalling. Desperately, Ned tried to get his aeroplane back up to speed and dived again. Jack watched in dismay as he looked up and saw the Fokker turn hard to the side and dive straight for them, his machine-gun ablaze. Ned heard the bullets pepper the fuselage behind him, then felt a sudden dull thump in his back and witnessed his own liver and shreds of his coat splatter the instrument binnacle with red gore. In that fatal split second before he lost consciousness forever he felt the first lick of flames in his face, but had expired by the time his petrol tank had been ripped apart. Through the blue, summer sky the BE2c hurtled uncontrollably earthwards, exploding in a ball of flame.

Clover answered the door on Saturday morning to a boy in uniform who handed her the telegram. It was half past nine on 17th July. As she sat on the old armchair in the scullery she looked at it in a mixture of disbelief and sadness, for it could contain only bad news. Her heart started beating fast and her throat went dry. She turned it over and over in her fingers before she plucked up the courage to open it.

'Oh, God, no!' she said under her breath as she read it.

Her first thought was for Posy who played in the back yard trying to catch a butterfly that had settled on one of the rose trees Ned had planted. Should she tell her now and face the barrage of questions and the inevitable tears? Or should she say nothing? As the weeks and months of Ned's absence had slipped by, Posy was asking less and less about the man she knew as her daddy, and his letters home had always been few and far between to remind her. Maybe Posy was forgetting him. Maybe, therefore, it was best to tell her straight away. The sooner she knew, the sooner she would get over it.

She dreaded having to tell Florrie and the old man. The grief would kill them. They were so proud of their younger son. But she would have to do it. There was no point in dilly-dallying either. So when she had spruced herself up she called Posy and told her they were going to see Granny and Granddad Brisco.

As they walked down Hill Street hand-in-hand, Clover said: 'We've got to give a message to them, sweetheart. I had a telegram this morning to say that daddy's aeroplane has been shot down.'

Talk she'd heard over the past few months had expanded Posy's vocabulary. She'd heard people saying words like, telegram, Zeppelin, Dreadnought, explosion, troops, massacre, retreat, tragedy; phrases like, killed in action, tactical withdrawal, German offensive. She wasn't sure what they meant but nowadays they were familiar words and they gave her a distinct impression of gloom for nobody smiled when they uttered these words. At only six years old, she knew already that war was not a pleasant thing, that everybody feared it and its consequences. Thus, she did not expect to feel any great elation at what her mother was trying to tell her. Rather, she expected to hear something bad.

'Does that mean he's dead?'

'Yes, he's dead. Killed in action.'

'That means we won't see him again, doesn't it?'

'I'm afraid it does.'

'Are you sad, Mommy?'

'Yes, I'm very sad. Of course I'm sad.'

Posy looked up at her mother anxiously. 'Are you going to cry?'

'Well ... I might, but I'm trying not to.' She looked down on her daughter with love and care in her eyes, and sniffed. If only she could protect her from this scourge of war and the turmoil of emotions it roused in folk. 'How about you?'

'I'll try not to as well.'

'It doesn't matter if you do, sweetheart. Sometimes it's better to cry over something as sad as this. We have to tell Granny and Granddad and if they start crying, I might.'

They arrived at the house in Watson's Street and went in.

'It's Clover and our Posy,' Florrie said, stating the obvious, but rather coldly, Clover thought. Had she upset Florrie somehow?

Posy went in and draped herself over the arm of Granddad Brisco's chair, all the time anxiously watching her mother.

'Well? Have yer heard from him this wik?' Florrie asked pointedly. There was definitely a chill in the atmosphere.

'No, Florrie... But I ... I had a telegram a few minutes ago...' As she fished in her pocket for it, Florrie looked aghast and the colour drained from her face. Clover handed it to her mother-in-law and held back the urge to weep. 'It's bad news, Florrie.'

Florrie read it and, without a word, handed it to her husband. A tear trickled from one eye, rolled down her cheek and dripped off her chin as she watched his reaction to the news. He sighed heavily, closed his eyes in despair and handed the telegram back to Clover.

'Am yer surprised?' Florrie asked with a great shuddering sigh.

'I suppose not,' Clover responded quietly. 'Flying over enemy lines in wartime must be one of the most hazardous things anybody could do. I read that we've lost scores of aviators already.'

'Then why did you let him go?' Oh, there was acid there all right, burning to get out of Florrie, to be spat at Clover.

'I couldn't stop him, Florrie,' Clover answered defensively. 'Flying was in his blood. It's what he wanted to do. You know that.'

'Piffle! I never heard such damn piffle.' She wiped her eyes with her handkerchief and pointed a finger at Clover accusingly. 'You could have kept him here if you'd only loved him.' Clover looked down at her shoes to avoid Florrie's piercing gaze and wagging finger. 'Less than a wik ago he wrote to me and told me the truth of how things stood between you pair. He wanted me to know the truth. The last confessions of a chap as knew he was about to die, it strikes me. He told me as you've never loved him, that you never even wanted to marry him, even though you was carrying his babby. He told me as how you've been having it off again with that chap what you was engaged to before, and how you was leaving young Posy here wi' me so's you could slope off and meet him. He told me as you was leaving him in the house at night to look after her while you went about your dirty business. Well, I never heard of anything so damned wicked and deceitful. He told me an' all as how you ain't lived a proper married life since the day you wed. Well, you drove him to his death, Clover, and no two ways.' She prodded her forefinger animatedly into Clover's shoulder. 'By God, you did. As sure as God med little apples. You drove him away from his child, from his own mother and father to volunteer, knowing full well as he might never come back...' Florrie broke down and a flood of tears ran down her anguished face. 'You should be ashamed...' she blubbered.

Clover did not know how to respond. It was bad enough merely trying to deal with the loss of a husband, however unloved he might be; now she was being blamed for that loss. There seemed little point in telling Florrie that, from the outset, Ned knew she didn't love him, that she'd made him no promises, that she had never misled him. Now Clover was the villain, poor Ned the victim of her audacious duplicity. But at least he'd withheld some things; he hadn't confessed he was not Posy's father. Obviously, it would not have been in his best interests to do so.

'I can't deny it, Florrie,' Clover said softly, reeling from the unexpected tirade but trying to maintain her composure. She glanced at Posy, lolling over Granddad's arthritic knees now, but with a worried expression. 'I won't deny it. Any of it. But I question Ned's judgement in believing that you needed to know... In any case, I don't think we should be discussing this in front of Posy.'

'No, I don't suppose you do.'

'Look, Florrie, he knew I never loved him in the first place. I held nothing from him.'

'Except yourself.'

'Yes... Except myself... But he knew what to expect. His judgement in the first place must have been questionable for him to take me on, knowing I didn't love him.'

'And yours wasn't for accepting? For Christ's sake, Clover, do me the courtesy of not blackening his character, especially now he's dead and gone, fighting like a hero for king and country... 'Cause our Ned was brave, and no two ways.'

'He *was* brave, Florrie,' she agreed inadequately. 'He was very brave...' He was also an incredible fool, she wanted to say.

'Well, here's your telegram back... Tek it and I hope you'm proud of yourself, young Clover.'

'I can't help the way I am, Florrie...'

'Praps it'd be better if you left us alone now, so's we can grieve in peace.'

Clover hesitated, unable to believe that she was being dismissed so abruptly, not being allowed to share their grief for just a little while, not being allowed a few words to make her own position understood. But they would never understand. They would never see it from her viewpoint. He was their son; and now they had lost him. She must take the blame because she had been having an affair with another man. The war was not to blame. The enemy was not to blame. She alone was to blame. She was as much to blame as if she had shot him down herself.

'If that's what you want,' she answered eventually. 'I'll call back in a day or two to see how you are. I might have some more news by then.'

'The only news we want to hear is that it's all been a big mistake and he's still alive.'

'That would be the best news of all, Florrie, I agree... Come on Posy. We'd better leave Granny and Granddad to themselves.'

What were you supposed to feel when you learnt that your unloved husband had been killed in action? Sorrow? Regret? She felt all those things but it was obvious she did not feel them with the same intensity as would a woman who truly loved and wanted her man. She was immensely sad that the gangly lad she had helped build aeroplanes in Joseph Mantle's old stables was dead and gone. He had been her friend, her companion. She had liked him as a friend. And yet that very friendship, which she had truly valued, had evaporated like steam when they married.

Now, she felt relief that he was out of her life, and she did not like herself for it. Rather, she felt somewhat ashamed; ashamed that maybe she had been too self-centred, ignoring Ned's aspirations for their marriage. God knows what emotions he must have felt that he was unable to express in words, for he was not a person who might know how to phrase his innermost feelings. Maybe she had treated him too shabbily. Maybe she should have tried harder to understand him, to accommodate his hopes and dreams. But at what cost? At the cost of her own hopes and dreams?

It had been impossible married to Ned. He had been such a fool. Always a fool. But he did not deserve death even though he had stood on death's path. Now, she would be branded the villain of Kates Hill, for no doubt Florrie would blab everywhere the truth of the matter – as she saw it. She would be denounced as a whore, spoken of in the vilest terms. She would have to be strong to withstand the affronts, the insulting comments, and the sneering folk who would soon shun her and Posy. And what of Posy? Would all this anticipated hostility manifest itself in the children of those who were about to ostracise her?

They were due to visit Tom and Daniel later that morning. Clover was yearning to see him, to discuss everything, to wallow in his support, for she needed it. So, at about quarter to one they left home and walked to his studio where Daniel would also be. As soon as Tom saw her he could see she was perturbed although he said nothing, apprehensive of what it might be. She would tell him what was on her mind soon enough.

She did so as she was standing at the sink preparing dinner at his house in Salop Street.

'Ned's been killed in action, Tom.'

'Oh, my God.'

'I had a telegram this morning.' She stopped what she was doing and looked into his eyes disconsolately. 'Presumably he was shot down.'

'I could see something was on your mind. I didn't like to ask. Leave off peeling those potatoes, my flower, and come and sit down. Tell me about it. Tell me how you feel.'

She dried her hands and went to sit by him. 'I don't know how I feel, Tom... No, that's not true. I do know how I feel, but I don't like myself for it one bit. The trouble is, I don't know how I *ought* to feel. I'm sad – of course I'm sad, I've lived with him years and known him even longer – but I'm relieved as well. You know how much I regretted marrying him, you'd expect me to feel relieved – wouldn't you? Tell me you would, Tom. Tell me I'm not a wicked, unfeeling woman.'

He put his arm around her. 'Of course I expect you to feel relieved. You're free of him. It's what you've always wanted.'

'But I didn't want him to *die* ... I didn't want him to *die*.' As yet she had shed no tears, and she had not really expected to. But now tears welled up in her eyes. 'When I think of how he might have died, how he might have suffered, I blame myself. I keep thinking it's all my fault, that he didn't have to go to the Front, that I drove him there.' A tear rolled down her cheek and she mopped it up with her handkerchief. 'God,' she sniffed, 'these are the first tears I've ever shed over him... He was such a mundane creature, Tom. So unassuming.'

'It's not your fault, Clover. There's no sense in blaming yourself.' He hugged her tight and her tears flowed the more. She cried for some time, drenching one handkerchief while the children were playing in the back yard, oblivious.

Eventually, Tom said: 'Have you told his mother and father?'

'Oh, yes...' She rolled her eyes. 'As soon as I knew myself... But he wrote to Florrie ... less than a week ago. Obviously just before he got killed. He told her everything about our marriage. Everything. I don't have to spell it out. Now she blames me for his death.'

'And that's why you blame yourself because Florrie blames you.' He sighed with exasperation. 'But that's ludicrous, Clover. It's not your fault. He was a flyer. He would have gone to the war whether or no. Even if you'd been lyrically happy with him, he'd still have gone.'

'Do you think so?' Hope returned to her eyes.

'It's obvious. And if Florrie thinks otherwise she's living in cloud-cuckoo-land.'

She sniffed and wiped her eyes again, red now. 'You make me feel so much better, Tom. So much better.' She forced a smile. 'I hope Florrie comes to realise it as well.'

'Don't count on it. She obviously perceives him as being a victim of your indifference. You'll always be the villain in her eyes. But never in mine.' He smiled at her lovingly.

'So ... I'm a widow now... Don't you think I'm a bit young to be a widow?'

'I'll tell you something, Clover. There'll be thousands more widows your age and younger before this war's over. On both sides.'

'There already are,' she said. 'Just think – when it's all over there'll be thousands of women, all seeking new husbands, and only a handful of men to go round. Still ... I won't need to, will I? I've got you.'

'So, you've already got me marked down as your new husband?'

'You know I have. Wasn't it always on the cards if anything happened to Ned, or he divorced me?'

'I don't know. Was it?'

She smiled uncertainly. It seemed a strange response. As if he didn't already know. She looked at him curiously, alarm bells ringing inside her head. This was definitely not the reaction she'd expected.

'What do you mean, you don't know? You know very well. Did you think all this time that I was just a lie-by? Somebody you could have your way with, then send packing and forget about till the next time? Did you think I was not serious about us, Tom, after all we've been to each other?'

'Not at all, Clover,' he asserted. 'You're jumping to conclusions. It's just that you must let me get used to the idea first. I didn't expect you to be available so soon. If ever.'

'No, let's get this straight. Are you saying you don't want to marry me – after a suitable period of mourning for Ned?'

'It's not that simple a matter, Clover. There are a lot of things to consider. I think that ... that it's something we *should* talk about... After a suitable period.'

'So you're saying you don't want to marry me

after all? Now the opportunity is there?'

'I'm not saying that at all. You're trying to put words into my mouth. What I'm saying is that there are many things to consider... *Many* things... Not least of which are our children...'

Clover was staggered by his hedging. After all this time, after all the happiness he'd brought her since their reconciliation, after the promise of perpetual happiness in the future, she could not believe his reticence now – now that he was blessed directly with the prospect of marriage; now that she was available.

She got up from the sofa in a huff of over-sensitivity, called Posy and collected her coat from the back of the scullery door. She would not stand to be so humiliated, especially on this of all days, when she needed, desperately needed some support, when she was so highly susceptible to negative emotions after the awful news of Ned.

'If that's how you feel, Tom, you'd better cook your own dinners. Today and every day.'

She called Posy and quickly put her cardigan on while the child complained bitterly at being dragged away when she was enjoying herself so much.

'Why are we going?' she screamed. 'I want to play with Daniel.'

'Evidently, we're not wanted here either,' Clover said touchily, wiping more tears from her eyes.

Chapter Thirty-One

Tom's attitude left Clover in ferment, tortured by uncertainty. She could not think why he had manifested this lack of commitment when all the time, apart from a hint when they went walking in the castle grounds, she had believed it was his dearest wish that they marry and spend the rest of their lives together. She contrived one reason after another as to why, and felt inordinately sorry for herself that this trauma had come on top of the dreadful shock of Ned's death. Just when she needed comfort and support from him there was none. But hadn't her life always been like that?

She and Posy alighted from the tram at the corner of Priory Street and Stone Street in the centre of Dudley town. Posy, in a juvenile huff that she'd been hauled away so rudely from her playmate, was still complaining sulkily. To pacify her, and to try to take her own mind off events, Clover waltzed her around the shops. They gazed into shop windows and Clover said wouldn't it be nice if they could afford this dress or that piece of furniture? She bought Posy a quarter of dolly mixtures which, little by little, put a smile back on her face. From the market Clover bought fresh vegetables and two pork chops from a butcher for their dinner tomorrow, for it was certain they would not be asked to the Briscos'.

As they walked home, past Tom's studio, Clover never even deigned to look in his window, reminded of the misery of those times they had become estranged before. Emotionally, she was back where she started; she was single all over again and had just had a another massive disagreement with Tom. Would fate always confound them? Would they never get together? Would they always have to suffer an on-and-off relationship?

That night she went to bed and could not sleep. As the climbing moon traversed the slit in the curtains, casting a streak of eerie, silvery-blueness that moved obliquely across her counterpane, the devils of night distorted all her thoughts, all her fears. Ned was gone. Ned, who would have moved heaven and earth to have her love. Tom was gone too – yet again. Tom, who possessed her love but seemed not to know what to do with it. Her thoughts drifted incessantly between both. She began to wonder what must happen next. Where would Ned be buried, assuming they had some remains to bury? What would happen to his things? Would somebody issue a death certificate? She had visions of being swamped by his superfluous unwashed underwear and smelly socks, of grubby handkerchiefs sticking together disgustingly, of his sweaty shirts. Thoughts of clothing reminded her that she had better find something black to wear. Also, she must remember to keep the curtains shut for a week.

She listened to the heart-rending yowls of a cat in one of the yards close by, sounding more like a distressed baby than any baby. The moon hid behind a cloud and an even darker gloom pervaded her. A dog barked irritatedly, as if offended by the presence of a cat in his personal back yard, and then she heard Posy in the next room mutter something unintelligible in her sleep. Posy had taken the news of Ned's death exceedingly well; but maybe she was too young to understand, too young to understand even the concept of death.

Ned is dead, she kept telling herself, trying to convince herself of the truth and the significance of it.

Ned is dead. Ned is dead.

Mere words. If you keep repeating them they sound funny and have no meaning.

They had no meaning anyway. She tried hard to feel something appropriate to the awful circumstance, to the loss. But she could not. She felt no emotion, no sorrow; no sorrow that induced her to weep at least, and she berated herself for being so contemptible. A life had been lost; her own husband's life. But while he had been away she had not missed him. While he had been away she had felt released from the constrictions of a marriage she did not cherish. So why should she feel sorrow now?

Had she left Tom's house a bit too abruptly, giving him no chance to explain? Maybe she had, but only because she wanted to make a show of her indignation at what appeared to be his rejection of her. But Tom could be just as awkward, matching fire with fire. Even though she had received that terrible news, she was sure he would oppose his natural inclination to sympathise, just to prove he would not be manipulated by womanly guiles, even though it might hurt him to do so.

The following morning, Sunday, she kept inventing little jobs to keep herself occupied. She would occasionally peer behind the curtains in the front room to see if she could see Tom walking up the street, come to claim her as his bride. Conscious of her role as mother despite her heartache, she gave Posy lots of hugs and read her several stories between the necessary tasks of preparing their dinner. Later, she tickled Liquorice's soft, furry belly for some time afterwards, deep in thought, while the cat purred with unconcerned pleasure. Again, she peeped from behind the closed curtains, but there was no sign of Tom.

Next day, washing day, presented something of a dilemma, since it was her custom to take the laundry round to the Briscos' and work on it with Florrie. But, after she had taken Posy to school, she returned home and did the laundry herself. She nattered over the wall to Mrs Bellfield next door and related the bad news about Ned. Tom could not come today; he would be at work, and then have to collect Daniel from his mother's house.

On Tuesday she ran into Zillah Bache and told her the sad news.

'So what'n yer gunna do about money?' Zillah asked, typically.

Clover shrugged. 'I don't know. I don't know whether I'm entitled to anything as a war widow or what. My allowance for his military service will stop. I'll have to find a job, I suppose.'

'You could always work at the Jolly Collier.'

'Never,' she scoffed.

A week went by and still no sign of Tom. Clover's yearning to discover what was wrong turned to impatience, then from impatience to animosity. Well, if he ever did come now, she would be so cold and indifferent towards him... She was fed up with his deliberately avoiding her, fed up with his lack of care and consideration.

The postman delivered a parcel with Army markings on it. She signed for it. Ned's things, obviously. Half-heartedly, she cut the string that was wrapped around it and broke the seal. Gingerly, she opened it. There was a letter inside addressed to herself. She opened that first and read it. It was from a Major Camplin, Ned's Commanding Officer. It told of his bravery in battle, of his natural flair for aviation and expressed deepest regrets at the beastly loss of a beloved husband and father. His remains would be interred in a military cemetery in France. The letter was rather more personal and rather more poignant than the telegram she had received a week earlier. Major Camplin went on to say how Ned's belongings had been hastily assembled and despatched as soon as it had been expedient, and he trusted she was comforted to have his personal effects returned.

Clover put down the letter and looked into the cardboard box. There was nothing of any significance except for the japanned metal money-box he'd taken with him, which she took out and tried to open. It was locked. A lot of small change was rattling about inside, albeit rather restrictedly. She rummaged through the cardboard box for the key but there was no key. Of course, he would have been carrying it with him when he was killed. It was lost now. A thought struck her; there might be a spare key in his tallboy. She trotted upstairs, scavenged the backs of its shelves and then the drawers in his chest until she came across a small metal key. If this failed to open the box then she would have to ask if Mr Bellfield next door could prize it open. Downstairs again she went to the table and offered the key to the japanned box. It slid in easily. To her surprise, it turned easily too. She opened the lid.

Inside lay a small pile of envelopes all tied together with white fabric tape. Letters from Florrie, no doubt. There were coins and bank notes, a whole treasure-trove, money he must have saved. She was aware that, as a flyer, his pay was many times that of an ordinary soldier, so he was evidently able to save. Well, he neither gambled nor drank, nor smoked either. She counted out the money. Forty-five pounds; enough, with the money she had herself saved, to pay off that damned loan. At last. Thank God she would be free of it. She would deliver it next week. But she was so ashamed it had taken so long to repay, she didn't feel brazen enough to show her own face. She would send Zillah to Julian Oakley at the *Dudley Herald* with the money and her apologies – and ask him for a receipt, of course. She put it all in the loan jar.

She turned her attention again to the envelopes. Just what did Florrie have to say to her absent son? She opened one, withdrew the letter and was struck by the sweet scent of a pleasant perfume ... Florrie's?

My dearest, darling Edward,
It has been three long months since you went away from me and I am counting the days till you return in May. May is always a delight in Hampshire and I so look forward to your leave, (you can't imagine how much) when I can show you more of it...

With a perplexed frown, Clover glanced at the address; Fareham. He had been sent to Hampshire for his training – and he'd evidently been due to return there for some leave; leave Clover knew nothing about...
The monkey!...
She realised she was smiling. So, he'd found himself a lady friend. Good for him. She read on...

Violet Lingfield came to see me yesterday complete with three incredibly energetic and friendly dogs which much cheered me up. She was kind enough to bring me chocolate which I find such a comfort on these long, lonely days and nights. All in all she and the dogs had an enormously cheering effect on me. She believes her husband is presently in the Dardanelles on his battleship, Albion. She's missing him terribly and is so worried that they might get torpedoed. Thank God Rodney is in the Pacific. He might get torpedoed too, but even if he doesn't, at least he won't be home before May when you return to me, my love.

Oh, my true darling, I am so longing to see you, to feel your arms about me...

A married lady, Clover reflected, a Navy wife, and no mention of any children. Well, wasn't Ned a dark horse? She read on, picking up more and more of Ned's intimate secrets. The letter was signed, *Evelina*. Clover smiled again to herself, not out of disdain, but out of pleasure. It made her feel so much better knowing that Ned had found love at last, however fleeting. He deserved some devotion in his life.

She sat down and opened another letter... Full of love and yearning, the intense, recorded feelings of somebody who had found a true soulmate and who was acutely missing him. Clover began to feel unutterable sadness for Evelina, and for Ned. She finished that letter and opened another. The sentiments were the same. This time Evelina referred to his last letter when she told him how reassuring it was to read his expressions of love and to note how much he was missing her. Another letter confirmed that they had spent time together in May and referred to romantic incidents that meant something special to them both. Well, it was quite developing into something of a love story.

Clover read them all. The sadness that had eluded her over Ned's death hit her now like a forge hammer. Poor, poor Ned. He had found love at last, albeit with a married woman, but he had not lived long enough to enjoy it. Life was too short. That fact had been pointed out to her before when Ramona died. All that mattered was being happy. All that counted was finding your one true love and making the most of the joy you brought each other, not the heartache. Avoid the heartache, whatever it took. If only Tom could realise that. Poor, poor Evelina.

It struck her that maybe poor Evelina would be wondering why she had received no mail from Ned over the last week or so. So she was moved to take her writing-pad from the drawer in the sideboard, and her pen and ink.

Dear Mrs McMichael,
It is with very great regret that I write to inform you that my husband, Edward Brisco of 14 Squadron, Royal Flying Corps, was killed in action over Champagne on the 15th of July. I am aware of his relationship with you, and I do not mind one bit. I am beholden to you for giving him the love and affection he deserved that I could not give him. I am only sorry that he has been snatched from you too soon.

Do not feel obliged to reply to this note, but if you do, I shall consider it an honour. At least you brought him some happiness where I failed. I am left with those of his personal possessions that have survived. If there is anything of his that you would like as a keepsake, please do not be afraid to ask.

In the meantime, I remain,
Yours very sincerely
Clover Brisco

She would have offered all her letters back but she did not feel inclined to let Mrs McMichael know she had been nosy enough to read them. In any case, Mrs McMichael would not want evidence of her extra-marital affair with Ned to incriminate her when her husband returned home, even if she was not happy in her marriage. Rather, Clover had another idea of what to do with those letters.

She went out into the warm sunshine and called Posy who was playing hopscotch in the street with other children. She asked if she was all right. The child answered that she was and, fearing being dragged away to accompany her mother, begged not to be.

'I'm going to see Granny and Granddad Brisco...'

'I don't care,' she rigorously pouted. 'I want to stay here and play.'

'All right. I'll be half an hour. Be good. You know where I am if you want me.'

Clover shoved the letters, once more tied up in Ned's tape, into the pocket of her skirt and made her way to the Briscos'. Rather than walk in without knocking, as she always used to, she tapped on the back door.

Florrie answered. 'Oh, it's you.'

'Can I come in?' Florrie opened the door wider and stepped aside as Clover entered. 'The Army sent back Ned's things and I got them this morning,' she explained. 'I think you should have these...' She handed Florrie the bundle.

'His letters?'

'Letters from his lady friend–'

'Lady friend?' Florrie snapped sternly.

'Yes, his lady friend. A Mrs Evelina Mc-Michael. She was evidently very fond of him, and he was fond of her as well.'

'I tek it as you've read 'em, then?' Florrie sounded disapproving.

'They actually belong to me, Florrie, as does anything that was Ned's. He had a leave from duty in May. Evidently he spent it with Mrs Mc-Michael in Hampshire. I just wondered whether he'd told you about her. His last letter to you told you all about me and my affair with Tom Doubleday ... I just wondered if he'd said more... Something about her...'

Florrie hesitated to reply.

Clover went on. 'I'm just sorry that he was snatched away from happiness before he had the chance to enjoy it, Florrie. She sounds a very nice lady, despite the fact that she's married. I've already written to her to tell her about Ned's death, but once you've read the letters I daresay you'll be moved to write to her as well. I suggest you don't judge her too harshly yet. I think she was as unhappy in her marriage as Ned was in his.'

Still Florrie said nothing.

Clover turned to go. 'Oh – and by the way – I haven't given you all Mrs McMichael's letters. I kept one ... I'd thought about showing it to Zillah Bache, but then I realised you probably wouldn't like me to do that in case word got around, especially as I imagine you've said nothing to anybody about me and my friendship with Tom Doubleday – well, at least I hope you haven't...'

Still there was no response.

'I'd better go now, Florrie. Posy is playing in the street and she'll fret if I'm away too long. Cheerio.'

'Clover...'

Clover turned to Florrie.

'Clover... Don't let's fall out, eh?... Call and see us... As often as you've a mind. You see, we don't want to lose Posy as well as Ned. That would break our hearts even more...' Florrie tilted her spectacles up and wiped tears from her eyes. 'And I'm that sorry about us having words the other day. You can't imagine how upset I've been, what with everything an' all.'

'I know...' Clover touched her arm reassuringly, guilty that she too had been unfeeling, too brusque. 'Don't worry, Florrie. We shan't neglect you. There was never any intention to.'

On the following Wednesday, Tom Doubleday had a visit at his studio from Julian Oakley of the *Dudley Herald*. Tom was surprised to see him and his first thought was that he wanted to commission him to take some photographs. He greeted his visitor cordially and, with his usual hospitality, asked if he would like a cup of tea.

'No thanks, Tom,' Julian replied. 'I've got something for you. I just wanted to get rid of it and wend my way back to the office.' He felt in his briefcase that he'd put on the table and pulled out an envelope that was stuffed with paper. 'Looks like that loan you made to Ned Brisco has finally been repaid.'

Tom looked at him in open-mouthed disbelief

as he took it from Julian.

'Well, aren't you going to count it?'

'Did Clover bring it in?'

Julian shook his head. 'No, it wasn't Clover. Unless Clover has turned into a big fat old woman since the last time I saw her. Whoever it was, she made certain I gave her a receipt.'

'Zillah Bache. Clover would've sent Zillah with it.'

'Well, aren't you going to count it? Aren't you going to make sure I ain't pinched any? It's all there, I can assure you. All two hundred pounds.'

'Good God!' Tom said quietly. 'I never expected her to... Not the way things are. Not in her straits.'

'Her straits? I thought she was married now – to Ned.'

Tom explained that Ned had been killed in action.

'Never! I'll run a piece on him in the *Herald*. But the poor madam,' Julian remarked solemnly. 'You and she had a bit of a fling a few years ago, eh, Tom?'

Tom nodded.

'Handsome-looking piece, as I recall. I don't suppose she's changed that much. You're a widower now, eh, Tom? Why don't you pay her a visit? I bet she needs a bit of comfort to get over the shock. She'd appreciate that. You could get back into her good books. Who knows where it might lead? Dammit, I've a good mind I'd go myself.'

Tom sighed. 'Can you keep a secret, Julian?'

'Sure.'

'Clover and me have been seeing each other for a couple of years now. The day she heard about her husband being killed I upset her by letting her think I didn't want her.'

'You what? You heartless bastard!'

Tom shrugged. 'I know. It all flared up in a minute. I was trying to explain but she wouldn't give me time. She suddenly left in a huff and I thought, oh, she'll get out of her mood soon enough. But she hasn't. I keep waiting for her to come back and say she's sorry.'

'Bloody hell, Tom. The way I see it, you're the one who should be apologising. Fancy putting her through that when she'd just had that dreadful news about her husband, whether or not she was still in love with him. She must have been upset to start with, and then you rubbed salt into her wound. You're a heartless bounder, Tom Doubleday. I would never have thought it.'

'I saw it as her fault...'

'Evidently, she doesn't. Neither do I. Christ! How could you treat a poor grieving woman so?'

'She wasn't grieving that much.'

'I expect she needed comforting nonetheless. It would still have come as a shock. And you turned her away.'

'Think I should go and make it up to her?'

'Don't *you* think so? Especially now she's paid off his debt as well.'

'But she never knew it was me who lent the money in the first place.'

'All the more reason to go and see her.'

Tom grabbed his appointment's book and flipped it open. 'I'll go right now. I've got nobody else coming this afternoon.'

Julian made his exit and Tom packed the large envelope into his hold-all and locked up his studio. When he arrived at Clover's house in Hill Street he tapped on the door and waited.

Clover was sitting in the scullery mending one of Posy's frocks. She was thinking about Tom Doubleday at that very moment. When she heard the tap at the front door she put down her mending and answered it.

'Tom!' All at once her resolve to be haughty with him vaporised and she found her legs trembling. 'Won't you come in?'

It was the first time he had ever been in her house. It was not like his own. The furniture here was well-worn, shabby. There was a darn in the tablecloth and a hole in the teacloth that hung over the fire grate on the drying-rack. There was no fire, just a few pieces of screwed-up newspaper and some sticks of wood in the fire basket, ready to burn but not alight. The fire grate was black-leaded to perfection, the curtains were fresh and everything was spotlessly clean; but he saw here evidence of financial hardship compared to his own modest but comfortable home.

'What brings you here? I wasn't expecting you.'

'Well, Clover, I think there are one or two things we need to discuss.'

'Oh? Such as?' She sounded indifferent, her animosity revealing itself at having been neglected and avoided for too long.

'I think you know.'

'Can I make you a cup of tea or something?'

'Later maybe. First, I want to get one or two

things straight.'

'Sit down then.' Her heart was beating fast and her tongue seemed to fur up with dryness. 'So what do you want to get straight?'

'You and me.' He sat down biddably and shifted the hold-all so that it sat on the floor between his legs. 'I apologise for being so ... so unsympathetic the other Saturday. I should've realised you were upset having just heard about Ned. I wasn't much help, was I? I'm really sorry, Clover. I feel very guilty about it.'

She shrugged, merely pretending to be indifferent now.

'You see,' he continued, 'I've been in love with you for so long, and too many times we've been on the verge of committing ourselves finally to each other then had it snatched away at the last minute... What I'm trying to say is, although I've loved you for so long, because you were married to Ned I never really expected us to be able to become man and wife. It's not that I don't want you, Clover. It's just that, suddenly faced with the opportunity, it struck me that over these last few years I'd overlooked two important facts that would affect such a circumstance and...' He shook his head, and she looked into eyes that revealed his sincerity and the struggle within him as he tried to choose the right words. 'Well, before I say anything more, I need to know how you feel. Otherwise I might be wasting my time explaining.'

'I feel hurt and angry that all of a sudden you should shun me after all we've meant to each other,' she replied vehemently. 'You turned away from me as if I was just a casual bit on the side and you were safe from having to marry me. But as soon as you realise I'm suddenly marriageable again you run a mile. How am I supposed to feel?'

'But do you still love me?'

'I don't know,' she answered sullenly.

'You must know, Clover. You just can't turn love on and off like a tap.'

'*You* can, apparently.'

'I can't. If I could I would've turned off my love for you ages ago, because sometimes it's just too painful to bear.'

'Says you.'

'Yes, says I. And it's the truth. I still love you, Clover, with all my heart... Always I've wanted to be your husband. Ever since I've known you...' He paused.

'But?' She could sense there was a but ... and this was the crux of the matter.

'But there's Posy to consider.'

'She'd like nothing better than for us to be married. She'd have a permanent playmate in Daniel.'

'I wasn't thinking of it from Posy's point of view, Clover...'

'From whose then? Mine?'

He shook his head. 'No... Mine... You see, I'm not sure I could cope with taking on another man's child.'

'*What?*'

At once Clover burst into tears, unable to cope with the unspeakable irony of his unwitting presumption. She could have hit him. She wanted to

562

hit him. She *would* hit him, damn him. So she punched him on the shoulder as hard as she could and hurt her fist. But this was worth hurting her fist for. She punched him again, incensed that he was such a prize fool, that never in his life had he bothered to count months, that he accepted everything at face value, while he winced under the pummelling. Unsuspecting, he had taken on Elijah Tandy's child as his own. Yet his own flesh and blood he did not recognise. He deserved a good thumping.

'Stop fighting me,' he earnestly beseeched, trying to defend himself by parrying her punches. 'Christ, you fight like a man.' He grabbed her wrists and held them. As she quieted, drained of strength and emotion at his exasperating lack of guile, he looked into her eyes and saw her tears of anguish. 'I can't help the way I feel, Clover. I have to be honest with you.'

'It's time *I* was honest with *you*, Tom Doubleday,' she croaked, her voice hot with fervour. 'Let go my wrists... *Let go my wrists!*'

'Only if you'll stop thumping me. What d'you think I am, a punchbag?'

'Oh, I could *kill* you,' she shrilled. 'You're so stupid. You're such a fool.'

'That much I know. But in what particular this time?'

'Posy *is* your child, Tom... Oh, you great lump...' She broke a wrist free and hit him again. 'Did you never bother to work it out? Did it never occur to you why I didn't marry Ned until the very last minute? Well, I'll tell you. It was because I wouldn't let him sacrifice himself on another

563

man's child. If the child had been Ned's, don't you think it might have suggested I was in love with the poor devil? In which case I would have married him earlier. But you, in your blindness, never thought that deeply about it, did you?'

Tom looked as if he was in a state of shock.

'And what about me? Did it ever occur to you how I might feel about taking on Daniel? Another woman's child?' This would have been the perfect opportunity to enlighten him as to Daniel's parentage, but still she could not do it. She could not fulfil Ramona's dying request. It would introduce too much trauma, too much hurt. Both Tom and Daniel would suffer. There had been suffering enough already. As far as she was concerned, the secret died with Ramona.

He ignored her question. He had not heard it. He was totally preoccupied with what he had just been told. Posy was his own daughter? She was his? Not Ned's?

'I had no idea, Clover,' he uttered quietly.

'God, you only have to look at her. She's the image of you.'

'She's the image of you, Clover.'

'To you. But not to me. I can see you in her all the time. Look next time and you'll see it yourself.'

'And there is no doubt about this?'

She rolled her eyes in impatience. 'I have never been with anybody but you, Tom. Not even Ned... Not all the time we were married. Not *ever.*'

'You didn't?'

'Never.'

'But this puts an entirely different slant on things... If she's my child...' He broke down, put his hand to his face and his shoulders started shuddering.

Clover sat beside him and put her arms around his shoulders. She ran her fingers lovingly through his hair while he wept uncontrollably, overcome by emotion for his daughter and all those lost years he had never spent with her.

'Oh, Tom,' she cooed softly, consolingly, hugging him tight. For some minutes she held him like this, realising what an absolute shock it must be.

'I never realised,' he blubbered. 'All that time... You were carrying Posy ... at the same time Ramona was carrying Daniel. If only I'd known... Why didn't you let me know? I would never have married Ramona...'

'I couldn't let you know, Tom, because I didn't know myself till after you were married,' she whispered calmly. 'Besides, if I'd done that, it would have been just as terrible for Ramona. Better this way, I think.'

'You must have felt terrible. It must have been awful for you...'

'My mother knew,' she said and stroked his cheek, avoiding his question. 'There was no fooling Mary Ann. But she couldn't say anything because of Jake – because he was your father-in-law ... Zillah knows as well. But she's sworn to secrecy.'

'And Ned ... Ned was still prepared to marry you, carrying another man's child?'

'Yes.'

'God,' he sniffed. 'He's more of a hero than ever I gave him credit for. He's a better man than me, Clover. I feel so ashamed now at what I said a few minutes ago ... at being reticent about taking on Posy.'

She gave him another hug. 'Well, at least you know the truth now.'

'Why did you never tell me before?'

'Out of respect for Ned. While he was seen to be Posy's father there seemed no point in gainsaying it.'

'No, I suppose not.' He took a handkerchief from his pocket and dried his eyes. 'I feel such a dope, Clover,' he sniffed. 'But at least it's determined one thing.'

'Which is?'

'That we'd be fools not to get married. Will you marry me, Clover? Say you'll marry me. We're a family, for God's sake. We should be together.'

She sighed, a profound sigh. 'That's all I've ever dreamed of, Tom. Of course I'll marry you. After a suitable time. How long do you think is a suitable time?'

'I don't know, sweetheart. Three months? Two months? A week?'

She laughed. The first time she'd laughed in ages. 'As soon as we can. I don't feel so bad about Ned any more... All his things came back... He had a lady friend, you know...' She explained, and Tom made some comment about him being a dark horse. 'At least he didn't get himself killed deliberately over me, which had crossed my mind. He had something to live for after all.'

'You know, I'm glad for him, Clover – about his lady friend, I mean.'

'So am I... So shall we live at your house in Salop Street? I want to get away from here. There are too many sad memories here.'

'As you wish,' he said, and kissed her on the lips as if to set a seal on it.

'I'll make that cup of tea now.'

'No, wait... There's something else...'

'Oh, Lord,' she replied with a sigh of apprehension. 'What?'

He felt between his shins and opened his hold-all. He withdrew the thick envelope and placed it in her lap.

'What's this?' she asked with a puzzled frown.

'Your money. Take it back.'

'My money?' She laughed as if he was perpetrating some outrageous tease. 'What are you talking about?'

'The loan that was made to Ned – how long ago? – seven years? That two hundred pounds.'

'So?'

'Well, I have a secret as well... It was me that loaned the money.'

'You? I don't believe you.'

'It's true nevertheless. It was me.'

'What ever possessed you? You must have been mad.'

He shrugged. 'I think I *was* mad. But I also felt guilty. Do you remember those photos of him and his *Gull* that I sold to the *Dudley Herald?* Ned believed that the five guineas I got for them should be his to go towards an engine. Do you remember?'

'Yes. Now you mention it, I do.'

'I just felt I had to make amends.' He shrugged and sighed. 'In any case, I admired then what Ned was trying to do. I just wanted to help him on his way...'

She sighed with exasperation. 'Tom Doubleday, you're a bigger fool than ever I thought you were. But why are you now trying to hand me more money ... I don't deserve it. Just because I'm his widow—'

'It's your money.'

'How can it be?'

He laughed. 'Now you're teasing me. You evidently sent somebody to repay it earlier today.'

'I did no such thing. As a matter of fact, I was going to do it tomorrow. Here...' She got up and went to the cupboard where she kept her jar. She grabbed it and waved it at him. It was full of money. 'I've been saving for it for years. Then, when Ned's things came back there was more money in that. Enough, with what I'd saved, to pay off everything.'

'So where did this money come from?' he asked, mystified, waving the envelope in front of him.

'How should I know?'

'Zillah delivered it to Julian Oakley this morning. At least, the description fits her. He brought it to me straight away. I assumed you'd asked her to deliver it.'

'Zillah? Oh, no,' she cried animatedly, realising she'd discussed not yet paying the loan with her. 'Zillah can't afford it. Oh, I'll have to go and pay her back...'

568

'Then let's go together,' he suggested. 'We could announce to her that we're getting married.'

Chapter Thirty-Two

Clover collected Posy from the Board School while Tom went to his mother's house to tell her he would be late collecting Daniel. Then the three of them sat down together for tea, and after six o'clock they walked to Zillah's house in High Street, Kates Hill, Posy between them holding the hand of each like the new family they were. It would have been pointless visiting her before then, since she would still be at the Jolly Collier working. When they arrived, they walked up the entry in single file and Clover, who headed the small procession, knocked gently on the back door.

'Hang me!' Zillah exclaimed when she saw them. 'Come on in.'

At once Zillah made a fuss of Posy and held her on her lap while Tom and Clover flashed affectionate glances at each other as they explained everything.

'Well I'm that pleased as you'm a-going to get wed, the pair of year,' Zillah proclaimed. 'It's a pity you missed one another the fust time round though. So when's it gunna be?'

'We don't know yet, do we, Tom? After a suitable period of mourning, though. It's only fair.'

'So ask her about the money,' Tom prompted, anxious to get the matter clarified.

'Money?' Zillah gave Clover a sheepish look.

'Yes, Zillah, what about all that money you paid to cover that loan? It was very kind of you, but we've brought it back. You can't afford it and I won't let you pay it. I'd saved up enough to pay it off myself and I was about to tomorrow.'

Tom reached into his hold-all again and pulled out the envelope containing the two hundred pounds. He placed it on the scrubbed wooden table in front of him.

'Well, there's no sense in denying as I took it,' Zillah said. 'But how did you know it was me?'

'Because Tom was the one who originally lent it Ned. When Julian described you—'

'*Tom* lent it? To Ned? Christ, Tom, you must have more perishing money than sense.'

Tom distorted his mouth in a look of resignation and nodded. 'It seems that way.'

'Well, I got news for the pair of yer,' Zillah said with a gleam in her eye. 'It wasn't me as coughed up. I mean, it ain't my money, so you'd best have it back.' There was a look of self-satisfaction on her big, round face.

'So who did pay it then, if it wasn't you?'

'Who d'you think? It was your mother. It was Mary Ann.'

'My mother?' Clover glanced at Tom incredulous. 'She'd never do that, Zillah. I'm not in her good books.'

'Clover, as sure as I'm sitting here, your mother gi'd me that money to tek to pay off that loan. I happened to mention to her the other day about it, when I told her as Ned had got killed over France. I told her as I was worried about yer, as how I didn't know how on earth you was a-going to manage, specially as that loan hadn't bin paid.'

'But my mother?' Clover said again.

'Yes, and she can afford it these days. But if you'll tek my advice, the pair of you, you'll go and see her. Go and mek your peace with her, Clover. I know Mary Ann as well as I know meself, and her's a-mythering to see you and to meet her granddaughter. Why else do you think her did it?'

Clover and Tom exchanged glances again, seeking consensus.

'I think you should,' he said. 'It was a grand gesture.'

'Be ruled by me, Clover – go and mek your peace. And don't forget to tell her that you and young Tom here am gunna be wed.'

'But what about Jake?' Clover asked warily. 'What's he likely to say?'

'Jake's a reasonable man, Clover,' Zillah said. 'As you know well enough. Just tell him the truth. He understands the ways of the world. If there's one bloke on God's earth as will be pleased about you and Tom, it's Jake Tandy. He might even get to see his grandson a bit more often when you'm wed.'

'Come with me then, Tom.'

'Course I will.' He stood up at once. 'Let's go now. I can pay your mother her money back.'

'Zillah, you're a treasure, and I love you.' Clover said, as she stood up and kissed the old lady. 'Come on, Posy. Leave Aunty Zillah alone now and we'll take you to meet you Grandma Tandy. She'll let you have some ginger beer, I bet.'

During the short walk to the Jolly Collier Tom and Clover speculated on the sort of reception they were likely to encounter while Posy speculated on what her unknown grandmother might look like.

'Is she big and fat, like Grandma Florrie and Auntie Zillah?' she asked.

'Not the last time I saw her,' Clover replied. 'She's quite slender for her age... But then, she wears a corset,' she added mischievously.

'So does Grandma Florrie, but she's fat,' Posy reasoned.

They reached the Jolly Collier in George Street. Clover held Posy's hand as she and Tom looked at each other, summoning the courage to enter.

'The taproom?' he queried.

She shook her head. 'The scullery. She'll be in there clearing up after tea. Jake will be in the taproom. I'd like to see Mother on her own first – without Jake, I mean.'

He nodded his understanding and they walked along the passage, Clover first. The place looked eminently more spruce than last time she saw it. Everything had been repainted, was clean and bright and welcoming. But the familiar smell of beer and tobacco smoke remained, evoking a thousand memories and as many doubts. They walked past the closed doors of the taproom and the snug, and carried straight on down the passage, conscious of their footfalls on the newly re-laid quarry-tiled floor. The door to the scullery was ajar and Clover caught sight of Mary Ann working at the sink, her back towards her. Clover gently pushed open the door, her heart beating fast.

'Mother...'

Mary Ann looked over her shoulder, then seemed to reel, putting her hands to her breast as she realised it was her long-gone daughter. She snatched up a cloth, quickly dried her hands and seemed to leap towards Clover. She flung her arms around Clover's shoulders and drew her close.

'Clover... Oh, my babby...' She held her daughter tight, uttering a string of impassioned words that were largely unintelligible in the sudden upsurge of emotion. 'Oh, I've missed you, our Clover. God knows how I've missed you... Why as you never come a-nigh? Why did you leave me to myther, to grieve? I've worried meself sick...'

'Oh, Mother...' As she screwed up her eyes in this moving embrace there was a lump in her throat and she tried to force back tears that would not be stemmed. The two women, mother and daughter, unexpectedly but magically no longer estranged, held each other tight for some time, trying to compensate for all the empty years they had not set eyes on each other, those long, long years when scorn, defiance and a lack of compassion had conspired to keep them apart. Now all those negative forces seemed distant and irrelevant.

'I've brought somebody to see you,' Clover said, smiling through her tears. She stood aside so Mary Ann could cast eyes on her granddaughter for the first time.

Mary Ann sighed profoundly. 'This is Josephine?' She held out her arms as she swept towards her, then scooped the child up and hugged her tight.

'We call her Posy,' Clover said, wiping her tears but laughing now.

'Posy?... Let me have a good look at you, my little flower.' Mary Ann scrutinised Posy's face. 'I thought the day would never come when I would cast my eyes on you, you little angel... Well, you'm like your mommy and no two ways wi' your dark hair and your big blue eyes.' She wiped away more tears and smiled with infinite pleasure at the child. 'I daresay you'll break a few more hearts as well when you get older.'

'Do you wear a corset?'

'I do, young lady,' she answered straight-faced and looked at Clover suspiciously. Clover cringed but saw the expression in Mary Ann's eyes, saw that she was not offended, merely amused. This was indeed a changed Mary Ann. 'And when you grow up you'll wear a corset as well, if you've got any sense. Don't listen to what your mother tells you about corsets.'

'Tom's here as well,' Clover said, interrupting Mary Ann's sincere advice.

Mary Ann clung to Posy proprietorially. 'Tom... By God, I reckon I ought to be surprised at seeing you... But after hearing about our Clover's husband being killed p'raps I shouldn't be. I know what you two meant to each other. Does this mean you'm about to sort yourselves out at last? It's about time...'

574

'We're about to sort ourselves out, Mrs Tandy,' Tom affirmed. 'But we'd like your blessing – and Mr Tandy's.'

'Specially Mr Tandy's, eh? Since you was married to Ramona before and you'm the father of her child? Well, you'll be able to ask him for it soon enough and I daresay he'll be happy enough to give it. But sit yourselves down. Let me put the kettle on... No, no, let's have summat stronger. This is a time to celebrate. And we've got a lot to talk about.'

Clover smiled and sat down. 'So where shall we begin?'

'Oh, we'll find a beginning somewhere. We've already got a happy ending by the looks of it.' She gave the child another squeeze. 'I'm that glad to see you at last, my little flower, you'm beautiful and I'm gunna spoil you rotten...' She turned to Clover. 'We've got a woman comes to work in the taproom nights nowadays. Her husband's away in France, fighting. Her'll be here in a minute or two. Then, Clover, you can go and ask Jacob to come in here.'

'Well before I do,' Clover said, and glanced at Tom. 'That money you sent to pay Ned's loan off...'

'What about it?'

'It was very kind of you, Mother, but I'd already saved enough money myself. I was actually going to deliver it tomorrow. Tom's got it in his bag to give you back. It was Tom that lent it in the first place, you see.'

'It's true, Mrs Tandy,' Tom admitted. 'And my conscience won't allow me to accept your money

575

in payment, generous as it is.'

'You'm intending to get married, ain't yer?' Mary Ann asked, unfazed.

'That's the general idea,' Tom replied.

'Then consider it me wedding present. I won't take it back. It's enough to buy a decent house and no mistake. Better than renting, I can tell yer. Tek a tip from me and buy yourselves a nice house... Our Posy, I'll have to put you down. You'm a weight on me poor arms. Here, I'll sit down and you can sit on me lap, eh?'

'That's more than generous, Mother,' Clover said. She bent over and gave Mary Ann a kiss on the cheek. 'Thank you.'

As Tom echoed the sentiment, Jake appeared at the door and there was a broad grin trying to escape from under his massive moustache. 'Charlie Harris just told me as he'd seen you three come in. Lil's here now so I thought I'd come and pay me respects. By God, it's bin a long time, Clover, but it's nice to see you again. And Tom...' They shook hands. 'How's me grandson since last I saw him?'

'Oh, he's well, Jake.'

'Good, I'm glad.' He looked from one to the other and spoke to Posy, ruffling her hair gently as she sat contentedly on her new grandmother's lap, enjoying the attention. 'And you'm a pretty little thing, eh? You must be Josephine?'

'Posy,' Mary Ann enlightened him.

'Posy, eh? Well, God bless you, Posy... It's good to see all three of you. So is anybody gunna to tell me what this is all about, or can I guess?'

Tom felt it his duty to explain and did so, fully.

'But what I want you to understand, Jake, is that Posy is actually my own flesh and blood. She's *my* daughter, Jake, not Ned's at all, contrary to what you've believed all this time. I didn't know myself till today. I did right by Ramona, Jake, as you know. But Ramona's gone – and so has Ned. Now I want to do right by Clover. So, as soon as we can, we want to get wed ... Jake, it'd mean a lot to both of us if we could have your blessing.'

'Have me blessing?' Jake queried. 'Course you can have me blessing. I ain't daft. I could always see how it was with you two. Good lad! I'm pleased for yer. There's no fun being a widower, and I should know.' They shook hands again. 'I'm pleased for all three of you – all four, 'cause you can't not count Daniel, can you? Hey, the sadness and the heartache is in the past, Tom. Get wed, the pair of yer, and enjoy the rest of your lives together.'

'We should celebrate this, Jacob, with summat decent to drink,' Mary Ann chipped in with an enthusiasm the like of which Clover had never witnessed. 'Have we got summat special in the cellar as we can open?'

'I do believe we have,' Jake said brightly. 'There's a crate of champagne left over from Coronation Day. I'll fetch two or three bottles, eh? And don't forget as Elijah and Dorcas am a-coming tonight as well.' He took the fob watch out of his waistcoat pocket and checked the time. 'Why, they'll be here any minute, I bet. Looks like we'm in for a proper family get together tonight, eh? And about time.'

As Jake left them to fetch the bottles from the

cellar, Clover said: 'Elijah and Dorcas ... I haven't seen them for years. How are they?'

'Oh, they seem all right,' Mary Ann replied. 'Elijah's working hard in the business. The brewery's thriving and he keeps trying special brews.'

'And Dorcas?'

'Helping her father run his firm. He's bin ever so poorly and Dorcas started to help him out. Now I think she runs the show.'

'No children then yet?'

'I reckon they've bin too busy to think about kids, Clover.'

'Fancy,' Clover said, pondering. 'I take it their marriage is a success?'

'They seem happy enough,' Mary Ann responded. 'I take it yours wasn't?'

Clover glanced at Tom, then at Posy sitting with her head resting on Mary Ann's shoulder as she quietly watched her grandmother talking. 'Hardly. It was doomed from the start. I think it was only Ned who never realised it.'

'Well, the truth's out now, that's all that matters. Posy'll soon get used to Tom, I daresay.' She turned to her granddaughter. 'Tom's going to be your new daddy. You'll like that won't you?'

Posy nodded and smiled coyly. 'Does that mean Daniel will be my brother?'

'Stepbrother. You'll be his stepsister.'

Posy smiled cheerfully. 'Can I have some ginger beer, please?'

'Course you can, my flower, when Granddad Jacob comes back from the cellar.

'What d'you think is a decent gap after Ned's

death for us to get married, Mother?' Clover asked.

'That's up to you, our Clover. Normally folk would reckon on two years—'

'Two years?' she said incredulously.

'Maybe in view of the truth of the circumstances, one year.'

'No, we're not waiting a whole year, Mother. Three months at the outside.'

'Oh? Am yer pregnant again then?'

'No...' She laughed self-consciously. 'Course I'm not pregnant. It's just that we don't want to wait more than three months.'

'Well, suit yourselves. It's nobody's business but your own.'

Jake returned carrying three bottles of champagne. He set them on the table and set about opening the first. 'I tek it as you'll have a bit of a do here on your wedding day?'

'Oh, I should think so, if that's all right with you,' Clover said, and Tom nodded his agreement.

They heard footsteps in the passage and everybody fell quiet waiting for the door to open. Elijah walked in, followed by Dorcas. Dorcas had put on weight though her face was just as lovely, while Elijah simply looked older and leaner.

'Jesus, look who's here,' he exclaimed in astonishment. 'Well, I'm buggered, if it ain't Clover and Tom. And who's this pretty little madam here?'

Elijah made a great fuss of Posy. Dorcas fussed around Clover, took a kiss on the cheek from Tom and introduced herself to Posy. Elijah and

Dorcas also had to have the latest news and developments and duly congratulated Clover and Tom on their imminent marriage. Jake fetched some glasses from the taproom, poured the champagne and several different, separate, animated conversations developed, during which time Clover found herself conversing alone with Elijah. He wanted to know all about Ned and what had gone wrong with her marriage and she told him, all the time conscious that here was the real father of Ramona's son, conscious that everything that had occurred since the child's conception had been a direct consequence of it.

'And what about you and Dorcas?' she said evenly. 'No children yet?'

'There's no sign, Clover,' Elijah answered. 'Nor is there likely to be.'

'Oh?'

'I've been to see the doctor a few times. I mean, when you've been married more than seven years and there's no sign of e'er a babby, you begin to wonder, especially when you do your bedtime duty regular. He had me in and did some probing about in me nether regions. He reckons there's some congenital defect. He told me I'm not capable of fathering a child...'

Clover tried to conceal her utter astonishment. 'Does Dorcas know this?' she asked stupidly. Suddenly, she thought of Ramona believing she'd had his child, and her mind was in a whirl of confusion. If Elijah was incapable of fathering a child, which of them was Daniel's father?

'Oh, course she knows. But what can we do? She gets ever so broody. She'd love a child.'

'I'm flabbergasted, Elijah,' she proclaimed. 'Is there no cure? Can't you have surgery to rectify the problem?'

'The doctor said I could, but it'd be bloody uncomfortable and there'd be no guarantee as it'd work.'

'I would have thought it more likely that the problem lies with Dorcas,' Clover suggested, unconvinced. 'You'll just have to keep trying. The doctor might be wrong.'

'I hope he is.'

Clover Brisco, née Beckitt, was married on Sunday 7th November 1915 for the second time and realised the one true ambition, that at one time looked as though it would elude her for ever, in taking the name Doubleday. The ceremony was held at St John's Parish Church on Kates Hill and the bride, statuesque in a beautiful cream brocade dress diligently made by Bessie Roberts of Brown Street, was given away by her step-father, Jake Tandy. James Doubleday, the groom's brother, was best man. The stark contrast between the two bridesmaids – Posy in a tiny red dress, Zillah Bache in a huge one – was regarded with benign amusement among the guests and elicited even greater affection for both. Daniel, fair-haired and looking innately more angelic than his mother had ever contrived to, was pageboy. Mary Ann, once the indifferent mother and now the doting grandmother was moved to tears.

The celebrations afterwards were naturally held at the Jolly Collier, where drinks flowed freely and Lil Bowater, the recently acquired barmaid, demonstrated unanticipated catering skills by preparing a fine beef dinner for all the guests. Clover sat with the new husband she adored on one side and Jake occupied the other. While Zillah and the children occupied Tom, Jake engaged Clover in conversation and, the more he drank, the more he seemed inclined towards sentimentality.

'I love your mother, you know, Clover,' he said sincerely. 'She's a fine woman—principled, and as honest as the day is long.'

'I know,' Clover responded cheerfully. 'But she's a funny woman as well, Jake. And yet you can't help loving her, for all her little quirks.'

Jake smiled, acknowledging it as the truth, and turned his glass around pensively on the table cloth in front of him. 'It broke her heart when you left us, you know, Clover. But you know Mary Ann. She wouldn't bend... Although she regretted it after. It was a relief to her when Zillah told her you was living with her.'

'I wish I'd known that, Jake,' she said wistfully. 'I'd have come back home if she'd asked me. I wouldn't have taken much persuading, especially the state I was in – carrying Posy, I mean. Not that I didn't like being with Zillah ... but if I'd had Mother's support I wouldn't have felt the need to marry Ned when he asked me. I'd have been happy to bring Posy up by myself, without a husband. I could have put up with the snubs and finger-pointing of others. I just needed that bit of security being here would have brought.'

Jake nodded solemnly then took another quaff

of beer. 'It's easy to see all these things with the benefit of hindsight,' he commented, wiping his luxuriant moustache that was showing streaks of grey these days. 'I must admit, I was surprised when they said as it was Ned Brisco's child you was expecting. I din't need hindsight to see as he was never your type, Clover.'

'God rest his soul,' Clover remarked.

'Yes, God rest his soul... Funny chap ... I never thought he was Ramona's type either, but there you are...'

Clover looked at him, curiously. 'What do you mean, Jake, he wasn't Ramona's type either?'

He took another swig of beer and licked his lips. 'Well, I know as she used to see him occasionally – when there was nobody else about. He took her out once a long time ago. Nothing come of it o' course. Then, after he bought that motor car of his, he started to tek her out again. Oh, only for a week or two, mind.'

'I didn't know that.'

Jake chuckled. 'I know you didn't. When I found out I was sworn to secrecy not to tell you. He never called here for her. She always met him on Dixon's Green by the Shoulder of Mutton. So as you wouldn't see 'em.'

'I didn't know that,' Clover repeated, astonished.

'Well, it don't hurt to tell you now they'm both gone. There was no love there. Leastwise, I'd be surprised if there was. At that time Ramona was in love with somebody else. She never said, but I could tell. Moping about and distant, she was ... clinging. You know what I mean? I never knew

583

who it was she was pining for but it certainly wasn't Ned Brisco. It was somebody who was giving her a hard time, I reckon, and she used to get her revenge, I suppose you could call it, by going out with Ned. Well, let's face it, having a chap with a motor car was a bit of a novelty for her, and one in the eye for the other bloke I suppose.'

'I never knew that, Jake,' Clover said again, rapt in this momentous piece of information. 'Well, I never...'

'Ned always seemed happy to let anybody walk all over him. Our Ramona included. That's why I never imagined him to be your type, Clover. Then, when you fell out with Tom, and our Ramona and Tom started courting and you started courting Ned, nobody was more flabbergasted than me.'

'But I wasn't courting Ned, Jake. He was just company.'

'Like he was for Ramona I reckon. When she was pining.'

Oh, like as not, Clover thought dubiously, knowing her late stepsister as she did.

That night, the Doubledays were staying the night at the Jolly Collier. The children had been allowed to stay up late, enjoying the attention of their grandparents and the wedding guests, and the games they contrived to play in the back yard. But, by half past midnight they were seriously flagging. The last lingerers had drifted away in a haze of alcohol, good wishes and good humour, so Clover nudged Tom, who had also drunk more than he was used to, to retire to bed. While Tom undressed in the bedroom that used to be Clover's where they were to sleep, Clover supervised Posy who was in Elijah's old room, and Daniel who was to sleep in Ramona's.

She could see with satisfaction that they were both capable of performing the necessary bed-time routine, interrupted only by fits of giggling and teasing each other, as all young children do, before they parted for the night. So she went to her old bedroom and prepared herself for her 'first' night with her new husband, and told the children she would be along to tuck them in presently.

'Well, we made it to the altar at last,' Clover said, unpinning her hair.

'And we got a ready-made family to start with,' he replied with a benign smile. 'Let's see if we can't add to their number.'

She smiled happily and shook out her hair as she sat on the stool at her dressing-table. 'Oh, I'm sure we shall. Another two, at least.'

'I'd like daughters, I think. I've got a son.'

'You've got a daughter as well.'

'I know,' he said proudly and grinned. 'But I'd like more. I always wanted daughters, don't you remember?'

She stood up and, with her slender fingers, unfastened the dress she'd changed into for the party. 'I'll see what I can do...' She smiled knowingly. 'When the time comes.'

'I love you, Clover... By God, I do.'

'I love you, Tom.' She looked at him with all her affection in her eyes. Funny how drink made him

585

so sentimental.

'I love our kids as well, Clover. And they love one another...'

'They do,' she said, stepping out of her dress. 'There's no doubt.'

'We all love one another... You do love Daniel, don't you?' It was as if he needed her reassurance.

'Course I do,' she affirmed, and took off her chemise. 'As if he was my own.'

'Good,' he whispered. 'I'm glad... Are you coming to bed now?'

'In a minute. I must go and tuck the children in. I promised I would.' She peeled off her stockings and pulled on her nightgown, then she brushed her hair by the light of the oil lamp while Tom watched her admiringly.

All was quiet and Clover tiptoed barefoot across the landing, first to Posy. She was settled but not asleep. Her lush, dark hair was spread over the pillow and she looked heartbreakingly beautiful with blue eyes that were clear and bright with juvenile contentment. She bent over and kissed her daughter and, as the child told her what a lovely time they'd had, Clover, in one fleeting second, saw Tom in her expression, unmistakably. 'Goodnight, sweetheart,' she whispered softly. 'Sleep tight.'

She blew out the candle and tiptoed across the landing to Daniel's room. His mop of soft, curly hair gave him a look so cherubic. Poignantly, he held his arms up to Clover, appealing to be loved, and she leaned over and hugged him generously.

'I've got a mommy to love as well now,' he

whispered as he flung his arms around her neck readily and squeezed her with uninhibited affection. 'I'm glad you and my daddy are married now.'

At this unbidden show of affinity, a tear fell from Clover's eyes in response and was mopped up by his pillow. 'I'm glad as well,' she said, almost choking with emotion on the words. 'I'm glad I've got a son now, as well as a daughter.'

She blotted up her tears on Daniel's pillow and looked at him, only then realising just how much he must have missed a mother's tenderness. At the same time, she tried to discern a likeness to his father in the same way she'd seen Tom's likeness in Posy. But all she saw was Ramona. Ramona's features were too strongly represented in her son, overwhelming those of his father. Long may it remain so. But what did it matter whose child he was? He was delightful and she was not sorry he was in her own tender care now. She would cherish him, like she cherished Posy. She felt she had a duty to, irrespective of Tom, especially after what she had learned tonight. And Tom need never know the truth of it.

The publishers hope that this book has given you enjoyable reading. Large Print Books are especially designed to be as easy to see and hold as possible. If you wish a complete list of our books please ask at your local library or write directly to:

Magna Large Print Books
Magna House, Long Preston,
Skipton, North Yorkshire.
BD23 4ND

This Large Print Book for the partially sighted, who cannot read normal print, is published under the auspices of

THE ULVERSCROFT FOUNDATION

THE ULVERSCROFT FOUNDATION

... we hope that you have enjoyed this Large Print Book. Please think for a moment about those people who have worse eyesight problems than you ... and are unable to even read or enjoy Large Print, without great difficulty.

You can help them by sending a donation, large or small to:

The Ulverscroft Foundation, 1, The Green, Bradgate Road, Anstey, Leicestershire, LE7 7FU, England.
or request a copy of our brochure for more details.

The Foundation will use all your help to assist those people who are handicapped by various sight problems and need special attention.

Thank you very much for your help.